THE WAR CRIES ROSE AGAIN.

Alryc took a deep gash under the eye as a barbarian arrow sailed by, thundering into the wall behind him. Stacy plunged her dagger through the heart of a hairy bestial man who had flung himself at her. Around them were the sounds of swords crashing against mail and flesh and animal skin and axe blades alike. Stacy felt the blow of a fist and stumbled to the ground, resigned to plunging a knife into her breast before her assailants could take her.

She was dimly aware of the grisly shouts, but through the fog of her mind she swore she could hear the howling of wolves. The ultimate irony, she thought. Now that the *things* had ravaged the city from below and the barbarians from above, the wolves would seek their own vengeance too.

THERE HAD BEEN TOO MANY
ENEMIES FOR TOO LONG,
AND NOW SHE AND
THE CITY WOULD HAVE TO
PAY THE PRICE. . . .

LADY OF THE
HAVEN

ADVENTURES OF
THE EMPIRE PRINCESS
BY GRAHAM DIAMOND

PLAYBOY PRESS
PAPERBACKS

Published simultaneously in the United States and Canada by Playboy Press, Chicago, Illinois. Printed in the United States of America. Library of Congress Catalog Card Number: 78-55733. First edition.

Books are available at quantity discounts for promotional and industrial use. For further information, write our sales-promotion agency: Ventura Associates, 40 East 49th Street, New York, New York 10017.

ISBN: 0-872-16477-2

For Rochelle
and Leslie:
IN WHOSE EYES
I FIRST SAW STACY
COME ALIVE.

ACKNOWLEDGEMENTS

For his knowledge of the sea and ships, John G. Leinung; for their helpful assistance in the study of wolves, The New York Times Reference Library; for being my catalyst, George Woods.

PART ONE
THE VALLEY

CHAPTER ONE

From the beginning there was the forest, a primeval expanse sprawling across endless scapes. Complex and mystifying, alluring and compelling, it has been spoken of endlessly in folklore and fable—sometimes darkly, sometimes sweetly, but always with awe and respect for as long as men have known it. Mighty nations come and go, great empires rise and fall—but the forest always remains. And to the forest the busy schemes of men last no longer than the blink of a never-sleeping eye through the long passage of time. Some claim the forest is like the sea, receding with the tides only to return to begin the endless cycle once again when the proper time has come.

And Fara, the Fate in the heavens that watches over the forest, makes certain that this is so. The forest Dwellers are her children, and Fara must always protect them.

Of all the Dwellers perhaps none understands the Great Forest better than the wolves. None has been more favored by Fara than they; none has been given more cunning or intelligence, save, of course, for men, whom Fara does not guide or protect. Even as they know the wood that surrounds them, the wolves know the sun and they know the moon, for these, too, are Fara's agents. There are few secrets in the forest, and all Dwellers understand that the wolf is king, even as the lion is king in the jungle. Wolf lore is filled with many wondrous sagas and tales that have been repeated down through countless generations from one storyteller to the next. Their culture and history abound with these tales—tales that they are happy and more than eager to pass on to those who will take the time to listen. And the wolf who remembers and recounts them, well, he is a wise wolf, indeed. Such a wolf is Cicero, a brave and noble lord of his pack. His stories recount many adventures, not only of wolves but also of other Dwellers, and even of men. Yes, even of us, for the wolves know us well, better perhaps than we even know ourselves.

The tale you are about to read was told to me by Cicero over many long and sleepless nights. It tells of wolves, it tells of men, but most of all it tells of a young woman and the many adventures that befell her in the land in which she lived. Cicero was part of her tale, so in many ways it is his tale as well. It is a story of a far different time and place, a place that for now can only be reached by imagination. But do not be misled; the tale is real. And if you believe, then Fara will take the mist from your eyes, and you will know and understand.

And so I begin, putting words to paper, telling it to you exactly as Cicero told it to me, not so very long ago.

CHAPTER TWO

The first hints of autumn were in the air. Bright leaves of gold and red from the holly and maple trees peppered the damp earth as a soft, chill breeze whistled through the rushes of the meadow. The sun, a flaming ball of red fire, dipped below the western horizon, leaving a lingering glow in a sky fading into azure and purple. All across the hills flowers closed their petals and bowed their long stems to the lengthening shadows of the night. High in the trees the owls began to stir, and all around fireflies danced in ritual. Great lumbering bullfrogs hopped to the banks of the ponds, peered meekly about and began to croak. And from some distant unseen point in the wood a lonely jackal wailed his mournful cry at the moon.

At the crest of the highest hill in the meadow stood an aging gray-furred wolf, eyes searching the thicket below. He was a large animal, with long pointed ears and dark slanted eyes that dimly glowed in the dark. His snout was long, and his jaws were still powerful despite his advancing years. Sharp fangs, slightly curved, protruded from his upper lip. Lightly he stepped through the thick grass, ever keeping his gaze on the shadows below. Suddenly he stopped and growled. At the foot of the hill, nestled beneath the hovering branches of a tall oak, he saw her—a girl. A child of men. She was lying peacefully, with her eyes closed and her lips slightly parted. Her head rested

13

against the trunk of the oak, her legs stretched across the curving roots.

The wolf walked quietly down to the bottom and approached cautiously. She was asleep, completely unaware of his presence. The wolf lowered his snout and nuzzled it gently against her face. The girl began to stir; she opened her eyes—dark eyes, almond-shaped and bright, that crinkled at the corners as she smiled. Long black hair fell softly over her shoulders, cutting an oblique line against darkly tanned skin. Her mouth was small, her lips thin, her cheekbones high. A royal sign, the wolves claimed. The girl wiped the sleep from her eyes and looked about at the encroaching darkness.

"You promised to be back before night," growled the wolf.

The girl sat up, brushed a scattering of leaves from her jacket, then rubbed gently behind the wolf's ears. "I'm sorry, Hector," she apologized. "But the afternoon sun was so warm, and I only intended to rest for a little while."

The wolf growled again. It could be dangerous to be alone in the forest at night. She should know better. But then again, she *did* know better: for this was no mere girl come from the Valley to the forest—this was a child who had spent as much time in the wood as she had among her own. He knew she could take care of herself as well as any Dweller. Still, she was under his protection, and Hector knew he must treat her no differently than any other huntress from his pack who had disobeyed the rules. "We must get back to the hollow," he snarled gruffly.

Stacy nodded. She got up slowly and flexed her arms. The forest was beautiful at this time of year, she thought. The trees were awash in swirls of rich color, the grass tall and damp and glistening from the soft autumn showers. It had been good, this past summer with Hector's pack; and the sudden realization that tomorrow she would have to leave made her sad. She would miss them, miss them all. Especially Hector. "Don't be angry with me, Hector," she said as the wolf led her along the escarpment of the hill. Rows of berry bushes hugged on either side. Stacy paused and touched lightly at a small bunch hanging down between several overgrown leaves. "I wanted to have this last day to myself," she said with a sigh. "That's why I went off alone."

Hector glanced up at her soft eyes and wagged his bushy tail slowly from side to side. "I understand," he said quietly. "Parting is always difficult."

Stacy leaned over and kissed him lightly on the forehead. Hector turned away, knowing she could not stay. Stacy was a child of two worlds: that of men and that of the forest. And each world carried its own responsibilities. It was only right that she return home, just as it was right that rain should follow the sun.

They crested the hill and walked down between the sycamores and over the moss field that bordered the brier patches. Neither spoke. They both had so much they wanted to say, yet neither could find the right words.

Dressed as she was in a simple cotton tunic and light woolen jacket, many would have taken her to be but a simple country girl. In truth Stacy was far from that. She was of high and noble birth, a lady, a lady of the Haven. At home she could have commanded royal treatment, with servants and suitors to do her bidding. But Stacy chose not to live that kind of life. She loved the forest and its Dwellers and sought only to be among them. She needed to be free, to live without the restraints that her family's titles imposed upon her.

Many people said Stacy was just like her father had been in his own youth—restless, never content unless he was far from the Valley, seeking some new mystery or exciting adventure. And Stacy was proud of the comparison. If she could lead the same life that Nigel had once led, then she would be more than content. When teased about the absurdity of a woman doing the same things as a man, she would be quick to show her temper.

Standing tall and proud, head thrown back, eyes flashing, she would show her breeding.

It had been evident that Stacy was a leader from her earliest days when she first was brought to live among the wolves. Most children would have cringed and cried at the sight of the barking cubs—but not Stacy. She had demonstrated time and again her fight and her zeal and her spirit. And it had not taken long for the wolves to respect it. Often cubs ran whimpering back to their mothers, bruised at the hands of this brazen daughter of men.

At the foot of the ridge that led down to the meadow below, Hector paused. A small flock of sparrows fluttered above his head. They were small birds, and usually the sight of wolves would have made them fly away in fear. But Hector was no enemy, they knew. Nor was the girl who walked beside him. In this part of the forest all birds knew Stacy, and they greeted her now with chirps and songs. Stacy laughed and waved as the sparrows made one last swoop just above her head before they glided up past the treetops and far into the sky. Hector watched all this and smiled. Few from the Valley, men or women, seemed to be so beloved by the Dwellers as was Stacy. She was special. And it would be a sad day if the forest were to lose her.

Again without speaking the two inched their way to the sunken hollow in the meadow. Stacy moved softly over the damp grass and bare soil, never so much as snapping a twig or turning a pebble. She moved with grace and ease, as the wolves had taught her long ago. Like Aleya, the wind, as she sighs and breathes through the leaves; like Aki, the dragonfly, whose presence is rarely known until after her sting has been felt.

Hector was proud of Stacy; in many ways he was prouder of her than of his own grandchildren. For as children of Fara all these things were expected of them. But Stacy was of men, youngest cub of his man-friend Nigel. When Nigel had first brought her to the forest,

Hector had fallen in love with the child at once. But he had never shown his favor. No, not a single time. If the girl were to learn the ways of the Dwellers, then she must act as one. And if that meant bruises and pain, then so be it. There was no other way.

But Stacy had learned her lessons well. Hector glanced at the silver dagger strapped tightly around her waist, her father's dagger, given to her some years before. And Hector was certain that Stacy could use it if necessary. Sly as a cat, agile as a hunter, swift as a doe—all this, plus the cunning of men. Indeed she was a child of two worlds. And hence her wolf name: Khalea, the bridge between the moon and sun.

The hill tapered softly, evening out onto a narrow belt of thick grass surrounded by tall columns of hazel and chestnut trees. At the edge of the hollow there ran a small stream, twisting and winding along the edge of the clearing. Beside the stream, several dozen female wolves were tidying up their infant young, licking at their coats and waiting for the return of the hunters. Some of the older cubs were tumbling and rolling in the grass and occasionally chasing each other up the escarpment of the brown hill at the end of the meadow.

Now, from all around, wolves began to appear beside the stream. Some were quite old and infirm and had to hobble down from their resting places; others came bounding from behind the ridges and trees, tongues hanging low, tails wagging in anxious anticipation.

"Are you hungry, Khalea?" asked Hector as they joined the procession to the stream.

Stacy felt her stomach growl. "Starving," she replied happily. "And I think I smell fresh meat on Aleya's breath."

Hector grinned. There *was* a scent of meat on the wind. "And how long before the hunters return?" he asked.

Stacy sniffed at the breezes and furrowed her brow. The scent was getting stronger with each moment. She squinted her eyes and peered out at the top of the highest hill. There was a tall oak tree, solid and firm, with huge branches encompassing the top like loving arms. "They come now," she said, pointing in a sweeping gesture.

And so it was. Barely a moment later, twelve fierce-looking wolves appeared darkly at the zenith. They walked slowly, eyes glowing. Behind them came another twelve wolves, younger ones. New hunters. And they were dragging behind them the carcasses of two fine young bucks, throats bloody, eyes glazed in death but still wide with terror.

The hunters turned the carcasses over and rolled them down the hill. Cubs leaped up from everywhere and bounded to greet them, barking and snapping at the glassy eyes of the fallen prey. Pleased at the eagerness of the cubs, the hunters stood back and smiled. These cubs would one day be fine hunters themselves.

Stacy knelt beside the stream and washed her hands and face while Hector and two of the other elders instructed on the carving of bucks and apportioned the meat. The old and sick received the first pieces, then the cubs and females. Once everyone had ample food, the rest was apportioned to the hunters. Among the wolves no one goes hungry.

A stunning dark-furred female scurried toward Stacy carrying a large chunk of blood-dripping meat between her teeth. She lowered her head as she approached the girl and stretched out her front paws. Stacy reached out and took the meat gratefully. "Thank you, Dedra," she said.

The female smiled, then turned and raced away. Stacy walked to the shade of a hazel tree and sat down with her back against the trunk, legs dangling over the burrowing roots. She nibbled slowly at the raw meat, finding that she really had no appetite after all. Living with wolves makes one acquire a taste for raw meat, but with her departure

for home so close at hand, it was of a fine, hot meal that
she dreamed. And how long had it been?

It was evening now. The moon, bright and full, hung
low behind the trees as the pack sat quietly and ate. Stacy
watched the wolves lick their lips and paws and gnaw at
assorted bones. Some of the wolves rolled over contentedly, tails beating gently against the grass. Cubs huddled close to their mothers; young hunters and their mates
strolled to their places along the sides of the hills. The
night was pleasant enough, but there was a nip in the air.
Stacy leaned back and rubbed at her arms. She had spent
the entire summer without once having to make a fire for
warmth, and now, on her last night with the pack, she was
not about to start. It was not that the wolves would be
frightened or even complain about the fire, but rather that
she tried not to be different than they were, though they
had fine furry pelts to keep them warm, and she had only
a tunic and jacket.

"Are you cold, Khalea?"

Stacy glanced sideways and smiled as Hector slumped
down beside her. She ran her fingers through the thick,
bristly fur. By Fara, it felt warm, she thought.

Hector looked deeply into her eyes and searched her
face. Somehow, thought Stacy, he seemed to know everything she was thinking. Like now, keeping her warm with
his body.

They sat in silence for a while, Hector closing his eyes,
Stacy staring up at *Balaka,* the stars. After some time,
Hector growled. "We'll miss you this winter," he said
sorrowfully.

Stacy sighed. "And I'll miss all of you. You know I
will."

"If the snows are not heavy, will you visit with us for a
day?"

The girl nodded and cleared a growing lump in her
throat. "Of course. The first chance I get. . . ."

Hector's eyes brightened. "And ask Nigel to come,

also," he added. "It's been too long since we last saw each other."

Stacy returned his gaze. "Hector, why not come home with me? Tomorrow—we can leave the forest together. Spend the winter in the Valley. You know it will be much warmer there for you. Your illness. . . ."

Hector flinched and drew back slightly. "These old bones are far too weary to make the journey," he said sadly. "Besides, there is so much to do here, preparing for winter, seeking better shelter for the pack. No, there is too much to do. I am needed here."

Stacy forced a weak smile. Hector still refused to talk about his growing illness. But she saw it plain enough, as did the hunters. She often had cried when she heard him cough and moan in the middle of night. "Aleya soon will blow cold," observed Stacy, "and who will look after you in the night when you shiver?"

Hector stared for a long moment at the dazzling stars. "Fara will care for me," he noted softly, sagely. "As she always does. And if she should call, I'll be ready."

Stacy turned her head to the side and avoided his fatalistic look. On this last night she wanted to hear nothing of this sadness because it would make leaving all the harder.

"You are upset, Khalea. I see it in your face."

She dismissed the matter with a wave of her hand.

But the aging wolf would not let the matter be. He pushed his snout only inches away from her face and felt the warm breath from her mouth pass over his nose. "Tell me, child," he said gently, "what is wrong? What is it that troubles your heart?"

Stacy looked at his piercing dark eyes and felt again that he was reading her innermost thoughts. "I don't know if I'll be back," she said, turning her eyes toward the ground.

Hector nodded glumly. He had expected as much. "Then you have chosen the Valley over the forest?"

Stacy laughed a short soundless laugh. "Of course not. You know me better than that. I hate the Valley. If it weren't for my parents, I'd never return. But I can't spend my life here in the forest, either, as much as I love you all. I need to find a place among my own, but far away."

Hector nuzzled closer and sighed. "You'll travel across the mountains, won't you? To Newfoundland?"

Stacy nodded slowly. Newfoundland. There was magic for her in the name itself. The new frontier of rugged hills and fjords and roaring rivers that led to the sea. There were many from the Valley in Newfoundland, adventurous men and women who had left the comforts of the Valley to seek a new life in the open wilds. It was a hard life but a satisfying one.

"Is your mind made up?" Hector asked.

Stacy wiped away the hint of a tear from the corner of her eye. "I can't find any other answer for myself," she said truthfully. "I only know I can never be happy the way I am."

"Your parents will be sad," said Hector, trying not to speak of his own feelings toward her inevitable departure.

"I know. But what else can I do? Perhaps somewhere in the Empire there'll be a place for me. I know it's not in the Valley. It has to be Newfoundland."

Hector hung his head low. He knew that to try and talk Stacy out of this would only cause her more unhappiness, and that was the last thing he wanted. The Valley confined her; and the forest gave her freedom but not the companionship of her own. It was that she needed most. Hector frowned because it was also the one thing the wolves could never provide.

"You'll be giving up much," he told her. "Your title, position. . . ."

Stacy shrugged. "I don't care about such things. I never did. Besides, most of the ladies at court will be glad to be rid of me." Here she smiled wryly. "I make them uncom-

fortable. Behind my back they gossip about me and . . .
the wolves."

Hector laughed. "Indeed?" he snarled. The world of
men could be cruel, he knew, and the idea of them laughing at one such as Stacy made him all the more contemptu-
ous of their ways. Still, not all men behaved in such a
fashion. In fact, Nigel had once been the best friend he had
ever had. The adventures they had shared so many years
before had become legends in the forest. And of all men
in the Valley, was it not Nigel who had been the first to
forge the friendship between men and wolves? And was it
not he and Nigel who had found the way out of the forest
and discovered the lands now called Newfoundland? Hector closed his eyes and sighed. That was all so long
ago, like the magic of a dream. In many ways it seemed
to Hector that his friend had forgotten the wolves. Like
other men he was too preoccupied with the building of
man's Empire to pay much attention to his old friends in
the forest. But there had been Stacy to take his place. And
now even she would leave them—leaving him as lonely as
before.

As he sat, with Stacy running her hands through his
fur, he heard the laughter of cubs. He opened one lazy
eye to the small gathering under the old willow tree at the
side of the stream. In the center of the half-circle of gig-
gling cubs there was a large white-furred wolf sitting up
on his hind legs, growling softly. The cubs were staring
at him in anxious anticipation as the elderly white wolf
spun one of his fabulous yarns. It was a tale of times long
past, a fable of ancient wolf lore. And Hector quickly
noticed that Stacy was listening, too. Hector smiled wistfully. It seemed like only yesterday that she had sat under
the willow tree with Old One and had listened every bit as
eagerly as the cubs did now.

Hector stirred and wagged his tail discontentedly.
"Doesn't Old One ever tire of those fables?" he muttered
under his breath.

Stacy glanced down at him and smiled. "Does any wolf tire of fables?" she retorted.

"But he keeps the cubs up past their bedtime!" protested Hector with annoyance. "Someday I'm going to put a stop to all this nonsense."

The girl pinched him lightly on his forehead. "Why be so angry? He's been doing this for years, ever since I can remember."

"And sometimes I curse the day we ever found him," snarled Hector, trying to act the role of patriarch. "Did Old One ever join the hunters? No, he didn't. And did Old One ever take a hand in giving lessons to the cubs? No, he did not. He never even helped the females with the chores. He never even helped in seeking our winter shelter. All he's *ever* done is sit back under that blasted willow tree of his, eat a hearty supper and spin outrageous tales."

"You're the one who always said the pack had to be kind to Old One," recalled Stacy after a moment's thought. "And you're the one who took him into our pack."

Hector nodded glumly. "I know, I know. But if I had only realized what he would be like. . . ." He shook his head ruefully.

"You'd still do the very same thing," laughed Stacy. "You know you would. You found him cold and dying in the snow, with nowhere to go——"

"He could have gone back to his own land," snapped Hector before Stacy could finish her thought. "Back to his land of miracles."

"Wherever *that* is," she replied with a shrug.

In all the years that Old One had been with the pack, no one, not even Hector, who after all was lord of the pack, had ever been able to find out just what land that was. But wherever it was, it was nowhere in this forest. Indeed he was the only white wolf Stacy had ever seen.

Hector curled up and once again closed his eyes as Stacy continued to stroke his fur. Old One seemed to be at a very important point in his story, she realized. The cubs' eyes were wide with astonishment, and one or two of them were actually trembling with the expectation of what was yet to come and how it all would end. Old One cleverly let the tensions mount, as any master storyteller does: he rolled his eyes in his head, glanced at his listeners carefully, looking from face to face, and let his words roll painfully and slowly off his wet tongue. Stacy strained to hear the outcome of the tale, of how Fara had spun her magic and finally slew the demon that had imprisoned her.

But it was odd, she mused, that like everyone else in the pack, she had known Old One for so long yet really knew nothing about him, not even his true name. He was called Old One only because when they found him, that day so long ago, he was already getting on in years. And now, by far, he was the oldest wolf she knew of all the wolves in the forest.

The crisis was solved; Fara returned to her stars. The cubs sighed with relief, for it had been touch and go for quite awhile. A few begged for yet another story. Old One shook his head and laughed. "Not tonight, young hunters and huntresses, the hour is late and well past your bedtime. But tomorrow," Old One winked, "ah, yes. I have a *special* tale. One I have been saving."

And at the barks of their mothers the cubs scampered away. Old One smiled as he watched them leave, then looked longingly at the stars, as if listening to them speak. Did his many fables come from the stars? Stacy wondered. She answered herself with a shrug; a child of men would never know.

Long moments passed; Hector dropped his head from Stacy's lap and rested it on the soft earth. Then he began to snore. All the camp was asleep, Stacy saw. All but her—and Old One.

Quietly, without disturbing Hector or any of the others, she got up and walked to the willow tree. Old One turned his head and smiled. "Khalea," he whispered, surprised and delighted. "They say you leave the forest tomorrow.

How kind of you to remember to come and say good-bye to me." He stared at her with tired eyes, kind eyes, filled with warmth.

"I'd never forget to say good-bye to *you*," answered the girl. She knelt down and kissed his muzzle. Old One returned her affection with broad sweeps of his tongue across her face. Stacy plopped down and hugged him with all her strength, something she had not done since she was a little girl, a cub.

A sudden gust of wind swept through the trees and sent a scattering of leaves tumbling around them. Old One raised his head and sniffed at the breeze. "The snows will come early this season, I fear," he said knowingly. "Aleya speaks it on her breath."

"Your senses are good, Old One," replied Stacy.

The white wolf smiled. "Ahh, but not as good as when I was a hunter. When I was young. . . ." The words trailed off like a wisp of smoke.

"Don't stop," pouted Stacy. "Tell me about when you were young. I'd love to hear."

"*When I was young*," repeated Old One, "I could sense Aleya blowing from the mountain to the meadow; I could catch the scent of a fine young buck or elk clear across a valley. But that was a long time ago, Khalea. A very long time ago."

"How old *are* you?" asked Stacy, the words blurting out before she could stop them. Among wolves, such a question was considered rude, and she was sorry for her outburst.

But if Old One felt slighted or hurt, he did not show it. He gazed again to the stars and wagged his tail from one side to the other. "How old am I?" he asked with a shrug. "How shall I measure the time? How old is the great oak at the top of that hill?" he wondered rhetorically. "How old are these pebbles that rest in the stream? How old is this fine willow that lends us its shade? Truly, Khalea, I cannot count the years."

Stacy stretched out upon the grass and rested her head in her hands. "But there are many ways to measure time," she said. "You can count the summers, or the new moons, like tonight."

Old One nodded somberly. "What you have said I know to be true. Back in my own land we count the time by the long nights of winter and by the snows that begin with the first frost. Summers are far too short."

Stacy shivered involuntarily. She could never be happy in a land where summer was a mere brief encounter. "It sounds like a very cold place," she told him.

Old One shook his head. "Oh, no, Khalea! It is a *beautiful* land. A rich land of snow-capped peaks that rise right to the heavens. A place where a wolf can feel Fara's presence everywhere. My own pack dwelled in such a place, high above all. And sometimes you can feel as though Fara herself were standing at your side as you peer down at the world below."

"But to have no sun! No summer!"

Old One stared at her incredulously. "No sun? No summer? Not so, Khalea! The lands come alive during the warm months. Lush and fertile, the meadows and valleys overflow with wild flowers, even more beautiful than this lovely forest."

Stacy saw the wolf's eyes light up with pride as he spoke, but in a way that told her that this was no mere fable. These were true memories. Fond memories, told with love. "Have you never wished to go home?" she asked, wrapping her arms around her knees.

Old One sighed a deep sigh. "How can one ever hope to cross the sea?" he said.

Stacy grimaced. He was speaking in riddles.

And Old One saw the frown at the corners of her mouth. "Such a journey cannot be made twice," he continued after a time. "Now I must be content to live with but memories."

For a moment Stacy was startled; was the wolf being

serious? Was he saying he *had* crossed the sea? Literally? Then she leaned back and smiled. She should know better. This was another tale after all, another yarn to while away the long, early autumn night.

Old One lowered his head and sighed. "I see that you do not believe. But who can blame you? Whenever I have recounted the adventure, I am laughed at. So I speak of it no more. I'm sorry that I began to tell you."

Stacy glanced up. The pained look in his eyes told her that he had been telling the truth and that this was not one of his fables. She gazed deeply into his eyes. "Forgive me for laughing, Old One. But no one can cross the sea. It's just not possible."

The wolf kept a sharp steady look. Dryly he said, "*I* did."

"But . . . but how?" sputtered Stacy. "Even the bravest Newfoundland mariners haven't yet crossed the sea in their ships. How could a wolf?"

Old One sat in stony silence. Stacy leaned back and bit her lip. She was sorry again for the outburst. "Please tell me how you came to our land, Old One," she said softly, eyes downcast. "I'll not make fun of you. I swear it."

The wolf drew a long breath and let it out slowly. It had been such a long time, and so much had happened since then. But he wanted Stacy to know; he had found someone who might believe him. And if she did, then that alone would make it all worthwhile.

And so he began. "I was quite young at the time, in fact not much more than a cub. But already I was considered one of the finest young hunters in the pack. Many were the times that I had led the other young hunters down the mountain to seek the wild game of the meadows. Often my father, who was lord of the pack, would look at me with amazement when he saw the fine game my companions and I had dragged home. 'My son is blessed by Fara,' he would tell the elders proudly. And truly it was so, for no other hunter, no matter what his experience, was able to have the success that came so easily to me. And I was a proud tracker; indeed, I often scorned the caution and wisdom that many of the wizened hunters tried to instill in me. And that was my undoing."

Here Old One paused and gazed back at the stars through watery eyes.

"The next winter, times were hard. The cubs and the old whimpered in the caves for lack of even an old bone to chew. Our hunters made constant forays down into the meadow, but each time without success. The land was bare, Khalea, bare like I pray no wolf shall ever know again. The hunters came home and wept at the sight of their starving families. My father, great lord that he was, despaired. And despite the pleas of my sobbing mother, he set out alone one night to go down the mountain and see what he could find. One moon passed, Khalea. Then another. And still another. But my father did not return. I decided that I, too, must go down the mountain—and if not find food for the pack, at least seek out my lost father.

"Aleya grew colder and colder that winter morning. The sage warned me not to stir from the cave. 'There are terrible snows about,' he told me, 'And the touch of death breathes on Aleya's lips.' But as I have said, I was a proud hunter. And nothing, not even Fara herself, could stop me in my determination. 'I will go nevertheless,' I told the sage. And as he bowed his head sadly, I left our lair. Little was I to know that I was leaving forever.

"The path down the slope was perilous, but using my wiles and cunning, I managed to reach the plateau before dark. I paused beside the smooth rocks of the ledge and searched the white meadow below. But there was no sign of any other—not even of my father. All through the night I searched, traveling over hills I had never seen before. By the next morning I was exhausted.

Beside a mound of snow there stood a huge pine, and under that pine I nestled, burrowing a small hole in the snow like a rabbit. And there I fell asleep.

"I woke to hear a cry. *'Father!'* I screamed, *'Is it you?'* But no. It was Aleya blowing more fiercely than I had ever known. And with her rage came swirling snow. Frightened like an unweaned cub, I wept and bemoaned my fate, for surely this day I would die.

"The storm ended. Starving and lost, I wandered aimlessly, seeking I know not what. Was I delirious? Perhaps. I cannot say. But delirious or not, I was still too stubborn to give up. Soon I was in the lowlands of my home, a place of barren rock and shrubs. How I managed to have walked all that way I'll never know. But walk it I did. The sun warmed my fur and melted the snow at my feet. I was alive. Hungry and bedraggled, to be sure, but alive. Now if only I could find food. And no sooner had I thought the thought than Fara herself delivered a tasty meal. From some ugly hole in the ground a jackrabbit raised his head, sniffed with his nose and bounded into the open. Like a panther I leaped. The rabbit had not even time to run. Believe me, Khalea, to this day I remember that meal more than any other in my life. That lowly rabbit saved my life.

"After some searching for the way home, I became sleepy again. And as darkness was close and the chance of finding another rabbit for supper remote, I once again went to sleep in the snow. Only this time far more contentedly than the last, as you can well imagine. And it was a sweet dream I had that night. I dreamed that Fara was cradling me in her arms and rocking me back and forth. And it was a wonderful feeling, but then I woke, and the feeling became quite something else. I looked about in total fear. Indeed, I *was* rocking—on a sheet of ice! And what a strange sight I saw. The land was rolling by me. Had some demon taken the land and moved it? I was horrified; what would become of me now? But soon I calmed, and the truth became apparent. My sheet of ice was upon the frozen river, and now the sun had broken the ice and I was drifting upon it. I could not leap to shore, for shore was too far away. Nor could I possibly hope to swim to safety, for the water was too cold to survive. Helplessly I gripped the ice with my paws, praying that soon it would hit against a bank.

"But Fara had turned from me that day. I could see my mountain home recede into the distance until it was no more than a speck on the horizon. And with night I grew cold again, and again I became frightened. Where would this disastrous adventure lead me next? I shuddered at the thought. Soon my sheet of ice began to pick up speed. I was up on a strong current of the river. The ice pitched this way and that, making me sick to my stomach. My head began to spin; my eyes became blurred. I covered my head with my paws and whimpered. If only I had listened to the sage, I would still be at home.

"And it was only then, in my darkest moment, that Fara smiled down upon me. A school of tiny fish swam directly alongside my sheet of ice. I plunged my face into the frigid water and found myself rewarded with a fine young salmon. The fish squirmed and wriggled, and I felt compassion for this water dweller. But it was either his life or my own, and so there was little choice. With a gulp I swallowed it whole. Then eagerly I ran to the edge of the ice to see if I could find another. Again it was easy. I ate that one, too, then sought out a third. And the last one I saved, knowing that tomorrow I would again be hungry.

"By dawn of the next day my fate had become clearer to me. Fara must have a special purpose for me, I knew, for look! My sheet of ice was no longer up on the river but had floated onto the very sea itself. I was far from land, with nothing around me save endless water as far as the eye could see. Have you ever seen the sea, Khalea?"

Stacy shook her head. "No. But I hope to . . . one day."

"Ah, then I cannot explain it to you," sighed Old One. "The waters spread farther than ten birds can fly. And here I was, totally isolated from any form of life, with just my single fish to eat when I became hungry. Truly all hope of survival was gone."

"Yet you survived," said Stacy breathlessly. "How? With a single fish to sustain you?" Stacy was incredulous.

Old One laughed. "By heaven, no! There were others to catch. It took me days to learn how, but learn I did. A hunter is still a hunter. And so I drifted on alone for many more nights. It was only the warmth of my fur that kept me alive against Aleya's howl. And after some long period of time that I cannot count or remember, I drifted at last within sight of your shores. To the lands you call Newfoundland. There I met with many strange things, but that tale is for another time. Suffice it to say that I wandered south, over the mountains, and at last came to this forest, close to your own Valley. And here I have spent the years."

Stacy sat there numbed, absolutely speechless.

"And so, my Khalea, the bridge between the sun and moon, now you know why I can never go home again to the Land of the White Wolves."

"Is . . . is that what your land is called?" asked Stacy, trying to regain some of her shaken composure.

Old One nodded.

"And the white wolves? Are they masters of that land?"

The wolf growled, and a sudden look of malice crossed his face. "We are masters in the meadows, in the hunting lands, across most of the mountains. But unlike here we keep far distant from the civilization of men. Once, across the seas, I wandered close to man's city, and their hunters tried to kill me. They would tear the pelt from my body and wear it themselves."

Stacy's mouth gaped wide. Had Old One said what she thought he said? Her lips pressed together, and her hands began to slightly tremble. "Are you making this up, Old One?" she demanded. "Tell me the truth!"

Old One looked at her with stinging hurt. "Khalea, I swear it! By heaven, I swear it! A city of fabulous riches ruled by cunning men."

"Are you telling me that in your homeland there are people like me?"

"Many such as you, Khalea," he vowed solemnly. Then, bashfully, "But their women are not as beautiful as you."

Stacy was in no mood to be flattered. The implications of what the wolf was saying came rushing at her, and it took a few long moments for her to clear her head. *Another civilization!* Impossible! It could not be! Her civilization had stood for more than two thousand years and never in all the time of the Empire's existence had there been the slightest hint of other civilizations. "Tell me again, Old One," she growled. "And swear under *Balaka,* under the stars. Swear by Fara herself. Tell me that what you have said is the truth."

Old One looked her squarely in the eye. "May Fara take me now, Khalea. I swear I have told the truth." Then he lowered his head submissively.

Stacy drew a deep breath. If Old One was right, then everything the Empire believed was wrong. The books would all have to be rewritten. Her people were *not* the only descendants of mankind. But second thoughts about Old One's tale still nagged at her. Perhaps he truly believed what he said but because of age or senility had forgotten the real truth. Maybe he was confusing men of the Empire with some vague distorted memory of his home. How could she be sure?

"I'll have to relate your tale to my father," she said at last. "And probably to some of the others of the Council. What you've told me is a startling revelation—

one they'll not find easy to believe. They might want to question you."

"Let them come," growled the wolf. "I'll tell them everything I know."

Stacy rubbed at her eyes and saw that dawn was coming. Without realizing it, she had stayed awake the entire night. But if what she suspected were true, then it was well worth the effort. She got up and brushed the leaves and damp dirt from her tunic. She was about to leave the wolf when one last thought crossed her mind. "Old One, I know everyone has always called you that. But what is your name? Your real name, I mean."

The wolf stared hard at her. "Does it matter?" he asked.

Stacy shrugged. "No. Not if you don't want to tell me."

"I will tell you, Khalea, but don't tell any of the others. My father gave me the name Garth."

Stacy winced and looked startled. "Garth. That means 'royal one,' doesn't it?"

Old One smiled mysteriously. "Not exactly, my lady. It means 'prince.' "

CHAPTER THREE

After brief farewells, Stacy placed the bit gently into the mare's mouth, fastened the bridle around its head and mounted. The horse stood docile, and the girl took hold of the reins and arched her body forward. She clasped the mare's body tightly with her thighs, and nudged gently with her heels. And the black mare galloped off. Riding bareback, the way she loved, she left the wolf lair without looking back. Leaving was painful enough as it was; long good-byes would only make it worse.

Hector watched sadly from under a leafy hickory, never letting his gaze falter until the girl was out across the knoll and gone from sight. "Go with Fara," he whispered after her. Then he sighed a deep sigh, growled menacingly at a staring rabbit and raced back into the forest.

The early morning sky was dull and overcast. Black thunderclouds rolled ominously as Stacy made her way along the old forest path. On either side loomed tall chestnuts and lofty pines, branches bowed as if in respect to the coming winter. Already the wind's chill was making itself felt, whipping cruelly over the dales.

At the crest of an angular hill, Stacy stopped to get her first look at the Valley since she had left. For as far as she could see, there were gentle rolling hills dotted with stone farmhouses beneath lofty trees. Beyond them she could see a large village nestled in a dale—houses of brick with red-and-green-tiled roofs. There was a large apple grove running in a straight line at the right of the village and long fields of wheat somewhere behind it. Water mills towered over streams, and the muddy road was filled with wooden wagons rolling slowly to the west, laden with produce.

And off to the west, no bigger than a handful of dirt, loomed the high walls and towers of the Haven. And the very highest of the towers poked clumsily almost to the sky itself, overseeing all. There would still be soldiers in the tower, she knew—some things would never change —but their need was minimal. There was no danger, no threat from anyone. But soldiers of the Haven had stood guard there for two thousand years, and as long as the Haven stood, they would always be there.

It was a long ride home and Stacy took it slowly, letting the mood and the feel of the Empire come over her gradually. When you had lived in the forest, the sudden change could be startling. You had to reorient yourself from the way a Dweller thinks to the way a man thinks— and at times this was extremely difficult. She'd have to constantly remind herself not to snarl, not to growl, not to use the common tongue of the forest, except, perhaps, when speaking with birds. It would be hard, by Fara, she thought. *By Fara.* Stacy smiled. That would have to go, too. Anyone ignorant of the canine tongues would look at her more than strangely if she let that one slip.

She wound down the hill and onto the Old Road, glancing from side to side, taking in as much of the scenery as she could. Produce wagons rumbled past down the middle of the road. Almost everyone seemed in a hurry these days. There was a zeal in the Valley, indeed even to the farthest reaches of Newfoundland: the building of the Empire. The tasks were never ended. In fact, mused Stacy, they had hardly yet begun. Scattered far and wide, across hundreds of leagues of forest, the Empire continued to grow and grow and grow. But this was an exciting time, she knew. And she wondered what part in it she would play.

She took a shortcut away from the road that ran along a narrow outland meadow. There was a shallow brook winding down from the escarpment of a small hillock. There she stopped to drink. The water was ice cold. As she finished, her attention was caught by some muffled cries and shouts from the top of the hill. Stacy peered up. A squad of blue-tunicked soldiers was surveying the slope. Their commander, obviously an engineer, was bellowing instructions. His men swarmed like ants, making markings in the earth, charting each location. The engineer used wooden stakes to mark each plot, paying no heed to the nearby farmer who stood staring incredulously as they ran over his land.

Stacy smiled. Typical, she thought. Give the Council half a moment to work up some new scheme and you might find your very bed dragged out from under you as soldiers ran amok in their urgency to build a new road, a new mill, a new silo, a new *anything*.

"You there!" came a harsh voice.

Stacy looked up slowly. "Me?" she asked innocently.

"Yes, you! What are you doing here?"

Before she could answer, the bearded young engineer was dashing toward her in a huff. "Didn't you hear me calling you?" he barked testily. "We're clearing this whole meadow. What's the matter with you? Can't you see?"

Stacy's eyes flashed angrily. "My horse is tired. I've been riding all morning. We only stopped to rest—"

The soldier glared at her, this brazen girl standing in the way of his progress. "Well, you'd better move," he grunted. "Go rest somewhere else. This area's restricted. Go back to your farm—now!"

Suddenly his jaw dropped; he stared, dumbfounded. From inside her blouse she had pulled out a gold necklace. The charm showed a flying falcon with red jewels for eyes. "I . . . I'm sorry, my lady," he stammered, "if I had realized. . . ."

Stacy threw her head back, trying to calm her surging

anger. Only his realization that she was high-born had stopped him from treating her like dirt.

The engineer bowed stiffly, then forced an embarrassed smile. "You can stay here as long as you like, my lady. It's just that you were blocking my sextant." He gestured to show her.

Stacy rudely turned her back on him and mounted her mare. "Build your road, soldier," she hissed and quickly rode away.

By late afternoon she had reached the flat lands of the Plain, that fertile stretch of rich land that was the Valley's breadbasket. The New Road was as busy as she had ever seen it, with the endless flow of wagons coming and going on either side. And straight ahead of her, its high walls looming into the sky, stood the Haven, city of the Empire, center of man's world. The black and gold iron of the Great Gate swung open, giving entry to the city that gleamed like a bright flame in an otherwise black night. And beyond it she could see the swelling crowds of people along the broad avenue that led to the central markets. Stacy leaned forward and stroked the mare's forelocks. "We'll be home for supper," she whispered. And once more the old excitement began to race inside her. Home. She was *home*. And despite all, it was a good feeling.

The way through Old Town was a short ride. The streets were arched and narrow, consisting of simple two-story houses of stone and brick with side windows. There were small groups of children playing in the streets, never noticing the wagons that rumbled past. After a while, the street widened and trees and hedges lined either side. The homes became larger, less clustered, with gardens beside every one. These were the homes of wealthy merchants and tradesmen, well kept and trim. But soon even these fine homes began to look pale as Stacy wound down the avenue and came to the quarters reserved for the nobility. Here the houses were not houses at all but estates, each one larger and finer than the last. There were stables and servants' quarters at the sides and great yards and gardens behind tall hedges set behind taller trees.

Stacy stopped in front of a small black gate. The house was a magnificent three-story structure with broad glass windows and terraces. Its roof was of red tile, and boughs of ivy twirled and twined along the sides all the way to the chimney on the roof. As she leaned over and un-latched the gate, she could see the slightly bent form of a man racing from the main house. He was dressed in a dark woollen tunic and sandals, and from fifty paces she could see the broad grin across his face.

"Welcome home, my lady!" shouted the servant, bound-ing to the gate and opening it wide. He grinned from ear to ear.

Stacy got off her mare, smiled and kissed the servant lightly on the cheek. "Thank you, Olaf," she said. "It's good to be home."

"We've missed you, Anastasia," he told her truthfully.

Stacy grimaced at the sound of her real name. "Are my parents home?"

"Lady Gwen is out," said Olaf, "but she's been expect-ing you. She asked me to——"

"And my father?" Stacy interrupted.

Olaf sighed. "He's in, my lady, but I can't tell him you're here just yet. There's been some sort of problem at Deepwater, and he's having a meeting."

Stacy threw back her head and laughed. "There's al-ways some problem at Deepwater," she said. "And he's always having a meeting. Where is he, Olaf? In the study?"

The servant nodded. "He asked that he not be inter-rupted. Lord Desmond is here."

Stacy pinched Olaf on the cheek. "I'll not disturb them. Don't be worried. But take my horse to the stable, will you? And feed her if you can. It's been a long ride."

Olaf smiled and led the mare toward the stable as Stacy walked slowly to the house. Before she had even opened the front door, she could hear the muffled shouts coming from within the study. That was Lord Desmond's voice, she knew. Des always took to shouting whenever he was upset. Her father's oldest friend would never change.

Standing outside the study door, as if on guard duty, stood a blue-tunicked soldier. He bowed stiffly as Stacy looked at him. "Are you protecting us from pirates?" asked Stacy sarcastically.

The soldier shook his head awkwardly. "No, my lady, I was told by Lord Desmond to stay outside and not to let anyone in."

Stacy tilted her head to the side questioningly. "Oh? Well, this is my house, too," she said. "Why can't I go in and see my father?"

The soldier looked at her sternly. "It's Council business, my lady. I can't let you in. Really, I am sorry."

Before the soldier could move, Stacy brushed past him and gently opened the door. She combed her hair with her hand, fixed her tunic and slipped inside the study unnoticed.

Inside there were half a dozen men, all peering intently at a large sheepskin map that was spread across Nigel's desk. Not one of them heard or saw her as she entered. But off in the corner, sitting calmly on his hind legs was a wolf, a hunter, Stacy saw right away, with shiny dark-red fur and wide glowing eyes. The wolf's ears slanted forward; he growled at the intruder.

Nigel looked up; his mouth dropped. "Stacy!" he cried. He squeezed her and lifted her a foot off the ground. "Where have you been?" he asked. "Your mother and I expected you home days ago." He beamed as he held her at arm's length.

"I'm sorry for interrupting your meeting," Stacy said apologetically.

"Not at all," laughed Nigel. He turned to his guests and swept grandly with his hand. "Gentlemen, my daughter, Lady Anastasia."

Des looked at her and grinned. He walked over, bowed

low and kissed her hand softly. "Welcome back, Stacy," he said sincerely.

Stacy glanced at his face. The blond hair was showing a little more gray than the last time she had seen him, but his eyes were as blue and piercing as ever, and his face, although lined, was just as handsome. And with his new title and Council robe he looked every bit as dashing as she could remember. In fact, except for the obvious stiffness in his right arm, due to an old battle wound, he still seemed fit enough to lead a regiment of cavalry. "And *you* look well, my lord," she told him, with a ladylike curtsy.

Des winked. "A beautiful woman always brings out the best in me," he replied.

Stacy laughed, her eyes flashing. He handled her with ease, she knew; the old charm was still there.

"But let me introduce you to the others," said Nigel. He pointed to a dark, well-built man. "This is Captain Mace," he said, "our top engineer at Deepwater."

Mace bowed stiffly. "An honor, my lady."

"And this," said Nigel, "is Commander Trevor."

Stacy winced. The young man rubbed at his trim beard and smiled sheepishly. He was the soldier who had chased her away from the stream.

"Your daughter and I have already met," said Trevor awkwardly.

"Oh?" said Nigel, looking to Stacy.

"We had something of a run-in, I'm afraid," added Trevor hastily. The girl gave the soldier her hand and bit her lip as Trevor took it limply.

"It was nothing," she said. She tossed her head back to push away a lock of hair that trailed across her eyes. "And who are the others?" she asked, purposely to avoid Trevor's eyes.

"Ah, yes," said Nigel, "these are guests from Newfoundland."

It was obvious they were not from the Valley. Their

tunics clearly were cut from rougher cloth; their boots, of thick leather and rawhide, were certainly not Valley-made.

"This is Edric," continued Nigel, gesturing to a small stocky man with closely cropped light hair. "And this is Elias."

Elias was tall, easily the tallest in the room, with curly black hair that curled at the nape of his neck and a trim black beard showing hints of gray around his mouth. His eyes were deep-set, cheekbones high. Around the open neck of his tunic he wore a silver chain with a medallion. "I've heard your father speak of you," he said.

Stacy blushed. "Good things, I trust."

Elias laughed and nodded.

"Elias is a river captain," said Nigel.

A riverman! Stacy felt her heart leap and her eyes widened. "I've always wanted to meet a riverman," she said. "We hear so many tales about you."

" 'Good things, I trust,' " said Elias, repeating Stacy's words, flushing with pride.

The girl laughed. "Of course."

Nigel took Stacy by the arm and together they stepped closer to the wolf. "This is Cicero," he said, "a lord from the Newfoundland packs. He came to the Valley with Elias."

"Fara has graced you well," said Stacy with a growl.

The wolf's eyes widened and he bowed, wolf-fashion, with his head low and paws outstretched. "You speak our tongue?"

Stacy nodded. "I speak all canine tongues. Wolf, Jackal. Even in the cry of Hyena."

To the others in the room the conversation was little more than growls and barks, but it was clear from the look on his face that Cicero was most impressed. Many men had learned basic words and phrases in his tongue, which was common, but this girl spoke it freely, clearly, almost as if she were a wolf herself.

"Perhaps we can all talk later," said Nigel after the last

of the introductions. "But now I think we'd better get back to business."

"Yes, please do," said Stacy. "I'll leave."

"No, no," said Des, "stay and listen. It might do us all some good to have you around."

Stacy looked questioningly at her father. Nigel smiled. "It'll be all right, Stacy."

Stacy walked over by the windows and stood with her back against the long drapes. The wind was mild, but there was a slight chill in the air. Hands folded, she listened intently as the discussion began again.

The stocky Newfoundland man, Edric, planted a stubby forefinger squarely on the map on the desk. "That's the trouble spot, right there," he said, rolling his r's in the soft Newfoundland burr. "No wagon is going to negotiate that pass without some real difficulties." He shook his head sourly.

Lord Desmond pursed his lips and rubbed at his chin. "Then we've got to move our wagons around it. The project's too far behind as it is."

Edric looked at him coolly. "And how're we to do that? It'll take a new road, to be built across the range—and that'll take us years."

Des took a deep breath and exhaled slowly. A nerve in his cheek began to pound. "Well, we haven't got years," he snorted. "We've got to get that hardwood delivered from Aberdeen by summer."

Edric put his hands on his hips. "Fat chance o'that!"

Des seethed. "We had your word on it, Edric."

"Aye, that you did. But that was before the mudslide," growled the Newfoundlander. "My wood's cut more than a hundred leagues downriver. And I can't bring it up to Aberdeen any quicker—even if that damned new road you promised me was already cleared."

Des glanced to Captain Mace. The engineer avoided the icy stare. "What about it, Mace?" asked Des. "Can you be done by spring?"

Mace shook his head. "I've got a work force of one

hundred thirty men," he said, with a deep sigh, "and about a third of them had to be taken off my road to help with the old road clearing. There's no way it can be done. I'm sorry. In another six weeks the snow'll be chest-deep." He shrugged noncommittally.

The wolf began to stir. He glanced from one face to the next, searching their eyes. "I think Elias has the only solution," he growled in the common tongue.

Des turned to the riverman. There was a slight look of distrust in his eyes, though Stacy and Cicero were the only ones to detect it.

"I've discussed it with Lord Nigel," said Elias, "and we think it can work."

Des shuffled his feet. "Let's hear it, then," he said impatiently. "At this point I'm willing to try anything."

Elias smiled. "Well, it won't be easy," he admitted. "But my plan is to pick up the lumber at Edric's site, tie it down on barges, then haul it downriver." He spoke rapidly, with a cocky Newlander air of assurance in his husky voice—a tone that rattled most Valley folk.

Des stared for a few long moments, then said, "I think you could do it as far as Aberdeen. But what about getting the rest of the wood up to Rhonnda? What about the rapids?"

"I said it wouldn't be easy," answered Elias.

Des shot a glance at Nigel. "You think it's worth the risk?"

"Those downriver currents can be treacherous, no doubt of that," said Nigel. "But Elias knows the river like the back of his hand. And if he thinks it can be done, I believe him."

"I can barge about five metrics on a single trip, I'd say. Maybe a little more. Depends mostly on the weather."

Des whistled with some surprise. "You can barge that much? Even at this time of year?"

"I'll have to. Rhonnda's depending on it. We need the bulk of the wood before winter."

Stacy's ears perked up. Ah, she thought. So Elias is

from Rhonnda. The settlement that was the farthest out-post of the Empire. The town that bordered on the sea itself. The sea! Her mind flashed back to Old One and his strange tale. Already the first pieces of her own schemes were fitting into place.

"If I agree," said Des hesitantly, "I'm going to have one of my own men sent along with you."

Elias glared. "To take charge, you mean."

"I think this is a mistake," said Mace. "Captain Elias is promising too much, too soon."

"You don't think it can be done?" asked Des.

Mace laughed sarcastically. "I've spent too much time in Newfoundland to believe in their schemes. These New-landers are all dreamers. The rapids will more than likely rip his barges to shreds, and we'll wind up losing every-thing we cut."

Edric's mouth twitched angrily. He darted his eyes toward Mace. "You Valley folk scorn everything you don't think of first, don't you? Because you fail in your own tasks, you degrade anyone else's ideas."

Mace's own temper began to flare. "I don't have to listen to this," he barked, his face flushed.

Des held up his hand and gestured for Mace to hold his anger. "I've been to the rapids myself once," he recalled, "when I helped survey the lands for Aberdeen. And I think Mace has a good point. It will take quite a ship to grind its way downriver tugging five metrics of lumber. You'll lose all maneuverability."

Elias's face grew stern. "I make my fortune on the river," he replied. "And I know what can be done and what can't. My ship can take a lot more stress than you give it credit for. I've made the trip between Deepwater in the south and Rhonnda in the north a hundred times and more. You may be masters on the land, my lords, but on the water I'm the master. And let there be no misunder-standings between us. I expect to be paid and be paid very well if I succeed. If I fail"—he shrugged—"we're both losers. The settlements don't get the lumber, and I don't get the money."

"I didn't know you were such a mercenary," drawled Mace.

Elias's eyes narrowed. The old feud between New-landers and the Valley was beginning to flare.

"I've been on the river with Elias," said Nigel, "and he has my confidence. Two years ago, when I was at Deep-water, I spent a week on the river aboard the *Brora*. And Elias is right. His ship's a tough old wench. Her keel and ribs are built with the finest oak I've ever seen. Her last captain sailed her for almost twenty years. In fact the *Brora* was one of the first to carry cargoes to Rhonnda. I think Elias deserves a chance. And if he's right, if it can be done, we can have a dozen ships barging wood for us. The day might even come when we won't need the Old Road at all. Then we could recall Mace and his men and give them other assignments closer to the Valley."

Des nodded slowly. He met Elias's gaze. "All right," he agreed, "we'll try it. But I'm still going to insist that one of my men go along with you."

Elias shrugged. "That's fine with me. But you'd better pick him quickly. I plan to leave for Newfoundland no later than tomorrow."

It hardly took Des a second to decide. All through the conversation young Trevor had stood aloof, listening carefully but not saying a word. "Can you be ready by the morning?" asked Des, looking to his first young engineer.

Trevor nodded. "If you want me to go, I'll be ready."

Lord Desmond nodded. He looked again to Elias. "Now how soon can your ship be made ready?"

"She's ready now," replied Elias with a hidden smile of satisfaction. "She's sitting at Deepwater with the barges at her side. I anticipated your agreement."

"Can the first shipment be delivered before the snow?"

"If the road to Deepwater's still there," Elias said, "I'll be there within a week. Aberdeen will get her supplies before the month is out, and then it's on to Rhonnda."

CHAPTER FOUR

Stacy luxuriated in a hot bath for almost an hour, the first hot bath she had taken since leaving the Valley. She lingered for a long while, then got up and began to dress for dinner. And the thought of a hot meal was almost as pleasing as the bath. Sitting before her vanity mirror, she carefully braided her hair and let it fall over her breasts. The black hair shined and felt as soft and fluffy as a rabbit's pelt. It curled slightly upward at the tied edges and bounced ever so gently with each breath. She slipped out of her robe and dressed in a light-yellow tunic with white lace at the collar. The tunic was a smart fit, one that hinted at the firm and toned body underneath. Stacy stood fully before the mirror and smiled. She wore no makeup; she never did. She took the gold pendant, clasped it firmly and let it dangle in full view. And the transition was made; once again she had become the fine lady of the Haven she had been brought up to be. Then she slipped out of her room and made her way down the winding stairs that led to the dining room.

Olaf held the doors wide and bowed slightly as she entered grandly.

"Anastasia," came a joyful cry.

Lady Gwen, Stacy's mother, bounded up from her chair and ran to Stacy, hugging her tightly and smothering her with wet kisses. Stacy held her mother at arm's length and

46

stared at her. "I'm sorry I didn't see you when I arrived. But you look wonderful, mother. Ravishing."

It was true. Gwen, despite her years, was still an attractive woman. The almond-shaped eyes were as large and sparkling as ever, the ashen hair just as silken to the touch.

Gwen blushed at the compliment. "And you look lovely, too, Anastasia. You could turn every eye at the Great Hall."

Stacy laughed grandly, now blushing as well.

"Why just yesterday Lord Brendon was asking about you," Gwen said. "He wanted to know when you'd be back."

"Oh, really?" Stacy mumbled, feigning interest. Inwardly she groaned. Was her mother trying to push a husband on her already? And Brendon of all people! Of all the marriageable lords of the Haven why must she always be pestered by *him*? Anyway, marriage for her was a long way off. If her parents did not know it now, they surely would know it soon.

"Perhaps next week I'll drop by to see Brendon and say hello," she said at last, sounding bored.

Nigel rose from his place. "Come, Stacy. Sit down. Your mother had a special dinner prepared for your homecoming."

Stacy moved to take her place, then tensed. Standing at the far end of the table was a guest for dinner. Trevor.

The soldier smiled with embarrassment. "Your father invited me to stay," he told her, somewhat awkwardly. "We have a lot of matters to clear up before I leave for Newfoundland."

"Commander Trevor was just telling us about his new duties," interrupted Gwen. "They sound really exciting. But never mind about all that. We haven't seen you all summer. Tell us everything about the forest, and tell us about Hector."

Stacy eased into her chair and put the grinning soldier out of her thoughts. "I have a lot to tell you," she said, "but first I want to hear what I've missed in the Valley."

"Well, you haven't missed much," laughed Nigel. "Trevor here is building a new road. But I understand you know about that."

Stacy nodded icily; she knew more than she wanted to.

"Last week we got a letter from your sister," added Gwen happily.

"From Newfoundland? From Lorna?" There was real excitement in Stacy's voice. It had been about five years since Lorna had married and left the Valley. "What does she say?"

Gwen laughed. "Well, her writing is so scribbled it's hard to make out what she wrote. But she had a lot to say. Simon has received a post from Governor Bela. It seems he's a young man with a future. He's been named Royal Medical Commissioner."

"For Deepwater?"

Nigel shook his head. "For Rhonnda."

Stacy frowned. She loved Simon like a brother and thought that he deserved better than that.

"Don't be displeased," said Gwen. "It seems Rhonnda is not the muddy backwater town some people think. Lorna says it's already become the biggest town in all of Newfoundland."

"Remember, Stacy," said Nigel with a glint in his eye, "it is the only part of the Empire that touches the sea."

The sea! thought Stacy. If only I could see the sea!

"Newlanders are moving there in droves, they tell me. Even Valley folk. That's why there's so much urgency in Captain Elias's mission. And Trevor's." Her father looked at the soldier and smiled. But Stacy didn't hear; her mind was racing.

Perhaps if she went to Rhonnda herself. . . . Yes!

"Ah, dinner is ready," said Nigel, interrupting her thoughts. And from the kitchen came an elderly woman carrying a large silver tray laden with hot beef and steaming potatoes. Stacy felt her mouth water as the servant set the tray down and filled her plate.

"Well, I think our conversation can wait until we've finished," said Nigel, seeing the hungry look on his daughter's face. "Don't you agree?"

Stacy laughed. "For once, father, we agree completely."

The meal was wonderful, and Stacy ate slowly, savoring each morsel.

After the main course was done, the servant brought a large bottle of sweet wine and a bowl of fresh fruit. Nigel sat back, wiped his mouth with his napkin and raised his goblet. "To you, Stacy," he said. "Welcome home."

Gwen and Trevor eagerly joined in the toast. Then Nigel raised the goblet toward Trevor. "And to you, Commander. May your journey to Newfoundland bring nothing but success."

Stacy politely raised her glass and took a small sip. For all she cared, this arrogant soldier could drown in the deepest part of the Newfoundland River.

Trevor acknowledged the toast with a bow of the head, then proposed a toast of his own. "To the Empire," he said sincerely. "May it stand forever." And to that they drank again.

"Well," said Nigel after a while, "that's more toasting than I've done for a year. Now, Stacy, tell me. How is Hector?"

Stacy frowned. "Not well, I fear," she confided sadly. Nigel raised his brows and stared. "He tries to hide his discomforts," she went on, "but they become more apparent all the time. He doesn't sleep well anymore. And he whines in his sleep. Sometimes he shivers. But he won't talk about it. He just shrugs it off. I think sometimes he's in great pain."

Gwen put her hand to her mouth and glanced at Nigel. "Can't we do something for him? After all, he is such a friend."

Nigel rested his hand in his lap and half closed his eyes. Sadly he shook his head.

"Isn't there some medicine we could bring?" asked Trevor. "Surely there has to be something to ease such pain."

Again Nigel shook his head. "I see you don't know much about wolves, Trevor. They're a proud species. For Hector to accept our drugs would shatter his pride." He sighed, quickly adding, "but I suppose I could bring him some morphine—when his time comes."

"That's right," said Gwen. "There's nothing to be done now. Why not let him spend his last years in dignity."

Stacy's eyes flickered sadly. "I don't think he has years, mother. Hector spends most of his time staring idly at the stars."

"Waiting for Fara to call," whispered Nigel knowingly.

Trevor stared dumbly. "*Fara*?"

"The Fate that guides all forest Dwellers," explained Stacy, with a trace of impatience in her voice. Only a sharp glance from Gwen stopped her from saying any more.

"I asked Hector to return to the Valley with me," Stacy continued after a while, looking at her concerned parents.

"And?"

"And he refused. He said there were just too many things that had to be done for the winter." She looked away to conceal her sorrow.

Nigel gave an understanding nod. That would be like Hector—too concerned with his pack to even think about himself. He leaned forward at the table and rubbed lightly at his temple with his fingertips; a dark shadow crossed his features. How the years had slipped away!

Gwen reached over and touched his hand with her own. "Hector's lived a rich and rewarding life," she reminded in a very low voice, "and he'll never be forgotten. He has sired more than a dozen hunters, known as many wives and even helped raise a brood of grandchildren. Strong and healthy grandchildren."

Nigel looked warmly at his wife and smiled through his saddened eyes. "Was there ever any doubt?"

Trevor glanced sideways at Stacy and saw that the girl was showing every bit as much emotion as her father. Like many soldiers and officers of the Empire, he had often come into contact with Dwellers, sometimes even friendly wolves, but this was the first time he had come into contact with a family who spoke of the wolves as though they were members of the same race. Nigel and Stacy, and even Lady Gwen for that matter, were treating this as though it were a deep personal loss.

"The two of you must have been very close," he said.

Nigel looked at him curiously. "*Close*?" he repeated, as if the word were new to him. "Yes, we were close. I don't know if you can understand this, but we were almost, well, almost like brothers. But that was a very long time ago, Commander, before Stacy was even born—and I daresay before you were, either. Hector was the bravest, most clever wolf I've ever known. I could tell you stories about him—but never mind. I guess they really wouldn't make much of a difference, anyway. . . ." His words trailed off into a whisper.

Trevor looked totally bewildered.

Gwen noticed and smiled softly. "I don't suppose any of this is easy for you to understand."

"No, my lady." He smiled back gratefully.

"But my husband is prouder of his accomplishments with Hector than of anything else he's ever done. It was Hector who first brought friendship between us and wolves —and he did it at a time when the easier and safer course would have been to fight against us."

"The Forest Wars," said Trevor, with a touch of awe in his voice.

Gwen nodded. "No doubt you're too young to remember them."

"They concluded three years before I was born, my lady. But every schoolboy has read the story."

Nigel gave a short, curt laugh. "Hector and I *lived* the story, my young friend. It was a bloody period in our history, and in many ways if it weren't for the wolves, our Empire probably wouldn't exist. We'd be no more than Stone Age hunters eking out a bare subsistence on what we could find or steal, and with a frightened eye ever on the forest. But we won that war and the Empire flourishes, all the way from the Valley to the Newfoundland Sea. And you can thank the wolves for that, Commander. Most of all, you can thank Hector."

"I didn't know," whispered Trevor. "Forgive me if I seemed cynical, but I really didn't know."

For a long moment there was a stillness in the room, broken only by the soft chirping of a hummingbird perched in the hickory tree outside in the garden.

"I see I have a lot to learn about wolves," said Trevor thoughtfully. "Perhaps when I get to Newfoundland."

Stacy laughed. "An unweaned whelp like you? Why, those Newland wolves'll chew your ears off."

"Stacy!" cried Gwen with a glare. "That's no way to speak. I'm sure Trevor would be gracious enough to forgive you—if you apologized." She looked at her daughter with smoldering eyes.

And Stacy could tell by her mother's tone that the apology was not just requested, it was demanded. She pressed her lips tightly together and glanced at the embarrassed young officer. "I was rude, Commander. I do apologize."

Trevor dismissed the thought with a wave of the hand. "And I was rude to you this morning," he said. "Will you accept my apology for that?"

Stacy grinned. "Certainly, Commander. Let's call it even."

Not certain as to what they were referring, Nigel avoided the exchange entirely. Turning to Trevor, he said, "You know, Stacy has a point, though. Have you ever been to Newfoundland, Trevor?"

The soldier shook his head. "This will be my first trip, Lord Nigel. And I don't mind telling you I'm really quite eager. I have a brother at Deepwater I haven't seen for, oh, must be about six years now."

"Well, you'll find Deepwater and the other towns pleasant enough, I suppose, but the route you're taking with Elias, across the rapids and downriver to Rhonnda, that's really going to tax your energies. Newfoundland can be a rugged place, and you won't find many comforts there like you have here in the Valley. Outlanders, those who live in the farms and settlements away from the towns, are a rough bunch of fellows. And you're going to need a good guide."

"Ah, but you forget, my lord. We have one. Cicero, that wolf who came with Elias."

"I've been meaning to ask you about him myself, father," Stacy said. "Where's he from?"

A glint came back into Nigel's eyes as he recalled adventures long past. "Cicero's a mountain wolf, Stacy. And they're a breed like no others I ever knew. I met him for the first time two years ago when I went to Deepwater on Council business. Cicero's a cagey devil. And clever as sin. Something of a brigand himself, I understand; but I'll tell you one thing, if ever there was a wolf with a nose for getting out of trouble, it's him."

Stacy's mind began to click. Somehow things were falling almost perfectly into place. But now was not the time, she knew. Later perhaps, or even tomorrow. But not just yet.

"And what's his relationship with that riverman? Elias, is it?"

Nigel chuckled. "Bless me if *I* know," he said. "Elias is a Rhonnda man, and you know what they say about *them*. Close your eyes in front of one and your wallet's gone—along with your teeth."

"I get the feeling you don't trust him," said Stacy wryly.

"Don't put words in my mouth. Elias is a good man and a fine mariner. But all these rivermen are adventurers. Why else would they *be* on the river? And if there's a quick profit to turn, Elias won't lose any time turning it. And that's why Desmond was so intent on having some-one from the Valley," he glanced to Trevor, "someone we can trust to go along and make sure there are no games played with our timber."

"How long will you be gone, Commander?" asked Gwen, her chin in her hand.

Trevor glanced at Nigel. "I'm afraid I can't say, my lady. At first I thought I'd be home as soon as we got this matter of the hardwood squared away. Now it seems Lord Desmond has other duties in mind for me while I'm up there. I'll probably find myself stationed in Rhonnda for at least a year."

"Oh?" said Stacy. And in her mind she said, *Now! Tell them now!* "Well, perhaps we'll see each other. I hope to take the first caravan next spring to Deepwater and from there sail on one of those exciting ships up to Rhonnda-by-the-Sea."

"Then you must make a point of looking me up," the soldier said happily. "It'll be wonderful to have a friend from the Valley." His smile turned sheepish. "I hope we *can* be friends?"

"Yes, Commander, we can. And I *will* look you up."

The smile returned. Rising, he said, "But now I really must be going. I still have a great many orders to carry out and some bags to pack." He turned graciously to Gwen and took her hand. "My lady, I want to thank you for a wonderful meal and a delightful evening."

Nigel stood at his place and shook Trevor's hand firmly. "Good luck, Trevor. Keep your eyes open and be alert at all times. Don't forget that you're acting in the name of the Council. As far as Elias goes, you're to make all the decisions, not he."

"I'll remember, my lord. And thank you." And with that he strode through the open doors. A few moments later Stacy heard his horse gallop off into the night.

"A very nice young man," said Gwen with a gleam in her eye. "Don't you think?"

Nigel sat back down in his chair and furrowed his brow. "Never mind that," he rattled. "Now, Stacy, what's all this business about going up to Newfoundland in the spring?"

"I've been turning it over in my mind for a long time now, father," replied Stacy. "And it's time I tried to make a life for myself."

Somewhat aghast, Gwen said, "You think you can make a life up there? In that *wilderness?*"

"Lorna and Simon did."

Nigel pursed his lips. "Your sister has a husband to take care of her."

"And you're still a child!" snapped Gwen.

Stacy's eyes flashed. "I'm twenty, mother. I'm a woman. And I don't need a man to take care of me."

"We know you don't, Stacy," said Nigel softly. "You've always been independent and free to come and go as you choose. But Newfoundland's a long way from here, Stacy. And can you blame us if we'd be worried?"

Stacy sighed and let the harshness of her feelings subside. "I have a reason for going, father," she answered. "I don't want you to think that it's just a girlish whim."

Nigel waved his hand. "Let me finish. I know you're restless, even as I was until long past your age. That's why I brought you to Hector back when you were just learning to walk. You're a lucky young woman, Stacy. You've had the best of two very different worlds, and of that I'm proud. Few others can claim that distinction. And I understand the pains you've suffered because of the way you are. Men are crueler than Dwellers, I don't have to tell you that, and I know about the nasty, snide things said about you behind your back. But Stacy, you can't run away from it; you can't stop being what you are. If you think that living a frontier life in Newfoundland will hide and shelter you from the pains you've had here, you're wrong. You were right in one respect, Stacy. You *are* a woman. And we can't stop you from doing what you feel you must. But the answers you seek won't be found in Rhonnda, despite the glamour of adventure. Nor can they be found in the Valley or the forest. The wolves have a saying: '*Avanora*'."

"Seek inside yourself," whispered Stacy.

Nigel nodded. "Exactly. Look inside yourself. That's where the answers will be found. The *only* place they'll be found."

Stacy got up, walked to the open window and stared out into the garden. It was filled with rosebushes on either side of the small walk. In the center of the walk was a tiny fountain used by birds, and Stacy paused to watch the hummingbird peck his beak ever so gently down into the water. "If you had told this to me a week ago, father," she said, "I'd have said that everything you told me was true. I *was* planning to run away from myself, to hide in the wilds. I want something else in life—other than marrying some pompous noble and raising ugly children. No, I'm not saying that I won't marry, only that first I have to feel fulfilled, feel a sense of accomplishment."

"You *can*, Stacy, right here at home. Believe me, you can."

"Please, father, now let *me* finish. I wasn't going to discuss this with you now. I was hoping to wait until the right moment. But now that things are out in the open I'm going to tell you."

Nigel frowned. "Tell me what?"

Stacy lowered her gaze to the tiled stone floor. "I have to speak with you alone," she said. "Not as my father but as a member of the Council."

Nigel shot her a long questioning stare. Then he looked at Gwen and shrugged. "All right, Stacy, if that's what you want. Let's go to my study."

Nigel got up and walked to the dining-room doors, tall cumbersome doors, made of heavy oak that creaked ever so slightly when swung wide. Stacy passed through while Nigel kissed Gwen lightly on the cheek and said, "Don't wait up for me. We might be quite some time."

And as Gwen watched, perplexed, the two of them walked slowly down the long hall to the study.

Stacy stood impassively at the center of the room as Nigel struck a match and lit the small lamp atop his desk. Dark shadows immediately leaped across the walls and ceiling as the flame sputtered, grew large, then finally settled down into a low, steady glow. Nigel gestured to the round wicker chair opposite the desk.

"Sit down," he said, taking his own seat.

The girl slumped comfortably into the chair, which had been bought from a Newfoundland merchant. Then Nigel leaned over the desk and clasped his hands together. "Now," he said, "why don't you tell me what's on your mind—and why we need this secrecy from your mother."

Stacy crossed her legs, rested one arm on the back of the seat and toyed with her braids with the other. "There's no secrecy," she answered honestly, "but I was serious when I told you I wanted to speak with you alone, officially, as a member of the Council."

Nigel nodded and bit at his lip. "All right. I'm listening."

"Father, who sets the goals of the Empire?"

Nigel looked at her oddly. "The Council, of course."

"And what are those goals?"

"Look here, Stacy. You said you had something important to discuss with me. What's all this for?" He shifted restlessly.

Stacy frowned. "Please, father. Bear with me for just a few minutes. I need to clear up a few things in my mind before I tell you."

"Fair enough. But I'm afraid it would take a volume before I could enumerate all the goals the Council has set. Briefly, though, our first commitment is to the well-being of our citizens. To assure adequate shelter, food, schooling and trades for the children."

"And beyond that?"

"Beyond that? To place our banners in the farthest reaches. To expand the Empire as wide as we can."

"To *explore*?"

"If you want to put it that way, yes. The discovery of Newfoundland opened a whole new frontier for us, a world we didn't even dream existed until thirty years ago, during the Forest Wars. And since that time we've used every resource at our command to ensure that Newfoundland is colonized and settled for the Empire. Thirty years ago we were locked into the Valley and surrounded by enemies in the forest. I don't have to tell you that that's all changed. Changed forever. Men have tasted the vastness of the world outside, and the goal of the Council is to bring as much of that world as we can under our banner."

"And when Newfoundland's settled and properly colonized, what then?"

Nigel leaned back in his chair and let his eyes glance to the flickering flame in the lamp. "To do what men have always dreamed, I suppose. To cross the sea."

Stacy felt her heart begin to race; she stayed calm and cool, though, and did not show the slightest emotion at what her father had said.

"But that's a long way off," continued Nigel with a sigh. "Our knowledge of the sea is minimal—and that's being kind. A voyage of that nature is fraught with risk. We'd have no proper course to set, no set goal to reach. It would be a matter of blind luck—if our ships didn't sink or get blown away in some storm."

"But what about the rivermen? Surely they'd be willing to try."

Nigel shook his head. "The Council would never permit it, I'm afraid, even if some captain *were* foolhardy enough to volunteer. Empire ships are fine for the river, even for exploring the channels. But to cross the sea?" He left the words hanging and shook his head.

"But once civilizations *did* cross the sea," said Stacy, pressing the point.

Nigel drummed his fingers on the desk. He knew his

daughter well enough to know when she was trying to lead him somewhere. "Yes, Stacy," he drawled, "once men did cross the sea in mighty sailing ships. In the days of the Old Time, when men lived all across the world. There once was an age of expansive travel, when men knew every continent, every island. Sadly that's all changed. We, the Empire, are the descendants of those men, and their knowledge is all but lost to us."

"And isn't another goal of the Empire to regain some of that lost knowledge?"

"A definite goal, Stacy," Nigel was quick to concede. "But we haven't the ability or the manpower to do so much at once. Before you were born, Stacy, there were about twenty thousand men and women in the Empire— for that matter, in all the world. We've been prosperous since then, and now we number more than twice that. And about half already live in Newfoundland. That territory proved to be far more expansive than we thought. It could take us a hundred years before we actually need to find more space or different lands to colonize. Right now our hands are full just trying to deal with what we have. The Haven can't even find the manpower to properly govern the Newfoundland wilds, so what business would we have in promoting a dangerous voyage to cross the open sea?"

Stacy kept quiet for a long moment and let her father's words run through her mind. It had been a convincing argument, she knew, but one that was based on faulty logic. "Father," she said after a time, "how do we know that somewhere there aren't other men, other civilizations? After all, we know so little of the world . . ."

Nigel stared blankly. "We know because in the two thousand years of our own recorded history there has never been the slightest indication that other civilizations flourish. In all our explorations of Newfoundland, of the Uncharted Territories, there has never been a single sign of anything that would lead us to believe another civilization or culture exists. Not a single artifact—not as much as an arrowhead or copper trinkets. But you know that as well as I. Even the wolves, who have wandered the length and breadth of the world, claim to have known no other men."

And *that,* thought Stacy, was where his logic was wrong. Indeed the logic of the entire Council was wrong. "Yet just a moment ago you spoke of mighty sailing ships."

Nigel looked at her impatiently. "Dead civilizations, Stacy. All ashes scattered to the winds. But come on now, why all these questions of goals? And why all these questions about crossing the sea? What is it that you feel you have to tell me?"

"A story, father. A very strange story—probably the most fantastic and incredible either of us has ever heard. And all I ask is that you listen to it with an open mind." She leaned forward in the wicker chair, made a pyramid with her hands and recounted Old One's tale exactly as he had told it to her.

For a long while after she had finished, Nigel sat perfectly still, his own hands folded and eyes closed. At length he looked at his daughter and said, "Do you really believe all of this?"

Stacy nodded seriously. "I do, father. I'm convinced of it."

Nigel stared glumly. He inhaled deeply and exhaled slowly. Then he said, "If you had told me this before an open Council meeting, you know what would have happened, don't you?"

Stacy cast her gaze to the floor. "They would have laughed," she sighed.

"That's putting it mildly," retorted Nigel. "They'd probably have had you gagged and thrown into the asylum."

Stacy turned her head away to hide the tears that were ready to flow. She had done her best to convince him— and she had failed. What more could she do?

"But," said Nigel, disregarding her hurt, "most members of the Council have never dealt with wolves. They don't know them as we do."

Stacy spun around and glanced wide-eyed at her father. "Then you do believe me?" she asked, breathless and hopeful.

Nigel put out his hands, palms forward. "I didn't say that. But I am willing to concede that *some* of this wolf's adventures are possible. For one thing, no one has ever seen a white wolf before, either in our forests or in the Newfoundland wilds. So I am willing to accept the fact that he comes from some unknown land. Also, I've heard some of the rivermen at Rhonnda speak of ice drifts during the winter that roll in with the swells and do reach the Newfoundland channels. Now it's not easy to believe that anyone could actually float on a sheet of ice for weeks on the open sea. I mean a man would die just from exposure to the elements."

"But a wolf has a pelt!" cried the girl jubilantly.

Nigel smiled. "I know, Stacy, I know. And because of that, I'm even willing to accept that Old One did it."

"Then why can't you accept the rest of the story?" protested Stacy.

"Because the idea of a city of men, of *living* men, is just too fantastic. If he had told of some sort of ancient ruin or the like, well, perhaps that could be so. But a *living, thriving city*?"

"Father, believe me, if Old One were making this up, spinning another of his yarns, I'd have known it. But he swore. He swore by Fara!"

Nigel leaned forward with a stern look. "I believe Old One *thinks* he was telling the truth. And in his mind he probably was. But he's very old—some say senile—and his mind could very easily be confused. He might have recalled true memories of his faraway home and then somehow tangled them together with us. The men he spoke of are probably real—but men of *our* Empire. Soldiers or settlers with whom he probably came into contact years ago."

"But these men tried to kill him!" cried Stacy. "Surely that tells you it wasn't Empire men. Our friendship with wolves forbids it!"

"That may be so," Nigel admitted. "But many things go on in Newfoundland that our Valley law forbids. Many Dwellers have found themselves at odds with our settlers. Who can say if some foolish soldier at one time didn't brandish his sword at Old One just to chase him away or something? The soldier may have done it in jest or actually may have *tried* to kill him. I don't know. And I doubt there'll ever be a way of finding out. But what I'm saying is that Old One may recall this event and in his mind somehow believe that this 'attack' took place before he came here."

Stacy sighed. This time her father's argument was not faulty. But by no means was she convinced. "All right, then," she said, "I admit that a wolf could conceivably have been attacked by one of us. But there's one thing I won't admit. Old One says the men of his land wear skins as clothing from the cold—wolfskins! No Empire man would dare do that!"

Nigel pondered on that briefly. "You're right about that much. If a man killed a wolf here, he wouldn't display the murder by wearing his victim's pelt. But Old One's word on that won't sway many opinions."

"But what if the story *is* accurate? What if Old One isn't confused in his mind? What would you say to the fact that somewhere across the sea, in some northern clime we know nothing of, there actually is a rich city of men?"

"I would say," said Nigel, weighing his words carefully, "that it would be the greatest discovery I could imagine. But, alas, I don't believe it's possible."

"Why, father," said Stacy with a mock laugh, "you sound more like those pompous fat politicians every day! *Any-*

thing is possible—you of all people should know that. Thirty years ago who would have believed that there was a way out of the forests, or that men could align with wolves?"

That was a good point, Nigel knew. If he had predicted today's facts when he was Stacy's age, *he* would have been the one locked in the asylum as an incurable lunatic. "Ahh, Stacy," he whispered, "I've forgotten how it is to be young. To you, there is nothing that can't be overcome, no mountain that can't be climbed, no forest that can't be conquered."

Stacy's eyes flashed happily. "And no sea that can't be crossed!"

Nigel smiled and wistfully shook his head. Indeed to be young again! "I know what you're thinking, Stacy. That the Council must prepare an expedition. And believe me, I'd love to see it done. But planning such an expedition is an enormous task, and a costly one, to boot. Before I even dared to hint at it, I'd have to be able to show the Council some sort of genuine proof that this faraway land really exists."

"The proof," replied the girl, "will be in the success of the voyage." And she looked him straight in the eye.

Her father shook his head. "No, Stacy. That's not the way it works."

Stacy fidgeted in her chair and felt her temper beginning to rise. "How can we prove it exists unless we go and find it?"

Nigel glared. "I need proof now, child! Now! The Council isn't about to risk a hundred lives on the open sea without something to assure them the risks are worth taking. And the storytelling of a wolf will not serve as proof."

"Your own belief in the matter would help to sway them."

Nigel looked at her oddly. "My belief? Founded on what? The word of some crazy canine who spins fables all day? I'd be an idiot even to attempt to sway the Council with such gibberish."

Now Stacy was really angry. It was one thing for her father to listen and sympathize, and maybe even in part to believe. But that was clearly about as far as he was willing to go. Stacy was livid. "I'll wager there are plenty of folk in Rhonnda who'd be willing to listen!"

Nigel threw up his hands in total exasperation. "Who?" he barked. "Let me tell you something, Stacy. Sailing the Newland rivers and channels is a far cry from sailing a thousand leagues of open sea. Any captain would have to be crazy even to think about it, and, if you don't believe me, go and ask them!"

Softly, Stacy answered, "I intend to."

"And what does that mean?"

"A few moments ago you said that the finding of another civilization of men would be the greatest discovery you could imagine."

Nigel nodded hesitantly. "So?"

"Well, now we have the opportunity to do just that. And I want to be a part of the discovery if I can. Right now we could be standing on the threshold of the most significant encounter the Empire has ever faced: the chance to come into contact with another culture, one that has as little idea of our existence as we did of theirs. Father, don't you see the potential of such a meeting? Think what we could learn from each other after all these thousands of years. It will change the face of the world—not just the Empire's world, but the *entire* world. There could be trade between us and a constant flow and exchange of thought. The potential is unlimited."

"Hold on, Stacy," said Nigel. "You've said an awful lot. But did you ever consider the other side of the coin? What if your dream turns into a nightmare?"

The girl furrowed her brows questioningly.

"I can see you haven't," said her father a moment later. "All right, let's assume that one of our ships is able to battle across the sea and somehow reaches this elusive Land of the White Wolves. Do you expect the men of this land to be waiting on shore with open arms? It's been many thousands of years since men have come into contact with one another. How do you think they'll react to seeing our lads? They might be frightened out of their wits by the sight of our ship and pack up and head for the hills. Or worse, they may look on us as invaders. They might attack us before the first words of friendship could be uttered. Are you prepared for that possibility in your dream, Stacy? Remember, you told me that Old One was afraid of these men, so it's clear they have no love for Dwellers as we do. And if the men of this land did indeed try to kill him, that only tells us they're warlike. And, if they are, what do we do? Should we send a dozen ships filled with Valley soldiers to protect you? For all we know, this civilization across the sea may be no more than a bunch of savages wielding clubs and spears and howling at the moon like jackals. What would you think then? Would you still be so eager to make their acquaintance?"

Stacy listened intently and in her mind admitted that these were possibilities she had not considered. "I never said there would be no danger—only that the opportunity of finding this city is worth the risk. We have much more to gain than we do to lose. If our ship were to be lost, what of it? A handful of adventurers would be gone, but the Empire would not change. Things would continue as always, and the Empire need never set out to cross the sea again. But if we find this city and *if* its people prove to be like us, look what benefits it would provide. By combining our knowledge, we might conquer the world! Newfoundland is only our backyard; there are entire continents still waiting for us. And I intend to help by carrying the first banner."

"Brave words, Stacy," retorted Nigel. "But all this talk is quite meaningless. As I said, the Council would never fund such an expedition without some concrete evidence that the sea *could* be successfully crossed and that this 'city of men' really exists. And without the Council to provide its help, what man would be willing to risk his life on the strength of a fable?"

"You're wrong, father. Some of these rivermen would give their eyeteeth to do it. They've dreamed of it for years. Why the glory alone would make it worth the effort—not to mention the lure of adventure and wealth. Remember, Old One said this city is rich."

Nigel laughed. "And what would you do, Stacy? Sack the city of its gold?"

Stacy's temper rose with her voice. "That's not what I mean!" she flared. "A wealthy city means a wealthy land. And what does the Empire need more than anything for its growth and expansion?"

For a moment Nigel seemed puzzled, then he smiled. "Raw material."

"Right," cooed Stacy. "The Empire is rich in timber, salt, granite. Our granaries are overstocked; Newfoundland is a breadbasket."

"But we're desperately short of metals," observed Nigel. "Nickel, zinc, copper, tin."

"Now do you see, father?" said Stacy excitedly. "They could have an abundance of the very things we need so badly. Our furnaces are constantly in short supply. Our expansion is hampered. But if we could reach out and *trade....*"

Nigel's mind began to click. "What exactly is your proposal, Stacy?"

The girl leaned back and smiled widely. "Simple. The Empire must reach this land and send an emissary to represent it. If the men of Old One's city are anything but total barbarians, they'll see the mutual advantages and seize upon them. They'd be fools not to."

"And how will you even find this city? Your ship could find itself moored in a wilderness. How will you locate it?"

Stacy winked. "The white wolves will show us. And that's where I come in. Who in the Empire knows wolves better? But don't worry, I plan to take a pack of hunters with us. Together we'll seek out these white wolves, gain their friendship and find the city."

"What makes you think any of our wolves would be interested in our ambitions? After all, wolves are still Dwellers."

"I think you're right," replied Stacy. "Most forest wolves would not be eager to come. But what I have in mind are mountain wolves. They're a very different breed. Half-wild, you might say. Like Cicero. They're daring and adventurous, and it's from their packs I'll find the hunters I need. I understand wolves better than I understand my own kind, and I guarantee you, father, these wolves will be interested, if only to find these white-furred cousins and breed with them."

Stacy had it all figured out, Nigel had to admit, right down to the smallest detail. And although he was not yet ready to concede it openly, much of what she said made sense. Good common business sense, if you like—the kind the Council understood. "This has all come very fast and furious," he said, "and it's something that we can't just jump into. I'll need time to consider, weigh it over in my mind."

"Of course," answered Stacy happily. "We have the whole winter to mull it over and plan. But I must remind you that by spring, when the Newfoundland road is open again, I intend to be with the first caravan. And I'm going to seek out a riverman, one who's not going to cringe at the idea of danger, and with luck we'll set sail from Rhonnda by the first days of summer."

"You know you can be stopped," said Nigel roughly. "The Council can instruct any ship trying to head for the open sea to be confiscated and put under military order. We can see that you never leave harbor."

Stacy glared at him sharply. "No, you can't," she

retorted. "If I have to, I'll seek out a brigand, a smuggler, and run your damned blockade. You know it can be done."

Nigel tensed. "Yes, Stacy. I know it can be done. All right, then. Maybe we can strike a bargain, you and I."

Stacy's brows rose, and her eyes grew wide.

"I'll be going to see Hector when winter begins," said Nigel. "Perhaps I'll be able to find something to ease his pain. And when I go, you'll come with me. While we're there, I'll speak with Old One and try to get a clearer picture of what he knows about this city and how we could reach it. And I give you my word, if I can't prove to your satisfaction—and mine—that his story is only a fable, then I promise to put my own prestige on the line. I'll ask the Council to back such a voyage. We'll get you all the supplies you'll need and scour Newfoundland for the best mariners, even order a squad of crack Valley soldiers to accompany you. How does that sound?"

"That sounds fine," replied Stacy with a smile. "But what must I do in return?" She leaned forward with interest.

"Your part of the bargain is simple. You'll do absolutely nothing. This matter will be discussed with no one." His eyes narrowed and darkened. "Your mother must know nothing about it. You'll make no hasty plans until then; put the matter out of your head. And if it's proved that this 'Land of the White Wolves' is sheer fantasy, you'll forget this scheme forever."

There was a sly smile in Stacy's dark eyes. "You won't be able to prove Old One wrong," she said with conviction.

Nigel grinned. "Then I'll lose and you'll win. What do you say?"

"Father, you drive a hard bargain. But, of course, I agree."

CHAPTER FIVE

For those in the Valley the ensuing weeks passed quickly. The harvests were reaped, the grains carefully and painstakingly stocked in the silos and warehouses. As the weather grew colder, the pace of activity slowed. The last caravan across the mountains to Deepwater left, and the Old Road to Newfoundland was closed until the next spring. This was a peaceful and quiet time for those of the Valley, a time to rest from the long months of labor and enjoy the benefits of their work. Activity now centered on plans for the next year and growth of the Empire.

But to the Dwellers winter is seen very differently. After many months of watching her children and caring for them, Fara is tired. She can no longer spend her time in the forest slipping unnoticed among the Dwellers. She must sleep. And when she does, the world changes. One by one the trees shed their leaves and stand lonely and forlorn; the grasses wither and die; the hills and dales become dulled and pale; the earth cold and hard. No longer are there splashes of wild flowers to color the meadows, no longer is there the thick, lush grass to cover the ground. In his sadness, Khal, the sun, no longer bathes the land with his warmth, and Lea, the moon, becomes restless and hides behind the clouds. In anger at her sleeping sister, Aleya sweeps down from the mountains and brings the bitter frosts that cause the animals to shiver and tremble. And then one day, often in the stealth of night, when the sky is burdened with thick clouds, the snows begin. At first it is little more than a touch of gentle flakes that fall, more often than not melting before they touch the ground. But the flakes are deceiving, the Dwellers know. Before the night is done the land will be covered in white, the streams and ponds frozen to ice, and so they will stay until Fara awakes. Rabbits burrow deeper into their warrens, and only the bravest among them dare to venture outside. The birds fly away to seek the shelter and relative warmth of the Valley, leaving their nests empty and cold, untouched save by the frosts on Aleya's breath. Even the mighty bear, most hated Dweller in the wood, knows that he may no longer roam and hunt at will. With his mate he returns to his caves and like Fara herself sleeps a long, deep sleep. The industrious beaver and the tricky raccoon also hide and rest; the bullfrog is gone; the snake crawls beneath his rock; the butterfly dies. And life in the forest becomes still.

Yet not all Dwellers sleep with Fara. Fara would not have it so, for she dare not leave her children unattended, lest men or other enemies come and take them from her. Someone must guard and protect the forest in her absence —and the task is an important one, one that cannot be taken lightly. It is said that once, long ago, Fara entrusted the great cats to take care in her name. They were graceful and sly creatures—many said they were as cunning as Fara herself—but they proved lazy in their ways and showed little concern for those in their charge. Through their own deeds they lost her trust, and now they can be seen roaming only in the mountains, still shamed by their disgrace. But now who was Fara to trust? Should the responsibility go to the fox? Fara thought not. He was too devious a creature to leave so much in his care. Who then? The mighty elk? He was powerful enough and a good leader, but he had neither the wiles nor the cunning. The hare? He was smart and quick on his feet, but one so puny could never rule. The caribou? Too gentle. Reindeer? Too meek and docile. Fara was deeply troubled; she pondered for many long nights, delaying the winter. But one morning, after a long night of consideration, Fara smiled. The choice became clear—she should have known it all along. Of all her domain there was but one who was worthy of the task—the wolf. He and he alone possessed all the qualities needed to protect the forest. She knew that none would dare harm her children while he was on the prowl. Only a foolish creature indeed would even dare to try. And so, many ages ago, Fara came to meet with the wolves. In the guise of a she-wolf, Fara came among them and offered the task. Filled with awe at her sight and proud that they had been chosen above all the rest, the wolves readily accepted. And yet again Fara smiled. She had chosen well. Such an important duty would not go unrewarded, she promised. While many Dwellers would be forced to go hungry during the lean months while she slept, the wolf would always find the means to keep his belly full. Cunning and intelligence they already possessed, and their swiftness was hard to beat; so in her wisdom Fara added the ability to organize into packs and hunt together. Thus blessed, they could not help but catch their prey. If a Dweller must die so that her guardians stay strong and healthy, so be it. That is Fara's law: the law of the forest. And never once has she regretted it.

Not so very far from the meadow where Hector's pack lived there was a large clearing, a place of flat, soft earth surrounded by sharply sloping hills filled with many varieties of trees. And in the center of the clearing, not far from the brook that rambled down from the hollow, there was a large pond.

Today the clearing was so still that even the snap of a twig would sound like a crash of thunder, and the pond was covered with a layer of ice. As the sun began to drop behind the western horizon, a small herd of deer cautiously made its way down the rugged slope from the top of a hill. They were white-tailed deer, a small but swift breed. Just then the wind gusted fiercely all around, swirling the top layer of snow above their heads. The deer stood frozen. Not because of Aleya—they were accustomed to her song—but because of what lay on her breath: danger!

The deer began to race across the clearing. From behind the ridges of the nearby hills leaped a pack of wolves. Fanning out, they snarled and barked to frighten the already petrified deer. The deer scattered and began to run helter-skelter in all directions. But the wolves were too clever for that ploy; they concentrated their efforts on just several, paying scant heed to the others, who managed to dash from the clearing and back up the slopes.

Soon one wolf had felled a buck and after dragging the carcass to the thicket gave a low, throaty growl that pierced the frigid air like a knife. The hunters at the farthest edge of the clearing stopped immediately and turned around. The cry was clear. Enough food had been caught and the hunt was over. Slowly they made their way back to their companions.

"The grandfather will be pleased," growled one of the hunters.

The wolf from the pond snarled. "It's the best we've done in a week," he replied.

"You chose the timing well, Casca," barked a third.

Casca shrugged in wolf-fashion. "We were lucky. I never dreamed so many would come. They made it easy for us."

It took some hours before the hunters had managed to drag their prey back to the winter lair of the pack. About a day's travel from the meadow there was a tall, craggy hill filled with rock and tall pine and fir trees. The pack had chosen this place carefully, noting that the shelter of the boulders would provide good walls from Aleya's winter wrath, while the denseness of the trees gave a blanketlike protection from the snow. Along the hill's broad ridges the pack had dug its dens, deep, open holes beside the rocks, cavelike, from which the females, many already pregnant and ready to deliver in the spring, could rest easily and watch for the hunters to return.

As Casca and the others approached home, they were greeted with the familiar cries of the cubs hailing their arrival. Within moments the entire pack came out into the night and stood happily, tails wagging and beating against the snow as the hunters dragged their prizes along the escarpment for all to see. A large she-wolf, with icy silver-gray fur and slightly slitted eyes, dashed from her den and stood panting before Casca. Momentarily forgetting both his prey and his hunters, he nuzzled his snout beside her own. The female smothered his face with long wet kisses from her tongue and a soft purring sound, strangely catlike. Casca stepped back slightly and let his eyes gaze up and down her sleek body. Then he smiled in that curious way that only wolves can. "Who do you love?" he asked.

The female, Athena, growled complacently. "Wild flowers and fresh meat," she replied.

Casca snarled jokingly. "I asked *who,* not what."

Athena laughed and again smothered him with wet kisses. After a few moments together in this fashion, Casca barked several commands and watched as several wolves, those either too young or too old to hunt, began to tear chunks of juicy meat from the deer's belly and apportion them properly.

"Where's the grandfather?" asked Casca, looking about in some bewilderment. It was unlike Hector not to be in the forefront when the hunters came back. And he had always demanded that he personally make certain that each member of the pack was fed his due amount.

Athena lowered her eyes and turned her head away from Casca's sharp stare. "He rests in his den," she whispered sullenly.

"Then let's wake him."

Athena shook her head. "He cannot be awakened. I tried. Dedra tried. Even Old One tried. He's in a deep, deep sleep." Athena fought back tears.

Casca felt his heart miss a beat. "Has the sage tended to him?"

Athena nodded. "He's with him now. But there's nothing he can do. Grandfather will not wake. Not for me, not for anyone."

Casca lowered his head, beating his tail against the snow in the rhythm of a clock, back and forth, back and forth. Perhaps this deep sleep was a blessing, he thought. Perhaps it would be better if the grandfather never awoke. At least there would be no more pain for him. Ever since the day Khalea had gone back to the Valley, Hector had become worse—and now.

"I want to see him," said Casca flatly, commandingly, more in the tone of a lord than a husband.

"Is it wise?" asked Athena. "Surely the sage——"

"I'm not awed by that hocus-pocus and mumbo jumbo," snapped Casca. "The sage can do nothing for him. You told me that yourself." And without waiting for an answer, Casca ran along the slope to the last den on the side of the hill, the side that was the first to see the light of dawn.

The cave was dark. Even with his superior night vision Casca was hard pressed to see anything inside. But his ears heard much. There was the low growl of the sage, praying lowly to sleeping Fara, and there was a heavy rasping sound from Hector as he lay in his coma. Casca felt a cold chill race through his body. With his right paw forward he stepped warily inside. The sage, an old wolf with brittle brown fur and bloodshot eyes, faced Casca and stared without missing a single beat of his chant. Bowing wolf-fashion, Casca lowered his head and stretched out his front paws in submission. In this way he told the sage that even he, soon to be lord of this pack, respected him for both his office and his wisdom.

"How long has the grandfather been like this?" he asked after the sage acknowledged his presence.

"Since before you left this dawn. Dedra tried to wake him this morning but was unable."

"Will his lips accept water?"

The sage shook his head glumly. If a sick wolf turned from water, it could mean only one thing—that death was at hand. Or so the wolves have always believed.

Casca sighed. At that moment he felt like an unweaned cub, frightened and forlorn, with no mother or father to raise him. And he recalled how, when his own father had died under the hooves of a wild moose maddened with fever, his grandfather had taken special pains to see that he was trained and raised by the best family in the pack. And the grandfather had always favored him, even as he favored the child of men, Khalea.

"What's to be done, then?" he asked at last.

The sage cast his eyes above, as though looking to *Balaka*. "We wait for him to slip from us," he said sadly. "We wait for him to run with Fara. But for you, Casca, there is much to be done. You will be our lord now. You must go among your flock and speak with each wolf. It's our law. The pack must accept you."

"And the other packs must be told of Hector's grave sickness. There will be many lords who will wish to pay their respects."

"You must send out the messengers tonight, Casca. There is no time to be lost. Lord Hector is known far and wide in this forest. Even beyond. As you said, there will be many to mourn his passing."

Casca felt a searing glare from the sage. The wolf was sizing him up, he knew, looking to see if he were truly wolf enough to follow in his grandfather's tracks. To be a leader of the pack was something that he had often craved, yet now that it was close at hand, perhaps only a day or two away, he was not so sure of himself. The responsibility involved would be a heavy weight on his shoulders. If now, as the sage observed him on the sly, he were to show the slightest hesitation or indecision, the sage and others would proclaim his weakness, and some other wolf would challenge his right to lead. And that other wolf would be doing exactly as he himself would do had circumstances been different. A weak lord is no lord at all, and the entire pack would suffer for it. A leader must not waver in his judgment or commands. He cannot afford to. Too many lives depend on him.

For a long moment Casca stood silent, pondering these thoughts and gazing down at the shivering body of his grandfather. He wanted to cry and howl at the moon like a jackal, but now was not the time for the luxury of grief. Important tasks were at hand, the pack must be reassured, encouraged to respect his authority and have confidence in his judgment. Tall and proud, he turned and faced the watchful eyes of the sage. "Fetch a female to lie beside my grandfather and keep him warm," he commanded. "There's no more you can do for him."

The sage raised his brows. "But the prayers, Casca."

Casca stared icily. "You can pray outside."

And at that moment the sage bowed his head with respect. Young Casca had proved equal to the task. He said, "Yes, my lord," crisply and clearly and strode from the den to find the female. Casca stepped to the entrance and looked about. Two of his best and closest hunters were standing meekly a few paces from the den. One held a large piece of meat between his jaws.

"You didn't have any supper," the hunter said, laying the meat at his paws.

"I can't eat now, Pireaus. But thank you for the thought. I'll leave it beside grandfather. Perhaps he'll awake after all."

Pireaus looked at him quizzically. "Allow *me* to place it before Lord Hector," he entreated. "Such work is no longer your task, my lord."

Casca winced slightly at the words. When the sage had

called him "my lord," Casca had thought nothing of it. But Pireaus was a friend. Such a title seemed awkward coming from a friend. "Grandfather will die soon," he growled, still referring to Hector in his familiar rather than proper title. "I'll need a messenger to run through the forest. And I want someone to leave for the mountains tonight. Grandfather has many friends there, and they'd want to be here."

"I'll go myself," said Pireaus. "I'll travel as fast as I can."

Casca nodded gratefully, wearily.

"Shall I go, too?" asked the other wolf.

"No, Sonjii. I have other duties for you. Someone has to go to the Valley and find Lord Nigel. I know grandfather would want him to be here."

Sonjii and Pireaus bowed low and scampered out of sight. Casca watched them go, then turned back into Hector's den, the meat between his teeth. And while he waited for the sage to bring the female, he closed his eyes and cried.

CHAPTER SIX

All night long Nigel tossed and turned fitfully in bed, restless and tense, unable to sleep. Something dim, something he could not get at, was nagging at the back of his mind. An uneasy feeling, the kind that made him shiver and clutch tightly at the blankets.

From the tightly shuttered window came a low rapping. A single sharp sound that almost sent him leaping from his bed. Nigel stared at the window. Was it his imagination? The wind, perhaps? No. The shutters were locked as tight as drums. It couldn't be the wind pushing against them. Again the rap—this time three short knocks, in sequence. He bounded from the bed and clumsily began to unlatch the bolt, afraid to find what would be waiting outside. A strong gust of wind blew harshly against his face as the shutters were slightly cast to the sides. Nigel stood dumbly. On the ledge there was a bird, a large falcon. Small eyes stared up at him, blinking furiously.

The falcon fluttered his feathers slightly. "A message for you, Lord Nigel," he squeaked in Common Tongue.

Nigel held his breath and whispered, "From the forest?"

The bird nodded darkly.

"Is it . . . Hector?"

Again the bird nodded. "Lord Casca bids that you come at once if you care for your friend. There is a hunter waiting to escort you."

Nigel glanced down toward the hickory tree in the garden. He could see the silhouette of a young wolf standing in the shadows beneath the lengthy branches.

"I'll dress at once," he said, unaware of the urgency in his own voice. "Please bear with me. It will take just a few minutes."

"Be swift, my lord," answered the bird. "There is no time to lose." And before Nigel could turn from the window the pointed wings fluttered and the bird soared off into the clouds. Nigel hastily threw off his nightclothes and began to pull his tunic over his head. Gwen opened her eyes, watched silently for a moment, then asked, "What's wrong?"

Nigel sighed. "It's come," he said glumly. "There was a bird at the window. Casca's calling for me. There's a hunter waiting in the garden."

Gwen sank back against the pillows and covered her eyes with her hands. "Is it . . . the . . . end?"

Nigel shrugged. "It must be. Casca would never send for me like this in the middle of night if it weren't."

"I want to come, also."

Nigel shook his head firmly. "I can't wait for you, Gwen. I'm sorry, but I just can't. I have to go *now.*"

Gwen looked at him through watery eyes. "What about Stacy? You promised to tell her—"

"I know, I know. But I can't wait for her, either," he said. "When she wakes, tell her what happened. Have her horse saddled. She'll know where to find me." He leaned over and kissed his wife long and hard on the lips. "Take care, Gwen," he whispered. "I'll send word back to you as soon as I can."

He clambered down the stairs, raced into the courtyard and quickly made his way to the stable. He paused to have a brief exchange with the waiting wolf and saddled his horse. Then the dull clatter of hoofbeats sounded in the night as he raced down the street on his way out of the Haven and toward the forest.

* * *

When a wolf dies, all the forest knows. The howls of the pack fill the air, and the other Dwellers stop and listen, for they know that Fara has taken one of her children into her arms. And for that they are glad, for life would be meaningless without the assuring knowledge that after it is done there is a new forest to greet, a golden forest where food is plentiful and enemies cannot enter. In Fara's own forest Aleya never blows cold; Khal never dims. But only Dwellers who are deserving may reach Fara's wood. They must be pure in spirit and mind and must have led a life that was unselfish. As for Hector there could be no doubt. Was there ever a more noble and worthy wolf? Was there ever one more devoted to his duties and obligations to his tribe? The question hardly needed to be asked. Many believed that Fara would even wake from her winter sleep to have the joy of greeting one so noble into her home.

From far and wide they came to the winter home of Hector's pack. From the deepest reaches of the forest they traveled, league upon league, never once pausing for rest. Some came from the south, the land of steamy swamps and bitter soils; others marched proudly from the east, the lands of windswept plains and rugged grasslands; and still others came from the west, from the mountains that divided the Valley from Newfoundland. For these it was the hardest travel, over treacherous passes and peaks deep with winter snow, iced rivers and thunderous winds that blew down from the sea. Yet even all this did not deter them one whit; Lord Hector was waiting.

In all the land, from the fjords to the southern forest below the Valley of Men, no wolf had ever been more revered than he. He was not a king—although he might have been had he desired—but a humble hunter, a lord who sought neither glory nor ambitions, whose only wish in a long, rich life was to see wolves and men live in peace together. When he passed on into Fara's arms, it would create a void that wolves could not recall, for Hector, if not in name, truly *was* their king. And when he died, would there ever be another wolf like him?

Stacy jumped from her mare and left her standing awkwardly beside a cluster of firs. From the top of the hillock she could see the deep tracks in the snow from the steady stream of wolves who had made their way to the sloping, craggy hill near the hollow where the pack, already being called Casca's pack, had their lair. The forest was quiet. To Stacy's surprise there were no howls from the hunters, nor even soft moans or whimpers from the females. Along the escarpment of the hill, standing in snow almost up to their bellies, was a line of hunters. Their faces seemed impassive, as though they were wearing masks to hide their grief. Immobile, save for an occasional tail that beat softly in the snow, the hunters formed a line of mourners, waiting for the sage to bring word the moment Hector left this life. And when that word came, these hunters, many of them Hector's grandchildren, would begin the task of running through the forest and howling the word for all to hear.

Moving slowly, face partly covered by a scarf, Stacy tightened her woolen coat, flicked snowflakes from her collar and made her way along the narrow path between the juniper trees. At the foot of the hill she saw the gathering. There must have been hundreds of wolves all squatted together along the small ice-filled stream, growling quietly among themselves. Many Stacy recognized. There was Bruli, Lord of the South, standing beside Athena with his head hung low and his tail curled between his legs. Off to his left she saw old Sula, the once-feared black wolf of the eastern wood, whose packs were renowned for their fierceness and martial abilities. All wolves organized themselves in military fashion, she knew, but few with the skill of Sula's breed. Once upon a time men had feared wolves such as he more than they feared the vicious wild dogs that once ran rampant near the Valley. And with good reason, for Sula was the true descendant of kings, great-grandson of Dinjar, who lost his life fighting valiantly in the Forest Wars. When a wolf such as Sula growls, all take notice. And his presence here at Hector's side was all the more honor because it showed just how much affection everyone in the forest felt for the dying wolf.

Yet apart from these and several others, there were many that Stacy did not know at all. There were New-foundland wolves all around, their black-and-gray-flecked pelts blazing wetly as soft flakes fell upon them. They were larger than most of the others, eyes seeming to signal an awareness that this terrain, this forest, was alien to them. They were wild wolves, free to march across the highest peaks of the Empire, often taunting even the great cats with their presence—and even daring to battle with them over some fine caribou or moose.

As Stacy slipped among them all, hardly a head turned, so used to her presence had they become. Some of the finer ladies of the Haven often laughed and snickered that the reason Stacy was able to move so freely among wolves was that she smelled like them. But there was more to their poor joke than they realized. Although to men such a scent could not be recognized, to wolves it was obvious long before she had reached the lair. Her scent was carried by Aleya even as she first entered the forest. And Casca was waiting to greet his sister.

"Welcome, Khalea," he growled lowly as he moved from among the crowds to her side.

Stacy knelt down on one knee and ran her fingers through his fur. "I would have come yesterday, with my father, but he——"

Casca nodded. "I understand. Your father did as he had to do. He has been with grandfather all through this day."

Stacy looked about. "Where is he now?"

"In grandfather's lair. But you must not go, Khalea. Not now. Only the sage and your father can be there."

Stacy's mouth opened slightly, and her eyes began to water. "Am I not permitted to see Hector before he passes into Fara's kingdom?" she cried.

Casca shook his head sadly. *"No one* is allowed. Even I cannot go."

"But a lord need not die in solitude," Stacy protested. "There is no law against his loved ones being close by!"

"Only your father is permitted, Khalea. Believe me, my sister, I am sorry. The sage has begun the chant. Now we must all remain here and wait, listen to our own thoughts and rejoice in the knowledge that we were beloved by him."

Stacy made a noise, a brief high-pitched squeal, the way wolves do when they are in pain. A few heads turned.

"Please, Casca, let me see him. Only for a moment."

Again Casca shook his head, only this time with an air of finality. He was lord of the pack now, Stacy saw. She was only a huntress. Casca's word was law.

From among the Newfoundland wolves Athena came. Her head held high, eyes wet from crying, she nestled close beside Stacy. "Come rest with me," she said. "I have a warm den nearby. We can wait together, if you like."

Stacy nodded sadly. Athena led Stacy along the stream, moving upward toward the ridge. About halfway up, almost hidden by the bushes and snow and by a stately spruce, there was a long, narrow tunnel dug at a slight downward angle into the side of the hill. Across the floor was a smattering of twigs and dead leaves, which made the ground somewhat dry and comfortable. Here and there Stacy smelled the fresh scent of pines. A few fallen branches had been dragged into the den recently, she knew. And she wondered if Athena had not dug this place especially for her.

Stacy followed Athena to the farthest wall and then slumped down on the floor forlornly. And there, in the dark and solitude of Athena's den, she buried her face in her hands and began to weep—not the long, mournful cries of the wolves but the deep, wrenching sobs of girls; young *hu-*

man girls who, for the first time, have had to come to grips with death. At that moment her wolfishness was totally gone; there was no feeling of joy that Hector would find new happiness with Fara in her wood, only the harsh reality that a friend, almost a second father, was actually going to die—to be buried in the earth, and neither she nor anyone else would ever see him again.

After quite some time, Stacy drew a small handkerchief from inside her coat and dried her eyes. Athena sat on her hind legs, mouth open, eyes fixed on her. She smiled kindly.

"Do you feel a little better, Khalea?"

Stacy nodded and blew her nose. "I'll be all right now, Athena. Really I will. But thank you for bringing me here and giving me a place to let out my——"

Athena smiled. "Human emotion?"

Stacy tried to laugh. "Yes, human emotion. I guess this all came so fast. I woke up this morning to find my father already gone and my mother in tears, and I ran out of the house like someone crazed. Then the road was snowed in. I had to ride across the foothills to get to the forest, and, once here, I almost killed myself racing through the snow to reach the lair. I'm afraid I was in a bad way before I even arrived."

Athena nodded knowingly and growled, "Have you eaten? Your strength must not be diminished."

Stacy shook her head. "Nothing since last night. But I can't eat now, Athena. My stomach's in knots."

"It will all be over soon, Khalea. The chant has begun."

"I know. Casca told me."

"Then you know that the end will come at any time. The howls will begin across the forest and will last until morning."

"And if Khal is bright at morning," said Stacy, "then we'll know that Fara has taken him into her arms."

"And if Khal hides," whispered Athena, "it will mean that Hector was found unworthy."

Stacy smiled. "That won't happen, Athena. You and I know it won't. As certain as Lea shines tonight, Khal will greet her at dawn."

And no sooner had Stacy finished her thought than there came a loud wail from the lair. Stacy bounded up to see what was happening.

"It's the sage," said Athena. "The chant is done. The grandfather will be gone in moments."

Stacy put her hand to her mouth; she felt her heart pounding like a drum. She wanted her father to be here now, to comfort her. But that was impossible. If there was one thing she was certain of, it was that Nigel would stand by Hector's side until the end.

Slivers of pale moonlight filtered dimly into the den, giving only the faintest light. Nigel's coat was off, placed under his knees as he leaned over the still body. With his left hand he stroked Hector's fur, with his right he nudged gently at the wolf's muzzle. The body stirred for an instant, then went limp again. Nigel sighed. All day he had tried to bring a moment's recognition into the glassy eyes, and all day he had failed. Not for an instant had the wolf known that he was there. But now time was getting short, he knew. Hector's breathing had become laborious, his nostrils dry and stiff. With a tear in his eye he leaned over to Hector's ear and whispered, "I've come to see you, old friend. Will you not wake from your sleep to say good-bye?"

And from somewhere within his pain-wracked mind the wolf heard these sweet words. The eyes opened and stared hazily. He tried to raise his head but couldn't. "Ah, Nigel," he sighed in the barest of whispers, "is this a dream?"

Nigel shook his head. "No, my friend. I'm here. I'm really here." His voice began to crack with grief. Hector looked evenly at him and smiled. And in his eyes Nigel caught a glimpse of their old luster and sparkle.

"You look well, my friend. Forgive me that I was not

able to greet you when you came. I have another appointment, you see. One I fear that cannot be delayed."

Nigel raised his head and turned his eyes away from the wolf's. "Fara is a jealous lover," he said. "I know she——"

Just then Hector began to cough violently, and his body began to shake. With the back of his sleeve Nigel wiped Hector's mouth. "Are you in much pain, my friend? I brought something with me that I can give you, something to lessen your hurt."

Hector slowly shook his head. "Fara would be angered. She would meet me as I am. You understand that, don't you?"

Nigel wiped away a tear. Yes, he understood. "And tell her that when my own time comes, I'll expect to see you standing at her side."

Hector began to speak but was racked by another spasm of coughing, one that left him barely able to whisper. "That . . . much . . . I promise, Nigel. But now you must forgive me, old friend. I hear her call and I must hasten to answer."

Nigel stood in the shadows and heard the wolf sigh deeply. Hector's eyes began to close, and his ears picked up as if he were listening to something or someone far distant. But to Nigel and the old sage, who was sitting meekly in the corner, there was nothing to be heard but silence.

"Good-bye, my guide and companion," whispered Nigel. "I'll not make you keep her waiting any longer."

The wolf forced his eyes open and tried to smile. "Kiss . . . Khalea . . . for me." Then the old head slumped across his outstretched paws, the body gave a small jerking motion and the bushy tail wagged. And then it was still.

Like a small child, Nigel bent down on his knees and banged his fists into the cold dirt, all the time weeping and sobbing unashamedly. And from the hill came the howls.

At first a single long cry that pierced the forest for a mile; then it was joined by others and then by still others. Soon every wolf at the lair joined in the ritual. They wailed and sang their mournful song until the very sound became so overwhelming that no Dweller remained unmoved. Nigel stayed beside the limp body of Hector and shivered uncontrollably. There was no doubt that a part of him had died with the wolf; the bonds between them were just too close for it to have been any other way.

CHAPTER SEVEN

It had been a long night, a painful night. But now it was over. Just as Stacy had predicted to Athena, Khal came bright and strong with the new dawn. Khal climbed high into the early morning sky and bathed the forest with the most warmth they had known in months. It was more like a mild day in spring rather than midwinter, and the wolves rejoiced, for Khal was again happy because Fara had stirred briefly from her slumber, pleased by the arrival of Lord Hector into her fold.

The hour of sadness and mourning had passed; the hour of joy had begun. Indeed Lord Hector had been well received. Now the wolves must get on with the matters of this world, lest Fara be angered at them for not getting back to the task of protecting the forest.

Stacy lay sleeping peacefully inside Athena's den. Using her long coat as a blanket, she had stayed snug and warm through the lengthy and difficult night. The early morning sunlight filled the den with its brightness; its warmth pressed against her face and made her stir. Bleary-eyed, she sat up, yawned and looked around. At her side she found the leather pouch she had left in her saddlebag. Someone, obviously her father, had fetched it for her. Gratefully she opened the straps and pulled out a handful of dried corn, which she ate slowly.

Before she was finished, Athena poked her head inside.

There was a contented smile written across her face. "It's done," she said with a sigh.

Stacy looked at her curiously. "What's done?"

"The sage and the other elders have appointed Casca as lord of the pack. The meeting was held before dawn."

"That's wonderful," said Stacy, forgetting last night's tears for the moment. "You should have wakened me. I'd have liked to have been there."

"Your father asked that we let you sleep, Khalea. But now that you're awake I can bring your visitor."

"My visitor?"

Before Athena could answer, another wolf slipped by her and slunk slowly into the den. His fur was dark red, paws large. His eyes glowed. It took a few long moments for recognition to come, but when it did, she smiled.

"Cicero! I never expected to see you here. I mean not all the way from Rhonnda."

Cicero lowered his head, bowed wolf-fashion and waited politely for Stacy to gesture for him to sit beside her. "I wasn't at Rhonnda," he growled. "There had been some trouble among the mountain packs. Not much really, just some petty squabbling among wolves and a few Newfoundland farmers who took it into their heads that the herds of caribou belonged to no one but them. It could have been a nasty situation if things weren't calmed. Seems these men were actually ready to fight."

Stacy pressed her lips together. "Fight? Men against wolves?" She was incredulous.

Cicero nodded. "But don't be concerned. An agreement was reached. I helped to mediate the matter along with one of your Valley soldiers. A good chap, actually. In fact I think you met him. Trevor's the name."

Trevor! In all that had happened these past days, Stacy had all but forgotten. "Of course I met him. He left with you and Elias. Tell me, Cicero, was Elias successful? Did he manage to barge the hardwood up to Rhonnda?"

The wolf smiled slyly. "Elias never makes promises he

can't fulfill, Khalea. I think the rapids gave him more problems than he bargained for, but nevertheless Elias is a resourceful man. I'm told he made three trips before the snows came."

Stacy whistled. Elias's profit would be a pretty penny, indeed.

"Anyway," continued Cicero, "one of Casca's hunters, Pireaus, reached the mountains early yesterday with the news. I set off on my own at once to be here. I never knew Hector myself, you know, but like any hunter, tales of his deeds had filled my head since I was a cub. And I knew that no matter what, I'd have to make it here in time."

"And did you?"

"Alas, no, Khalea. Heavy snows across the mountain pass made the going slow. I arrived here a few hours ago."

"No matter," said Stacy. "It was the thought that counted. I'm sure the grandfather, er, I mean, Lord Hector, would have been pleased to know."

"When I saw your father and he told me that you were here, too, I was all the more glad that I came. To tell you the truth, this Trevor fellow, while we were together and all, well, he never stopped talking about you. It was Stacy this, Stacy that." Cicero rolled his eyes around in the way that most wolves do when they are speaking of the confusing ways of men. "Anyway, Khalea, there was no way to shut the fellow up. I never saw a man talk so much. You'd think he was in love."

Stacy blushed. Unlike men, wolves were quite frank. When they had a thought, there was no embarrassment in speaking it. "And, er, how is this Trevor fellow? Is he keeping well?" she asked.

"Wraps himself in blankets at night and walks about with a bear pelt for a coat in the day." Cicero chuckled malevolently and shook his head. "The man is always cold!"

Stacy could not contain her own laughter at Trevor's expense. "Come on now, Cicero. That's not nice. He's from the Valley. You know he's not used to the frigid Newfoundland weather. I'd be cold, too."

"Which reminds me, Khalea," growled the wolf, "this Trevor fellow insists that you'll be coming to Rhonnda. Is this true? Or is the man more out of his head than I thought?"

Stacy paused for a moment before answering. She had promised her father not to discuss the voyage across the sea with anyone. But speaking of Rhonnda should not matter; at least it could do no harm.

"Trevor is right," she answered at last. "I have a sister at Rhonnda and I plan to visit with her."

The wolf grinned. "That *is* good news. And Elias will be glad to hear it."

"Elias?" Her eyes looked questioningly at the red wolf.

"Another of your admirers, Khalea," laughed Cicero. "He never speaks his thoughts like that Trevor fellow, but he can't hide them from me. I can read him like the sage reads *Balaka*. I never understood these things about men. Tell me, is this time of year your mating season?"

Stacy roared with laughter. How much more simple life was among wolves!

"Some men are always in mating season, Cicero. But in our way of measuring years I'm hardly more than a cub. It'll be some time before I choose my mate."

"Very wise, Khalea," nodded the wolf. "But come! I'd almost forgotten. Your father asked me to fetch you. Seems he's deep in conversation with that white wolf. Old One, is it? Whatever, he asked that you be there. He says it's important."

Stacy gulped down the last of her corn. "It *is* important, Cicero. I can't explain it to you just now, but it could have significance for you, too. For all wolves. Where is he?"

Cicero gave a puzzled glance and pointed outside with his long snout. "He said for you to come to the hickory tree."

Stacy got up excitedly. "I know where it is. Will you come with me? I think you'll find it worthwhile."

Cicero laughed soundlessly. "Of course, Khalea. You've tamed me. Lead and I'll follow."

They crossed along the ridge of the hills and at length came to a small brook. It was not iced over, so the brook was a regular watering spot for all the nearby Dwellers. And at the right of it, just in front of a lumbering oak tree with bent branches that dripped icicles in the warm sun, there was the hickory. A tall old tree, probably as old as the forest itself.

Stacy shaded her eyes and glanced ahead. Her father, red-eyed and weary looking, was sitting with his back against the trunk, legs stretched out and crossed, boots almost at the bank of the brook. Old One, beside him, was lying in the sun, beating his tail against the damp, snow-melted soil. Nigel was speaking to him in a low soft voice, and here and there she could see Old One either nod his head or shake it. Without disturbing the mood of their peaceful encounter, Stacy and Cicero slipped down near them and sat a few paces to Nigel's left. Nigel and the white wolf looked over and nodded, then, as if no one had come to join them, continued with the discussion.

"And this city can be reached only by crossing the plains?" asked Nigel, toying with a wet twig.

Old One growled. "Mostly. You can cross the peaks of the Satrian Mountains, but such a route is never used by men. The big cats dwell in the mountains as well as wolves, and most of the men are loath to risk their lives doing it."

"I see," drawled Nigel. "Yet you yourself encountered them. Where?"

"I told you. I strayed too far from our lairs. Near the foot of many of the mountains there are villages. The men hate us; they loathe all Dwellers who spoil their hunting."

"And some of these men tried to kill you?"

Old One looked about with a glare of frustration. "Yes!

I told you that, too. They came at me, screaming and shouting, barking their terrible war cries."

Nigel furrowed his brows questioningly. "War cries? What sort of weapons do the men of this land carry?"

The wolf half-shrugged, half-trembled. "In the villages only a few. They fly their arrows much like your own hunters. They carry sharp teeth at their sides, even as your Khalea does."

"Daggers? You mean daggers?"

"Yes, daggers, if that's what you would have them called."

"And swords? What about swords?"

Old One thought for a moment. "I have heard tales of the soldiers of the city. They, I believe, carry these swords. But I never saw them. Only the arrows and daggers."

Nigel pursed his lips and rubbed at his stubbly chin with his hand. Stacy watched him carefully and saw that he was deep in thought and that he had not, so far at least, been able to shake the wolf's story. After a long while, he began to talk again. "You say that these men wear wolf pelts to keep them warm."

Old One nodded emphatically.

"Yet you said that men hardly ever venture into the mountains where the white wolves live. How do they catch you?"

Old One's eyes narrowed, and he snarled lowly, as if recalling some evil that was yet to be repaid. "They make traps for us, my lord. Vile things made of iron and steel. When a wolf becomes snared, he has no way to escape. One wolf I knew did, though."

"How?" asked Nigel.

"When the vise closed about his leg, the poor animal howled in pain, so much pain that he chewed off his leg rather than endure the agony or wait for the men to come and kill him."

Stacy could not control her shudders at the thought.

"And he hobbled away from the trap as best he could,"

continued Old One, "leaving a trail of blood behind. It was a steep climb up the slope to his den, and the beggar was just too weak to make it. My father and I found him dead in the tundra. He had bled to death, you see, alone and frightened. There hadn't even been anyone to sing the chant for him at his death."

"A cruel way to die," said Nigel, wincing.

"Such it is with men," sighed the wolf. Then hastily added, "But of course I don't mean the men of this fair and pleasant land. Here I have known only kindness." He smiled at Stacy. "But in my land such traps and devices of men are a constant threat to us. Can you blame us if men are our enemy?"

Nigel recoiled at the idea of the traps and the brutality with which they did their work. And just the fact such traps existed assured him that the men of Old One's land were not only clever in their methods but could be cruel as well.

"What other things of the men can you tell me?" he asked.

Cicero, sitting with his front paws outstretched and enjoying the warm sun, began to stir. "Why all this interest in a faraway land that doesn't concern us?"

"It may one day concern us, Cicero. But we'll talk about that later. Well, Old One?"

The wolf bowed his head to shade his tired eyes from the brightness. He stared down at the ground for a long while, hardly moving except to occasionally beat his tail softly against the thin snow. Then, after some deep thought, he peered up. Nigel and Stacy at once saw that his eyes were watery. "Forgive these tears," he growled softly, slipping out of the common tongue and back into his own, "but they come all too easily at my age. Before I tell you any more, Lord Nigel, I must ask you, do you believe what I have already said? Or do you think that this has been but another fable?"

Nigel leaned back, rubbed lightly at his bloodshot eyes, took a deep breath and exhaled slowly. Without looking, he could feel Stacy's glare upon him, and he knew how important to her his answer would be.

"Yes, Old One," he whispered. "I believe you. Many would consider me to be mad, but I do believe what you've told me."

At that the white wolf's face lit up with a look of sheer happiness, like the cub who hunts for the first time with success; like the female, who after so many months of labor and pain, smiles down on her cubs for the first time and forgets all the hardships that came before.

"I have hoped and prayed to Fara that such a day as this would come," he said proudly. "And for most of my life I never dared to dream that it would. To be believed! No longer to be scorned and laughed at as just a spinner of fables! And I thank you, Khalea, for my joy. Once again I can hold my head high."

Stacy flushed and let her eyes drift from his stare.

"But to answer what you asked, my lord," went on Old One, "yes, there are many things I could tell you of my land and the men who share it with us. What would you know?"

Nigel propped himself up beside the tree. "The riches of this city of men, where do they come from?"

Old One blinked his eyes and gazed in the direction of the faraway mountains of Newfoundland. The snowcapped peaks were dazzling in their brilliance.

"From a place called Satra," he said, speaking in a soft tone, with a tinge of fear and respect in his voice.

Stacy glanced at her father. It seemed Old One knew far more than he had told her. "What is Satra?" she asked.

"A mountain, Khalea. I know little of men and their ways, but only a fool in my land would not know of Satra."

"And what is so special about this mountain?" asked Nigel.

"Not merely a mountain, my lord, but a mighty peak that reaches to the heavens. And it is there that the men have their city. It is there that they rule their empire."

Stacy felt her heart race. An empire! She should have known all along!

"Do the white wolves live on Mount Satra?" asked Nigel.

Old One shook his head emphatically.

"But they do know where to find it?" Stacy asked hastily.

"Certainly, Khalea. But we never dare venture too close. As I told you, there is war between us."

"But the white wolves could show the way if they wanted?"

Old One looked at her oddly. "You ask strange questions, Khalea. To whom would the white wolves show the way?"

Stacy smiled thinly at him and said, "Me."

Old One's jaw dropped, as did Cicero's.

"There are those of us," said Nigel, "who would like to find this place and meet with the men of Satra if we could."

"But how would you reach my land?"

"With our ships," replied Stacy. "But that needn't concern you. Tell me this, Old One, if men from here, from the Valley, came to the shores of your land, would the white wolves help us to find Satra?"

Old One looked at her darkly. "Men are enemies, Khalea. I told you as much before. At best, if you set into the mountains, the white wolves would run and hide. At worst, they would kill you."

"But I am a wolf," growled Stacy. "Would they attack me, also? Would they not accept me as one of you?"

Old One sighed deeply. "I don't know, Khalea. Perhaps if you came to them alone, perhaps if they had time to speak with you, to see for themselves that you are one of us, maybe then they would take you in among them."

"And what if I came with other wolves? Wolves from Newfoundland or the forest? Would they attack them, too?"

Old One glanced first to Stacy, then to Nigel, finally to Cicero. "Explain to them how it would be, my lord," he said.

Cicero growled. "When a strange wolf comes upon a pack, he will be accepted—provided that he means no harm nor demands too much. If a wolf comes meekly, in submission, the pack will take him in, just as Hector took in Old One."

Stacy smiled. "What you're saying, what you're both saying, is that any wolf will be treated as a friend by any other wolf—no matter from where he comes."

"Not exactly," answered Old One. "A wolf will not kill another wolf, unless he is driven to it. The white wolves would likely be suspicious of even one such as Cicero. But if he proved to be a friend and meant no harm, then yes, Khalea, he would be treated as such."

There was a lull in the conversation as Nigel picked up a few scattered pebbles and threw them into the stream. His eyes focused on the ripples they made, and in them he saw the Empire. First there was the Haven, that was the pebble, the foundation. The first ripples were the Valley and the near forests where men hunted and cleared. Then came the Newfoundland ripples, larger than the others, reaching out far and wide; and lastly there were broad outer ripples, the ones that spread from shore to shore, ever becoming wider, ever becoming thinner until they mingled with the ripples of another pebble. And in those tiny pebbles splashing into the icy water he saw the future. Not for him, for his years were already numbered, but for Stacy and for her children, and their children after them. A growing Empire that would know no bounds, no limits; a universe to be conquered and a better life for all. And his own youth flashed back before his eyes; the fires began to burn again. He would never make the voyage across the sea, he knew. Such adventure was for the young. For Stacy. And for him to try to stop her, even if it might mean an untimely death on some foreign and inhospitable shore, would be wrong. How else would the Empire grow and thrive if not by the daring of the young? If Stacy failed in her voyage, there would be another, and if that one failed, there would have to be yet another—and so it would be until there was success.

And Stacy's success would only be the start.

"The Empire means to send a ship across the sea," stated Nigel flatly, showing all that there was no longer any doubt in his mind. "And we mean to find Satra if we can. For too long we've sheltered ourselves from the rest of the world. Now it's time that we reached out and established contact."

Cicero glanced up. "And you would send Khalea to seek these white wolves?"

Nigel nodded. "If our ship managed to cross the sea, it would likely find itself completely lost in a strange land. We'd need the white wolves to guide us, just as Hector once guided us through the forest years ago."

Old One began to weep. "It would be a glorious day," he said proudly, "when Khalea comes face to face with my own. Would that I could be there to see it! But my bones are too old and tired. I ask nothing more than to die here, close to Hector's spirit."

"You've already done more than we could have hoped," encouraged Nigel. "It's because of you that the Council will undertake such a perilous expedition. You and I are both too old, my friend. I would never ask that you do more than you already have."

"Then who will guide Khalea to the white wolves?" asked Old One, a sad glint in his eye.

"I had hoped to find some Newfoundland wolves to accompany me," said Stacy. "And with luck, the white wolves will show us the way to Satra."

"*AnaFara*," Old One whispered. "AnaFara, the daughter of Fara." And although he did not mean it literally, it was clear to Cicero that this white wolf did indeed see her as an earthly messenger of Fara herself. Not only as Khalea, the bridge between the sun and moon, but also as the bridge between all Dwellers and men.

PART TWO
NEWFOUNDLAND

CHAPTER EIGHT

Outside the tent a swirling wind scattered the newly fallen soft snow about in a frenzy. Inside the tent, the only occupant lay soundly asleep on a small cot, hugging tightly at a couple of thick quilted blankets.

It was well before dawn when he awoke to the clatter of hoofbeats along the mud-tracked road outside. He heard a few muffled words as the sentry on duty questioned the rider.

There was a moment of absolute numbness as the closed flap of the tent was pulled back and a gust of bitter wind rushed inside. And with it came a soldier, a Valley soldier, he saw, dressed in a heavy dark-blue tunic and covered from shoulder to belt in a thick fur-lined blue-gray jacket.

As he peered at the intruder, the soldier snapped smartly to attention. "A message for you, Commander," he husked in a raspy voice. "It is a message from the governor."

Trevor scratched his chin. "From Deepwater?"

"Yes, sir."

"Do me a favor, will you? Take a match and light that lamp for me."

As the soldier fumbled in the dark, Trevor took the envelope and roughly tore it at the edge. All of a sudden the tent grew bright with a rich red glow as the wick caught the flame of the match. He rubbed his eyes and began to read. At the top of the heavy brittle paper there was a red seal, slightly smudged from the wax imprint. It showed the colors of the Empire, gold and red, in the form of a great soaring falcon. This was indeed an official letter, written by Governor Bela himself.

The message inside was brief, though, only a few scrawled lines: "To the Officer Commanding, Noatak Valley, Newfoundland." Then it became less official: "Trevor, it is imperative that you leave your present duties on the Line and return to Deepwater at once. A special dispatch reached me yesterday, one that I think will require your attention.

Congratulations on your ending the dispute on the Line. I look forward to seeing you again." It was signed *Bela.*

Trevor sat back and smiled complacently.

"Good news, I hope, sir," said the soldier meekly as he noted the wide grin on the commander's face.

Trevor shrugged. "Maybe. I'm not sure. But I'm being pulled from the Line, and that's good enough for me. I never thought I'd leave this place."

"Then you'll be returning to Rhonnda?"

"No, at least not yet. I'm being called to Deepwater." He opened the flap of the tent, searching for the soldier on watch. "Have a horse saddled and ready," he barked to the sentry. "And get my tunic washed and pressed."

"Now, sir?" asked the puzzled guard.

"Yes, now! I'll not go to the governor looking as if I just came from a stable."

Even at the best of times Deepwater was a quiet town, made up of several hundred pleasant and simple frame houses with tiled roofs and pastel colors. The only real activity at Deepwater came either from the small garrison of Valley soldiers that stood off at the northern edge of the town, or at what was called Dockside, that busy cluster of warehouses and wharves where the riverships were loaded and unloaded as they made their way downriver to the channels and to Rhonnda. A few taverns and one inn at the center of town were really the only places that a weary traveler could find a ready meal and a warm bed.

Yet inside the house on the hill, unknown to Deepwater's uncaring citizens, the whole future of Newfoundland, indeed of the whole Empire, was being planned and considered. It was one thing for the elderly gentlemen of the Council at the Haven to make the laws by which Newfoundland was to live, but it was quite another to implement them. The governor was the only real authority in Newfoundland, and his job, as meaningless as it might seem at first glance, was perhaps the most important there was. The Council told Newfoundlanders what had to be done; it was the governor's job to do it.

The room was oval, with large windows across one entire wall, facing east so that the room was always filled with early morning sunlight. From the windows one could see groves of apple trees clustered directly below, and beyond them, league upon league of newly plowed land. That morning, as the governor sat at his desk briskly thumbing through mounds of papers and notes, he felt in no mood for the humdrum tasks of the day. There was some absurd request from a cattleman to buy up five thousand more acres of Huddlesford land; an urgent request from a group of planters in the Sama Plain to provide them with a construction crew for their damming project across the Visi tributary; a note to remind him that that same petitioner, the merchant from Aberdeen, was again requesting to see him about setting up a new post station on the Rhonnda Road.

The other letter was a dispatch from the Council, bearing the official seal, wrapped in sheepskin. And the letter was one of the most curious he could imagine. Written personally by his old friend, Nigel, it was a request, which meant a command, that he personally take charge of finding and fitting a rivership that would leave from Rhonnda with the intent of crossing the sea. That in itself was queer enough, but the oddest part of all was that Lady Anastasia would be arriving with the first spring caravan, along with a wolf called Casca, to seek out a group of wild mountain wolves to accompany them on the voyage.

Bela scratched his head. A ship with women and wolves to cross the sea? Had Lord Nigel gone completely out of his senses? Was the entire Council mad, also? He could do nothing but wonder and wait for Stacy's arrival, hoping that she could explain these matters a little more to his satisfaction.

No wonder that he was in no mood for dealing with the other matters on his desk!

As Bela sat reflecting, staring out from the window at the distant mountains, he was suddenly startled by an abrupt loud knock. He swung around in his chair and peered up. "Enter," he said in a quiet tone.

A youth in a dull brown tunic entered and bowed stiffly. "There's a soldier here to see you, my lord. A ragged-looking fellow."

Bela waved his hand to quiet the servant. He was in no mood for a lengthy description. "His name?"

"Commander Trevor, my lord."

Bela smiled fully. "Well, send him in, send him in! And bring us some lunch, will you? Some hot soup and bread." Then, almost as an afterthought, "And some good wine."

The servant bowed and strode from the room. Right on his heels came the tall engineer. He came in meekly, eyes darting about, taking in the paintings and colorful tapestries on the wall, trying to familiarize himself with civilization again.

Bela stood up, walked around the desk and grasped Trevor firmly with his hand. "Good to see you again, Commander. Here, take off your cloak and come sit beside the fire."

Trevor unclasped his cloak at the neck and flung it

haphazardly over the back of a great wicker chair. Then rubbing his hands together, he stood beside the fire.

"You must have made quite good time," said Bela as he sat back down at his desk.

Trevor nodded wearily. "The road was a muddy mess. The stuff splattered all over me. I had to wash myself clean in some iced springwater."

"*Brrr*," said Bela with a shiver. He knew how cold the mountain road could be at this time of year: frigid enough to turn one's fingers into icicles.

"But at least most of the snow's melting," added Trevor happily. "In a couple of weeks it'll almost be spring."

The governor smiled. "This is your first winter in New-foundland, isn't it?"

"Yes. Why?"

"Well, I'm afraid you'll find that spring comes a little bit later here than it does in the Valley. The last snows tend to linger up this way, you know. We've got a good six weeks to go yet."

Trevor groaned and forced a wan smile. "Well, at least I won't have to spend it all on the Line," he said, grateful for that.

"That you won't," said Bela with a hearty laugh. "But speaking of the Line, how are things out there these days?"

Trevor, at last feeling the first rush of warmth through his body, slumped down into the divan opposite the governor's desk. "Quiet," he sighed. "It took nearly the whole bloody winter to do it, but we finally got those agitated farmers settled down. There shouldn't be any more trouble."

"And the wolves? Did you manage to placate them as well?"

"Oh, I guess they did a lot of howling and growling," admitted Trevor, "but they came around in the end. I'd never have done it, though, without that big red wolf on my side. You know, Cicero. The one who sometimes accompanies Elias."

Bela could not help but chuckle. "Ah, yes, Cicero. I've never met him personally, I don't think; but his name's crossed my desk at least a dozen times. A couple of years back he and a pack of mountain wolves were raiding the farms out Fiana way. Those angry farmers damn near killed him, and I wouldn't have blamed them if they did. His blokes tore up half the Fiana countryside, what with their sheep-stealing and all. Some men I know swear that we lost more than three hundred sheep that winter."

Trevor whistled. Cicero certainly did live up to his reputation.

"But I understand he's tamed somewhat since then," Bela added hastily. "Now he spends most of his time hunting caribou and elk."

"Or on the river with Elias," agreed Trevor. "At least that's what he told me."

Bela smiled and shook his head slowly from side to side. "Can you beat that, eh? A wolf on a boat? Still, it is an interesting thought."

Just then, the servant came into the room with a tray filled with two ceramic bowls and a small pot of hot soup. He placed the tray down on the small table beside the fireplace, left, then quickly came back with another tray bearing two silver goblets and a large flagon of wine.

Bela stood up and gestured for Trevor to follow him to the table. "You *are* hungry, aren't you? I took the liberty of ordering us some lunch."

"I could eat a wolf," said Trevor, grinning. And for the next few minutes they hardly spoke as they sat back and ate. To Trevor, a hot meal was a most welcome treat.

After lunch, his belly full, head slightly tipsy from the strong Deepwater wine, he returned to the divan and slumped down. He cleared his throat. "Governor, your message said my presence here was important, so I guess that you must already have some other duty planned for me before I can go back to Rhonnda."

Bela forced a sour smile and sighed. "There's been some

trouble, some real trouble. I got this letter three days ago from the captain of the Aberdeen garrison."

Trevor's face slid out of his smile, and the boyish youthful flair seemed to disappear instantly. The grimness of the governor's lined face assured him that the business ahead was not something he would ever be able to think back upon fondly.

"What's happened?" he asked with rising trepidation.

Bela drew a deep breath and half closed his eyes. "Two Valley soldiers are dead. They were murdered," he said flatly. "The Aberdeen captain is certain it was the work of smugglers who were caught trying to evade paying taxes on a whiskey cargo headed for Rhonnda. And if rivermen are behind this, it'll take an expert on the river to track them down."

Puzzled, Trevor looked at him. "But I'm not——"

Bela nodded curtly. "I know you're not. But I'll need some good Valley soldiers to be there when the fighting starts." Here his eyes narrowed and his face grew dark. "And there *will* be fighting, Trevor. Those brigands murdered two men in cold blood. And they're going to pay for it, by Fara, they're going to pay for it. I've commandeered a ship from Rhonnda to find them. We think they'll be hiding in the channels near Fiana Fjord."

Trevor blew the breath out of his mouth. "That's tough country, my lord. A man could hide there forever, if he wanted."

"But a ship can't," rejoined Bela. "We're going to find those swine and keelhaul them until they drown."

"Who's the riverman you paid to bring them back?"

Here Bela smiled slyly. "Elias. The best man for the job."

"He's the best," concurred Trevor. "But you know in Rhonnda they say he's a bit of a brigand himself."

"Ah, Commander, that's the beauty. Don't you see? Who better to send after a thief than another thief?"

Trevor swallowed hard. "May I ask why you chose me

to lead the Valley soldiers on this mission? After all, Governor, I'm really just an engineer. My job is building things."

Bela looked at him impatiently.

"I called for you for several reasons, Commander. First, you've been on the river. Most soldiers haven't. Second, you've had good contacts with wolves—and in a job like this we'll have need of wolves in our tracking. And thirdly, perhaps most important, you've sailed with Elias and you know him. When these brigands are caught, you'll make sure that our friend doesn't find any sympathy for them. You say you build things, Trevor. Well, good. When you get back, I want you to build the highest gallows you can. Murder in Newfoundland is never to happen again."

CHAPTER NINE

As the long months of winter drew to a close, even before the last snows had fallen in the Valley, the first caravan set out to cross the mountains to the Newfoundland coast. The road wound an uneven course through the peaks until it came out of the thick forest at the Shara.

More than three hundred people set out from the Valley in the first caravan. They were an odd mixture, almost half of them were new settlers, deeds in hand, ready and eager to begin their new lives on the tracts of land set aside for them along the Aberdeen Plain. Most of the others were Newfoundland traders and merchants, who after spending winter in the Valley now came with wagons laden with goods to be sold throughout the Empire. Fifty wagons and four hundred horses, the caravan formed a long line through the wilds overlooking the Cottonwood. A squad of Valley soldiers led the way, plodding on through mud and slush, until at last they overlooked the sleepy town of Deepwater and its endless sprawl of farms beneath the towering mountain ranges in the north. That Stacy and Casca had joined them on the journey was a small matter. Her rank and title meant little or nothing, the wolf-companion merely an odd quirk that raised not a single brow. But had anyone been aware of her true purpose in Newfoundland it would have raised many an eyebrow indeed.

Stacy stood at the crest of a hill, a heavy scarf wrapped tightly around her neck. The hill was cluttered with pines, their leaves exuding a strong, spicy scent. Her long hair tossed to and fro in the wind, and her riding boots were grimy and caked with layers of thick mud and clay, a testimonial to the long journey she had endured. At her side her mare stood meekly, occasionally digging a hoof into the earth to seek a root or plant. Casca, restless with the slow pace of the trip, had already left the caravan and was somewhere out in the foothills, seeking a more appetizing game than that which he had been forced to eat.

As she stood watching the last of the wagons negotiate the road that led down to the town, Stacy was approached by a Rhonnda merchant who had befriended her.

"Well, there she is, my lady," he said gesturing grandly out at the town. "Been quite a trip for you, eh?"

Stacy smiled at him and pulled her fur collar higher over her ears. "I feel as if I could sleep for a week," she said with a gaping yawn.

The merchant laughed and rubbed at the side of his nose with a stubby finger. "The Ax Blade Mountains are always the hardest part," he drawled in the Newfoundland burr. "But it's done now. There'll be plenty of time to rest at Deepwater."

"I don't have very much time, Spooner. I'll only be at Deepwater as long as I have to. Governor Bela's expecting me."

Spooner grinned toothlessly. "See that grand house atop the hill?"

Stacy peered past Dockside and the couple of small boats in the harbor, followed along the winding street and fixed her gaze at the spacious, pastel house with the red-tiled roof. With all the open land and gardens around it, it was hard to miss.

"That's it," said Spooner. "That's the governor's place. Know it well myself. Many's the time I've stopped there to see the governor on business. He's a fine man, Bela is, yes, indeed. And a fair one, too. A very fair man."

"I know he is. It'll be good to see him after so long. He's an old friend of my father's."

Spooner laughed and clapped his hands together. "Well, bless me, I should have known! A fine lady like yourself, I should have known, yes, indeed. I'll wager my sheepskin coat he's counting the hours until you arrive. He's got a fine eye for the women, Bela has. Yes, indeed, a fine eye."

Stacy blushed and looked back down at Dockside. "Are any of those boats headed for Rhonnda?" she asked, changing the subject.

"Those old tugs? No, my lady. Those aren't Rhonnda ships. They're just for the locals. Channel skiffs, you might say. They bounce up and down along the river to the Cottonwood and carry mostly small cargoes to the nearby settlements. When a Rhonnda ship comes into harbor, you'll know it. Their sails are as high as the tallest pine in Newfoundland. Their flags fly still higher atop them. Yes, indeed, my lady, when the Rhonnda ships come, you'll know."

Stacy frowned. "I have to get to Rhonnda as soon as possible."

Spooner grinned at her. "Have you a young man waiting for you? Never mind. Youth is always impatient. But look. I'll tell you what. There's an old cargo ship due in any time now. She's short on comforts and plays all Hel going down the rapids, but she'll be Rhonnda-bound. I'm taking her myself, you know. And I'm sure old Sykes, her captain, can find room for a lady and her companion, even if it is a forest wolf. If you like, I can arrange the passage for you."

Stacy's eyes flashed happily. "Could you? I'd really appreciate it."

Spooner bowed. "No problem at all, my lady. None at

all. You go see the governor and carry out your business. I'll look out for Sykes and see what I can do. But there won't be any problem, I'm certain of that. Old Sykes always has room for one more. Then we'll both be Rhonnda-bound, my lady, aboard the *Lady of Newfoundland*."

CHAPTER TEN

The morning was bright and dry, with a fresh wind blowing from the north, clearing away the low, rumbling clouds from above their heads. "Unfurl the sails!" came the cry, "unfurl the sails!" And the tunic-clad sailors scrambled across the pine decks and tackled the halyard ropes. They worked swiftly, sure-fingered, with the tight precision that comes with long experience. Barely moments later the heavy canvas of the main and topsail was swelling with the breezes, spreading to the fullest as it caught the wind and caused the boat to lean hard to the starboard side. It swayed and leaned even harder as the Cottonwood currents cut directly underneath the bow. Slowly the boat straightened, veering hard from the Cottonwood channel and into the wide expanse of the New-foundland River.

Stacy stood aft on the deck, her back against the railing. Her eyes stared in awe at the size of the mighty river. The nearer bank, the one at Dockside, was a good three hundred meters distant, and the far side, a gravelly steep bank already showing the first signs of spring peat moss, was at least twice that distance from her. The tiny Deepwater homes became increasingly smaller with each passing second as the *Lady of Newfoundland* dipped and rose, cutting against the waterline. What was it Governor Bela had told her? The river, the great river, was the blood of Newlanders; when her waters flowed warmly in the spring, then and only then did Newfoundland begin to breathe. It was their life source, from which all, men and Dweller alike, drew their sustenance. Without it there would be nothing.

The cry of shouting voices pulled her from her daydream, and she looked back to the frantic activity on the deck.

Captain Sykes, a tall, graying fellow, was standing close to the mast, hands on hips, darting his eyes and barking commands. His face was ruddy in color, deeply lined—a telltale sign of his years on the river. As the ship rounded the first in a series of sharp bends, he called to his mate, "Steady as she goes, Mr. Wren; bear with the flow." And from behind him the steersman gave the reassuring reply, "The currents are with us, Capt'n; they'll be no problem tonight."

Just then there was another call, a shrill voice from atop the sail. "There's a ship to portside, Capt'n, I can see her sails!" cried the lookout.

Sykes leaned over the rail and shaded his eyes. "Can you see her colors, Mr. Woolsey?"

"Aye, Capt'n. Gray and green—out of Fiana. She'll pass us in a minute. Her flags are already lowered."

"Then dip ours, Mr. Woolsey! And as she passes, raise 'em high!"

As Sykes spoke, a burly youth began to tug at the ropes and carefully began to bring the flags down. No sooner had he done it than there came a great lumbering ship from around the curve in the river. It had a single square sail of blazing gold. Emblazoned at the center was the black likeness of a flying hawk with silver-black talons. The ship was larger than the *Lady of Newfoundland,* yet clearly faster on the water. As the two ships passed each other at a distance of about two hundred meters, the crews of each began to shout and exchange greetings. Then the larger ship took down its gray Fiana flag and hoisted another of maroon and blue in its place.

"She flies Rhonnda colors, Capt'n," shouted Woolsey from his high perch.

"Then we'll show her ours!" called back Sykes. And the youth at the ropes hoisted a similar banner, triangular, maroon in color with thin blue stripes.

Stacy leaned with her hands clutching at the rails and with her eyes followed the wake of the fast ship.

Spooner, the merchant, came by her side and grinned. "Impressed?" he asked.

Stacy nodded without looking back at him. "Very. Are there many like that?"

Spooner laughed, his pot belly quivering. "No, my lady. Only a few. But that one's perhaps the finest of the lot. Yes, indeed. She's a *Rhonnda* ship."

"How can you tell? By the flag?"

Spooner looked at her thoughtfully. "Yes, the flag tells the port. But did you see the gold sail? And the flying hawk? Well, they tell more than just a port or a destination. Indeed they do. That ship's rigged for danger and battle. It takes more than just a desire and knowledge of the river to sail her, I'll tell you."

"Sounds important," said Stacy, impressed.

"That she is, my lady. There're stories I could tell you about that ship that would curl your hair. Yes, indeed. Why, her captain's a man who'd dare anything if there'd be a quick profit to turn. Some say that back in the Valley he was a lord, a man of stature, but he gave it all up to come here and sail the river." Spooner's old eyes began to glitter with a tinge of envy. "And he made a name for himself like no other. Yes, indeed. He's married to that old ship, they say. He and the *Brora* are like one, if you get my meaning."

Stacy stared at him breathlessly. "The *Brora*?"

"Aye, my lady. Have tales of her doings even reached fine folk such as you?"

"Her captain," said Stacy, excited, ignoring the question, "is it Elias?"

"Well, bless me!" said Spooner with a silly grin. "Don't tell me you know him, too?"

Stacy smiled. "Sort of. We met once last year. But only for a few minutes."

The merchant roared. "Now don't tell me. Is it Elias that you're to meet in Rhonnda? Is it because of him that you're in such a hurry?"

Stacy tried to conceal an embarrassed smile but could not help it. "Strictly business, Spooner, strictly business. I, er, my father has a proposition for him. One that could prove most rewarding."

Spooner's eyes twinkled even more brightly than before. "Then Elias will be your man, yes, indeed. But what a pity! Here we are less than an hour out of harbor, and the man you're on your way to see is headed back from where we just left."

"It'll wait, Spooner. Anyway, I'm sure that Elias will be in Rhonnda within a few days after us."

Again Spooner laughed. "A Rhonnda man always comes home, my lady. Sure as cod in the sea, a Rhonnda man always comes home. And when he does, there's always a tale to tell!"

Barely two weeks before Stacy and her caravan reached Newfoundland, the *Brora* slipped out of the Deepwater harbor under the cover of night. Elias had been searching for the pirate ship and its murdering crew. To Elias and his rivermen this crime was a betrayal—of them, of Newfoundland, of the great river itself. The brigands had used their skills and wiles viciously, committing the foulest of crimes on innocent, unarmed victims.

Also on this journey were eight crack Valley soldiers, hardened veterans of Newfoundland duty, men who would not cringe at the sight of pirate daggers or blades. They knew and understood only one thing—Empire law. And they were sworn to uphold it. And Trevor, who commanded them, knew as well as any how difficult the task might be. The hills of Fiana were wild and rugged, and Valley soldiers would find few friends among the scattered settlers who called them home.

Thus it was that Trevor took action of his own. Men were not adept at the foul work that must be done. These strange hills would pose new threats behind every rock and tree. Wolves, though, could do what men could not. Mountain wolves, savage and free, wild as the rapids and the ice sheets of the Axe Blades. They would not flinch from their work, no matter what the cost, and Trevor knew he could trust them as a man trusts his right arm. And who better to lead these wolves than Cicero, the most cunning and daring wolf any man had ever known.

Out in the Fiana, where the Scourie River sharply narrows before flowing into the still waters of Kilkiddy Lake, the *Brora* stood silent in the moonless night, waiting, eyes watching, like a great cat that has found its prey and pauses to consider the best plan before striking.

A thin fog rolled down from the far mountains and settled unevenly over the lake, hazing all but the sharpest points of the gravelly bank from view. Elias, red-eyed from lack of sleep, peered evenly across the bow, teeth clenched, face impassive and cold. The pirate ship stood nestled at the far shore, near the channel that led down to the fjord. The channel was narrow, he knew, having been this way several times before, and his ship would not be able to negotiate the rocky bottoms and maintain good speed at the same time. But neither would the other ship. The pirates were cornered, trapped, with no chance to turn before reaching the fjord itself. And then there would be but two choices: Turn and face the *Brora,* or head for the open sea, which, at this time of year, was asking for an almost certain death. But in his heart Elias knew they would not run. They would turn and fight, burn the ship and run for the hills if they had to. No, devils such as these would not face the open sea, no more than they would have given their innocent victims a chance. Still, they were rivermen, and when finally faced, whether on land or water, they would hold their last inch of ground. And they would fight to the death rather than surrender.

Elias fingered his dagger and inhaled deeply. Cicero, at his side, began to growl. Elias spun around.

Trevor strode forward and held his hands slightly up, palms forward. "Only me," he said uneasily, noting that Elias's dagger was almost half out of its sheath.

Elias put it back clumsily. "I thought you'd be asleep with the others," he said.

"Couldn't. Tried to but couldn't. Have they moved?"

Elias looked up at the fog. "If we can't, they can't. They'll do like us, sit it out until the mist lifts, then make a run for it."

Trevor frowned and involuntarily shivered. "Then they've seen us, you suppose?"

Elias laughed curtly. "If we saw *them,* they saw *us.* A ship as big as mine is hard to miss."

"But how do they know we're after them? Maybe they think we're just carrying cargo out this way. Maybe——"

Elias interrupted sourly, "They'd all know the *Brora,* and they'd also know that we don't sail this way to bring whiskey to the trappers."

"Were they flying any flags?"

"A black flag, Commander. Know what that means?"

Trevor shook his head.

"It means fever. A warning for other vessels to keep far away. It means they've got disease aboard."

Trevor sucked a cold breath between his teeth. "I assume that's just a ruse—to keep everyone far away."

Elias shrugged. "Probably. But who can say for sure? We'll know when we catch them."

"Wait a moment. If they *have* got fever aboard——"

"Shall we run, Commander?" asked Elias, looking icily into Trevor's eyes. "Isn't that what they're hoping?"

The soldier frowned. "Well, just in case, hadn't you better get out your own black flag? They might have to quarantine us when we get back."

"It's already done, my friend, it's already done. But I wouldn't spend too much time worrying about it. I think I know that ship out there. Her captain's a swine if there ever was one. One of the boys from out your way in the Noatak. He was a bully then, a renegade who used to befriend stray wolves and murder them for their pelts."

Cicero snarled; his eyes narrowed hatefully.

"What's your plan, then?" asked Trevor.

"We'll probably break out of this weather by dawn. Then we'll chase them through the channel to the fjord. What happens next . . ." Elias shrugged. "If they choose to stand and fight . . ."

"What if they ground their ship?"

"Then you soldier boys take over. And our wolves, too. We'll lead you inland for as far as the channel allows. Then you're on your own."

"My troops will be ready. How long until dawn?"

"Couple of hours or so. You'd be better off catching that sleep, Commander. Tomorrow, take my word for it, you're going to need it."

Dawn spread quickly across the eastern sky, a splash of purple that grew brighter and brighter. And as Elias had said, the fog began to dissipate.

"She's moving, Elias!" came a muffled cry.

The captain glanced to the sailor perched high in the nest atop the mast.

"Damn!" Elias pounded his fist against the rail. "They must be crazy," he hissed. "They're trying to outrun us through the channel!" Then, hands on hips: "Full sail across the Kilkiddy, Mr. Boniface! Trim 'er for the channel. They might want to smash themselves on the rocks, but I damn well don't!"

"Aye, Capt'n. Full sail it is!"

Trevor came running from the leeward hatch, hastily strapping his sword onto his belt.

"Morning, Commander," growled Elias. "Seems they're going to give us more of a run than I'd thought. They're trying to cut through the channel like it was an open canal."

"But they'll smash up on the rocks!"

"Maybe, Commander. But we've got to follow. Fly the colors, Mr. Ashcroft!"

"Aye, sir. Rhonnda colors, it is!"

"Not Rhonnda colors, Mr. Ashcroft! This is Valley business. Empire colors! Let those bastards know who we are and what we intend! And by Fara, I hope it makes them shiver!"

With the swelling wind the *Brora* picked up speed and cut sharply at an angle across the Kilkiddy. Gold sail blazed in sunlight; the black hawk shimmered and glistened. High above, the brown and green banner of the Empire flapped wickedly in the wind. It was a sight to be seen, this proud Empire ship, bow dipping and rising, speeding across the lake, every moment gaining on the sloop now dangerously making its way through the hazardous channel.

Trevor stood close to the bow and felt his heart pound as the pirate vessel loomed larger and larger. He could make out the frantic scrambling of swarthy men racing across the tired deck, drawing more sail.

With a soldier's instinct he fell to the floor as an arrow whistled over his head and smacked against a spar.

"That'll teach you a lesson, Commander!" shouted Elias, signalling for all hands to keep low.

The Valley soldiers, who by this time had all clambered onto the deck, knelt low against the railings at the starboard side.

"Let's show these lads a thing or two," called Elias. And about six of his own men came running to the forecastle, crossbows and arrows in hand. They formed a line near the bow, then, almost as a single entity, shot. There was a quick *twang* as the arrows loosed and smashed helter-skelter aboard the other boat. Then, ducking before their own shots could be answered, they reloaded and shot again.

"Good at it, ain't they?" laughed Elias. "Didn't know Newland lads could be so sharp, eh?"

Trevor mumbled: "I guess they didn't learn that on the river."

"No, Commander. Not on the river. My lads——"

"Capt'n, she veers!"

Elias grimaced and leaned hard along the portside. The pirate ship had set itself a dangerous course against the shoals and the reefs close to the left bank of the ever narrowing channel. The *Brora,* meanwhile, had all but cleared the deep waters of the Kilkiddy and was swiftly approaching the dangerous channel currents. Elias could feel the growing swells along the hull and feel the dramatic surge of the *Brora* as she lurched ahead.

"Trim our sails and tack 'em a quarter off the wind!" he shouted, glaring at Ashcroft and Boniface. Without so much as a blink the two officers were barking at the crew. Slowly the great canvas began to shift.

"Close-hauled, she is, Elias," called Ashcroft.

"Then set her straight down the channel and keep her by the wind."

Confused at what was happening around him, Trevor sat in his crouched position along the rail and began to give commands to his own men, who had crept closer to the forecastle. As Elias returned to the prow, Trevor inched closer and peered ahead. The *Brora* had already passed the banks of Kilkiddy and was ever steadily negotiating its way through the channel. He felt his body quiver as the ship reared at what seemed only inches away from the sharp rocks along both banks that jut like icebergs above the water.

"Is this safe?" cried Trevor, in a near panic.

"Don't concern yourself," replied Elias, his gaze on the ship ahead as it zigzagged at a fierce clip. "That captain knows his only chance of escape is to run us ragged and hope that we smash onto the reefs."

"Then aren't we playing his game? We're doing exactly as he wants." Trevor was aghast at the terrifying maneuvers.

Elias chuckled. "Not quite, Commander. Not quite. His ship is smaller than ours, but she's too light to be forcing such speed in these waters. His sails are almost full—the first good strong gust that sweeps down will send him reeling."

"The wind's shifting to dead stern, Elias," shouted Boniface, worried.

"Then run with her, Mr. Boniface. And feel for the swells. There's rough current ahead, and I don't want to get bogged down while those brigands head for open sea."

Tense minutes passed. Trevor wiped his brow as the pirate ship began to loom larger. The *Brora* was catching up to her, closing in fast. He could almost smell the fear of the pirates on board. Three swarthy men, dressed in thick fur jackets, were leaning over the after rail, aiming their crossbows. But no arrows were loosed. It was obvious they were holding their fire now until the last possible moment—when the *Brora* would bear down hard.

"Set for ramming, Mr. Ashcroft," said Elias coldly.

"Aye, Capt'n."

From the sailor in the mast came a frantic cry. "Capt'n, she's turning about!"

Elias's jaw dropped. "Damn that cagey devil!"

The pirate boat had twisted herself in the channel, run purposely aground, in the hope of forcing the *Brora* to smash her broadside.

"Can we trim sail enough in time to avoid her?" called Elias.

"I doubt it! We're running too fast."

Elias looked about anxiously. "Get the anchor over-board, Ashcroft!" he barked. "Fast!"

Ten sailors raced across the poop deck, untied the lines and hoisted the heavy iron weight over the side into the icy waters. The *Brora* lurched ahead with the wind full in her sails, then, reeling with a tremendous blow, pulled back sharply and came to a sudden, petrifying halt. The pirate ship was less than fifty meters away. Elias sighed with relief. A matter of seconds would have brought them crashing at top speed. He'd been caught off balance, he knew—badly off balance. And he cursed himself for not giving the pirate captain more credit.

A thick black cloud suddenly began to rise from ahead.

Trevor gasped. "They're burning their ship! They're burning their own ship!"

Elias spun around. "Furl our sails, Mr. Boniface! If the winds don't rip her, then those damned flying embers will!"

As the *Brora*'s crew scampered about, Trevor could plainly see what Elias meant. The wind, gusting madly, was sending flying sparks of timber in every direction. An open sail as broad as the *Brora*'s was especially vulnerable.

The yards bared, the ship began to toss and bob terribly amid the strong currents. "What now, Elias?" called Trevor.

Elias pointed glumly. "They're going overboard, Commander. We'll have to swim to shore after them."

Trevor glanced over the railing and groaned. The choppy waters looked cold and hazardous, indeed. It was a good hundred meters to the nearest bank. But as he stared, his eye caught a glimpse of the first pirates already reaching land. Swords and daggers in hand, they were scrambling along the muddy edges of the bank and racing for the thick spruce forest that lined the length of the Fiana hills.

"Prepare your weapons," he shouted to his men. Turning back to Elias he said, "I enjoyed the trip, Captain. Maybe we'll do it again sometime." Then, standing straight on the bow, he dived into the cold waters. Moments later his soldiers followed.

Cicero and his hunters dashed across the deck and jumped, too.

"Take charge of the ship, Mr. Ashcroft," shouted Elias. He looked down at the uninviting water and shivered.

"But what about the brigand ship, sir? Shouldn't we wait and see what we can salvage?" He looked fitfully at the burning ship beginning to sink.

Elias laughed caustically. "She's blazing out of control, Mr. Ashcroft. That roaring fire'll leave little to get a hold of. If there's anything left we can claim, then claim it. As for me, I'm going to follow Trevor and his lads." Ashcroft began to protest, but Elias shook his head. "Please, Mr. Ashcroft, don't try to talk me out of it. The more I look down at the water the more I'll probably let you change my mind."

Chilled to the marrow, Elias swam his way across the channel. As he reached the gravelly bank, he saw that Trevor and his men had already grouped and were running at a quick clip along the slope of a hill. Cicero and the hunters were well ahead, dashing atop the escarpment, barking and growling.

The land was filled with wild cranberry and partridgeberry bushes, tall columns of spruce, peppered here and there with stunted trees. Dagger in hand, panting, Elias caught up with the soldiers and ran alongside.

Near the crest of the hill, Trevor paused and stood perfectly still; ears straining, he listened to the dim sounds. He could hear the wind whistling down from the Fiana Mountains and could make out the soft slapping sound of the faraway channel waters lashing against the banks. But as for the sounds of men, there were none. Only silence.

He bit his lip and signaled for his troops to move slowly over the top.

The scape was flat and broad, and the spruce trees were as thick as molasses. A man could lose himself among them forever. Just then there was a rustle from among the bushes. Trevor spun, expecting to see a band of pirates, swords already lunging at his throat. But it was Cicero. The wolf had been slinking along the top, overseeing the directions in which his hunters had spread out and making careful observations for tracks.

"Have you lost them, too?" Trevor asked.

Cicero growled, his eyes flashing hotly in the manner of all wolves who feel slightly cheated by an escaped prey.

"Men?" he asked with a snarl. "Their stink carries on Aleya's breath like a bloodied buck. We'll find them for you, Commander."

"Then which way, Cicero? We've only got a few hours of light. By dark they could make their way to the Badlands."

Cicero sniffed at the air and wagged his tail furiously. "No tracks up here. I think they've taken a path along the lowlands, keeping as far as possible from high ground. Remember, the big cats prowl these hills, and even men like them would make a fine meal for their cubs."

"Then back down the hill it is." Trevor turned and began to lead his men down.

"No, not that way. Across the top to the other side. I've sent my hunters down first. The best thing we can do is follow."

Trevor nodded. Then, following Cicero as best they could, they raced across the top and began the arduous climb down. Thistle and brambles stung and tore at their wet clothes; the muddy earth made them slip and lose balance.

Once down they made their way along a narrow gorge that led between hills that seemed to grow ever higher. The afternoon sun was low, and as they moved, their shadows danced and bounced off the rocky ledges like fearsome beasts. Still there was nothing; no scent of the pirates, nor any sign of the hunters.

After another few minutes of fruitless search, Cicero stopped in his tracks. Nose wrinkling, ears twitching, he lowered his snout. "What is it?" whispered Trevor.

Cicero shook his head and inched off to a patch of fern. The earth showed an inconsistent burrowing, indicating that something had been dragged into the bushes. Trevor followed close behind. A moment later the wolf stopped and stared. The body of a hunter lay in a heap, eyes wide in a stare of surprise. Blood covered its face. Between the wolf's jaws a chunk of flesh hung from the side of its mouth.

Trevor gasped. But what had happened became clear. The hunter had found one of the fleeing pirates and attacked him, ripping savagely at his arm. But during the fight another pirate had evidently come to his companion's rescue, caught the wolf from behind and slit his throat.

Cicero raised his snout and gave a long, mournful howl —the chant for the dead, Trevor knew. The kind of wolf cry that for countless millennia has sent shivers up and down the spines of men.

Trevor stood silently by until Cicero had finished. And then from some far-off point the cry was returned by another of the hunters. An even more distant cry soon followed that one. Cicero had spread the word. A wolf had been murdered, and all his hunters would not rest until that death had been avenged.

Elias made his way through the bushes and glanced around at the ghastly sight. "I told you these pirates would be rough to catch," he grumbled, his teeth gritted.

The soldier swallowed hard.

"They must be close," growled Cicero. "Their smell is everywhere."

"Then which way should we track?" asked Elias.

The sleek wolf darted his eyes along the steep side of a nearby hill thick with trees. "That way," he snarled.

Moving quickly, the band followed the wolf in a single line and wound their way through the muddy ground. The stillness of the air returned, and they were greeted with total silence save for their own heavy breathing.

The trees encompassed them like a forest. Sunlight barely filtered through. Trevor paused uneasily and peered about. Where were they hiding? he wondered. Where might fugitives make themselves unseen by both other men and wolves? There were no tracks. Trevor bit his lip and studied the foliage carefully. If *he* were a pirate, where would he lead his band?

The knowledge came, but it came too late. *The trees!*

Arrows whistled. There was a shrill scream, and one of his soldiers staggered, clutching helplessly at his throat, where the snubbed arrow had struck.

War cries filled the air, and ten men leaped down from the branches. Swords were drawn and clashed against the blades of the pirates. Cicero leaped high and brought down a brigand before the man could plunge his blade into Elias's back. Once on the ground the wily wolf snapped his jaws tightly into the soft flesh of the throat. The man screamed in a frenzy, then slumped unevenly across the mud, with his stilled hand clutching a long, curved dagger.

Trevor whipped his sword and swung it about, catching one of the brigands squarely in his ribs. Reeling, the pirate fell and rolled around as the life drained slowly from him. Then he gurgled, gasped and died.

Another soldier fell to the pirates' knives, but as the battle continued long and bitter, the Valley troops gained the upper hand, pressing the foe backwards.

"They're fleeing!" cried Elias, seeing the remaining pirates dash through the trees to seek safety.

Cicero gave chase without looking to see what Trevor

or the others were about to do. But Trevor kept only a few paces behind, shouting back to his men to follow.

The climb was steep, the hill filled with craggy boulders and thornbushes; Cicero balanced on a ledge and jumped down among the pirates. Trevor could not see what happened next but the terrible scream of a frightened man told him that one of the pirates had been caught.

"Up to the top!" Trevor cried. Along the crest, standing in a line with bloodied weapons drawn, the remaining eight pirates stood with eager anticipation. One raised his crossbow—Trevor leaped and knocked him down, but not before the arrow was loosed and had hit another of his lads. The soldier tumbled back down the slope, the shaft of the arrow through his gut.

Elias crouched and wielded his dagger. One of the pirates glared at him and laughed. A huge burly man, with a ragged dark beard and rotting teeth. His eyes were small, his nose crooked and broken. He heaved himself at Elias, and the two men stumbled to the earth, clutching and tearing at each other savagely. The pirate rolled to the side and sprang to his feet, his weapon ready.

"I knew they'd send you after me, Elias," he rasped.

"You're going to hang, Krebbs," replied the riverman.

The pirate grinned. He toyed with his dagger, shifting it slowly from hand to hand. "Maybe, Elias, maybe. But first I'm going to kill you." And with that, he jumped again and knocked the mariner off his feet.

Elias grappled with him and felt a hot flash as the blade slashed along the side of his right hand. In a moment of sudden pain he dropped his own blade to the frosted earth. Krebbs stood over him and laughed. "You're a dead man, Elias," he bellowed with hate, "a dead man!"

Krebbs screamed like a wounded beast as a wolf sprang seemingly from nowhere and dug his fangs deeply into his neck. Elias pounced up and shouted to the hunter, "Don't kill him! We need him alive!"

Grudgingly the wolf inched away from his terrorized prey.

Krebbs lay still on the ground, eyes wide. "Don't let the wolves have me, Elias! Please, *not the wolves!*"

The hunter snarled; Krebbs shivered. All around him the other pirates were dropping; Trevor and his Valley soldiers had the fight won at last.

"On your feet, Krebbs," snapped Elias.

Painfully the pirate managed to stand. Cicero stood paces before him, poised to strike.

"Don't let those beasts get at me, Elias. I'll do anything you want." Krebbs' knees were knocking.

Elias turned to Cicero, then back to Krebbs. "Do you know who this wolf is?" he demanded.

Krebbs shook his head, but there was terror in his eyes.

"They call him Cicero," the mariner said dryly.

The pirate gasped. Cicero! He had heard tales of that one and he knew he was as mean and cruel as wolves come!

"Let me have him," growled the wolf.

"Not this one, my friend. He's special. I'm going to take a special delight in watching him hang."

Trevor wiped the blood from his sword and sheathed it. "Three of my soldiers were killed today," he hissed. "And the two Valley inspectors you murdered make five. Five men! You're the worst killer Newfoundland's ever known. And I'm going to make you suffer for it."

Krebbs shivered. "You . . . you can't harm me," he stammered, brow breaking into a cold sweat. "You're under orders."

Trevor laughed. "I make the laws here, not the governor. He's back at Deepwater, waiting for you to be brought in chains."

"Well, I won't give you a fight. Chain me, then! Do it! Do anything you want! But you have to bring me back *safely.*"

Trevor raised a brow. "Oh? Do I? Cicero, would you like me to turn this fine gentleman over to you?"

The wolf snarled; his fangs were eagerly bared.

"Elias! They can't do this! Not the wolves!" cried Krebbs in anguish.

"He's right, Trevor," said the riverman.

"Give him to me, Trevor," growled Cicero, his eyes ablaze. "Just for a while."

Krebbs, in total horror at the thought of being put at the mercy of wolves, fell to his knees and began to sob. He had killed many wolves in his time, back in the Noatak, and he knew how much they would like to get a chance to even the score.

"I'm begging you, Commander," he pleaded. "Let me hang! Don't let me die like some animal."

"You didn't show such mercy to those Valley inspectors, Krebbs," snapped Trevor angrily.

Krebbs looked up, aghast. "Their deaths were an accident! I swear to you, it was an accident! Some of my men were drunk. The inspectors threatened to take away my papers. We . . . we had no choice."

Trevor bent over and yanked him up by the scruff of his neck. "What about those lads lying dead over there? Were they an accident, too? And the hunter whose throat you cut, what about him?"

Krebbs whimpered and looked through pitiful eyes at Elias. "Don't let them have me, Elias! *Please!*"

Trevor threw him to the ground and kicked him sharply with his boot. "You're nothing but a mangy hound, Krebbs. Not worth the effort or the time for torturing. Thank the Fates for your luck, but most of all thank Cicero here. Because if he wanted you that badly, I'd give you to him!"

He spit on the crying Krebbs and turned back to the riverman. "Our job is done, Captain. Let's get back to your ship and sail to Deepwater as quickly as we can. The stench of death is in my nostrils, and I can't get it out."

CHAPTER ELEVEN

Stacy stood close to the forecastle, white knuckles clutching at the rough beams of the rail. Ever since the day before, when they had hit the rough waters of the rapids, she had felt sick. Spooner had advised her to stay in her cabin, and she had tried, but the constant tossing and bobbing below made it even worse. Besides, her cabin was hardly a cabin at all; more of a closet really, with a narrow hammock slung from wall to wall. And poor Casca had lain at her feet, whimpering. Sick as a dog himself, as it were. Too weak to even wag his tail.

Amid crates and boxes being brought up from below, she stood her ground and buried her head in her arms. Three days, that's all the trip to Rhonnda would take; but now, as Rhonnda drew ever closer, it seemed as if she had spent all her life on this boat.

The gray clouds were at last breaking up, and faint hints of pale sun were beginning to peek through. The breezes were mild, the air crisp. And Stacy felt brave enough to pick up her head.

Spooner, jolly as ever, made his way toward her, a cheery grin splitting his face from ear to ear. Stacy tried to smile back. She felt badly out of place here on this old ship and felt that if she were to take a single step or let go of the rail, she would topple over like so much refuse piled high into a trash can.

"Good morning, my lady," said the merchant with exhilaration, swelling his lungs magnificently.

Stacy sighed, her face white as a sheet. "Hello, Spooner. Forgive the way I look, but I'm still sick from yesterday."

The merchant frowned and cast an eye at the wolf lying sprawled at her feet. "He looks sicker than you do."

"Oh, he is. Poor Casca. I pleaded with him to make this trip with me, you know. He was most reluctant. Forest wolves don't like so much water."

Spooner knelt down and stroked Casca gently behind the ears. "Well, not to worry. We'll be there soon. Yes, indeed, quite soon."

Her eyes widened. "Be there? Rhonnda?"

Spooner nodded emphatically. "See that broad mountain a yonder? That's a sure sign. And take a deep breath, my lady. Smell the salt? That's from the sea. Seawater. Yes, indeed. The winds blow it right down this way."

"How long, Spooner?" Stacy groaned.

" 'Bout midday, I'd say. Thereabouts, anyway."

Stacy closed her eyes. *Thank Fara for that!*

Looking out to the shore, she saw that the soil had taken on a deeper and richer hue. Some of the fields had been plowed; an occasional fence was spread out across the hills. A few head of cattle grazed here and there between small, neatly trimmed farmhouses.

"Up this way we have some of the best grazing lands in the Empire," said Spooner proudly. "Are you interested in cattle, my lady?"

Stacy shook her head. "No. But I *am* interested in horses."

"Well, bless me! Then you'll want to take a little look at the Free Lands south of the city. Why, there's some fine ponies and mustangs to be caught. Trouble is, there's too few good people about to catch 'em. Say, maybe you and me can go into business together. I'll fund the expenses, you'll corral and break 'em, and we'll split the profits."

Stacy smiled. "Thank you for the offer, Spooner, but

I'm afraid I can't accept. The business I'm on is, well, kind of urgent. But I'll tell you what—should the day ever come that I settle in Rhonnda, you'll be the first one I'll come to see. And maybe we'll get something going after all."

Spooner grinned, his ruddy cheeks aglow. "All right, my lady. I can wait."

As they spoke, commands were barked from fore and aft. Captain Sykes stood at the prow and, as was his way, kept a careful eye. It was "Mr. Wren," this, and "Mr. Woolsey," that. There was a constant barrage of instruction as the ship began to slow.

Stacy looked on admiringly as the crew followed the commands smartly and with fervor.

"They're a fine bunch of lads, these rivermen," commented Spooner.

She readily agreed. "That they are. One of them, what's his name? Mr. Pine? He came to my cabin and offered to bring me some dinner last night."

Spooner raised his brows. "He did? Hmmm. I guess that lad has a fine eye for the ladies, too. Did you take the food?"

"Heavens no!" laughed Stacy weakly. "I was so sick that the very thought of eating made me want to vomit. But I was grateful for the offer. I always assumed that rivermen would be a rough bunch of fellows. But they're not. Most of them are, well, just like anyone else."

"As good a compliment from a Valley lass as I've ever heard. Yes, indeed. Captain Sykes would be pleased to hear it. And so would Mr. Pine, I'll wager."

Stacy gazed out to the snowcapped mountains in the distance. All of a sudden she felt good again. She was going to like these Newlanders and their odd ways. Quoting Spooner, she thought: "Yes, indeed!"

Her thoughts were broken by a frantic series of calls from the sailor perched atop the mast. "Port ahead, Capt'n! Port ahead!"

Captain Sykes dashed to the bridge and leaned hard from the starboard side. He smiled and gave the order for the sails to be trimmed. Then he came over to Stacy. "Rhonnda's in sight, my lady," he said. "You can't see her from here, but my lad up there can. Once we round the next bend she'll be in full view."

"And you'll see a sight like you've never seen before," chimed in Spooner gleefully.

Stacy felt her heart race. Rhonnda! *At last!* How long she had dreamed of it! Now that the time had come, she was bursting.

"Sorry if I haven't had much time to sit and chat with you on this trip," said Sykes, pulling her from her thoughts. "But as you see, managing a ship is a full-time job. And this being the first cargo from the Valley since last autumn . . ."

"I understand, Captain," said Stacy. "Your officers paid more attention to me than they had to, and well, Spooner here, he's just been wonderful."

Sykes laughed. "Glad to hear it. Well, back to my tasks now. Enjoy our sights, my lady. And have a good look at our coasts. I think you'll be impressed."

"I already am. They're breathtaking. I never dreamed that Newfoundland would be anything like it. Back home they talk about it like . . ." She flushed.

"I know," laughed Sykes good-naturedly. "They think we're little more than frontier barbarians. But folk who come out our way, well, they know better, don't they?"

Stacy pushed the hair back from her eyes and smiled fully. "Yes, Captain, indeed we do."

With that, Sykes turned away. "Fly the colors, Mr. Woolsey. We're going home!" The banners were raised; they flapped wildly in the brisk wind.

The *Lady of Newfoundland* swept in a broad arc and made her way around the bend. Stacy stood breathlessly, hands on her hips, gazing at the magnificent sight ahead. Even Casca managed to rouse himself from his sickness to peer across the bow. The river opened majestically, wider than Stacy could have imagined. Fully half a league on each side of the creaking ship, the water rolled as far as the eye could see, until it branched into two great channels at the foot of Rhonnda Island. The sight of the riverships, though, was the one that swept her breath away. There were swift double-masted sloops, sleek yawls cutting and bowing deeply into the water with each swell, small cats with tall single masts and flowing sails that reached out to the clouds. Some craft were old and weather-beaten, others as fresh and new as the fine coats of paint on their decks. But they all had one thing in common—the Rhonnda banners of maroon and blue. There must have been close to a hundred ships in all, each one proudly flying their flags both fore and aft as well as from the yardarms. It was a sight that Stacy knew she would never forget as long as she lived.

Way off to the west stood the high spiral towers of the city itself. Bright colors were everywhere, and even at this distance she could see the shimmering golds and reds of the tiled roofs, the purple of the towers, the deep grays and browns of the warehouses at the ever-busy piers. Rhonnda was all she could have hoped—and then some.

"Welcome to Rhonnda, my lady," said Spooner proudly.

But Stacy scarcely heard. She just stood at her place and stared and stared as the city grew bigger and more wondrous before her eyes. "It's . . . so huge," she whispered. "I never thought——"

"One day it'll rival the Haven itself," predicted Spooner. "Just you wait. We don't have the fine boulevards that you have. But we will. Yes, indeed. One day—and soon, I'll wager—we'll have the same grand statues and fountains, the same columns of marble. We'd have 'em already if the cost of hauling the stone from the Valley quarries wasn't so prohibitive."

"You don't need them," said Stacy, still in awe. "What you have the Valley can never duplicate."

Spooner looked at her, brows slanted in puzzlement.

"The river and the sea, Spooner. *The river and the sea!* What more could you need? My sister says that more than half of all Newlanders already live in or near Rhonnda. One day that'll be half the Empire. And believe it or not, in my own small way I'm going to make all of that come true." Then Stacy turned and gazed again at the city.

And so the ship *Lady of Newfoundland* at last came to berth at Rhonnda. And for Stacy-of-the-wolves, as many Newlanders came to know her, the first real adventures of her life were about to begin.

Stacy sat quietly on the small divan, gazing out the arched window. In the starry night she could plainly see the towers and lights of Rhonnda glittering and flickering brightly in the distance. Her sister's husband, Simon, got up from his own chair and reached for a worn, leather-bound volume on the highest shelf of his bookcase. Smiling, he said, "Let me read you something." He opened the worn volume to a yellowed faded page and skimmed his eyes across it. Large gray steely eyes, Stacy noted, set deeply in a strong-featured face. Except for a touch of gray peppered here and there across his curly hair, Simon was very much the same as she remembered him when he had left the Valley five years ago.

Softly, in a singsong voice, Simon began to read:

> "O Rhonnda-by-the-sea,
> with your spires of gold and your purpled towers
> shimmering like baubles in the softness of dawn;
> Like a tiger poised, like heaven's jewel
> you watch over as we bow in your shadow;
> As a man I live and die,
> but peace fills my heart and throbbing pulse,
> for you are of me and will be so forever,
> O Rhonnda-by-the-sea."

He put the book gently on the shelf and also stared from the window. Rhonnda-by-the-Sea glittered in return.

"That was a lovely poem," she said, glancing his way. "Who wrote it?"

"A mystical poet named Bartok, long dead."

Stacy sighed, closed her eyes and ran her finger along the rim of the goblet in her hand.

"He captured Rhonnda so beautifully," she mused. "It's exactly the way I pictured it to be, especially the part about the spires of gold and purpled towers."

"Interesting that you should say that," Simon told her. "Bartok died more than twenty years ago, long before the towers were built. Some people claim his mystical powers allowed him to see the future, to a Rhonnda that even we today haven't dreamed of."

Touched by this bit of Rhonnda folklore, Stacy smiled. She turned her head toward Lorna, who was sitting in the large easychair set close to the brick fireplace. The logs glowed dully, the light reflecting softly against Lorna's face, a gentle, soft face.

"As you can see, Stacy," Lorna said, "we both love Rhonnda. And I doubt we'll ever leave."

"I can see why. Really, I can. It's nothing like the way Valley folk talk about it."

Simon laughed and refilled the goblets with hot spiced rum, a local favorite. "There's a freshness in the air here, Stacy, like nowhere else in the Empire. To us the Valley is old. Stale, if you will. The future is here."

Stacy returned to the window and the sight of the high spires reaching ever upward. On either side of the river stood peaks and plateaus, jutting from the earth like great nimble fingers whose tips teased at the clouds.

"How long will you be staying?" asked Lorna.

Stacy shrugged. "The governor is the only one who can answer that. This business of finding the right ship and fitting it is in his hands."

Simon's face grew grim. "I don't understand all this

business, Stacy. Really, I don't. Why is the Council so intent on this voyage? There's so much to be done right here. We've got our own uncharted lands to explore, and that alone would be work for any man."

"And the dangers, Stacy," added Lorna. "From what you've told us . . ."

"It shouldn't be any more dangerous than sailing the rapids. But that's not the point. It's going to be a monumental achievement. The first of its kind."

"I understand that," said Simon, gulping down his rum. "But why *you?* Let these rough rivermen do the job."

Stacy shook her head. "Believe it or not, Simon, they need me. That's why I came. That's why Casca is already searching your Free Lands for the best mountain wolves he can find."

"Well, perhaps as time passes, I can change your mind. But we won't argue about that now. You've been here two days already and you haven't had a chance to see anything. Rhonnda Island is filled with natural wonders, you know. Like the waterfalls."

"I'd love to see them! I hear they're magnificent."

"The best in Newfoundland," promised Simon with a wink. "And in a month there will be the Rhonnda festival. You must be here for that. People come from as far away as Deepwater to attend."

Stacy laughed. "I've heard about the fair," she replied. "A merchant aboard the *Lady of Newfoundland* told me about it. A fellow named Spooner."

Simon stared at her. "Spooner? Not Spooner Morningglory?"

Stacy looked puzzled, then broke into a wide grin. "Is that what he calls himself? Morningglory? A small man with an impish smile who has a penchant for saying 'yes, indeed'?"

"That's the one!" laughed Lorna, clapping her hands.

"Why he's one of the shrewdest merchants in Rhonnda," said Simon. "He has a virtual monopoly on most spices shipped from the Valley. And from time to time he's been accused of smuggling untaxed whiskey to the loggers and traders in Noatak."

"Why that sneaky devil!" chortled Stacy.

"That's common in these parts," said Simon. "Rhonnda folk are always looking to find a way to get around Valley taxes, you know. We pay levies as the goods reach Deepwater, then we pay them again when the ships bring them to Rhonnda. Usually a small bribe will do the trick, but sometimes there's just no way around it."

"Is there ever any real trouble? Rebellion, I mean?"

"Not really. Except, of course, for that Fiana incident."

"It was just a few weeks ago, Stacy," said Lorna. "Troops from the Aberdeen garrison found the bodies of two of the governor's inspectors floating in Fiana Fjord. We know Governor Bela commissioned a Rhonnda ship to search out the pirates who did it."

Stacy looked aghast. "Murder?" She shuddered involuntarily, drumming her fingers against her thigh.

"But they sent one of our best men to catch them. A man named Elias."

"The *Brora!*" cried Stacy. "As we left Deepwater, we saw the *Brora* heading for Dockside!"

Simon looked at her sternly. "Did you notice what flags she was flying?"

Stacy shrugged. "Rhonnda flags, I think."

Simon smiled thinly; he knew the mission would be ended at last.

"What will happen to the pirates?" asked Stacy, concerned.

"They'll probably be hanged. Bela can't afford to do less. For all we know, by now they're already dead."

CHAPTER TWELVE

From the window of the governor's waiting room you could see the garden, a summer garden built on two levels. Wide brick steps led gently onto a grass terrace shaded by a row of tall elms. In summer the garden would come alive with a multitude of flowers, but now it seemed bare. Save for the first hints of spring grass and the colorful glitter of painstakingly landscaped rocks, it seemed merely a hollow shell of itself, waiting patiently for spring to arrive.

Trevor stood beside the window, holding the filmy curtains aside, and peered down. A workman dressed in a plain dark tunic and quilted jacket was whistling happily as he knelt beside the barren rows and, tools in hand, pruned out a scattering of weeds. Trevor turned around and nervously paced along the side wall of the antechamber. The events of that morning raced painfully across his eyes. The hastily built wooden gallows, the somber face of the hangman, Krebbs' scowl as the rope was placed about his neck—and the limp dangling body swaying and turning in the bright sunlight.

Trevor shuddered and tried hard to forget.

After a few long moments of pacing, he snapped to attention. The wide oaken doors of the governor's chamber opened wide and an unarmed sentry passed through and bowed stiffly.

"The governor will see you now," he announced.

Trevor threw his cloak over his shoulder and strode smartly into the room, the silver insignia of his rank glittering brightly on his collar.

Bela stood up from his desk, spread out his arms and smiled broadly. "I'm sorry if I kept you waiting, Commander. Please sit down. Shall I have something to drink brought for you?"

Trevor shook his head and slumped onto the colorful divan opposite the large stone fireplace. The embers were burning brightly, making the room warm and comfortable on this chilly day.

Bela sat back in his velvet chair and inched it away from the desk so he could comfortably cross his legs. "You'll be seeing your first Newfoundland summer soon, Commander," he said almost wistfully. "You'll like it here in summer, you know. The hills flood with dahlias and marigolds; the junipers come alive."

Trevor looked at him thoughtfully as the governor went on with his description of Newfoundland's natural beauty. And after a moment, he realized that this talk of flowers and trees was Bela's own way of masking the shock of the morning's terrible events.

As if reading Trevor's thoughts, Bela faced him again and said, "It was a bad business, this hanging. But it'll insure that another killing won't happen again. I hope people understand why it had to be done."

Trevor sighed. "I'll never forget it as long as I live," he whispered. "Their faces . . ."

Bela scowled. "Don't allow yourself to be haunted by all this, Trevor," he said, using the soldier's name in a soft personal way to show that he understood his feelings. "They had only themselves to blame. And we did what we had to do. You did a fine job, Commander. A very fine job. I'd like to have a man like you assigned to me full time."

Trevor stared at him with a mixture of concern and despair.

Bela laughed. "Oh, don't worry. I'll not be sending you back to the Line, if that's what you're thinking. It's just that a good officer is an asset I badly need. Do you like it here in Newfoundland?"

Trevor thought a moment. "Yes, I do. But by trade I'm an engineer, Governor. And when my tour of duty is up, I want to go back to the Valley. There's great work to be done."

"There's great work to be done here, Trevor."

"I'm not a fighting soldier, sir. My assignments here have been out of my line. If you need an engineer for Newfoundland duty, then I'm your man. But if you need a troubleshooter, I'm afraid not."

Bela sighed. "I'm sorry to hear that. I have another assignment for Elias. One that means a mission of no small importance to the Empire. I was hoping that I could interest you in being a part of it."

Trevor smiled. "I have six months of Newfoundland duty left, Governor. During that time I will be at your command."

The governor waved his hand imperiously. "This is something that could take a year. Maybe two. It would be a full-time commitment. But I assure you it would be something you're interested in."

"Right now all I want is to take my leave in Rhonnda. I have a week coming to me, you know."

"Rhonnda?" Bela broke into a wide grin. "Are you seeing a Rhonnda girl?"

"A Valley girl, my lord," he replied with an unmistakable gleam in his eye. "I met her last year in the Haven. Seems she's coming to Rhonnda any time now, and I want to see her if I can."

Before Bela could ask anything further the doors opened wide again, and the burly frame of Elias stepped inside. The mariner swung off his jacket and nodded stiffly. "I'm late, I know" he apologized. "Couldn't be helped. There's a lot of work to be done on the *Brora*. Right now she's at the Dockside yard, and I had to leave instructions with the carpenters."

"Please, Captain," said Bela, standing up, "no apologies. Just take a seat, if you will. I have something to discuss with you."

Elias glanced at Trevor, then slumped down at the far side of the divan.

"Shall I leave?" asked Trevor, ready to get up.

"No, stay," said the governor, gesturing. "I'd like you to hear this, too. Actually, it concerns what I was beginning to tell you." He leaned back, folded his hands behind his head, and smiled mysteriously.

"What's this all about?" asked Elias.

Bela fumbled among the papers on his desk. "At the same time I received word of the Fiana pirates, I also received an urgent letter from the Council. From Lord Nigel." He paused, measuring his words. "The Council has instructed me to fit a rivership for, er, shall we say, sea duty."

Elias grinned. "What is it the Council wants?"

"A voyage on the open sea," replied Bela.

The mariner's eyes brightened. "You want us to chart the Newfoundland coast? It's about time!"

Bela shook his head forcefully. "We want you to head for the open sea. The ocean."

"To do what?"

"To cross it."

Elias half-stood, features frozen in disbelief.

"Sit down, Captain," said Bela. "Let me ask you a few questions before you ask any of your own. Is the *Brora,* or any rivership for that matter, capable of making a voyage that could mean hundreds of leagues across open sea?"

"Capable, yes," replied the mariner. "But there are a lot of qualifications to that yes. Mainly the weather. If a ship were hit by a violent gale, we'd have no way of guaranteeing its safety. The sea is too unpredictable."

Bela pressed the point. "But is your ship sound enough to make it from one shore to the other?"

Elias shrugged. "Certainly. But what shore? Just where are we supposed to be going?"

The governor sighed and cast his eyes down at the Council letter. "Perhaps I should read this to you," he muttered.

"Not necessary, Governor. I know Lord Nigel. Just tell me what his scheme is this time."

"Not *his* scheme, Captain. This letter bears the official Council seal. It seems the Empire has committed itself to crossing the sea. A representative to accompany you on the voyage has already been here to see me and is now in Rhonnda making, er, other preparations."

Elias whistled. "Your first question was easy," he said. "You asked can a rivership cross the sea. Yes, I think we can. And I'm confident the *Brora* can. But what you haven't told me is why. Where would we go, and for what purpose?"

"As for where," said Bela, "I hardly understand all this myself. The only thing I can repeat is what Lord Nigel's representative told me. If you sail a northwesterly course from Rhonnda, you'll eventually reach a broad land of snowcapped peaks. The Council has reason to believe that another civilization will be found there."

Astonished, Trevor asked, "Is it possible?"

Again Bela shrugged. "How do *I* know? But the Council—and Nigel—believes it to be true. Nigel's letter takes great pains to assure me that their confidence is well founded. It's their hope we can find this land, explore it for minerals and seek out this civilization."

Elias smirked. "And how will anyone do that? It could take a lifetime to explore such an uncharted land."

"I know," sighed Bela. "That's where the wolves come in."

"Wolves?"

"It seems that wolves also dwell on this land—white wolves. And through them, we hope to reach the city we're seeking."

"I don't know," said Elias, shaking his head slowly.

"This time I think the Council is asking too much. Even if all this were true, the dangers of the voyage still would make me reluctant."

"We'd make it worth your while," reminded Bela. "The Council is prepared to fund the expedition entirely. They'll refit your ship from stem to stern, pay you a year's wages in advance and be willing to work out a contract by which you'd receive a percentage of any mineral or other wealth that might be discovered. In short, you could come home a very wealthy man. And so would any of your sailors who were brave enough to risk their lives by going along."

"Have you spoken to any other rivermen yet?" asked an astounded but perplexed Elias.

"I have."

"And what did they say?"

"One refused completely. Another may accept."

Elias's brows rose. "Who?"

"The captain of the *Moontide*."

"Pallant?" cried Elias. "Why he'd never make it! The *Moontide*'s one of the oldest ships on the river."

"Ah, perhaps. But we're going to refit her, remember? By summer we'll have her as fit as any new boat out of the Rhonnda shipyard." Bela smiled at the captain. "But I promised Pallant nothing. I wanted to speak to you first. Give you first crack at turning me down."

Elias leaned back on the divan and rubbed the edges of his mouth with his fingers. Right now he was of two minds. The voyage would be more dangerous than anything he had ever done before. Yet if he were to refuse, and the journey of the *Moontide* proved successful, he would have lost the biggest opportunity for adventure and wealth in his life. The offer of a percentage of what they might find loomed before his eyes like an elusive bauble.

"May I ask something?" said Trevor. "You said before that this mission would involve me if I were willing. Why? What part would I be asked to play?"

"An important part, Commander," Governor Bela said.

"Because the risks of this venture are so great, we're going to send along a contingent of Valley troops. We have no way of knowing what we may be facing, what dark shadows may loom beneath those snowcapped peaks. With luck we'll find the expedition to be both successful and prosperous."

"And you're asking me to take command of this contingent?"

Bela nodded. "Think of it this way: You'll face perils no man of our Empire has ever faced before—but look at the rewards. We have the chance to come face to face with a foreign culture. Men who have never heard of our Empire. It's the Council's hope that a meeting between our cultures could prove to be to our common advantage. Think of it, Trevor! Trading across the sea! What lad hasn't dreamed of it? The Council believes this land to be rich—rich in minerals and raw materials, the very things we so desperately need. Why, a successful expedition could advance our Empire a hundred years. But the choice is yours, Commander. You can be a part of it, if you want."

"Why me? I'd have thought that the man for this kind of job would be one of your more experienced commanders. A man with a proven record of fighting ability should it come to that."

Bela nodded. "A hardened soldier would prove a better commander in a combat situation," he said, "but such a man would be too rigid. We need someone who'd be prepared to take risks, bold chances. A gambler. You always speak about building things, Trevor. Here's your chance, don't you see? Build a bridge between cultures, man! As ranking officer you'll be in authority when you reach the lost city. Think of yourself not as a soldier but as an ambassador. An ambassador of peace come to represent our Empire. But it's not a command," Bela said. "Just say the word and I'll throw the matter back into Lord Nigel's lap and let the Council pick one of their own. What about it, gentlemen?"

Elias rubbed his hands together. There was a tinge of excitement in his voice. "We'd need at least a three-month supply of food. And we'd have to clear out my entire hold, but we might be able to fit fifty or sixty passengers below. It'd be hot as a helhole, but we could do it."

Bela grinned broadly. He knew his catch well enough to recognize when it had taken the bait. "What sort of specialists would you require?"

"A few men with good navigational knowledge for a start. Then I'd need some capable craftsmen. Carpenters and the like, in case of the need for emergency repair. Perhaps a physician? Definitely an astronomer."

"Done," said Bela dryly. "Whatever you need, we'll get it for you. Present a list to the quartermaster at Dockside. What we can't do for you here will be done at Rhonnda."

"You mentioned that Lord Nigel had sent a personal representative here," said Elias. "Where does that fit in?"

"To lead our wolves, Captain. In order to find the white wolves we'll need some tough ones of our own. Nigel's representative came with a forest wolf called Casca. Together they're going to look in the Free Lands. We want the fiercest hunters we can find."

Elias looked at him skeptically. "I don't know that you'll find any, Governor. Wolves don't take to water much."

"We'll find our wolves, Captain," promised Bela, showing a hint of annoyance. "The representative that Lord Nigel sent knows wolves as well as any in the Empire. Maybe better. And when the crossing is made, she'll know how to find the white wolves, too."

Both Trevor and Elias stared. "She?" gasped the riverman, wincing at the thought of a woman on board.

Trevor blurted, "Stacy! It must be Stacy!"

The governor grinned. "Yes, that's right. She's quite a young woman, I understand."

Trevor laughed merrily, his eyes dancing. "That she is, Governor. You may not believe this, but she's the girl I told you I was going to Rhonnda to see."

CHAPTER THIRTEEN

In Newfoundland they say that spring in Rhonnda is like nowhere else in the world. Sunlight bathes the landscape like sweet honey, reaching into the deepest canyons of the Fiana Mountains. And the land comes alive. Wild horses and caribou come down in herds from their nooks hidden high in the bluffs of the Free Lands. Elk and moose appear, to graze and play along the sloping hills beside the maze of fjords and lakes. And the world sparkles with color. White lilies splash across the horizon, and delicate violets blossom at every turn in the shady woodlands that stretch from Noatak to the banks of Rhonnda Island.

And the banners fly in Rhonnda. Atop every steeple, at the crown of every spire, at the bridge of every tower, they flutter endlessly in the wind, a maze of maroon and blue that can be seen ten leagues in every direction. And for every Rhonnda color that flies there comes another to answer its call. The brown and green banners of the Empire fly proudly from the old walls of the High Castle and the small distant garrison at the mouth of the sea. The dull gray and silver flags of ships flap from the harbor down along the estuary as far as the eye can see. And from the roofs of town flash the reddish-hued and bright gold of Aberdeen, the ocher flags of

Noatak Lake, and the orange-and-black-flecked banners of Deepwater.

Stacy stood atop the tower in the square and swooned at the breathtaking panorama spread below. From where she stood you could see it all: the hills, the mountains, the ships, the city. It was the best of both worlds, she mused, as her long hair swirled about in the mild breeze. Spring and Rhonnda, too. What more could she ask? Exhilarated and inspired at the same moment, she knew she felt exactly as the poet Bartok must have felt when he put pen to paper. Right now she believed that both spring and Rhonnda belonged to her and to her alone. And wistfully she wished that she would not have to part with either one. But the sealed letter in her hand, brought to her by courier, burned with a life of its own. Hands trembling with excitement, Stacy forced her gaze away from the beauty of the city and peered down at the letter. The message was short, but it meant more to her than anything she could possibly have hoped for. Eyes scanning quickly, she read it once again:

"My dear Stacy,

Your ship has been secured. Captain Elias of the Brora *has agreed to make the first voyage across the Newfoundland sea. The major refitting of his ship has already been completed here at Deepwater. She sails for Rhonnda today for the final work to be completed and should arrive about the same time you receive this letter.*

Thirty Valley soldiers are being immediately dispatched to accompany you as we discussed. Commander Trevor, of the First Valley Regiment, O.C. Noatak Valley, will take command of the expeditionary forces. I understand that the two of you are already acquainted.

I trust that Casca has been successful in securing the mountain wolves required and your own work in

Rhonnda will be done by the time Elias's ship is set to sail.

If there is anything else I can do for you or for the voyage, please send a dispatch immediately.

May the Fates bless you on your voyage,

> *BELA,*
> *Governor, Newfoundland"*

For over an hour now Stacy had stood at the tower intently staring out at the river and the dizzying array of ships. But nowhere in sight, at least so far, could she see the gold sail and emblazoned flying hawk of the *Brora*. Could the ship have been delayed? she wondered. This was a matter of no small concern. Except for the ship, everything else was just about ready. During the past week she had left Rhonnda for the Free Land Mountains to join Casca. And they had been luckier than she had dared hope. More than a dozen hunters had expressed a willingness—in fact, an eagerness—to leave their dens and join the voyage. And Cicero, barely back himself from the Fiana Badlands, a glint of adventure in his cunning eyes, had accepted the task of leading them. Fierce and savage, wild as the Free Lands themselves, these were wolves that Stacy knew she could count on.

Edgy and tense, she paced back and forth along the tower. The afternoon sun was beginning to dip; long shadows from the minarets and spires danced across the water. Another boat was slowly making its way around the bend where the great river turned. Stacy held her breath as she gazed at the sail. The black hawk with silver talons became clear. Her heart pounded. She stood on her toes and clapped her hands excitedly, almost causing Governor Bela's letter to drift down to the busy street below. It was the *Brora!* Home to Rhonnda at last.

Running from the tower, she bounded down the narrow, winding stone steps and made her way along the broad avenue that led to the docks.

The *Brora,* lamps blazing from her bow like hazy fires, cut her way through the narrowing channel and crept closer to her empty berth. Stacy could hear the faint cries of commands barked along the length and breadth of the ship. It was "Hard to port, Mr. Ashcroft!" and "Steady on the rudder, Mr. Boniface!" She paused to catch her breath in the dimly lit doorway of an old warehouse. Along the dock she could see a handful of tunic-clad workmen begin securing the ropes that had come flinging from the ship. Sailors ran to and fro, tugging at the black iron anchor. A figure stood silhouetted on the prow, hands clasped firmly behind his back, keenly watching. It reminded her of Sykes and the way he had acted on her own journey from Deepwater. But this man stood much taller. His stance was aloof, though, as if he did not have to keep the same careful eye over his crew as the *Lady of Newfoundland*'s captain did. Stacy drew a deep breath. It was Elias. She could not make out his face, or even a hint of his eyes. But it was Elias!

She inched her way forward along the wharf, as the *Brora*'s sailors began to debark. One, a young fellow with a drooping mustache, halted her at the gangplank.

"My name is Ashcroft, my lady. May I be of help?"

"Perhaps you can, Mr. Ashcroft. I'm waiting for Captain Elias."

Ashcroft, smiling and bowing politely, said: "This way, my lady. Hold the ropes as you climb these steps. By the way, who shall I tell the captain is here to see him?"

"Oh," she replied, pushing a lock of hair away from her eyes, "Just tell him that Stacy's here."

Ashcroft's face seemed to droop; his lips sputtered. "Stacy? *The* Stacy? I mean, Lady Anastasia? The girl with the wolves?"

Stacy threw back her head and laughed, her eyes flashing and sparkling. "The same." Before the stunned Ashcroft could say anything more, a head popped out of the doorway to the leeward hatch. "Who's up there?"

"Just me, Captain."

"Look here, Ashcroft," the voice said sternly, "you know the rules about bringing women on board. Next time have her meet you on land. Is that understood?"

Ashcroft gulped. "Yes, sir! But Captain, this, er, lady, is here to see *you*. I was only bringing her to your——"

The riverman squinted his eyes and stared at the shapely silhouette standing easily at young Ashcroft's side.

"It's Stacy," said Stacy.

Elias beamed and slid open the companionway door. He straightened his shoulders, self-consciously pushed a shock of dark hair away from his forehead and strode across the deck to the ladder. "That will be all, Mr. Ashcroft. Enjoy your leave. Wonderful to see you again, my lady," he said in a low tone, eyes gazing into hers. "I'm glad you came. We'll probably have quite a number of matters to discuss. Arrangements and assigning quarters, and the like."

Stacy nodded eagerly.

Elias gestured sweepingly with his hand and pointed to the small bridge on the forecastle. "It's a warm night, my lady. And the quarters below are stuffy and dank. Shall we talk under the stars for a while?"

The girl nodded and followed in his shadow as Elias turned and walked to the front of the ship. The stars were bright as jewels, and the moon, a curved crescent low in the sky, glowed as the famed lights of Rhonnda flickered in the distance. The view of the town from the harbor was almost as magnificent as that from the highest spire, mused Stacy, glancing at the silhouetted city, hardly aware of the gently swaying ship beneath her feet. *The lights of Rhonnda.* She turned her eyes toward Elias. The riverman was leaning with his back against the bulwark, fingers gripping at the rails.

"I can understand why Rhonnda's so loved by Newlanders," she said. "It's dazzling. I almost have the feeling that I'm in a dream, seeing a city of gods."

Elias smiled knowingly. "Rhonnda will one day be the Empire's monument, my lady. Our gift to whatever kind of world our children inherit."

Stacy nodded. She glanced again at the towers and sighed. "I feel so small beside all of this," she confided.

Elias laughed. "You're not the first to feel that way. Rhonnda, this whole land, in fact, does that to people. It's the mountains, it's the river, it's the hint of the sea beyond the channel. The very crossroad of the world. From here we want to reach out and touch it all."

"Perhaps we will," replied the girl, dark eyes narrowing. "Perhaps we *both* will."

Within a fleeting second, Elias felt his heart race and his mind yearn with desire. Who was this girl with the charms and powers to try and alter the course of the Empire? There was something about her that entranced him, something he could not fully explain. Her proud stance, her easy shifting and grace, those enchanting eyes.

"I heard about the trouble in Fiana," said Stacy, frowning, "and about the hanging. It must have been terrible."

"I hope to never go through anything like that again, my lady. It was a nasty business. But I suppose someone had to do it, and the governor asked me. But why speak of such things? We have a saying here in Rhonnda: 'Bury the past before it buries you.' So why not put this sort of talk out of our minds and speak of better things to come?"

"All right, Captain." Her eyes brightened, and she threw back her head. "Shall we talk business?"

Elias laughed heartily. "Why not?"

"Governor Bela wrote that you'd be completing your fitting work here at Rhonnda. How long will it take?"

"The heavy work, for the most part, is already done. But we'll need a new mast, one sturdy enough for open sea winds, as well as new fittings below for our passengers.

But the best craftsmen in the Empire are here, so it shouldn't take long for things to be put in order."

"We'll be ready to leave by the first days of summer?"

"Of course, my lady. We have to. This journey could take weeks, months even. We have no way of knowing. And by midsummer the sea gales begin. We have to try to avoid them if at all possible."

"That makes sense," agreed the girl. "With luck maybe we'll have a pleasant voyage."

"If not pleasant, at least endurable," said Elias with a grin. "You know, when the governor first proposed this to me, I was quite skeptical. But while at Deepwater I began to see just how monumental this journey could be."

Stacy rested with her back against the bulwark. "What made you decide to come? I was really quite afraid that no ship would dare the risks."

Elias smiled. "I'll confide in you, my lady. There's not a mariner in all the Empire who's not dreamed of crossing the sea. But there're precious few who'd actually try it. I suppose I want to be the one who does."

Stacy looked at him thoughtfully. "Why?"

Again the riverman laughed. "Why?" he repeated as he shrugged. "Why not? Like other mortal men, I want to make my mark upon the world. I want my name to be remembered. 'Elias—the first captain to cross the sea.' Look at the mountains, Stacy. They're immortal. And look at Rhonnda. She'll be immortal, too. But even a lowly sailor hungers for a piece of that immortality. And this voyage will give me mine."

Stacy listened with surprise. Speaking in a soft voice, she said, "I think I misjudged you, Captain. I thought you only cared for the riches."

The riverman stared out at the calm waters and the small waves as they beat against the shadowed quay. "Five years ago, my lady, you'd have been right. But not now, not any longer. You can say I'm doing this for glory, or even adventure, but it's more than that. I'm doing it because it needs to be done. And if we should fail, I hope and pray that others will take our place and succeed."

Stacy's mood turned mellow as she listened to the faraway sounds from the river. An occasional shout from some harried sailor aboard some dark ship, a muffled laugh from a drunken laborer among the shadows of the warehouses. The deep voice of Elias finally broke the quiet.

"But what about you, my lady? My reasons for going are rather simple. Yours aren't. What makes a young woman give up a life of ease and comfort to risk her life on the sea?"

For a long while Stacy did not reply. At last she turned, her eyes downcast. "Maybe I'm like you," she whispered.

Elias looked at her curiously. "How do you mean?"

"Why did you leave the Valley and come here?" she asked him forthright and interested.

"I guess I saw myself as something of an outcast, my lady," he sighed. "The world of the Valley was a world I didn't belong to. Newfoundland was a place where a man could make a life for himself and be free."

Stacy nodded slowly. "I know what you mean. In the Haven I'm looked upon as something of an outcast myself."

"My lady? I don't understand . . ."

Stacy waved her hand at the staring riverman. "Hear me out, Elias. Please. You know my father, you know his love for Dwellers. He wanted to pass that on to me. So when I was a very young girl, he brought me to the forest and to the wolves. I was taught by them. Everything there is to know about the forest and its ways. I lived with wolves, learned their culture, their way of life, how to survive as they do. And I grew to love them—so much that for nearly half of every year I'd keep away from our civilization. I speak in the canine tongues like one of their own. I track like a hunter and use my dagger as they use their fangs."

"I find that admirable," said Elias sincerely. "You have the best of both your worlds."

Stacy's eyes flickered. "Do I? Sometimes I feel that people stare at me like I'm a savage. At court the other young women stare as though I'm likely to leap and slit their throats."

Elias leaned forward and touched her sleeve lightly. "Stacy, I ... I never dreamed. But you're not the first to befriend wolves. Many have. Why right here—even I ..."

The girl looked away. "I'm a woman, Captain. The daughter of a famous lord. Eyes see me very differently than they do others. And those eyes can be cruel. They taunt, they mock. And they *laugh*." Stacy wiped at her eyes and gave him a wan smile. "I'm sorry if I seem bitter, Elias. But at least now you understand why I left the Valley. In Rhonnda my name and title are barely recognized. And no one seems to care, anyway. For the first time in my life I feel as if I'm no different than anybody else. It's a good feeling, Captain. I don't want to lose it."

"You won't, my lady. Here you can live as free as a mountain laurel. You need never face those cruelties again. But tell me, my lady, what about your part in this expedition? Have you found the wolves we need?"

Stacy nodded happily. "Cicero and eight of the finest hunters I've ever seen. Most of them were more than eager."

Elias laughed at the thought of Cicero. He should have known that the wily red wolf would have been among the first to volunteer. "Then things are right on schedule," he said. "And when our voyage is done, what will you do?"

"Stay close to Rhonnda," she replied in a low voice. "I've come to think of it as my home already. I met a merchant here, and he spoke of wild mustangs to be caught in the Free Lands. I think I'd like that. I'm quite good with horses, you know."

"And, er, what about Trevor?" Elias asked awkwardly. "Where does he fit into your life?"

Stacy looked up blankly. "I don't know that he does. I like him, if that's what you mean. But I have no commitments." She smiled. "Right now I'm as free as those mountain laurels you spoke of."

Elias felt his heart pound in his throat. Most rivermen vow never to marry, to be wed only to their ships. But now Elias began to wonder. If Stacy *were* free—and if Trevor had no hold on her. . . !

CHAPTER FOURTEEN

As the sky turned to purple and the flaming red sun lowered against a backdrop of azure mountains, the Rhonnda festival began. Under a crescent moon and early evening twinkling stars, the streets and plaza thronged. Acrobats and jugglers danced and performed while crowds oohed and aahed, and the puppeteers dramatically displayed adventures of ages long past.

All work stopped in Rhonnda during festival. Tinkers and weavers mingled in a friendly way with lords and nobles, sailors greeted and bought rounds of drinks for competitors and shipmates alike. Valley soldiers strolled the streets laughing and winking at shapely Rhonnda girls, who in turn teased and winked back at the shy Valley lads. Rebellion in their playful eyes, they let the Valley lads chase them, and if the poor boy was handsome and charming enough—well, who could say what marriages might come of it?

At a large round table, one of many set up close beside the riverfront, Stacy and her companions sat under the stars, joking and toasting one another and ordering new rounds of wine. Above their heads a clustered group of glow globes swirled, sending down pale glimmers of yellow and orange. Everyone was dressed in their finest garb: Trevor, handsome and dashing in his smart officer's uniform; Elias, in his spanking-new captain's tunic of deep, rich purple; Simon in a wine-colored toga. Lorna, eyes ever bright, was dressed in a pale pink shift, the latest and most popular style in the Valley, but to the eyes of Trevor and Elias it was Stacy who held the attention. She wore a soft amber tunic, and her hair was pulled back tightly by a slim bronze-colored band. Large earrings dangled and danced with every move of her head. She sat with her legs crossed, arms over the back of the wicker chair, breasts rising and falling slightly with every breath as she watched a group of brightly dressed dancers race along the pier to take up positions atop a small stage. The musicians began to play as the dancers, five lads and five lasses, twirled about, skirts flinging high, hands clapping in time to the music. Gracefully they encircled, then broke, formed partners, then encircled again. Stacy watched with glee as the men held out glistening swords and the women nimbly jumped and danced inches away from the threatening blades. One of the men grabbed two torches and, swinging a girl over his shoulder, then between his legs out behind him, leaped and threw the torches high into the air. He caught them both with perfect precision and at last took a series of deep bows as the watchers stood and applauded loudly.

"Magnificent!" Trevor cried. "That's the best dance I've ever seen!"

Elias winked at Stacy. "Valley folk don't have that, do they, my lady?" He toasted her with his wine.

Stacy shook her head emphatically. "Our dancers are amateurs by comparison. These were wonderful! What kind of a dance was that?"

"A Rhonnda folk dance, Stacy. You'll be seeing a lot of it in the years to come."

Stacy smiled, missing Trevor's puzzled glance. "I hope so." She sighed, feeling slightly tipsy, but good.

As a waitress returned and refilled the empty goblets, everyone suddenly looked up. There was a low dim sound, almost like a mournful wail, coming from some distant point on the river.

"What's that?" asked Trevor, glancing in the distance.

Elias put a finger to his lips and strained his ears. The sound came again, this time vaguely louder than before. Elias stood up. Already a small crowd of onlookers had gathered at the edge of the pier and was staring out into the black waters. "It sounded like a ship's horn," Elias told them.

"Now?" asked Lorna. "At this time of night? Wouldn't a ship stay out of port until daylight?"

Elias shrugged. "Usually. But why would he be blowing his horn? We only do that in——"

"An emergency," interrupted Simon. He put down his goblet and stood. "We'd better have a look." Stacy got up, too, and followed.

Elias pushed his way through the crowd, Simon and Stacy beside him. The blast came again, so loud that they winced at the shrill sound. From the shadows ahead they could see the silhouette of a sloop moving with care and caution toward the harbor. Her sails were furled, and she crept along at a snail's pace, carried only by the current.

"There must have been an accident," whispered Stacy, transfixed at the eerie sight.

"And look at the way she's moving," added Elias. "She's weaving along with the current. As if there were no one to sail her."

Simon shuddered. The sloop was coming closer; he could make out the shape of a lone sailor standing at the prow and holding a bugle to his lips. Save for him, there was no sign of life.

Suddenly Stacy gasped. She squinted her eyes. Atop the mast was a dark banner flapping unevenly in the breeze. "I can't make it out, Elias," she panted. "What colors is she flying?"

Elias drew a deep breath and shook his head. "We'd better command a skiff and take a peek on board. I don't like the looks of this."

"But the flag," said Stacy, pointing at the bare mast.

Simon looked back to the riverman and said, "Get us

a boat, Elias. I'll have to order the dockside to be cleared. I don't want anyone within sight of the sloop."

Stacy stood perplexed as Simon called to Trevor, and the Valley soldier, with the help of some nearby Rangers, pushed back the crowds. Almost too frightened to look, she forced her eyes ahead and began to understand. The sloop had come to a dead stop a few hundred meters from shore, standing silently. The only movement came from the fluttering flag—and the flag was black.

Thick cumulus clouds, grim as the night itself, scudded high above Rhonnda as the small skiff made its way across the still waters to the foreboding ship. Save for the soft splash of the oars and the moan of creaking wood the quiet pervaded.

Elias, face drawn and tight, stood fore on the skiff and counted the oar strokes drawn by the two burly sailors. In front, the hull of the sloop loomed large as life. He could make out the faded name of the ship painted on the side: *Sea Witch*. And his heart skipped a beat. She was a Rhonnda ship, now lost and forlorn, unsailed, at least by any living hand as far as he could tell, and somehow she had come home to port, perhaps by her own will. Waves slapped softly against the hull. The young bugler on the prow was suddenly gone. Vanished as swiftly as he had mysteriously appeared.

Elias could see the deck now, as plain as he could see the anxious face of Simon at his side or hear the heavy breathing of Stacy standing directly behind him. The sails were clumsily furled—if you could call them furled at all. Sections of canvas hung awkwardly down from the spars, torn at the edges. Water barrels, as well as various tools, could be clearly seen, scattered from prow to stern. Elias and Simon exchanged worried glances.

At last the oars were drawn; the skiff ebbed close beside a long rope ladder dangling over the ship's side. Elias reached out and grabbed hold. "Follow me, Simon," he said. "The rest of you had better wait for us." The sailors nodded without a word, but Stacy shook her head. "I'm coming, too," she said defiantly.

"This is no place for you, Stacy," Simon told her. "It'll be safer for you to wait."

The girl refused. "I'm coming with you."

Rather than argue, Simon reluctantly agreed. He waited as Elias climbed the ladder and boarded, then climbed the rope himself. Once over the side, he held out a hand for Stacy.

The deck was smeared with oil and grease. Elias looked around with apprehension. Rats and mice were darting from view behind old crates and boxes. There was a nauseating stench in the air.

"We won't find anything up here," he muttered. "We'll have to have a look below."

Stacy gulped. From the companionway door she could see that the cabins and storage holds below were completely dark. And the thought of the rats running at her feet made her tremble with revulsion.

"You can go back to the skiff, Stacy, if you want," said Elias, sounding gruff and tense.

The girl stared sharply at him and shook her head. She had come this far, and she would see it through.

Elias gritted his teeth. Then, leaning out to the bowsprit, close to the very spot the bugler had stood, he took hold of a musty, cloth-covered torch. He dipped it lightly into a pool of spilled oil and struck a flint. The torch jumped to life, long yellow flames dancing high and black smoke curling thickly above it. Then, cautiously, he kicked wide the companionway door. The blaze of light brought forth squeals from frightened mice as they ran over the steps and darted between his feet. Elias grimaced. Step by step he lowered himself below. Simon took Stacy's arm and together they descended in the shadows of the torch.

They walked a long narrow corridor that led forward to the captain's cabin. On the way they passed a large dormitorylike room. This was the crew's quarters, they knew—and, as fearfully expected, it was deserted. For an instant Elias poked the torch inside. The blackness gave way to the hectic light. Again small mice scurried to hide.

"Nothing to see here," he mumbled.

Stacy looked around. Her canine sense of smell led her to push open a storage room door on the portside. Strong currents of pungent meat filled her nostrils. She lurched back, her eyes scanning the dark. "Here, Elias! Bring the torch *here!*"

Elias turned quickly and followed her voice. The girl stood halfway inside the room, eyes closed. The flames flickered, exposing the decaying body of a sailor.

Simon ran to the body. With the expertise that comes easily to a physician, he studied and examined the yellowed, cold face. He touched the lymph glands and let his finges run lightly up and down the abdomen. The sailor had been dead at least three days, he realized. Perhaps more, but it was difficult to tell. Yet why had the body been left like this? Why hadn't his shipmates buried him? It made no sense. But nothing aboard the *Sea Witch* seemed to make any sense, anyway.

"Let's try the captain's cabin," said Elias after Simon looked up and indicated that he was done. For a few moments longer they continued on their grim walk. At last Elias stopped. The door of the captain's cabin was locked. He turned the torch over to Stacy and with all his might pushed his frame, shoulder first, against the door. With a thud the heavy oak gave way. Elias peered inside. Again empty. A few books and charts lay across the floor, and a chair stood at the side of a narrow bunk bed.

"I just don't understand," whispered Simon. "What could have happened here?"

Elias knelt down and thumbed through the scattered books. He grimaced. "This is the captain's log," he said. "If *anything* can give us some clues, this will." Eagerly he pored over the pages as Stacy held the light. After a while he found what he had been looking for. Elias handed Simon the book, and the physician began to read.

"Mr. Cady fell ill this morning. I have relieved him of all duty. His brow burns, and he cries for water. Yet he shivers and complains of the cold."

Simon ran his finger down the page, skipped an entry or two, then read again:

"Mr. Land and Mr. Deer are close to death. Cady died this morning. We buried him in the river. May the fates take his soul. Now Mr. Tiller has developed the same rash."

Stacy's eyes grew wider. The captain of the *Sea Witch* spoke of each of the crew, including himself, beginning to show various symptoms of the illness.

"His skin has become red on the neck, armpits, groin. His face is flushed, a ring of pallor shows around his mouth. I have tended to him, but I can see that he will die like the others."

Simon paused and looked anxiously at his listeners. Then:

"My face is marked with the same red spots, intense and diffuse. My throat has become inflamed. It will only be a matter of days until I die, also. Land and Deer were buried this morning. Cates became wrought with madness. Last night he tore off his tunic, and, burning with fever, he jumped into the river."

"They committed suicide!" cried Stacy.

Elias nodded glumly. "They were all out of their heads. Scarlet fever does that to men."

The girl turned white. *Fever,* she thought, *fever!* That ancient scourge that had so often wrought destruction on the Valley had come to Newfoundland.

A lunatic laugh suddenly rang out from the passageway. Elias turned and yelled, "It's the bugler! He's down here!" He pushed Stacy aside, nearly knocked Simon over and raced from the cabin. There was a muffled cry and a loud banging as the two men fell outside. Stacy ran outside. She saw Elias on top of a frail boy, a lad of no more than sixteen. His face was disfigured with dark pinpricks. His eyes raged with torment, and his mouth foamed even as he laughed and cried at the same moment.

"You'll die, too!" he chuckled as Elias held him down, pinning his shoulders firmly.

Elias slapped him hard across the face. The lad turned his eyes away and began to whimper. "Oh, mercy! Help me, please! *I don't want to die! I don't——*"

Simon knelt down beside him and winced as he felt the burning forehead. "Listen to me, lad," he said softly. "I'm a physician. I'm going to help you if I can. Your mates are all dead, but you're still alive. We have medicines. We might be able to cure you, but first you have to help me, all right?"

Choking back tears, the boy nodded.

"Where was your ship bound? And what cargoes did you carry?"

"We sailed from the Cottonwood, sir."

Simon bit his lip. "What stops did you make on the way?"

The boy stared. "None, sir. We're a Rhonnda ship."

Simon sighed. At least this was good news. If the ship had not stopped at any ports, then it was a safe bet that none of the river towns was contaminated.

"And how did you make it this far? Who sailed the ship?"

"There were three of us left until yesterday, sir. The captain, a midshipman and myself. We knew that by to-night we'd be in sight of Rhonnda. But they were too ill to go on."

"There's a body in one of the storerooms," said Elias. "Why didn't you bury it like the others?"

The lad stared at the riverman. Then he began to grin maniacally. He put his hands to his mouth and stared at Elias. "For the rats, sir! Don't you know? Aren't you a sailor?"

"For the *rats?*"

"Of course!" laughed the boy. "No one knows it's there but *me.*" He began to whisper. "But you won't tell the captain, will you? Or Mr. Cady, the first mate. He'll be mad at me again."

"What are you talking about?" asked Simon, scowling.

"You fool! The rats were hungry. *I* left Mr. Tubbs's body for them to eat!" He frothed at the mouth again, tongue swollen and purpled, hanging limply.

Stacy hung her head and cast her gaze away from the stricken boy. Elias let him go and peered up at the physician. "This ship will have to be burned," he said.

Simon nodded. "That's just for a start. We're close to port. If any of those disease-carrying rodents have swum to shore, they could infect the whole city."

Stacy glared at him. "An epidemic?"

"Too soon to know. But this bodes badly for us all, I'm afraid. Word will have to be sent to Deepwater. And I'm certain Bela will put a quarantine on Rhonnda. We can't take any chances of having ships pull in and leave carrying fever on board. It could spread like wildfire throughout Newfoundland. And even back to the Valley."

"But you can't quarantine all of Rhonnda;" protested Elias. "We need supplies. The city will die!"

Simon shook his head. "For the present there's nothing else to be done. My authority as medical commissioner gives me the right to declare a quarantine here and now."

"But why?" asked Stacy. "There's no evidence that the fever will spread."

Simon looked at her darkly. "And I pray that it doesn't. But there's an incubation period. Symptoms won't show until a week after exposure. Don't you see, Stacy? The *Sea Witch* has been drifting close to the shore for days. At any point some of the infected rodents might have jumped ship. At this very moment they could be in our fields, attacking our cattle—or worse. They might be running wild and free in the city. Any ship that drops anchor runs the risk of the same fate as the *Sea Witch*. I can't let that happen."

"How long will the quarantine last?" asked Elias nervously.

Simon shrugged. "If there're no outbreaks, no more than a couple of weeks. But if it spreads . . ." There was an ominous tone in his voice.

"The *Brora* is set to sail in three weeks," said Stacy pensively. "The quarantine won't affect us, will it?"

Simon looked at her sternly. "It will affect *every* ship, including the *Brora*. It's for your own protection."

"But we're not headed for any of the Newland towns," Stacy protested. "We're bound for the open sea!"

"No matter, Stacy. We can't let any ships sail. Nothing moves on the river, either to Rhonnda or from Rhonnda. That's the way it has to be."

Stacy's eyes smoldered. "If we can't sail on schedule, we might as well not sail at all."

Simon was not about to budge. "Then you'll have to postpone."

"But we can't postpone!" cried the girl, distraught and disbelieving.

Elias nudged gently at her arm. "In the meantime, Simon," he said, "things will continue in Rhonnda as usual, isn't that right? We'll at least be able to have the shipyard work continued?"

"Certainly. Make her as fit as you like. But remember, not a stitch of sail will be unfurled until we've dealt with this." He gestured to the creaking ship around them.

"I understand," said the riverman. "Then let's get on with it. The first order of business will be to get this poor fellow to land and to some medical care."

"And then we burn the *Sea Witch*," said Simon. "The rest is up to the Fates. We can ease the suffering and misery of fever, even cure most of the milder cases. But we can't stop it from spreading. Pray for Rhonnda, my friends. For if the worst comes to pass, the city will be dead within a year."

* * *

Under threatening clouds Stacy rode through the silent midnight streets. She wore a long, black-hooded cape clasped around her shoulders. Long black riding boots shimmered in the wet rain; her father's silver dagger gleamed at her waist. Swiftly she passed the fabled Jeweled Garden and came upon a small cottage nestled beneath the long branches of thick-leaved trees.

Straight from the Free Lands she had come, pushing her mare to the limits of endurance. She had crossed the channel to Rhonnda Island at its shallowest point on horseback, avoiding at all costs the bridges and the Rhonnda garrison. Leaving the city had been forbidden under the quarantine, even to go to the nearby Free Land Mountains. But with rebellion burning in her eyes she had defied Empire law for the first time in her life—and made her way to the waiting Cicero and Casca. Now, her business among the wolves completed, she made her way quickly back to Elias's house. He would be waiting for her. So would Trevor.

Lightning flashed; thunder crashed. The mare reared in fear, her iron-shod hooves striking sparks like flints against the stones of the narrow street. Flinging back her cape, Stacy grasped tightly at the reins and calmed the anxious horse. Then, leaping from the saddle, she quickly tied the reins to a small post at the side of the house, ran back to the front and eagerly knocked at the iron-braced door. A thin beam of light leaped out as the door opened and a pair of dark, questioning eyes peered at her.

"Stacy!" said Elias, flinging the door wide.

The girl threw off her hood and strode inside. There was a small drawing room off to the left, dimly lit by a small oil lamp. Trevor sat dejectedly in a small chair beside the unlit fire, pensively rubbing his knuckles.

Stacy looked at Elias. His eyes were sullen and brooding. "What's wrong?" she asked.

"Come in and sit down, Stacy. Please."

Elias poured a cup of wine from a large colorful urn

and handed it to her. She sipped slowly, letting its warmth
run through her body.

"Now can you tell me?" she asked.

Elias grimaced, then downed his own drink. "Another
case of fever's been reported, Stacy. Outside the city.
Trevor has just received word from the captain of the
Rhonnda garrison. They want his soldiers put under
Valley orders."

Stacy glared at Trevor. "And what does that mean?"

"It means," said Trevor sadly, "that I'm no longer in
command of my contingent. The troops are wanted to
reinforce the quarantine. There's even talk of a curfew—
dusk to dawn."

Stacy put her head in her hands and sighed. What else
could possibly go wrong? For almost two weeks since the
burning of the *Sea Witch* not a single case of fever had
been reported. Simon and the Rhonnda Council were all
but prepared to lift it. Then a young girl suddenly died. In
the next four days three other cases had been reported.
Now this.

"Without Valley soldiers the voyage will be ten times
as dangerous."

Trevor avoided her angry eyes. "I know. It makes it all
but impossible for us."

"And the weather won't be in our favor much longer,"
sighed Elias. "The governor intends to keep us out of the
water until Simon and his people are absolutely convinced
that all possibility of an epidemic is gone."

Stacy threw up her hands. "Then what's the use? We
might as well give up."

Elias scratched at his stubbled chin. "Perhaps. Perhaps
not. We could give thought to breaking the quarantine."

Trevor stared. "Leave without authority? We'd be
breaking the law! We can't do that. The Council——"

Stacy laughed hollowly. "Are you going to tell us about
the Council again? We've been through all that, Trevor,
remember? This is Rhonnda. The Council can make all
the rules and laws they like. But they're hundreds of

leagues from here. Who'll enforce them?" Seething with anger, she turned to Elias. "Can we do it? Can we pull out without Valley soldiers from the garrison on our backs?"

The mariner nodded. "We can. The garrison boys are no problem. Half of them are Rhonnda lads in Valley uniforms, anyway. They'd wink if they saw the *Brora* sail past."

"Then let's do it!" she cried.

"Are you serious?" asked Trevor. "You'd actually break an Empire edict?"

Elias sat down beside Stacy and frowned. "I know the way you feel. There've been angry words between the Rhonnda Council and the Valley authorities."

Trevor fidgeted, well aware that he, as a senior officer, was one of those authorities to whom Elias was referring.

"Some of our citizens are blaming the Valley for our problems," added Elias. "Merchants believe that the Haven is purposely letting our commerce suffer, using the threat of fever as a weapon to wield greater control over us."

"But that's impossible!" cried Stacy. "Governor Bela would never allow it! He loves this land as much as we do!"

Elias sighed. "He does love Newfoundland, that's true. But his first duty is to the Valley. Some of our more ill-tempered rivermen have been threatening to break the quarantine themselves and defy the edict just as you're willing to do. But do you know what that could mean?"

Stacy nodded. She understood full well what such open rebellion could mean.

Elias turned slowly to Trevor. *"Tell her,* Commander. If you don't, I will."

The girl seemed confused; she glanced up at the soldier and Trevor lowered his eyes. "Stacy, the governor received a letter from the Council, one signed personally by your father. The Haven is determined not to let the edict be broken. You have to understand. Fever conjures up terrible memories back home."

"I know," she whispered. "I've heard the stories."

"Get on with it," snapped Elias.

Trevor sighed sadly. "The letter from your father was explicit. Until this entire matter of plague is settled Rhonnda is to be considered under military law. As an officer, I'm bound to comply and——"

Stacy glared. "Stop the *Brora* from sailing?"

"I won't have to, Stacy. There's a fighting ship coming up from Deepwater. The biggest in the Empire, the *Windjammer*. She's been taken off duty exploring the uncharted regions of the Cottonwood and is being dispatched to Rhonnda immediately."

"But why?" Her face was drawn and troubled.

Trevor looked at her darkly. "To blockade the harbor. The *Windjammer* carries two hundred troops—fighting troops. Not roadbuilders like me." He sat back with folded arms, shaking his head and sighing.

A look of despair written across her face, Stacy slumped back. "And my father, did he give the order for the *Windjammer* to sail here?"

"Technically, Bela gave the order," said Elias. "But he never would have done it without the Council demanding the strictest action."

"And what action will the *Windjammer* take if we defy it and try to sail?"

"Board us by force, if necessary," replied Trevor. "And if that fails, sink us."

Stacy's bright eyes dimmed, and her cheeks paled. "Well, gentlemen," she said, forcing a weak smile, "it looks like we've lost the fight. Without Trevor and his Valley troops, we'd probably never have accomplished our mission, anyway."

Elias leaned forward and touched gently at her sleeve. "We're not completely out yet, my lady."

The girl looked up, puzzled. Elias grinned. "Despite all that we've just told you, it *will* be possible to break the blockade and head for the sea. That is, if you have a taste for danger and facing up to the *Windjammer.*"

"What are you saying, Elias?"

The riverman's face suddenly turned serious. "There are those in Rhonnda who'd be willing to help us. They have various reasons, mostly to see the Valley with egg on its face. Nevertheless, they'll give their support if I ask. But it's not just up to me, Stacy. This whole business is your dream. Say the word, and I think I can still make it happen."

Stacy looked over to Trevor, who was sitting awkwardly and staring sullenly at the floor. "I think this scheme is insane, Stacy. It's a conspiracy against Valley law. But I gave Elias my word that I wouldn't hinder you in any way. But as a soldier, you know I can't help you, either."

Stacy nodded with understanding. "What is it we have to do, Elias?"

"The *Brora* is ready to sail. She's a virtual fighting ship. And I plan to, er, make a few additions to give us the edge we need over the *Windjammer* should they try to stop us."

"But what about our own soldiers? Without Trevor and his Valley troops we'll be virtually helpless."

"Not quite, Stacy. We can replace them with locals. Rhonnda's Rangers. They're hard as nails, my lady. And with your fighting wolves . . ."

"That's begging a confrontation," replied the girl coolly.

"We're only asking the right to leave the harbor. Nothing more. But it *is* a risk."

"And I'm prepared to take a risk, too," added Trevor hastily. "I'll ask my lads to join you on board. They might follow my orders, they might not. I can't be certain. But you must understand that I can't offer any help should an actual confrontation begin. If the commander of the *Windjammer* orders me to lay down my weapons, I'll have to obey."

Stacy readily agreed. "I understand, Trevor. And I appreciate the help you're trying to give us. But surely this can only bring trouble on top of your head. Win or lose, you'll be accused of aiding and abetting criminals."

Trevor smiled sourly. "If the *Windjammer* attacks us, we'll probably all die in the fight, anyway. And if it doesn't, we'll probably drown in the sea. Either way . . ." He shrugged.

Stacy smiled. "And what about *your* crew, Elias? Will they be willing to risk tackling Valley troops?"

"They will. And I've already spoken to one of the Ranger captains. He's promised his help. You see, the Rhonnda Council has never sanctioned this blockade. In their eyes, we're not breaking any laws."

Stacy's face brightened at the thought of the voyage finally being able to get under way. "Very well, then, Elias. I accept your proposal, even if it does make us brigands. How soon can we sail?"

"How soon can your wolves be ready?" he countered.

Stacy thought for a moment. "Give me three days. One to ride back to the Free Lands, another to come down the mountains, a third to meet you beside the bluffs at the tip of the island. We can wait for your signal after dark. But look, there're still a few things unclear in my mind. You said that there were those here in Rhonnda who were willing to help us. Who are they? And why?"

Elias winked. He went to the door and called, "You can come in now."

A small balding man with a cheery grin entered the room from the dark hallway beyond. Stacy stared in disbelief. The idea of a conspirator had conjured up the image of some dark-hooded man with an eye patch and a dagger. This man smiled warmly, exposing crooked teeth and a bulging paunch; hardly the stuff of which brigands are made! This was no pirate of Rhonnda, no brigand of the river. She found herself gazing into the gentle eyes of none other than Spooner Morningglory, the happy-go-lucky merchant.

"Are you the man who's going to get us out of Rhonnda?" she gasped, astonished.

Spooner laughed deeply. "I'm going to try, my lady. Yes, indeed, I'm going to try."

"But why you, Spooner? I don't understand. You're an Empire merchant. Governor Bela is your friend. Why are you going to turn against him?"

"But I'm not, my lady," replied the crafty merchant. "The governor had no choice in sending the *Windjammer* up here. It was forced on him, if you get my meaning."

"But why do you want to help us? What's in it for you?"

"Quite a bit, actually. You see, the Rhonnda Council has been stirring the waters for years to find a way to rid us of Valley authority. We don't want armed rebellion, that's not our way. We love the Empire as much as your own father does. But we can't tolerate our affairs being constantly muddled into by men who have never been here. In short, we're seeking a confrontation. One that will show the Valley boys that we mean business. That's where you come in. This effort will be for mutual advantage, Lady Anastasia, I assure you."

Stacy shook her head. "I'm sorry, Spooner. I just don't understand how."

"We're willing to set the *Brora* on her way. The local garrison commander can be bribed." Spooner winked outrageously. "Believe me, I've been, er, doing business with him for years. Then you'll force the issue for us. A Rhonnda ship versus an Empire ship. The *Brora* against the *Windjammer*. If the *Windjammer* backs down, as I suspect she will, then the Valley blockade will be seen for the sham it really is. We'll have broken it and the quarantine as well."

"But what about the threat of fever?"

"The real danger has passed, my lady. Even Simon would grant you as much. Besides, your ship touches no Empire port. You're headed for the sea, if I understand this venture. No one can suffer by your leaving. The governor knows this."

"And what if the *Windjammer* doesn't back down, Spooner? What if she comes about as Trevor believes and *fights?*"

Spooner sighed. His cherubic face grew cold. "Then put your trust in the Fates and Captain Elias here."

"You haven't lived here long enough to understand us, Stacy," said Elias. "We resent having to seek permission for what any Valley village takes for granted it can do on its own. We don't need a law hundreds of leagues away telling us when we can or cannot sail. We're not the dolts or barbarians the fine lords would have you believe. The days of Valley-imposed restrictions are numbered in Rhonnda—with or without the *Brora* to fight the battle. I'm sorry if what I said offends you in some way, my lady, but that's the way it is. The time has come for Rhonnda to share in the Empire's growth as a partner, not a servant."

Stacy listened quietly and understood. She wondered if, in some way, all that had transpired these past months could have been fated, unalterable, in ways she did not comprehend.

Stacy thought of Bartok again—as she so frequently had these past weeks. What it was about his poems that swayed her so she could not tell; only that they did. Only that his visions were her visions, too. She was a willing captive; as if the Fates themselves had taken a hand in each event in her life. Bartok never wrote of a Rhonnda at odds with the Empire, she knew. He foretold only of a Rhonnda whose glory was to lead nations, even as beacons lead fog-shrouded ships into harbor. In a curious thought, Stacy wondered if Bartok had seen her, too, in his visions. Her dark eyes brooded as the final lines of another poem danced before her:

> "The city is the throne,
> Yet who will wear her crown?
> From where will Rhonnda find
> her Empire Princess?

CHAPTER FIFTEEN

A white gull soared overhead in the dim hours before dawn. It cried out shrilly twice, then flew off westward, to the sea. Elias stood nervously at the prow, took his eyes off his duties and watched as the gentle bird disappeared from sight. A gull before dawn, he mused, a good omen.

Behind him, Ashcroft stood watching over four burly sailors as they put slack on the anchor hawser, brought the anchor directly under the bow, then, with eager hands and muscles, broke it from the bottom with a mighty heave. The iron weight dripped mud and slime as it broke the surface. Hauled aboard, it was washed down with buckets of water, then smartly lashed to the rail.

"Anchor secured, Capt'n," said Ashcroft abruptly.

Elias nodded and clasped his hands behind his back. "Very good, mister. Prepare to get under way."

The sailor saluted, spun on his heels and called for the crew to stand at quarters. Elias looked with satisfaction at his new mast, smiled at the new heightened bulwark at the sides of the aft and forecastles and noted the protection these walls would afford from the screaming arrows of the *Windjammer*. The *Brora* was truly the finest ship in Rhonnda now, and he felt an exhilaration he had rarely known before. He would snap at the tail of the *Windjammer*, let his sails bite into the

winds and let the *Brora* meet the sea on her own terms.
He was now the captain of a true fighting ship.

The call from Ashcroft to clear the decks of passengers broke into his thoughts. He caught a brief glimpse of the anguished Trevor, sword dangling at his side, as he led the contingent of thirty Valley soldiers through the companionway.

Elias knew his best hope in the fight—if there was to be one—would come from his own wily lads as well as the twenty Rangers secretly brought aboard shortly after midnight. And, of course, Stacy, Cicero and the hunters. If the *Windjammer* tried to board, it would be to the tune of leaping wolves at their throats. Yet his total complement—crew, Rangers and soldiers—was scarcely more than a hundred. The *Windjammer* boasted a complement of twice that—as well as fighting hawks and falcons, birds of prey whose talons could tear out a man's eyes upon command.

Silently, the *Brora*, only one sail unfurled, slunk out of the shipyard under the cover of night and made her way across the left channel of Rhonnda Island. She sailed east, to the broad waterway opposite the Free Lands. There, hiding below the bluffs, he would drop anchor briefly and wait for Stacy and her wolves to come aboard. That part would be easy. But after that would come the real test: The *Brora* would have to turn and head west. And there, at the edge of the bay, the *Windjammer* would be waiting.

Cicero poked his snout out from behind a thornbush and darted his eyes at the dark waters. He snarled lowly, then waited as Stacy crept out from the thick, damp grasses.

"Can you see anything?" she asked, crouching by him.

The wolf growled. "A sail on the horizon, Khalea. Look carefully."

The girl raised her head and pushed aside unruly

hair that had partially curtained her vision. Squinting, she stared into the black and made out the vague form of a small square sail. Her vision was as sharp as any Dweller's, she knew. "They'll anchor beside the bluffs, Cicero," she whispered. "We'll have to wind our way down along the gully to reach them."

The red wolf looked at her sharply. "Soldiers use that path, Khalea. Horse tracks are still fresh."

"It's the quickest way, Cicero. Tell Casca and the others."

Cicero nodded, then let out a quick series of low howls. Not in the wolf tongue but in the coarse dialect of the hyena. If soldiers were about, he did not want them to know that wolves were, too. Better to let them hear, or at least think they heard, the idle foolish chatter of the wolf's cousins.

A moment later the howl was repeated from atop the knoll—also hyena. But it was Casca who had answered. Stacy would recognize his bark anywhere, no matter how much he might try to disguise it.

The signal had been given. Without speaking, Stacy and Cicero turned back from the thornbushes and inched their way along the sharp decline that led to the gully. For a fleeting moment they saw the silhouettes of Casca and the others racing ahead.

Stacy stood up, arched her back and rubbed gingerly at her aching muscles. Cicero snarled at her. "You've been among men too long, Khalea. You've lost your forest ways."

Stacy glared at him and growled. "Bite your tongue, brother! I'll outtrack you anytime!"

Slowly they moved together, each pair of eyes complementing the other. They moved cautiously, Cicero, nose ever sniffing at the air; Stacy, in a semicrouch, right hand toying unconsciously at the glistening hilt of her dagger. The sail of the ship began to loom bigger. Stacy could almost make out the forms of men dropping anchor. She could not yet see the iron weight, but she heard the splash as it hit the water. Suddenly her calm was shattered. Cicero leaped to the soft, gravelly shoulder and dodged behind the stump of an oak. Stacy whirled and caught sight of two fast horses swiftly bearing down. She waved a hand at Cicero and growled for him to stay hidden. She would handle the soldiers.

Moments later the soldiers were at her side. A rough-looking trooper sporting a brush mustache stared down at her, his hands clutching tightly at the reins.

"What are you doing here, miss?" the soldier asked gruffly.

The girl batted her eyes flirtingly and smiled. Faking the soft Newfoundland burr, she said, "I've been out walking with me beau, sir. Taking in the evening lights, sir. But in the dark I lost the poor lad. Now I'm trying to find me way home by meself."

The soldier's eyes tightened. "You live nearby?"

Stacy nodded emphatically. "Oh, yes, sir. Me dad owns a farm. Just a small lot of land, you understand."

"You don't look like a farm girl to me."

She giggled. "Why thank you, sir. These are me best clothes, they are. I wore it special for me beau."

The soldier glanced to his companion, and the other man said, "Do you always carry a dagger with your best clothes?"

Flustered, she replied, "Me father makes me take it, sir. One never knows if some brute of a sailor will catch a young girl and try to force his way with her."

The soldier frowned. "There's no sailor about in this part of the Free Lands. The docks are a league from here. Anyway, who is this beau of yours?"

Stacy kicked her boot into the soft dirt and looked down shyly. "I would tell you, sir, if you promise not to tell me father."

"You'd better come with us," said the second soldier. "We'll see that you get home safe and sound."

"Oh, no!" cried Stacy, her hand to her mouth. "Please, sir! Me beau is looking for me."

The first soldier reached over and held out his hand. "Perhaps you'd better give me that dagger before someone gets hurt," he demanded.

Stacy drew it clumsily. "This one? Oh, bless me! I hear me beau *now!*"

Before the soldiers could blink, Cicero leaped from the tree stump. The mares reared and whinnied as the wolf knocked one soldier out of his saddle and sent him sprawling across the ground. Stacy yanked the other soldier's sleeve, causing him to tumble into the dirt. As he tried to right himself, she poked the tip of her blade hard at his jugular. The dagger glistened in moonlight.

"If you so much as breathe the wrong way, I'll slit your throat!" she hissed. "Is that understood?"

Wide-eyed with fear, he nodded. His companion tried to get up but was met with Cicero's breath hot on his face. He slumped back down, shivering, not daring to move a muscle.

"Who . . . who *are* you?" stammered the soldier under Stacy's knife.

The girl glowered at him, and her eyes flashed. "A wolf," she replied coolly. "And a *sorceress!*"

She withdrew the dagger from his throat and wielded it slowly in front of his eyes. Then she growled something to Cicero, something meaningless; but the very fact that she could speak like a wolf frightened the soldiers out of their wits.

"Tell me, soldier, where is the rest of your patrol? Are you from the garrison?"

The man nodded nervously. "Our patrol split up. Two went the other way, and we came this way."

"And why were you out tonight?"

The soldier looked at her, puzzled. "To enforce the quarantine. We're to make sure that no one tries to cross over this way from Rhonnda Island."

Stacy nodded, buying his story. "Have you any cord in your saddlebags?"

"Cord?"

"Yes, cord! You know what that is, don't you? Rope! Have you got any?" Her eyes flashed hotly, patience gone.

The soldier nodded slowly, his eyes still on the dagger.

Stacy stood up. "I'm going to check your bags and find it. If you have the urge to move, I want you to know I can throw this knife as well as I can wield it."

"I understand," rasped the soldier, giving his promise.

She smiled. "Good." Then she walked over and soothed both trembling horses and dug her hands deep into the bags and finally withdrew several pieces of thick twine. She threw off both saddles, slapped the mares on the rumps and chuckled as they raced off into the night. Next she ordered both soldiers to sit up and, under the watchful eyes of Cicero, bound their hands and feet.

"I'm going to leave," she announced when she had finished. "And I want you two to sit here without uttering a sound until dawn. If you don't, my beau here will be back. Okay?"

"We'll not cry for help," assured one. "I give you my word."

Stacy winked at him. "I think I'll believe you. Good-bye, gentlemen. And thank you for a fun evening." With that, she and the wolf raced along the gully and fled from sight.

"You look ruffled, Stacy," said Elias as his arm was taken and the girl pulled herself up from the ladder.

She shrugged and grinned. "On the way we ran into a patrol."

Elias's face darkened. "They'll warn the *Windjammer.*"

"I don't think so," said the girl. "Right now they're too worried about a sorceress they met on the way."

Elias looked on dumbly as she passed by him and took a long draft of water from one of the barrels. Placing the ladle back on its hook, she faced Elias fully and laughed. "Stop looking so foolish, Captain. It's almost dawn, and we've got a long way ahead of us."

Ashcroft heard Elias mumble something about women, then the captain gave the order for the anchor to be lifted. And once again the *Brora* caught the breeze in her sail. She changed tacks and made her way down the channel, toward the city, to the lure of the open sea sweeping in the distance before them.

There was a good strong breeze blowing down from the sea as the first light of the new day splashed against the horizon. The purple towers of the city strung out high to their left, the gentle slopes of the Rhonnda Mountains to their right. Elias called for the sails to be slacked and stood tight-lipped as the swift ship passed the familiar shores of the island. Not a soul on land could he see, yet he knew the *Brora* would be watched from within every window that afforded a view of the river. The stillness was eerie; the whole quality of this strange day left him with a numbness to which he was not accustomed. His mouth remained dry no matter how much water he drank, and his stomach felt weighed down with lead. Yet he remained calm, coolheaded, and as certain of his purpose as he had ever been. He kept his gaze straight ahead, across the bow. Even his crew stood silent. Gone was the usual banter between Ashcroft and Boniface, his ranking officers. They both stood at their posts in similar posture, neither passing a word between them.

Stacy, standing amidships, held one hand tightly at the halyard line. She leaned hard to port, face strained and anxious. At either side of Stacy stood a wolf. Casca, his sharp eyes fixed on the brightening sky; Cicero, red fur blazing, his mouth twisted into a snarl. Both wolves were preparing for a fight, Stacy knew.

A cry from the crow's nest broke the glum silence.

"Sail, ho!"

Elias spun about. "Where away, Mr. Beecham?"

"Five points on the port bow!"

Elias was ready to give the call for general quarters when his eye caught sight of what Beecham had seen. A small skiff, rowed at a frantic pace by four soldiers, was cutting furiously across the channel. A tall man was standing center boat, waving his hands and shouting. But from the long distance Elias could neither make out who it might be nor what the fellow was trying to say. He was about to give an order when he felt Stacy's presence at his side. The girl was flushed. Her dark hair glimmered as the first rays of early-morning sun touched it.

"I think it's Simon," she gasped.

Elias furrowed his black brows. "Simon? Fates above! What does *he* want?"

The skiff came closer off the hull, bobbing and tossing amid the swells caused by the *Brora*'s cut against the channel's waters.

Simon seemed to have an awful time trying to balance himself as the skiff tried to keep pace. His hair tossed about; his tunic blew hither and yon. Several times a strong gust almost knocked him overboard, but he seemed determined not to give up until he had spoken his piece.

At last the skiff drew abreast of the bow. "Elias, listen to me," Simon called. "You've got to turn about!"

"No chance, Simon," called back the captain. "If we're to have a hope of crossing the sea, we've got to leave now, before the gales begin."

"But the *Windjammer*'s waiting for you! She's sitting in the bay, expecting you to try and defy the blockade!"

"We know she's there, Simon. But she'll not stop us."

"Do you know what you're doing, man? She's armed to the teeth! Please, Elias. Don't make them fight you."

"We're not looking for a fight, Simon. We're a Rhonnda ship, and all we ask is to sail from our own harbor in peace."

Simon shook his head. "But you can't! Not while the

quarantine's still in effect. Listen, Elias, it will be lifted soon. I give you my word. As soon as we're certain . . ."

"We can't wait, Simon. You know that. The *Brora*'s a danger to no one. We'll come into contact with no other port or town."

"But the *Windjammer* doesn't care! Their orders come directly from the Haven. They mean to stop you any way they can."

"And we mean to pass," growled Elias defiantly.

Simon glanced desperately toward the girl at the captain's side. "Stacy, make him see reason! Not for me, for Rhonnda! It it comes to a fight, it'll mean open rebellion against Empire law. The Valley will send more troops— an entire army if necessary!"

"It's too late for words," cried Stacy. There were tears in the corner of her eyes. "And I *am* thinking of Rhonnda! The Valley must see that we're masters of our own fate!"

Simon, shocked, was near tears himself. "Please, Stacy. Don't do this; The *Windjammer*'s twice your size. I know her commander. He's a fair man. He wouldn't hurt a soul if he could help it. But his orders are explicit. He won't let you pass! You'll be killed, Stacy. All of you! And for what? If you love Rhonnda—if you care what happens here after the *Brora* is either sunk or smashed, you'll turn around now while there's still time!"

Stacy choked back her flowing tears. "Good-bye, Simon," she called. "Take care of Lorna." Then she turned her head and paid no attention to the frantic shouts that followed. At length the skiff fell badly behind and the *Brora* surged ahead, white waves foaming fore and aft.

The green fields gave way quickly to a succession of jagged mountains. The water of the river was dark gray, but off in the west, Stacy, for the first time in her life, could let her eyes focus on the blue sea. She felt awed by its immensity. She watched a few clouds racing across brilliant sky, and the sun, now burning down from above the mountains, promised to be merciless.

But Elias noticed none of these things. There was a dark spot on the bay—and huge sails atop it. *"Windjammer,"* he whispered, with a mixture of awe and defiance. The *Brora* was now making breathtaking speed as she bobbed with the increasingly swift current and the wind at her back. The hull of the Empire ship grew bigger and bigger before their eyes. Elias could see the outlines of the coiled serpents emblazoned on each sail. Twin-masted, with canvas enough for two ships of its size, the *Windjammer* would be a formidable opponent, indeed. No creaking slouch she, as Krebbs's pirate vessel had been, but a double-decked brig with sailors every bit as sharp and cunning as his own.

Elias wiped his mouth with the back of his hand and prepared for the battle that was now only minutes away. As the river widened into the bay, he snapped, "Dead to windward, Mr. Ashcroft!"

"Aye, Capt'n."

The ship shifted into a short tack and veered hard to the leeward side. The wind was still increasing. The *Windjammer* began to move in a long tack of her own, wind straight off the bow. Plain as day were the blue-tunicked sailors scurrying at the lines to furl the top sails. The *Windjammer*'s captain knew his business, Elias noted grudgingly as the tall ship came about gracefully.

"At quarters!" he barked. While the *Brora* eased ahead, the crew took to battle stations. Crossbows were slung over every shoulder. "Ask Commander Trevor to come on deck," said Elias to Boniface.

The officer saluted and raced off to fetch him. Moments later Trevor came strutting toward the bridge, shading his eyes from the sun.

"That's her, Commander," said Elias, pointing.

Trevor gulped. He had never imagined the Empire ship to be so large. He glared at the sails and the literally tens of dozens of soldiers standing firmly at the rails.

Stacy, who had brought her wolves out on deck and had positioned them into leaping formation along the prow, gaped. Across the lines and rigging of the *Windjammer* she could make out the dark forms of a hundred birds. Predators! Valley hawks and falcons—trained to attack—and to kill.

"Will you look at that," whistled Trevor. The birds, clearly on command, began to take to the air and circle the *Windjammer*. "They'll be all over us!"

Stern-faced, Elias replied, "We can handle them."

Trevor shook his head incredulously. "Have you ever seen fighting birds in action?" he asked. "I have! They'll swarm across the deck, and their talons will claw at your archers' eyes. Why, they can blind a man before he can blink!"

Cicero growled. Casca snarled. The wolves were obviously less impressed than the soldier.

Elias turned back to Ashcroft. "Better sound battle stations. It won't be long before those birds attack."

"Battle stations!" cried the officer. The bells clanged loudly. From below, both Trevor's own men and the husky Rhonnda Rangers came running, weapons in hand. All along the bulwark they crouched. Stacy stared briefly at the Rangers and did a double take. Half of them—more than half!—were women! Many not much older than she was. But like her, they were all swift and eager. They held their daggers and crossbows with professionalism, eyes fixed on the enemy ahead.

"She's coming about!" called Beecham from the crow's nest.

"Thank you, mister," replied Elias. Then to Trevor, "If you want to try and speak with her captain, now's the time."

Trevor bit his lip. "Not just yet, Elias. Let's let him think I'm going to defy his authority. We'll wait until we have to."

"That sounds like good strategy," agreed Elias with a grunt. He spun on his heels and looked to Stacy, forward on the prow. "Are you ready, my lady?"

The girl nodded. "All set, Captain. Whenever you are."

Elias gritted his teeth and smiled grimly. "Mr. Boni-face, prepare to ram!"

"Aye, Capt'n. Oddfellow, prepare to ram!"

On both sides of the bow hidden catch-doors sprang open. There came the dull grinding sound of a pulley and chains tugging. Stacy and Trevor froze. Two long shiny beams of steel, pointed at the tips like knives, slid slowly out of the doors and gleamed in the sun. They pushed their way forward from the tracks and came to a stop before the bowsprit. They glistened inches above the waterline, waiting to pierce the hull of the *Windjammer* and rip it to shreds.

"Lock the battle rams, Mr. Boniface!"

The chains halted abruptly; a series of sharp clicks ensued. Elias nodded somberly. "Draw your bows!" The rugged men and agile girls raised crossbows to their shoulders and kept steady fingers on the hair triggers. Their stares across the water were met in kind by dozens of *Windjammer* marksmen. Elias strained to watch the face of his adversary, but there was little to be seen. The commander stood impassively, against the reinforced railing, undaunted by either the steel or the Rangers. Then slowly the Empire ship began to turn, broadside, straight off the *Brora*'s prow, defying her to try and ram.

Elias bit his lip anxiously. This captain was a cool customer, he knew, and it would take more than threats to make him run. The captain, virtually glaring eye to eye with Elias, cupped his hands around his mouth and called, "Turn about, Captain Elias! We give you fair warning. We'll not let you pass!"

The riverman clutched tightly at his own railing. A small pulse throbbed in his neck. "We're headed for the sea, Commander. Change your position, or we'll ram!"

But the broad-shouldered captain merely shook his head. "We can't do that, Captain Elias. In the name of the Empire I command you to turn about, or we'll be obliged to attack." And as if to show that this was no empty boast, he signaled for the full complement to man battle stations. Every soul aboard the *Brora* was impressed as the tough blue-tunicked Valley troops lifted their weapons and took dead aim.

Suddenly Trevor unexpectedly leaped to the prow at Elias's side. "This ship sails on the order of the Newfoundland governor!" he cried.

"My orders come directly from the Valley, Commander Trevor. Empire orders! They *cannot* be disobeyed. And I warn you to remember that we both wear the same uniform. Sheathe your weapon at once! And tell your contingent to do the same!"

This was it, Trevor knew. The moment of truth. The penalty for disobeying a superior officer would be harsh —but his heart defied his head.

"You have no right to stop this ship!" he answered defiantly.

"Think of your men, Commander Trevor," came the retort. "Do you want to see them killed by Valley arrows and swords? Brother against brother? Is that what you want?"

The point was well received. Trevor felt panic race through him. It was one thing to risk his own life, but how could he purposely direct his troops to die for his cause? He shied from the glances of Stacy and Elias. But he could not avoid the stares from his own men. They were looking to him for leadership. Was he their commander still, or not?

As the *Brora* stood poised to ram, he lifted his head and searched their faces. Most were wide-eyed youths, eager to do their duty and serve the Empire, but right now they were understandably confused.

"I can't command you to open fire on fellow sailors," Trevor said to them. "Nor can I ask you to break Valley law. But I will tell you this: This voyage has been approved by both the Newfoundland governor and the Valley

Council at the Haven. None of you were forced to board with me last night—but you all did. And none of you were conscripted—you all volunteered. Now I release you of any obligation you may feel toward me. Those who would obey the order of the *Windjammer*'s captain are free to put down their weapons and withdraw below."

With stunned and pensive looks the soldiers stood fast and held their places. "What will *you* do, Commander?" asked one.

Trevor wiped his brow and set his teeth. His words now could change the future of his entire life.

"I have decided to stand beside my friends, Captain Elias and Lady Anastasia."

Elias felt pride; Stacy, tears. But neither made any move during this tense situation.

The soldiers looked at each other nervously. Either choice could easily prove to be the wrong one, they knew, what with the fierce Rhonnda Rangers viewing them as potential enemies on one side and the *Windjammer*'s troops aiming bows at them from the other. A long minute passed. Trevor became edgy. Tension rose like the heat. One or two of the men began to place weapons down on the deck, but angry looks from comrades stopped them. One of the lads shouted, "You're our commander, Trevor! Give the order and we'll follow!" Soon the cry was repeated by all. "Trevor! Trevor! Give us the order!"

The engineer sighed and smiled. "Right, then! To your quarters! Draw swords and prepare to fight!"

In a burst of enthusiasm the Rangers and the crew cheered loudly as the thirty soldiers took up strong positions all along the ship's bulwark.

The gleeful Elias turned once more to the commander of the Empire ship. "Do as you will," he shouted. "Turn aside or fight. But either way the *Brora* will cross the bay!"

The *Windjammer*'s commander studied the faces of his opposition. They were cold and hard, angry and determined. He could find no sign of fright or doubt. They were fully prepared—and prepared men are difficult men. But neither was he ready to give in. He called to his bugler and a shrill sound filled the air. Overhead, the hawks and falcons began to flap their wings amid squawks and cries. They took up diving battle positions, ready to bear down hard on the surging *Brora*.

Elias took a long breath. This was it, he knew. No more words. "Mr. Ashcroft! Full sails! We're heading for the sea. And if that pile of junk gets in our way, we'll smash her to bits!"

Ashcroft licked a dry tongue across a drier mouth. "Aye, Capt'n!"

The sails swelled; the ship lurched ahead. The tips of the steel battering rams lay a mere hundred meters from the *Windjammer*. The Empire ship turned at an angle, three quarters off the starboard. Elias prayed. Was she turning to avoid his rams and fight? Or was she turning to let them pass? He could not be sure. The next few seconds would tell.

From Beecham in the crow's nest came the shout. "Capt'n, she veers! She's turning about!"

Elias and Stacy stared in disbelief. "So she is, mister!" cried Elias with sudden glee. The *Windjammer* was *not* going to fight!

Stacy laughed with joy, letting the tears flow freely, and hugged Casca and Cicero. It had all been a bluff! Her father had been behind this. She should have realized it all along! He was the master of such bluff. The *Windjammer's* purpose was to threaten, to cajole, to frighten. But never was she intended to harm anyone. Nigel would never let the Empire split itself apart. Spooner had known it all along. Even Elias had suspected it. How could she have been so blind?

Laughs and cheers rose as the fighting birds circling above the *Brora* returned to the perches of the *Windjammer*. The two ships slowly passed alongside each other in opposite directions. The *Windjammer* lowered her colors, acknowledging that the *Brora* had won the match of wits. Her commander saluted smartly, and with a wide grin the riverman returned it.

Stacy, amid the tumult of shouts and banter, ran to Elias. "That captain," she panted. "Did you see what he did?"

Elias shrugged. "No, my lady. What did he do?"

She fumed good-naturedly. "He . . . he winked! He winked at me!"

Elias chuckled. "The scoundrel. But you can't trust a sailor, my lady." Then he winked also. "You should have realized that a long time ago."

For a long while the fun and frolicking continued, even after the tall sails of the *Windjammer* were gone from sight. Elias looked admiringly at the dozen or so female Rangers as they tossed their bows aside. The girls would at least make the voyage more interesting, he mused, now glad they were aboard. And even the sight of the wolves, running madly to and fro, made him smile. Soldiers, women and wolves! What a combination to cross the sea!

At length the *Brora* had all but cleared the bay. Elias sighed and once more clasped his hands behind his back as he stood sternly upon the bridge.

"Mr. Ashcroft! Mr. Boniface!"

"Captain?"

"Wipe those silly grins off your faces!"

"Yes, sir!"

"Now clear the decks and prepare to sail! Do you think this ship is built for pleasure cruising?"

"No, sir!"

"Unfurl those sails, mister! I want every stitch we can draw. You see that body of water out there? They call it the sea—and I intend to cross it!"

The officers beamed. "Aye, sir!" Then to the crew: "Sound quarters! The party's over! We're on serious business—*Empire* business!"

Suddenly there was a flurry of frantic activity. Stacy stood aside and stared out at the ocean. Its vastness left her numb. It was beautiful, stunning to behold—even more so than Rhonnda had been that first time she saw it, aboard the *Lady of Newfoundland.*

Elias called her to his side. "Frightened?" he asked warmly.

The girl shook her head. "Excited."

The riverman laughed. "You might as well take a last look back while you can. It'll be a long time before we see home again. That is, if we ever do see it again."

Stacy smiled. "We'll see it," she said with assurance.

"Oh? How do you know?"

The Lady of the Haven laughed, her eyes sparkling with tiny fires. "Let's say I read it in a poem."

Puzzled by this exotic, dazzling wolf-girl, Elias shook his head bemusedly and turned his attention back to the matters at hand. The *Brora*'s bow dipped, then pointed its way from Rhonnda Bay and into the open sea. She swelled ahead gracefully, no longer with the river current but with the ocean's. Gold canvas blazed under hot sun, the emblazoned black hawk upon the mainsail shimmered, flexed its talons and seemed to come to life.

"Hard-a-lee, Mr. Ashcroft!" called Elias. "And set the course."

Proudly the sailor answered, "Aye, sir! And what course shall I set? What destination shall I log?"

"West by northwest, mister—the Land of the White Wolves."

PART THREE
THE SEA

CHAPTER SIXTEEN

"Ah, Khalea, the warmth of Khal upon me at morning, the whispers of Aleya through the leaves, that's what I yearn for. The forest, Khalea. Our forest. Would that we were home."

Stacy smiled warmly at the sleepy face of Casca. The wolf rested his head in her lap, and she ran her fingers through his fur. It was a sultry night on deck, with a moonless sky illuminated by glittering stars.

"Poor Casca," she whispered, resting her back against the smooth wood of the bulwark. From where they sat, beside the foot of the bridge ladder, she could see the mainsail swell like a flowing cloud, pushing the ship forward, ever forward, across the endless tide. Apart from the flapping of the flags and the gentle moans of well-aged wood, the only sounds were the light footsteps of Boniface pacing up and down the deck, watching and studying the constellations above, hands behind his back.

"Forgive me, Casca," said Stacy as the wolf closed his eyes, "you never really wanted to make this journey with me, did you?"

Casca growled. "I wanted to come, Khalea. Too much of the grandfather is within me. But on a night such as this," he glanced up at the half moon and sighed, "I can think only of Athena, and the pack, and our friends, and our own cub yet unborn."

195

"You'll come home to a fine hunter waiting for you," said Stacy. "And he'll be proud of his father's adventures. So will Athena. A huntress enjoys nothing more than to glow about the deeds of her mate. You'll be a hero."

Lazy eyes laughed. "I would trade it all for a single glimpse of home. Wouldn't you, Khalea?"

His question caught Stacy by surprise. In all the months since she had left the Valley she had not once thought of home, that is, her forest home. Her eagerness to make the journey, her idealistic visions of some great plan for the Empire had dazzled her. But here, on the endless sea, far from the spires of Rhonnda and even farther from the great walls of the Haven, she felt merely a speck against the colossus of the ocean. She wondered if, somewhere above, the Fates were laughing at the spectacle of this tiny ship daring the overwhelming power and authority of the sea. She bent over and kissed the wolf lightly on his forehead. "I do miss our home, Casca. Truly, I do."

Stacy smiled. The wolf was sleeping contentedly, wagging his bushy tail in deep slumber. Just as well, she thought. No purpose in letting him know that her own heart ached as much as his.

But to be homesick was one thing, to be unhappy quite another. Stacy was not unhappy. Here, aboard the *Brora* these past seven days, she had made some of the closest friendships she had ever known. Real friends, such as blue-eyed Sandra, the calm and level-headed captain of the women Rangers, and sensitive Robin, with yellow hair and an enchanting smile. But most of all she thought of Heather and Melinda. Dark-eyed and proud, fiercely independent, how very different they were from the stuffy and pampered young women she had known at home. Stacy felt good just being around them. In the dank depths of the tiny cabins they bared the secrets of their lives, exchanged hopes and dreams and shared whispered romance.

It was long-legged Melinda she first met, that being the work of Elias, who had paired the two and assigned them to the broom closet called a cabin. But she soon realized that wherever you found Melinda, Heather was close behind. Smartly dressed in their Ranger tunics, crossbows slung over their shoulders, they appeared hard and tough girls, indeed. But beneath this coarse exterior they were gentle-mannered young women, as feminine as the most elegant daughters of the grandest noble. Often had the stern-faced ship's officers been caught letting their eyes wander from duty whenever Heather and Melinda were about. And how proud Stacy had felt just the other day when Elias, in a fury about one thing or another, shouted to Ashcroft, "I'd appreciate it if you'd keep those women off the deck during morning hours!"

Frowning, the officer had said, "Aye, Capt'n. But which of the girls?"

"All of them, mister," came the surly reply. "But especially Heather and Melinda—and Stacy!"

Leaning back, Stacy closed her eyes and smiled. Heather and Melinda and Stacy—she loved it!

Musing, she fell into a light sleep. The weather this past few days had been tepid. Elias had given approval to sleep on deck, providing, of course, that they did not interfere with the duties of the crew. The feeling of a long shadow over her caused her to wake with a start. All around was the night, the darkened rails of the ship. For an instant she believed that the "shadow" had been merely a dream. But then, as she peered to the forecastle, she saw the silhouetted form of a man. A giant of a man. Easily half a head taller than Elias, who was up until then the tallest man she had known, he leaned his great frame along the rail and held at the brace. His eyes, brooding and narrow, scoured the sky carefully.

Stacy watched him curiously. She had seen him before —but who was he? In the seven days of the journey she thought she had met or at least been introduced to just about everyone. His tunic was that of a sailor, she saw, yet there was something about him that said he was something more. It occurred to her that he must be one of the special hands Elias had signed aboard in Rhonnda. He certainly did not fit the part of a ship's carpenter or cook.

She wanted to approach him, introduce herself and satisfy her curiosity. But something stopped her. Not that he frightened her, but she felt she would somehow be intruding on a very special privacy. So for a long while she stared in his direction, turning her eyes away whenever he happened to glance in her direction.

After some time the tall man moved from his place and stepped closer. Stacy looked up and smiled. His face was ruddy and lined, curly hair thick and white. His arms were muscular and powerful, frame awesome. He seemed capable of tearing a tree trunk out by the roots with his bare hands. Unconsciously she moved her hand down toward her dagger.

The big man smiled broadly. "You needn't be afraid of me, little wolf princess," he said.

Stacy blinked. "I, er——"

The half-giant laughed. "No need to explain, little wolf princess. Many folk shy away whenever I pass. It's something I've lived with all my life." He sighed deeply. "One learns to know his limitations."

From his way with words Stacy could tell that he was well educated. But his being a noble certainly did not mesh with either his dress or manner. Without meaning to, she asked, "Who are you?"

The man threw back his head and laughed. "They call me Alryc," he said. "Alryc of the Blue Fires. Perchance you have heard of me?"

Stacy shook her head.

Alryc shrugged. "It's not that I mean to brag, you see. But in Rhonnda I'm well known."

"I'm from the Valley," offered the girl. "My name is——"

"Your name is Anastasia, but you only answer to Stacy. Am I right?"

With an impish grin, Stacy said, "I'll call you Alryc if you call me Stacy. All right?"

The big man smiled warmly. "Agreed, Stacy. But tell me, why are you out on deck so late at night? You should be below with your friends."

Stacy tossed the hair away from her eyes. "I like it up here at night. I like the sea. But I'll ask you the same question. Why are you here? Surely you're not on duty?"

Alryc leaned against the bulwark and rested his arms at his sides. He pointed to the sky. "Do you see that star up there? The one that glitters more than any other?"

Stacy nodded breathlessly, staring at the black velvet sky and the thousand flickering lights.

"That's the North Star, little wolf princess. From its fixed position in the heavens we plot our course. And do you see that cluster of stars below it? That we call the Big Dipper. It, too, helps guide us."

Stacy smiled. "I see. You're a navigator."

Grinning, he said, "Now you know my secret, Stacy. I read the stars."

"Wolves read them, too," said the girl.

He chuckled. "So I've been told. But only men can guide a ship. Only men can discern winter constellations from those of summer. A woman can learn these mysteries, too, little wolf princess. Even a young girl like you —that is if she has the desire."

"I'd *love* to learn, Alryc," she replied breathlessly. "Will you teach me?"

The navigator laughed, bushy brows furrowing as he peered down at her. "You would be my pupil? You would spend long hours of your nights studying and observing?"

Stacy nodded eagerly. "I promise. Teach me everything!"

Hands on hips, Alryc bellowed. "Everything would take a lifetime, Stacy. But a quick mind can take in much. Look there, little wolf princess! Can you see the two bright stars low against the horizon?"

The girl stared hard to portside. And sure enough, above the black horizon, two dots shimmered and twinkled.

"Those are the shoulders of Orion," said Alryc. "And there, Stacy—low away from the North Star, see how the Little Dipper points to it?"

"I *do* see it!" she exclaimed excitedly. "And that cluster nearby—that's the Big Dipper you spoke of!"

The navigator grinned. "*Very* good, little wolf princess. Tomorrow I'll begin to teach you other constellations. There are many. And we'll watch Jupiter and Venus at twilight. And the yellow star, Capella. The orange glow of Arcturus will enchant you, and Mars will flicker above and take your breath away."

"You know them all?" asked the entranced girl. "Where did you learn so much? Certainly not on the river."

The navigator grinned. "I am not truly a sailor, although I did go with the *Swordfish* many years ago when we sailed the sea to chart the Rhonnda coasts and the Western Isles. But by profession I am an astronomer. One of the few in the Empire." He sighed wistfully.

"The time passes too swiftly," he added. "And my night's work is hardly begun. I still have my charts to plot. Forgive me, Stacy, but I must draw our first lesson to a close. Elias will be needing my charts by morning."

Stacy got up slowly beside the sleeping Casca, now comfortably stretched out on the deck. Fondly she clasped Alryc's hand. "I think I'll go back to my cabin after all," she said. "But perhaps I'll see you at morning."

Alryc smiled and bowed gracefully, as lithe as a man

half his size. "Good night, my lady." Then once again he
turned and lifted his long face to the sky.

"Stacy, is that you?"

The girl on the hammock peered up through sleepy
eyes. The room was fully dark save for a beam of moonlight hazily shining through the fogged porthole.

Stacy closed the door slowly and grimaced as it
creaked. "Sorry if I woke you."

Melinda yawned, shrugged and lay back on the hammock. "I thought you'd be asleep on deck," she whispered softly.

Stacy smiled, slipped out of her tunic and hung it on a
hook. She sat on the parallel hammock and let her
sandals drop to the floor. "I was asleep," she admitted.
"But a curious man woke me. Says he's an astronomer.
Calls himself Alryc."

Melinda raised her head. "Alryc of the Blue Fires? Is
he aboard?"

"You've heard of him?"

The Ranger girl nodded. "He's well known in Rhonnda,
Stacy. A strange man, they say."

"A mystic," offered the girl. "But he seems kind and
gentle. I like him. He offered to teach me how to read
the stars."

Melinda looked at her in wonder. "Oh, Stacy! You
have all the luck! The stories about Alryc that I've heard
say he *never* speaks to anyone. Not anyone! They say he
gazes at the stars from the spires at night, returns home at
day and hardly passes a word. Some call him a lunatic."

Stacy's eyes flashed. "He's not! Eccentric, perhaps. But
surely not a madman. Anyway, he must be the best
navigator in the Empire, otherwise Elias would never
have brought him aboard."

Melinda sighed. "Well, never mind what people say,
Stacy. If you like him, and if he's really going to teach
you, you go right ahead. Maybe one night you'll introduce

him." Melinda winked. "After all, he is an eligible bachelor. And I've always had an eye for older men."

"Your hands are full enough already, I would think," laughed Stacy.

The Ranger girl stared at her in mock surprise. "Why, my lady, whatever do you mean?"

"I mean I've seen the way the crew looks at you. Especially Mr. Ashcroft and that junior officer. What's his name? Oddfellow? Why, I've even caught young Mr. Beecham in the crow's nest following you with his eyes."

"Look who's talking! The whole ship knows about you and Elias. I mean he stares at you even when he's looking the other way!" Melinda propped herself up with an elbow and glowered at her.

Stacy flushed. "That's not true! We're friends, but there's never been anything at all besides that."

"Tell that to Trevor," gloated Melinda. "That poor soldier is green with envy. And he takes it out on his poor lads during afternoon drills. Why, he runs them ragged!"

"Now be fair, Melinda! Trevor knows I like him; I've told him as much. But my future is far too cloudy to be making romantic decisions. But when the time comes. . . ." Her eyes gleamed.

"Now don't get haughty with *me,* Lady Anastasia! You don't pull wool over this Ranger's eyes! Admit it, Stacy. You love them both, don't you? And you can't choose!"

Stacy fumed, but in a good-natured sort of way. She knew Melinda was really not so far off the mark. Her heart *had* raced the very first time she had set eyes on Elias. Dashing, ruggedly handsome, he was definitely *everything* a girl could wish for. Yet in his own way so was Trevor. Bright, levelheaded, with boyish charm and the same kind of background as her own, he was certainly not one to be second best in anyone's mind. She fell asleep in the confused excitement of having two men from whom to choose.

The long morning passed slowly. The captain had put a skiff, with Ashcroft at the helm, over the side at dawn, with orders to catch fresh fish to supplement the ship's rations. Stacy stood at the rail, watching off the starboard quarters as the skiff rocked far out on the waves. It had been exciting to watch the brawny sailors haul in the giant cod at the end of their lines. Feeling good, she saw that they had hooked what she knew would be the last catch of the day. Then, suddenly, from behind the tiny boat she saw a great, dark lumbering form begin to rise to the surface. Her eyes opened wide, and she screamed.

Like lightning Elias was at her side. Stacy pointed frantically. "Look!"

Elias squinted. Off the portside bow, the creature rose higher and higher, then it dived and disappeared, leaving frantic waves in its wake. The skiff tossed about furiously. Ashcroft, now fully aware of the great thing below, began to shout for the sailors to row as fast as they could. A hundred meters from the *Brora* the fish rose again— huge, monstrous, water spouting from its back.

"What is it, Elias?" cried Stacy.

"A whale, I think," replied the mariner coolly.

" A *what?*"

"A whale. A mammal that lives in the sea. It's not dangerous, at least I don't think it is. But we've got to worry about our lads in the skiff. The whale could capsize it and smash it to bits."

From Beecham atop the mast: "Capt'n: She blows! Three points off the starboard!"

Elias turned. There, off against the darkening sky, he could see the mighty forms of not one but at least a dozen whales. A school of them, rising and diving, sending ripples all the way to the *Brora*. They pranced and danced, their spouts sending up great fountains of water. Stacy stared at the sight. Just then the whale near the skiff rose between it and the ship, causing near panic among the sailors. "Steady!" Ashcroft shouted as he tried to maintain his balance even as the skiff was knocked back under tumultuous waves. The sailors rowed frantically. Elias ordered lines thrown over the side, and eager hands began to clutch. For a long while again, the whale stayed out of sight and the skiff was hastily hoisted aboard.

Shivering and shaking, Ashcroft stood before the captain. His boots dripped and squeaked as he shifted his feet. His face was white and ashen; Stacy thought he looked about to faint. It was with great surprise then that he grinned and said, "All aboard safely, sir. But I fear our 'friend' will be with us for a while."

Elias grimaced. Bewildered, Stacy asked, "What does he mean?"

The captain scowled. "He means that the whale is playing a game with us."

No sooner had he spoken than the whale appeared again, this time right off the bow. It loomed like a giant and nearly shot into the sky before crashing beneath the water.

"This is a *game?*" asked an incredulous Stacy.

"I guess it is to a whale. Anyway, better for her to be on our side than against us. If she wanted to attack, our hull could have been torn to shreds."

Stacy looked to the school of whales still prancing off the starboard side. "But why's she staying with us?" she asked. "Why doesn't she go and splash with her friends?"

Elias laughed. "Oh, Stacy, how do I know? Maybe she thinks we *are* her friends. Maybe she's attracted by our sails. Maybe she's in love. In any case, I'm afraid Mr. Ashcroft is right. We've found ourselves a companion— and I think it'll be a while before she gets tired of us."

* * *

It was a grand evening. The fish was fried, spiced, salted and served steaming. Trevor and others told tales of the Line and the forest; Boniface and Oddfellow countered with adventures of the river. A jolly sailor called Leech recounted the old days when ships such as the *Snapdragon* and *Swordfish* sailed the rugged coasts of the uncharted lands. But none was listened to with more attention than Alryc when he stood and spoke of the secrets of the stars and their meaning for the Empire. In him, Stacy saw what Bartok himself must have been like. His eyes blazed as he spoke. Everyone listened, transfixed. And after he had done, there was silence.

And so the *Brora*, entering her tenth day at sea, unfurled her sails again and reset her course: north—with the prevailing winds.

CHAPTER SEVENTEEN

CAPTAIN'S DIARY

Day seventeen of our voyage. The weather, as it has been for the past week, remains good. Strong westerly winds have allowed the ship to hold a steady course. We are maintaining good speed; the crew works at their best. The blue whale, Salome, as she is fondly called by most, still tags alongside. In one of her more playful pranks she nearly caused a collision today when she dived directly off the bow. Fortunately no one was injured when her fin struck the rail. Day and night she remains within sight, never straying more than a few hundred meters in any direction. Sometimes I think that she actually considers herself our guide, flipping as she does and pointing her head in the course we take even before we take it.

Everyone aboard remains in cheerful spirits, although I am concerned that the first signs of tension are beginning to show. For all our efforts we have yet to see the slightest indication of land.

Commander Trevor has done a fine job of keeping his troops fit and trim. He maintains a daily program of exercise and drills on the main deck. The Rangers do likewise at different hours. All in all, they have high morale and genuine inspiration. Even our hunters are bearing up well.

*One noteworthy development I have noticed is
that Stacy has come to be regarded as a leader—not
only for her wolves but also for the Ranger girls.
She is beginning to show qualities that I had not
known she possessed. Thoughtful and levelheaded,
she dutifully spends long hours at night with Alryc
in the study of the stars. Alryc speaks quite highly
of her, often referring to obscure lines of poetry
written by Bartok. He says that Stacy already has a
basic knowledge of navigation and can plot rough
charts and fixes. If so, I must admit that she is far
more astute than I gave her credit for. I think
Alryc's influence has been good for her—but what
drives her with such intensity I cannot understand.
But she at last seems fully able to blend both her
human qualities and her forest ways—and with her
natural aristocratic bearing she seems a born leader.
I hope all this potential will not be wasted on a
voyage that leads us nowhere.*

Elias,
Ship's Captain

"Good, Stacy! Good!"

The girl beamed as Alryc put down the roughly
sketched chart. Overhead the stars sparkled in the black
night sky.

"You've fixed our position well enough, little wolf
princess. But see, you missed a point." His fingers ran
across the chart. "When you measure the angular height
of the North Star with our latitude, you must make
allowance not for where we expect to be but for our
dead position. You got ahead of yourself." He handed
back the assignment.

Stacy sighed. "You're right, of course. I guess I was
trying to second-guess the stars. But I promise not to
make that slip again."

"Nonsense, girl! You've done well! By the Fates,

you've done well! Every mariner errs from time to time,
but you've shown real *understanding,* and that's what
counts."

Stacy's face brightened. "I've had a good teacher."

Hands on hips, Alryc laughed. "That will *not* get you
better marks in this class, wolf princess, but I thank
you for the thought. Old astronomers love to be com-
plimented, but enough for tonight. Why not go below
and join your friends? I'm sure you have a good many
stories to exchange."

Stacy sat down beside her teacher and shook her
head. "They'll probably be asleep."

Alryc looked at her oddly. "Melinda, asleep? That
will be a change."

Stacy laughed. "Well, if not quite asleep, they'll be
whispering about the ship's officers and such. I don't
think I'm in the mood for all that."

"Oh? And why not? Is there something wrong in
pretty girls speaking of handsome sailors?"

"Of course not, Alryc. But tonight I feel as if my
romantic dreams would be better spent under the constellations. Look. See how Antares shines! I feel I could
watch for hours. Among wolves Antares is called *Ana-
Fara.* Know what that means?"

The astronomer shook his head. "Now I'll be the
pupil and you'll teach me the forest ways."

"It means daughter of Fara. That's the way stars are
named. Each by their relationship to Fara."

Looking at her seriously, Alryc asked, "Is that how
you still view life, child? As Dwellers perceive it?"

Stacy rested her back against the rough wood of the
bulwark and put her hands in her lap. Sad eyes flickered.
"I don't know anymore, Alryc. Since I left the Valley
I've never felt, well, more *human*—but how shall I forget my other life? The forest means more than home
to Dwellers—not at all like we think of a village, or a
house as home. To them it's everything. The universe.

It's hard to explain. I feel it, too, at least sometimes I do. The forest is my strength. Men and Dwellers die, but the forest remains. It's all there is, or ever will be."

"Yet you're not a Dweller, Stacy. Don't hide yourself behind a wolf's facade."

Stacy met his gaze. "What do you mean?"

"When the ways of men frighten you, as they sometimes do to all of us, you pretend that you're not one of us. 'Tis an illusion, child. Digest what you have learned from Dwellers and be the better for it. Take the Empire for what it is. And respect yourself for being a part of it."

"A lost soul finds shelter in wilderness," the girl mumbled disconsolately.

Alryc suddenly stared keenly at her. "Why did you say that, child?"

Stacy shrugged. "I don't know. It just sort of popped out." She smiled wanly up at him.

"No one has said those words to you before?"

"No, not that I know of."

The astronomer bowed his head and took Stacy's small hands in his own. "Those words have great meaning for me, child. More than I could ever tell. They were whispered to me so many years ago when a great man lay dying."

Stacy looked at him and felt a sudden chill. "Bartok?" she whispered. "Was it his thought?"

Alryc nodded. "The same words exactly as you spoke them."

"Perhaps I read it in one of his poems. I'm quite fond——"

The astronomer shook his head emphatically. "Those words are not written. But continue, Stacy. Finish the line!"

"I can't," she protested and looked away, feeling uneasy.

"Then I shall finish it for you." Eyes shut, the navigator recalled the last words of the poet. *"A lost soul finds shelter in wilderness; and from that shelter shall come a dream fulfilled. For who but a lost soul can better lead? And the world shall be one."*

For a long moment there was silence. Then Stacy, gazing at the prancing Salome, whispered softly, "I hope you're not reading something into this, Alryc. If I said something that Bartok might have said, I'm sure it's just coincidence."

They smiled, the pall of mystery suddenly gone. "Of course not, Stacy. Coincidence it must be. Besides, who but the Fates can alter destiny? Only fools would even try."

Alryc fell silent. It was not for him to tell her the rest of what Bartok had said. There had been more— much more. But to speak of it now might in some way alter its happening. And that must never be.

"I wonder what she's thinking," said Stacy.

Alryc snapped out of his thoughts. "Who?"

The girl smiled. "Salome. Look at her dive! She does it for hours on end. Don't laugh, but sometimes I think she's protecting us. The ship, I mean. Staying close and watching over us."

"Maybe she is," laughed the navigator. "Whales are odd creatures. Being mammals, they're as close to humans as a sea-Dweller can be. Who knows? Maybe Salome does know of passing dangers. Her prancing may be some sort of signal. Too bad we don't understand it."

"I wonder if it were possible," said the girl.

"Who can say? Perhaps the day will come when we *can* communicate with her. Just as we do with wolves."

Stacy glowed with the thought. "Wouldn't that be something! Imagine speaking with a whale! I'd wager she'd have a lot to say!"

Alryc laughed. "I've never met the female who didn't. But look! The sky grows light! Why, we've sat here until dawn."

Stacy stared over the side. "You'd better get below," she said worriedly. "The sun will be up soon."

Alryc nodded and was about to leave when from the shadows behind came a voice. "I wish you'd stay a moment. Both of you."

Startled, they turned to see the tall figure of Elias, his usually chipper face sullen and troubled.

Alryc studied the sailor. He saw a deep look of worry behind Elias's brooding eyes. "Does there seem to be a problem, Captain?"

"Perhaps you'd like to see this for yourselves. Come with me to the bridge."

Stacy and Alryc shared puzzled glances as they followed him. On the bridge Boniface was standing with his hands clasped firmly behind his back. The biting of his lip indicated that things were not as in order as his firm stance might otherwise indicate.

"Now then," said Alryc. "What is this all about?"

Boniface pointed out toward the west. Light was beginning to spread faster across the sky in the east. "Can you make that out?" he asked.

The navigator screwed his eyes and stared for a long while. "I . . . I see a haze. Is that what you mean?"

Boniface nodded. "I first noticed it several hours ago. It's lying right in our course. What do you make of it?"

"Fog," said Stacy without hesitation. "It looks like the mists that settle in the Valley."

Elias agreed. "But look how dense it is. It's spreading out like a wall across the horizon."

"Yes, and look," added Boniface, letting his worry become plain, "it's blue—the color of an evening sky."

"There's no such thing as blue fog," scoffed the girl. "It must be an illusion created either by the dawn or——"

"Or what?" asked Elias. "I've been in fog as thick as soup. But I've never seen anything like this before. And another thing—feel the breezes. They're strong. But the fog's not being broken up."

"Winds can be tricky on open water," explained Alryc. "The fog could be trapped by an inversion."

"Can't we avoid it?" asked Stacy.

"I don't see how," replied the captain. "It's already spread across half the horizon. By the time we reach it, it'll be all over us."

Alryc quickly agreed. "Best sail through as rapidly as we can," he said. "Perhaps by the time we reach it, the inversion will have lifted." Even as he spoke, the mysterious fog loomed larger, closer.

"Do we keep our course, Capt'n?" asked Boniface.

Elias nodded dourly. "We have to, mister. But put two men up on lookout and order all hands at quarters. We'll probably be reaching the fog by midday and I want to be prepared."

Stacy suddenly noticed a strange quiet on the sea. It took her a while to realize what was different. "Look at Salome," she gasped. "She's stopped splashing. She's——"

"She's seen the fog, too," said Alryc darkly. "It's frightened her."

Just then the whale moaned, a low cry, the likes of which men had rarely heard. She turned her great head toward the ship and went under the water. A moment later she surfaced off the stern, splashing and crying.

"She's trying to warn us," stammered Stacy. "She's telling us to turn around!"

Elias stared as the whale splashed frantically. There was another cry, this one longer and more sorrowful than before, and then she disappeared into the deep, leaving hardly a ripple behind.

Could it actually be possible that Salome was warning them, Elias wondered. Or were he and Stacy merely letting their imaginations run wild? After all, fog was fog. At length he said, "Full ahead, Mr. Boniface."

* * *

What began as a brilliant sunlit day soon became dull and gray. The ship braced for what seemed to be more rough weather. But there was none. Instead, the choppy waters suddenly calmed. Sails slacked and after a time hung limply from the yards. By midday they were almost into the fog. A vast shroud of dull blue blocked out the sky. It beckoned them, dared them to test the waters beyond. The crew stood by anxiously as the *Brora* slowly slipped into the haze. The mist at first seemed thin and wispish, like smoke from a candle, but soon it became thick—and frightening. Blue shadows covered everything; they were in a void, a world of blue, a twilight of haze. And the ship was powerless. Her bow dipped gently, and as if with a caution of its own, the *Brora* drifted ahead. Elias stood at the bridge and gritted his teeth. Not religious by nature, he did the only thing he could: prayed for rain and a strong wind.

A cold hand touched her shoulder and Stacy jumped. As she spun around, her hand grasped at the hilt of her dagger.

"Oh, Trevor, it's you," she said, putting her hand to her thumping heart.

"I didn't mean to scare you, Stacy. I saw you standing here, gazing, and I wondered if you were all right."

The girl smiled and pulled her shawl tightly around her shoulders. It had been cold these past days since the fog had overtaken them, too cold for midsummer. But in this blue world in which they found themselves nothing was normal, anyway.

Stacy stared back out to the hidden sea. Her dark hair shined a deep blue, her face, bathed in the eerie shadows, seemed more brooding and forlorn than ever.

"Why are you standing out here?" asked Trevor, worried about her.

Stacy turned to him and sighed. "You'll probably think I'm being silly," she confided, "but I'm listening for Salome. I have a feeling she's still out there. Somewhere near, but too afraid to show herself."

"She's gone, Stacy. You yourself saw her dive the moment the mist appeared. By now she's probably prancing a hundred leagues from here, happy as a summer lark."

Stacy shook her head. "No, Trevor. You're wrong. Salome's here. I don't know where, but she's still here. Still watching over us, protecting us."

The soldier smiled. She sounded almost as mystical as Alryc. "I'll take your word for it," he said. "But look, it's too cold and damp to be standing out here with just a shawl. Take my cloak." Before the girl could refuse, he unclasped the cloak and handed it to her.

Gratefully she swung it over her shoulders. "Won't you be cold without it?"

Trevor shook his head. "I'll be going below soon," he said. "After Elias takes the sounding."

"Sounding? Is Elias coming on deck? He's been locked away in his cabin with Alryc for days."

"Alryc found something in one of the journals, I think. Seems that the *Snapdragon* encountered thick fog a few days before it caught sight of the Western Isles."

"Then we might be close to land?" asked the surprised girl.

Trevor waved his hand. "Don't get your hopes up. This is just routine. Of course, if our line reaches bottom, it's a good bet we're close to some coast or other. But what land that'll be, we don't know. The ship's being pulled pretty well off its course."

"But land is land," cried Stacy, jubilant at the thought.

"You read Elias's mind. That's exactly what he hopes."

Elias and Alryc, ghostlike in the mist, suddenly came out from the aft companionway and looked about. If they saw Stacy and Trevor standing close by, they made no sign of it. Grim-faced, Elias turned to Ashcroft, who was busy fixing a deadweight at the end of a curled ball of heavy twine. The officer nodded at Elias and told him that all was in order. The captain frowned. Hands on hips, he said, "Over the side, mister. And take it slowly. Give me the count in tens."

Three sailors held the rope between loose grips as Ashcroft hurled the deadweight into the water. There was a dull splash as it sank. Slowly the rope disappeared. Ashcroft kept his eyes on the red-dyed marking that stained it.

"Ten fathoms," he whispered as it sank into the water. Elias stood impassively.

"Twenty."

A pause of a few seconds.

"Thirty, Capt'n." Moments later: "Forty."

Elias nodded. "Keep going, Ashcroft. There's still a lot of line left to drop."

"Fifty, sir. No bottom yet." Then: "Sixty . . . seventy . . . eighty. . . ."

Alryc frowned at Elias. The captain made no response.

Ninety and a hundred came all too swiftly. The deadweight had dropped as far as it could. Stacy could plainly see the end of the line being held taut by the sailors.

"All right," growled Elias. "That's enough. We'll take another sounding in the morning. Haul it back up." A dejected look in his eyes, he mumbled, "Thank you, gentlemen," and, with Alryc, made haste back to his cabin.

Stacy lowered her eyes and whispered sullenly. "So much for land being close. It was a good theory, though."

"Don't feel bad, Stacy," said Trevor. "Tomorrow we might touch bottom. And even if we don't, there's bound to be a good wind soon. This fog can't last forever."

The girl frowned and sighed. "It's been what? Almost six days now? We're in the fourth week of the voyage, Trevor, and we've no idea how far there is to go.

Can you imagine what will happen if we're still on the sea by winter?"

The thought of freezing to death was most unsettling, but Trevor knew that was one thing he'd not have to worry about. "Don't concern yourself with that, my lady," he said quietly. "The late-summer storms likely will smash us to bits before we have time to think about it."

With that, she wearily took his arm and they both went below.

On the twenty-sixth day of the voyage, the eighth since the fog had been sighted, a slight glimmer of sun poked its way through the mists. Cheering, the crew and passengers were sure they had at last found their way through. But soon the sun was covered again, and the fog became as thick as ever. The sails were unfurled in a vain attempt to catch the mildest of breezes. But no sooner had the ship gained a few hard-earned leagues than the breeze died completely and once again left them stranded upon a glassy sea. A superstitious lot, the crew began to wonder if the Fates themselves had not turned against them for daring the wrath of her daughter, the sea. Elias felt helpless. He watched his ship drift listlessly; his crew became tense and frightened. If something did not break soon, he knew that disaster was imminent.

Then, on the eve of the twenty-ninth day, matters began to change.

Ashcroft, face somber, eyes stinging from long hours on duty, almost missed seeing the single drop of fresh water that splashed at his feet. He knelt down and touched it, heart pounding. As he did, another drop splashed his face. He peered up at the eerie blue sky and then shouted at the top of his lungs: "Rain! It's beginning to rain!"

Startled, the crew stared. Then they, too, picked up the cry. Rain it was—and never more welcome. Elias bounded on deck, grinning from ear to ear. "Unfurl the sails!" he called, the first hints of a west wind blowing. Canvas swelled and the ship lurched ahead.

Stacy clambered up from below and stood hesitantly at the companionway door, gazing at the splashes at her feet.

Elias caught a glimpse of her and laughed. "Come up, Stacy!" he called. "This is a sight I don't want you to miss."

The girl laughed as she raised her face toward the sky and let the rain drench her. The threatening fog had met its match! Like smoke from a fire it rose and dissipated, almost disappearing before her eyes.

Thunder crashed violently all about. A strong gust of wind nearly swept her off her feet. She caught at the halyards and laughed. Breath swept away, she peered out across the bow. There was the horizon! A bleak one, to be sure, with dark nimbus clouds, but a horizon it was, nevertheless. The blue fog was gone and the ship at last was in the clear.

By dawn, though, it became clear that the ship stood at the edge of a severe storm. Furious gusts tore at the sails, and Elias ordered them furled before the canvas ripped. Swells and surges crashed over the side. Time after time the *Brora* keeled over and was nearly swallowed down. Lightning flashed like Hel's fire across the darkened sky. The noise of the thunder was so great, so shattering, that it caused men to quiver and wolves to howl. Elias gritted his teeth. Indeed, from the fog to the fire, he thought. From the unknown to the known—and which was worse he was unable to decide.

Desperately the ship turned about, topsail furled, mainsail half drawn. The winds shifted quickly and in a rage. There was no way Elias could maneuver the ship to run with her. Experience told him that it was better to cease futile resistance and throw both ship and crew at the mercy of the waves. If the *Brora* could hold fast, secured and well managed, they might yet come out of this storm unscathed. But until the mast could be bared the risks were high. And already the mainsail had begun to whip dangerously, trying in vain to counteract the violent thrusts.

"Bare the mast!" cried Elias, hands numb, face anguished.

Rain pounded like mailed fists as Ashcroft and his men held tightly at the lash lines and made their way across the deck. They grappled the halyards amid terrible frenzy. All around was chaos. "It's stuck!" cried the officer. "The lift is stuck! Jammed against a spar!"

The captain fought his way down from the bridge. In front of his eyes planks began to tear loose. The edge of the sail began to rip. Elias grabbed hold of the brace and stared. The mast itself was beginning to sway; the shrouds broke loose from their moorings, twisting in the air. Fins flew, mashed against rail and bulwark before hurling over the side into the crazed, angry sea.

"It's no use," cried Ashcroft, hands raw from the strain of tugging the line. "We'll never save her!"

"It's that or drown!" shouted Elias. "We need more hands!"

The sea roaring, unable to hear, Oddfellow nodded. The rip in the sail was worsening. His lads behind, he bravely inched forward against gusts that would have swept less stout men off their feet. But he never saw what came from behind. Elias's screams were buried. Water crashed against the bulwark, tore down across the aftcastle and crashed above their heads. Oddfellow held on, even as one of his lads screamed with the flowing wave and was heaved over the side. The *Brora* pitched, then suddenly was thrown back on her end beams. More screams filled the air. Oddfellow stared dumbly. Right before his eyes another sailor came crashing down upon him. Hands grasped frantically in search of the lash line. It gave. Six sailors were sent lurching, tossing and tumbling, smacking against torn railings. In rapid succession three more waves, each larger and more powerful than the last, crossed above their heads. Elias tried to reach the helpless men but was himself pushed back by a sudden gust that knocked him down. Only the sure hands of Ashcroft saved him from being tossed like a rag. With terror in their eyes, the two men watched young Oddfellow and the last of his lads as they were swept away.

Again the waves slammed. The companionway door at the forecastle was blown off its hinges and sent smashing against the mast. From below came a series of screams as water rushed down into the hold, flooding the passageways in seconds.

Panic-stricken, a handful of Valley soldiers fought one another to get to the deck.

"Get back below!" yelled Elias.

Perhaps they had not heard, perhaps they were merely too frightened to listen. As the ship wallowed, the wind sent them sprawling about like pins. One sailor jumped from the forecastle to help, his heart larger than his head. Along with the soldiers, he was smothered by giant white froth that heaved across the rail. Lungs filled with salt water; the limp bodies slipped over the side as the ship heaved.

Elias quickly leaped to his feet and went back to work at trying to free the halyards. If the sail were not furled—and fast—it would whip the ship even more furiously, adding fuel to the wind, and cause them all to drown. Prayers for the dead must wait.

Just then the winds began to slacken, and the rain began to ease. He gazed up to a grim foreboding sky. It grew dimly bright, a strange eerie light that almost revealed a few rays of the sun. He looked to the stunned Ashcroft and whispered, "The eye of the storm."

It was a brief respite, but one that allowed them to get to work. The torn sail was furled. Elias rushed to the helm to see what damage had been done.

Boniface, coughing and sputtering, smiled weakly. "So far, so good, Capt'n," he wheezed.

Elias grimaced. "We've a long way to go yet," he replied.

Alryc came running from the companionway. His clothing was soaked. "There's flooding below," he panted. "Cracks in the hull. We've been bailing by hand, but it's not much use. We'll have to seal it off and move everyone out into the crew's quarters. We can't take everyone in those tight quarters. Some of the passengers will have to come on deck and take their chances."

Elias groaned. The image of what had just happened to the Valley soldiers raced across his eyes. "All right," he muttered at last. "Mr. Ashcroft!"

"Sir?"

"Get out some more rope. I want lash lines drawn across the entire deck from the mast to the bridge. And reinforce them on the forestay if you have to. We've got to bring some of the passengers topside."

Ashcroft gulped. "Sir?" He looked at the captain incredulously.

"No time for questions, mister! Just do as I say."

The rains started again; the sea began to surge. Elias ran back to the mast, checked the lines and nodded evenly at the sight of Ashcroft busily at work with six sailors tying the lash lines as firmly as possible. He created a web; the ropes criss-crossed. If the Brora herself did not smash into pieces, those on top should fare well, Elias knew. At least as well as the crew, who had work to do and could not allow themselves the luxury of gripping onto ropes.

Then back to the helm he went. His eyes searched the sky, his hands felt for the direction of the winds. The Brora, as far as he could make out, was just off center of the storm front. And it was bearing down fast.

"Bring us two points off the wind to the starboard quarter, Mr. Boniface," he said. "Take note of the course and hold it—if you can. Then we'll try and run left semi-circle."

"Aye, Capt'n," answered the officer glumly. "But, sir, may I ask why you're allowing the women to come on deck?"

Elias glared at him. "What? Are you mad?"

"No, sir. Look."

From the flooded companionway came six girls, along with several Valley soldiers and Alryc. The captain shook his head and turned around. The ship was beginning to heave again. There was no time to argue. If these Rangers wanted to risk their lives, he was not going to fight them. But the thought that Stacy was among them weighed heavily.

The passengers huddled close to one another, hands firmly clutched at the lines. Next to Stacy were Heather and Melinda, next to them, Robin and Captain Sandra. Pitching and whining, the ship lurched amid the tumult. The rains came, slanting furiously—harder than they had before.

"Let her heave, Boniface," yelled Elias, wiping salt water from his tearing eyes. "The wind's shifting again. There's no purpose in trying to steer until we know which way."

Again the ship moved into the maw of the storm. The chaos that had reigned before was quick to resume. Drunkenly the *Brora* foundered between thunderous waves on either side. The bow pitched time and again; foam smashed left and right. One of the Valley soldiers, a lad at the end of the lash line, released a hand to wipe his eyes and that was all it took. When the wave hit, he was unable to grasp hold again. Another soul was washed helplessly over the side.

The ship whipped about aimlessly. A towering froth hit hard against the prow, splintering it. The forestay snapped like a spring; its rough edge caught an unaware sailor like a whip. The lad screamed as a thin line of blood spurted down his face. As the ship rocked, he lost his balance and fell against splintering rails. Arm waving frantically, he, too, went over the side, swallowed by the maelstrom.

Then there came a terrible grinding sound, then a groan. Boniface's eyes bulged. "Capt'n! The helm's begun to crack!"

Elias, fire in his eyes, slid across the quarterdeck and made it to the cockpit. The arm of the steering oar felt like weighted lead. He couldn't make it move in either direction without using the full force of his weight—and that would crack it in two.

"We'll have to manage without it," he hissed. "Not that we've been able to steer, anyway. Just stay——"

Suddenly his eyes tightened, and his mouth gaped. Holding his breath, he swore to the Fates. Coming ahead, straight off the bow, was a wave—a wave the likes of which no man had ever seen. It rolled slowly, foaming at the head, looming almost as high as the sky, half a league in width. It rumbled as it swelled, causing all other waves to bow their puny heads in respect. It was more than a wave; it was a monster!

Screams filled the air. The crew froze. A monster from Hel was upon them!

"It's going to hit head on!" cried Boniface.

"Not if we can help it!" shouted the captain in reply. He grabbed at the steering oar and turned it with all his might.

"Capt'n, it'll split!"

"What matter, mister? Look at that thing! We've got to turn about; otherwise we'll be smashed to bits!"

Muscles aching, the two men strained with every ounce of energy. With a groan the wood came loose—split at the beam. Now there was nothing to be done as the monster crept forward, gathering strength and momentum with every passing second. It hovered against the sky and roared. The thought raced through Elias's mind that it was laughing at them. The wave was looking down at this fragile pile of timber and humanity and bellowing at its audacity to face the wrath of the sea.

"Hold for your lives!" screamed Elias to all those within earshot. He looked to Stacy as the wave obliterated the sky and cursed himself for never having smothered her in his arms. His last look, he was certain.

The wave hit with tremendous impact. The mast groaned and split at the block; planks were ripped and twisted; rail shattered; the skiff was hurled from its moorings and crushed into bits of flying wood. Screams and cries were quickly muffled as salt water filled choking lungs. For a full minute the monster lumbered and rolled from stem to stern. The ship fell back on end beams; wood creaked along the hull amid flying debris and humanity.

But the *Brora* held her cut against the water and would not give. Painfully she eased with the blow and righted herself. She was shattered and taking on water, but her frame was still intact. With only her own will she fought for her life and the lives of those still aboard. Misshapen, savagely damaged, she stubbornly refused to die. And as if in awe of the gallant Rhonnda ship, the winds began to calm, the sea soothed her temper, the storm passed away. The *Brora* had survived.

CHAPTER EIGHTEEN

How lovely shine the lights after the storm,
How sweet the breeze, how warm the sun;
I glow with the leaves that shimmer with wetness,
And dream the faces of the girls of Rhonnda.

BARTOK

Heather looked up at the worried faces around her. Still kneeling, she slid a pillow under Stacy's head and put a cup of wine to the girl's lips.

Stacy coughed, vomited seawater, then slumped back on the blanket. Warm sun bathed her face and body and made her painfully aware she was still alive. Then slowly, her head spinning, she managed to open her eyes. Blurry, tense faces stared back. Melinda, eyes thankful; Elias, his frown turning to a grin; Trevor, sullen and anxious, a small bandage covering a cut above his brow.

"You'll be fine, Stacy," said Heather softly, now helping her to drink the wine. "You were much luckier than some of the others——" She bit her lip and cut off her words.

Stacy lifted her head and looked around. The entire deck was a shambles; ripped planks and boards were scattered everywhere. She could see a number of bodies under blankets along the side of the bulwark. Some were sitting up, heads in their hands, others lying still, gasping. On the other side of the deck were more blankets and bodies. Only they weren't moving at all. The blankets had been pulled taut above their faces. And under one such blanket she could make out the forms of wolves.

Aware now, her eyes widened in panic. "Where's Casca?" she cried, desperately looking for the wolf.

"Casca's fine," assured Melinda, bending down and touching her brow soothingly. "So is Cicero. Most of the others, too. But a few of the wolves didn't make it. They were drowned when the monster hit."

Tears came to the girl's eyes. None of the others realized that she was crying not because they were dead but because there would be no sage to sing the chant to bring them to Fara's kingdom.

"How . . . how bad was it?"

Heather began to sob. She put her head in her hands and let her tears flow. Stacy looked at Melinda. The Ranger avoided her eyes. "Boniface was swept overboard," she whispered. "He and Heather——"

"I know," said Stacy, recalling what a fine couple they had made. "What about——"

Melinda forced a weary smile. "Ashcroft is fine. He's too lucky a lout to have died."

Stacy squeezed her hand thankfully. "I'm glad, Melinda. At least for that."

"But many weren't so fortunate," continued the girl. "They say Beecham died trying to save Sandra from being swept over. Neither one of them had a chance. Heather saw them."

Stacy cried at the thought of Captain Sandra, a bold, lovely girl who so loved life and had barely begun to live it.

"Is Robin safe?"

"She's hurt, Stacy. The wave knocked her against the bulwark. The blow saved her life, I guess, but she's in a coma. Alryc and one of the others who know about medicine are tending to her. Most of the other girls are all right, though. Thank the Fates for that."

"Then we came through this fairly well."

Melinda gave a short bitter laugh. "We're mostly alive, if that's what you mean. But look about you, Stacy. The ship's a wreck. Our helm is broken, the mast is smashed. We can't even row. The *Brora*'s drifting slowly with the current, taking us wherever it leads. For now we'll survive. Some of the food's spoiled, but there's enough for a while. Anyway, we can probably catch some fish. But we're desperately short of fresh water. Most of the barrels were hurled overboard. But that doesn't matter, either. You see, if we hit more rough weather, we'll sink. The ship can't take any more. Fates above, she's done more than enough, anyway! We're adrift, Stacy. Helpless and at the ocean's mercy."

In the cool of the evening those who had perished were slipped into the sea. Alryc spoke, and his words instilled hope that all was not lost. The small Rhonnda banner of maroon and blue he held in his hand reminded them that no matter where they were, whatever course the sea had set, the Fates were still with them. The past was behind, he reminded them, the future ahead. Like the visions of Bartok. They must never look back.

And so the *Brora* sailed on, twenty-five of her one hundred companions left behind but never forgotten.

Days passed more slowly now; the breezes hinted at the early autumn that would soon come to these northern climes. The currents led them on a fair westerly course, and Alryc and Stacy saw that it was still close to the course they had planned. But after thirty-five days at sea, the gray horizon held nothing more than it had since the day they had left. There was no land to be seen.

Then, on the fortieth day, there was something curious upon the water that made Stacy cry with glee. Not land, which was still yet to be found, but the sight of a whale off the starboard side. A blue spouting whale that pranced and danced beside the shattered ship. When Elias came running to see what the commotion was about, Stacy happily pointed and said, "Our romance isn't over."

Elias threw back his head and laughed. Salome had come home.

The forty-fourth day of the voyage came bright and fair. The sky was deep blue, the sun warm and strong. Alongside the ship Salome pranced and dived in her early morning ritual. Stacy, sleeping peacefully on the deck, wrinkled her nose as a drop of Salome's cold spouting water splashed it. She opened her eyes. Her lips felt dry; she ran her tongue slowly across them. She felt her eyes adjust to the strong light. Sailing above her was a gull. Dreamily, she wondered if she was still asleep. The pale-blue bird soared higher and higher, then turned and dived down to the sea. There was a loud squawk as another gull, this one with broad, flecked wings, joined the first.

Stacy sat up with a start, now out of her dream. But this was no dream, she quickly saw. The gulls were real! *But how could they be?* she asked herself. Suddenly the meaning of their presence dawned on her and sent her mind swimming. There could only be one explanation.

Land!

Dizzily she sprang to the shattered railing. A brown, sandy bay, the shape of a perfect half-moon, came rushing up at her. Jutting reefs on either side broke crashing waves; white clean foam splashed cleanly against glittering rock. Stacy drew a deep breath, exhilarated. Real land, she knew. More than five hundred leagues from the shores of the Empire. And what a magnificent land it was.

Behind the shore stood row upon row of thick leafy trees, some rising twenty meters high. As high as the aged walls of the Haven itself. The hills were rich with a multitude of wild flowers, just as Old One had described; the grass was deep and tall. Behind it all stood a breathtaking panorama of smoke-colored mountains, like a huge tapestry woven across the sky. Each lofty peak towered above the last in never-ending succession. It took long glances for her to begin to grasp the enormity of it all.

Soft tears welled in the corners of her eyes, and she bowed her head in silent prayer. They were safe. Fara had taken care of her own, of all her children.

Cold salt water splashed against her face. Stacy turned to see the great whale break the surface beside her with a mighty roar. The girl stared blankly as Salome rose high and dived. In that instant there was a spark of communication. An exchange of thought between two minds.

Rest well, my princess, Salome had said. *I have brought you safely to land.*

And in that same instant, Stacy replied. *I knew you would. Thank you.* But before she could transmit another thought, Salome arched away from the ship and began to turn back toward the sea. Stacy gasped. The whale was leaving them, she realized, going home again, to prance far away upon open waters. One more time the whale broke the surface. Stacy called but to no avail. Salome dived again, deeply, leaving a wash of foam and ripples in her wake. Then she was gone.

The girl watched for a while, hoping she would come back, but her heart knew better. Salome was of her own world—and so she must return. Sadly, Stacy wondered if their paths would ever cross again.

All around, the haggard and weary crew began to stir. There were shouts of joy; everyone stared at the reefs and the sandy shores beyond. Elias leaned at the torn rail, Trevor and Alryc at his sides. Then there was a flurry of commands, as the mariner barked at his crew to prepare to lead the disabled ship into harbor. Harbor! What a wonderful word, thought Stacy.

Eyes closed, she stood with the breeze blowing through her hair and caressing her face. Her mind was on the smoky range of mountains so far in the distance, for it was there, she knew, that the real test was to come. It was there that the white wolves would be found. Elias had done his part; now it was time for her. The hardest part of all. For a moment she felt fear, then she calmed, knowing that whatever her destiny, it could not be altered.

It was Alryc who broke her mood. Standing before her, the navigator took her hand in his own and kissed it softly. She looked up at him awkwardly to find a soft smile written across his rugged face. He said no words, but his eyes told a tale: Again the visions of Bartok had proved true. Stacy, aware of this, smiled back, uneasy about the new role in which Alryc had cast her. She kept her gaze to the shore. The wind, tossing her hair in front of her eyes, could not make her lose sight of the mountains—and the alien land she had dreamed of for so long —now beckoning.

PART FOUR
LAND OF THE WHITE WOLVES

CHAPTER NINETEEN

The ship was moored close to the reefs, beside a tiny inlet that provided good shelter from further ravages of the sea. Leaning on her side, the broken ship looked lost and forlorn. But at least she was safe, and within days Elias would set the crew to work at making her seaworthy again.

Beyond the inlet there was a soft slope leading up to a broad flat ridge. Upon the ridge, camp was set. Tools were brought from the ship, trees felled, canvas spread. By nightfall camp tents were up and habitable. A fire was lit and the company sat around it thankfully, gazing about at the new world they had reached, already dreaming of its fabled mysteries and dangers.

The wolves, restless and tense, listened to the sounds, familiarizing themselves with alien songs on Aleya's breath and eerie rustlings from among the strange trees.

Elias, worn and tired, walked among the small groups of his company and gave instructions for the following day's work. Then he singled out Alryc, Trevor, Ashcroft, Cicero and Stacy and led them to a small open patch in the tall grass, well away from the others.

"It's going to take a lot of work to make some good winter shelters," he said soberly. "If the *Brora* weren't damaged, we could have stayed aboard her for the winter. But, as you all know . . ."

"There's plenty of good timber about," said Trevor. "We

can have my men start cutting down trees immediately. If we explore some of those hills, I'm sure we can find ourselves some sort of valley to give us better protection."

Alryc shook his head. "We can't afford to move too far from the ship," he said. "Better we build our camp here."

"I don't think I understand all of this," admitted Stacy. "I thought our whole purpose here was to explore. We need to find the white wolves."

Elias looked at her dryly. "I'm afraid that will have to wait, my lady. We're in a hostile environment. The best we can do is keep ourselves warm and safe for the winter and then, in spring, set out for the mountains."

"But that'll be six months! You're asking us to sit idle for half a year! We should be on the move right now."

"And do what?" said Trevor. "Winter comes early in these climes. Where will we find shelter? What will we eat? No, Stacy, Elias is right. First we have to build some sort of settlement. Then we can begin to send scouting parties into the hills."

"But don't you see?" pleaded the girl. "We must get moving right away, before the early winter sets in. If we can make it into the mountains———"

"We'll all probably die," interrupted Elias. "If the weather doesn't kill us, the wolves probably will."

Cicero growled. "He may be right, Khalea. These cousins know us not. They'll be suspect. Even Old One told you as much. White wolves are enemies of men. Better that Casca and I scout the hills alone. We can try to locate them and speak of your coming."

"What about it, Stacy?" asked Elias. "Does that suit you?"

Sourly the girl agreed. "I guess I don't have much choice. I can't go on alone."

"There'll be plenty of work for you to do here," promised Trevor. "We'll be needing hunters to provide food. It might be a good idea if you and some of the

Ranger girls began to scout around, starting tomorrow, and see what you can come up with."

"Old One told of great herds of caribou," recalled Stacy. "But I doubt we'll find them near here. We should be looking closer to the mounains. It's there they'll come down for the winter."

Trevor looked at her sternly. "You're not to stray anywhere near there," he ordered. "I mean it, Stacy. Aboard the ship Elias was commander, on land *I* am. And I'm warning you not to try and find the white wolves. We don't need caribou. Rabbit will be fine, thank you. Catch whatever you can—and stay within the perimeter we'll set down for you. Is that understood?"

There was no way she could disobey such an order, Stacy realized. Trevor was right. On land he *was* in command.

"All right, Commander. I give my word. I won't do anything more than you want me to. When shall we start?"

Trevor looked to Elias, then back to Stacy. "Tomorrow," he said. "Pick five or six of the best girls and take them out toward those thickets. I'll wager they'll find plenty of fresh game. Elias, in the meantime, will get everything off the ship that can be of use to us."

The mariner nodded.

The wolf looked to the soldier. "And when shall *we* leave?" he asked.

Trevor thought for a while. "Tomorrow you'll send your trackers up to the hills," he said. "Not all at once. A few a day. And I want each one back in no later than three days. That way there'll always be trackers out and others back to tell what they found."

Trevor stood and stared down at the anxious faces. "If we all do our parts, we should have no difficulty," he said. "Come spring we'll all set out for the mountains. By then we'll be ready and able to face whatever's waiting up there."

* * *

Dense broad leaves rustled inches above her face; a pale sun peeked between lumbering boughs. Stacy crouched beneath the tree, her eyes focused keenly on a large brown hare nibbling at a patch of peat moss. Then she stood erect, feet apart in a comfortable stance, and drew an arrow. Her arm bent slightly at the elbow, she swung the bow vertically and drew the string, one eye closed, the other gauging the distance to the hare.

Her fingers relaxed. The string rolled off them.

Twang!

The hare was thrown back off its haunches and went sprawling across the damp grass. Stacy drew her dagger and ran to the fallen prey. She swung the shoulder strap of her satchel over her shoulder, placed it at her side and threw the hare inside with the others.

"Good shooting, Stacy!" came a gleeful cry from behind.

The girl peered up to see the grinning face of Melinda. "Where did you come from?"

"Oh, I was on my way back to camp," she said happily, proudly pointing to her own heavy bag on her shoulder. "I've caught five rabbits already. But nothing quite as big as what you got."

"I've got four," said Stacy, getting up and flexing cramped muscles. "I guess that's enough for today. This bag feels as if it weighs as much as I do." She began to trudge away.

Melinda, crossbow in hand, slung the weapon over her shoulder. Not speaking, they walked across the knoll and followed a small winding stream that led down the hillock on the way back to camp. After a few minutes Stacy stopped and knelt down. Her eyes carefully scanned the fallen leaves and muddied bank of the stream.

"What is it?" asked Melinda.

"Deer tracks. A whitetail, I think. I saw them this morning."

The Ranger's eyes widened. "Deer! That's the first in these thickets anyone's seen. Think you can track her? A juicy buck will make us all a fine supper. Anyway, I'm sick of rabbit stew."

Stacy laughed loudly. "It's not all the cook's fault, Melinda. How many different ways can you cook rabbit?" She glanced forlornly toward the gradually steepening hills to the north. "I bet we'd catch that whitetail real quick if we were allowed to leave the thicket." Her eyes glinted with mischief.

"Promise me, Stacy," admonished Melinda, "you won't go trailing off out of the thickets on your own?"

Stacy looked surprised. "Why do you think I would?"

Melinda frowned. "I know you, Stacy. I know you watch with envy when our trackers leave for the hills. I know you want to be with them, exploring and searching for white wolves."

Stacy scoffed. "I gave my word, Melinda," she said, holding up a hand.

"I know. But I also know you're tempted to run away every time we set out to hunt. Sometimes I get back to camp expecting to hear that you're missing and nobody knows where you've gone."

The Valley girl threw back her head and laughed. "I give you my promise, Melinda. I won't leave on my own. And if I do, I won't go without giving you the chance to come with me. All right?"

Melinda smiled and nodded sheepishly. Then, packs over their shoulders, the two of them walked back to the camp, whistling happily at their discovery.

Under a moonless night sky Casca and two trackers came racing back to the ridge and the sleeping camp. Elias, standing guard with several of Trevor's soldiers, was the first to greet them. The forest wolf panted and looked about anxiously. "Where's Trevor?" he growled. "And Khalea?"

"Sleeping," replied the mariner. "You'll find Trevor near the fire and Stacy in the big tent with the other girls."

The wolf nodded and barked something in a low snarl to his companions, then returned to the common tongue. "I have news, Elias. Perhaps you'd like to come with me to find them."

Elias nodded and followed the wolf while the soldiers watched curiously. Trackers and hunters had been coming and going all week, at all hours. This was the first time any had returned with something to tell.

Elias rousted Trevor and Stacy from their beds, and the three of them followed Casca down toward the inlet, the roar of the tide filling their ears. The outline of the *Brora* loomed dimly against the black sky. There, everyone sat down along the sands.

Casca looked from one face to the next and in a low voice said, "We drew close to the white wolves this morning."

Stacy's heart leaped. "Where?" she panted.

"Far from here, Khalea. We followed the tracks of a herd of caribou that came down to graze in the hills. We suspected that white wolves would follow. We heard their howls, and we followed closely behind. We returned their cries with hunting calls of our own. The air became still, as if Aleya herself held her breath. There was no reply."

"Are you certain they heard you?" asked Elias, concerned.

The wolf nodded soberly. "They heard. Our call traveled as far as their own. But they made no reply. We continued to follow the tracks, but soon there were none to follow. They were gone. To where I cannot tell. But gone they were." And he glanced at his companions hesitantly.

Stacy put cold fingernails against her colder lips. "Do you think they saw you, even though you couldn't see them?"

Casca nodded. "They know these lands well, Khalea. A wolf could hide and observe from many places, and we would be none the wiser. Yes, I believe we were seen."

"I don't understand," said Trevor. "If they saw you, why did they hide? Why didn't they greet you?"

Stacy frowned. "It's possible the very sight of different wolves without white pelts caught them by surprise. Remember, they've never seen wolves like ours before. They might yet contact us."

"The hunters will return to the mountains, to their dens, and consult the sage," Cicero told them gloomily.

"The what?" asked Elias.

"The sage. The mystic. The wolf who reads *Balaka,* the stars, and serves the packs as soothsayer. He's second only to the lord of the pack—and frequently second to none. The hunters may well be frightened. The sage will tell them what must be done."

"And what might that be?" asked Trevor, shifting his weight uneasily.

"A number of things," replied the girl. "He could tell them to set aside their fears and greet our wolves openly, or he could tell them to send their best trackers and seekers down the mountains to watch us. The sage might want to know more before he takes further action."

"Like what?" Trevor demanded.

Casca growled uneasily. "If we are considered a threat, they will send a fighting pack against us. The warlords will sit in Council and call us out as enemies."

"But *we're* not their enemies," protested the soldier. "We've got to demonstrate that."

"Yes," growled Casca. "But as long as they hide from us, we cannot tell them otherwise."

"We should have gone into the mountains right away," said Stacy. "At least we'd have been in their lands, and they'd have been forced to deal with us."

"In light of this," Trevor said, "that would probably have been even worse. No, the best thing is to carry on as before. But we might have to go into the hills, anyway. From what you and the other Rangers have said, it looks like there won't be much winter game for us around here.

We may need to send out a hunting expedition to follow the caribou."

Elias peered up at the sky. Already the frosts had settled; the trees were withering. Any day now the first snows would begin. "We'll have to send out quite a large party," he said, frankly, "if we hope to bring back enough game to see us through."

Trevor nodded. "We will. A well-equipped one. Stacy and her girls can lead some of my men."

"The herds are large," growled Casca. "And don't forget, the white wolves will also be in the hunt. They depend on the herds as you do."

Stacy shrugged. "All the better. Let them see us and watch us. It should show our peaceful intent."

Trevor looked at her sternly. His eyes were cold. "Don't try to approach them," he warned. "If we go into the hills, it's for food, and food only. The other order still stands. Our wolves will be the ones to make contact."

Stacy's eyes smoldered, but she said nothing. She realized Trevor was intent on being as cautious as possible, but she believed that a clear opportunity at hand would be lost. But there was nothing she could do.

Elias held out his hand; a tiny drop of moisture fell across his palm. It was merely the lightest of flakes, but its meaning was clear. The snow had already begun.

Two days later, in the early evening, just after the first rough cabins were finished, the company of the *Brora* huddled close to their fires and the warmth of their new shelters. It was well past midnight. The snow had all but stopped, leaving the ridge ankle-deep in white. The fires were dim; there was faint candle glow from inside the cabins.

Stacy's restlessness made her bundle herself warmly and leave the Ranger cabin to walk among the trees. Her black boots dug soft tracks in the fresh snow. A tartan scarf was wrapped around her neck, half covering her face, leaving only her eyes exposed.

The feeling of the cold and the snow depressed her, but it was stunningly lovely country, she had to admit, what with the ever-present snowcapped peaks hovering against a starry velvet sky. It was exactly as Old One had said. But here, on the ridge, a stone's throw from the inlet and the sea, she felt trapped. The same feeling as in the Valley, when life came to a standstill and the cold, bleak winter months set in.

"A penny for your thoughts."

Stacy turned, startled, to see the silhouetted form of Elias coming toward her. He was wearing his river jacket, a heavy skin lined with a thick, bluish pelt. A bear pelt, she saw, glancing at the thick collar lifted up to his ears. Rugged leather boots were tightly drawn, knee-high, like her own. And she remembered that he had been wearing those same boots the first day they had met in the Haven, so many memories ago. Her heart beat faster, romantic dreams rekindled.

"Do you have a penny?" she asked.

The mariner shrugged and shook his head, smiling.

"Then I shan't tell you."

Elias pursed his lips in a mock pout. He looked into her dark eyes, ever mysterious, and caught the sparkle. "Shall I guess?" he asked, holding her gaze.

"All right."

He leaned his frame against the side of a snowbound pine and raised his eyes toward the stars. "Knowing you, I suppose you're thinking of the hunting expedition?"

Stacy shook her head. "I'd rather have been thinking of a forest of eternal summers," she said softly. "Do you think somewhere in this world of ours there might actually be such a place?"

" 'Somewhere' is a big place," said Elias with a sigh. "Somewhere is where you yearn to be if you're unhappy. But who can tell? Perhaps such a forest does exist."

"I'd like to believe it, Elias. And one day I'd like to find it."

The mariner moved his hand boldly and touched her chin with his finger. "Maybe we can find it together, Stacy."

His words were gentle and caring.

"Do you say that to all young women?"

"No, only girls with forest ways. And then only if they're aristocrats."

"That narrows it down some." Stacy smiled. "Why are you always teasing the nobility? Aren't you high-born yourself?"

He was slightly taken aback.

"I heard you come from an aristocratic Valley family," she said. "You gave up your title."

Elias frowned. "Who told you that?"

"Spooner did. A long time ago."

He cast dark eyes down at the snow and nudged at it with the toe of his boot. A strong gust of wind swept down from above and scattered fresh snow over their faces.

"Spooner was right," he said at last. "My family was aristocratic. But when my father died, my older brother naturally took over the household. He attained all the rank and title and land. Younger brothers are often doomed to secondary lives under those conditions, you know."

Stacy nodded. She knew.

"I came to Rhonnda, fell in love with the river and the city and never went back. That is, except for the Council business. But if I seem to make fun of aristocrats, it's because I know what they're like. As you said, I'm one of them. Cut my finger and my blood's as blue as your own."

Stacy laughed. "I feel better already," she said.

Again the wind gusted from above, sending the snow swirling. Elias shivered. "Brrr. Shouldn't we get back inside?"

The thought of the warm fire was enticing, but Stacy shook her head. "You go. I want to stay out a bit longer. I don't like that feeling of being confined. Out here, I can make believe I'm free to wander wherever I like."

"Like Cicero," said Elias with a smile. "I've known that wolf for years, and, you know, he'll never change. No matter how frigid the weather, how violent the wind, he'd rather shun a warm room and go huddle with his companions at the side of a cold hill."

"What did you expect? A wolf can't be cooped up like a hen. It makes us irritable."

"Ah," said the mariner with a grin. "Us? To whom am I speaking? To Lady Anastasia, or to Khalea?"

"*I* sometimes wonder myself who I am," she admitted. "I mean about who I *really* am. The forest ways are in me; they always will be."

Elias nodded. "Who do you want to be, Stacy? You can be Khalea if you like, but I'd like to think of you as just a girl."

His eyes were warm, his voice soft and kind and caring.

Stacy brushed loose hair away from her cheek and smiled. "Alryc thinks I'm a vision of Bartok."

Elias laughed and shook his head. "The old devil! He would! But everyone sees you in a different way. To your hunters you *are* Khalea, a huntress. To the Ranger girls, you're practically one of *them*—as well as their leader. To the soldiers and my crew you're your father's daughter, an aristocrat from the Valley. To a mystic like Alryc, you probably *are* some vision in Bartok's poetry. And to Trevor, despite all this military carrying on, well, he sees you like a fairy-tale princess."

"And to you?" she asked, batting snow-flecked lashes.

"Me? I suppose I blend a little of each." He let his eyes run over her shapely form. Even wrapped and bundled as she was she seemed lovely. He kissed her hand, then gazed lovingly into her eyes. "I won't fill your head with my personal feelings," he said. "I'll save that until we've done what we came here to do. Love clouds the mind. It's worse than wine—and the hangover lasts a lifetime."

With a dimpled smile she looked up at him. "That was very good, Elias. I didn't know you were a poet. Bartok himself would be envious."

Elias smiled. "Then consider it a gift, my lady. A present from me to you. Keep the thought with you when you go off hunting in the hills."

Stacy felt happy. All around snow continued to swirl; icicles began to drip from the boughs; wondrous peaks stared down at them from above. This new white world seemed to be pages from a book, and she was a part of it. And best of all Elias was at her side.

"I almost forgot to tell you," he said. "That's why I came out here, to look for you. Trevor and Alryc are going over the plans. The expedition's been set for the day after tomorrow."

"Who has been asked to go?"

"Besides you? Melinda and Robin. The rest will be soldiers. Except for Alryc."

The girl looked puzzled. "Alryc? Why is he going along?"

"To draw us some good maps of the hills while you're there. In any case Trevor will put him to good use one way or another."

"Trevor's coming, too?" Her brows lifted.

Elias nodded. "He insists on it. I'm to take charge of the camp and the work on the ship while he's gone. He may be afraid that the white wolves will attack, and he wants to be there. If you ask me, I think he's worried that you and the other girls will be in danger. He feels responsible."

Stacy sighed. That would be like him, she knew. Ever gallant, ever the gentleman. He would risk no life ahead of his own.

"I told him that letting the Rangers go at all was a mistake," Elias said flatly. "A hunting party of soldiers along with a few of our wolves could have done just as well. Trevor disagreed." Elias's eyes darkened, his lips pressed tightly together. "If anything should go wrong. . . ."

Stacy reached up and touched his lips with her fingertips. "Nothing will," she whispered. "Trevor was really right, you know. The Rangers and I know more about lands like this than his troops ever will. If there *is* trouble, we'll know how to handle it. Besides, Cicero will be with us. And together we're a pretty rugged duo."

He held her hand and kissed her lips ever so lightly. A lump rose in his throat. "I know you're tough and wily, Stacy. I know you could fight your way out of Hel if it came to it. But don't take any foolish risks. I'd hate to make that long voyage home without you."

"You won't. I promise. I'll be a good girl."

"I don't want a good girl. I want a smart one. Keep those bright eyes open and your dagger close."

Standing on her toes, she hugged him tightly. "I always do. That's the first thing you learn in the forest."

CHAPTER TWENTY

In the cold white hills the hunting party awoke to a morning of overcast and snow. They had departed from the inlet two days before, leaving Elias and Casca behind with the main body, and so far they had encountered no trouble, though Cicero and Snorri, another of the wolves, reported signs that white wolves were shadowing their movements. Stacy, Melinda and Robin prepared a breakfast of warm broth, while Trevor and Alryc rousted the others out of the tents. As they hunkered around the breakfast fire, sipping at the warm broth, Stacy breathed the cold morning air with satisfaction. The hunting had been good so far. Only the day before, she had tracked a small herd of white-tailed deer, felling two before nightfall had forced her to return to camp. The first task of the day would be to retrieve and butcher the two deer, lying hidden in the snow at about an hour's distance. At this rate, they would be able to return to the inlet within a week.

After breakfast they left camp and started off through the snow, bundled in hooded jackets. Stacy led the way, Cicero at her side. The others followed her tracks. The trail became laborious. Snow-laden boughs groaned above their heads as they inched slowly up the next hill and down the path that Stacy had marked.

Within minutes after their departure the winds began to

blow fiercely, and the snow began to deepen. Folds in the land filled with huge drifts. Their walking became more hazardous with every step. At this rate Trevor knew that by afternoon they would be trapped in a blizzard.

At last they came to the spot where Stacy had felled her two deer. The girl stood waiting for them, lips trembling, face as white as the snow. Trevor took one look and knew something was wrong. Stacy was visibly frightened; she ran to his side and pointed frantically to a small clump of thick brush leading past the iced stream and winding out of sight at the crest.

"They're gone," she panted, pointing to the site.

"Gone? What are you talking about? How could they be gone?"

"I don't know. But they're not here. Look—see that ravine? That's where I left them. They've been taken. Dragged away." She stood frozen in anguish.

Trevor's eyes narrowed. His face tightened under his tartan scarf. "Are you sure, Stacy? Maybe this is the wrong spot. The drifts——"

The girl shook her head fiercely, sending the mane of hair flying. "I'm not wrong. See that tree? I marked it with my dagger." She brushed aside a thin layer of snow from the trunk and exposed a deep K in the trunk. K for Khalea.

Trevor frowned uneasily. "I see it," he said. "Could white wolves have found them and dragged them off?"

Stacy fretted, and looked about. "I doubt it, Trevor. Wolves don't usually——"

Suddenly there came a faraway wail. A low cry that shattered the air and cut through the wind like glass. Trevor froze. Alryc reached for his sword. Melinda and Robin held their breath and quietly drew arrows.

Cicero twitched his ears and stood perfectly still. Once more that fearsome wail was heard—this time from an opposite direction. The mountain wolf snarled lowly and turned to Snorri, who stood listening from across the bank of the frozen stream.

"What is it, Stacy?" asked Trevor anxiously.

Stacy put her finger to her lips and listened keenly. The distant cry was repeated again, but louder, closer.

"It's a warning," she whispered to the soldier.

"A warning? To whom?"

"To us, I think. Trevor, listen. Something's wrong. I don't know what, but the white wolves are not threatening us. They're communicating danger."

"Then why don't they speak with us? Stacy, I don't understand this."

The girl whirled. From off in the bushes came another sound—but not the silent moves of a wolf. It was a low grunt. A strange deep-throated sound, one that she could not identify. She drew her dagger and stepped uneasily toward the bushes.

Trevor grabbed her by the arm. "Where are you going?"

"Something's lurking, Trevor. We've got to find out what it is."

"Stay put, Stacy. That's an order! I don't want anyone out of sight." The command was firm; she held her place.

The strange sound came again, this time from behind. Stacy spun instinctively, dagger in hand.

Something large and dark-furred leaped from the thick boughs of a tree. It happened in a blur, in the white swirl above their heads. One of the Valley soldiers screamed and tumbled to the ground with the creature swarming over him. Trevor drew his sword and raced to the stricken soldier's side. Animal eyes glowered. He saw long fangs protruding from a baboonlike face. As Trevor raised his sword, the animal dodged and rolled. A strong gust of wind blew snow in his face; he lost his vision. He heard Cicero's growl and caught a brief glimpse of the wolf springing at the now unseen attacker. Another grunt, low and evil, sounded from the opposite direction. Melinda drew her bow. She spun on her heels and loosed her arrow. An unearthly scream shrilled through the air. Another dark-furred animal bounded away, leaving behind a thin trail of blood in the fresh snow.

Shouts, calls, and Alryc raised his long sword. It cut against the trunk of a tree, missing another fiend set to strike. For the next few moments there was total confusion. Stacy crouched, wielding her dagger. A hulking form with a huge head and the muzzle of a dog dodged the point of her knife and scurried away into the underbrush. Then there was silence. Tense and forbidding silence.

The girl stood there, waiting breathlessly. Robin was shivering; Melinda bent low, lips parted and trembling. Trevor and Alryc had raced to the side of the first fallen soldier. Alryc cradled the lad's head in his arms and gasped. The face had been slashed beyond recognition—deep gashes criss-crossing his entire face. His throat had been severed at the jugular; glassy eyes stared. Painfully the astronomer looked up to Trevor and shook his head. "He's gone."

Trevor came to his senses and called for a tight military defensive formation. They gathered in a small circle, covering one another's backs.

"What were those things?" rasped Trevor.

At his side, Stacy shrugged. Her face was pale, her lips trembled. "Hel's fire, I don't know. I've never seen *anything* like that before."

The soldier turned to the crouching wolf. "Cicero, what do you make of it?"

The mountain wolf shook his woolly head. "It's not of the forest," he growled, "nor of anywhere in our land. Such beasts I have never seen."

"They'll kill us all, Trevor," said Stacy. "That must have been why the white wolves warned us. They knew these *things* were about."

"We've got to get out of this place," exhorted Alryc, stroking the hilt of his sword. His dark eyes scanned the white shrubs and thickets, and he knew that this fight had not yet ended. Whatever had attacked them would come again. And again. Until they were all dead.

"We'll try to make it back to our camp," said Trevor, also with an eye to the landscape. "Then we'll make all speed and get back to the ridge and the ship. The *things* might come again at any moment."

"We can't make it back to the ship in this storm," advised the girl. "We'll be followed and tracked. We won't have a chance."

"Well, we can't very well stay here," snapped Trevor. "Fates above! Look about you, girl! We'll be caught in a blizzard! Our only hope is to get away from this place as quickly as possible and find some shelter!"

Stacy glared at the swirling snow, now falling harder than ever. Just one glance confirmed her belief that they would never make it back. There was just too much distance to cover. And by night the *things* could be swarming all over them.

Nervously she looked to the closest of the never-ending series of snowcapped peaks. As rugged as they were, she knew they were a far better refuge than these open lands. At least up there, atop the ridges, they might find a cave for shelter. "Up there," she said at last. "That's our only chance."

Trevor looked at her, astonished. "To the mountains? We can't go up there," he protested.

"We have to. It's the safest place we'll find. There'll be caves."

"Wolf dens, you mean. That's white wolf territory. Are you suggesting we march blindly into it?"

Stacy's eyes flashed angrily. "Can't you see the danger down here? You saw those *things,* saw what they did. They'll stalk us at will! It's either take shelter up there, or die down here!"

"Khalea is right," growled Cicero. "The mountains offer refuge. We must seek it."

"Even if it means confronting white wolves? Invite them to attack us?"

"I don't think so," replied Stacy. "If they wanted us killed, they wouldn't have given us that warning. But in any case it's better to face them than to confront those *things* again."

"We can come down after the storm," said Alryc. "In clear weather we'd have a fighting chance. But not now."

Trevor sighed, and bit pensively at frozen lips. The snow was blowing worse every minute. A cave would be good shelter. Good protection, too. He peered at the mountains gloomily.

"We can't lose time," reminded Alryc. "We must start now, before the storm worsens."

"Decide, Trevor," said the girl. "Which way do we go?"

Reluctantly he said, "To the mountains." He spun on his heels and faced his men. "Keep your weapons drawn," he commanded. "We don't know what we'll face when we reach that peak. Melinda, you and Robin take rear guard. Stacy, Cicero and I will take the lead. Alryc, you take the center with the others."

With hesitation they left the slain soldier lying in the snow. Alryc covered the limp body with the soldier's cloak and offered a silent prayer to the Fates. Then they moved out onto fresh snow in the direction of the mountains. Cautiously they crested the hill and stared at the huge peak that loomed before them. The wind blew bitter cold. Scarves bundled about their faces, they moved on, single file, farther into the desolation.

A thick layer of ice covered a winding stream. Cicero had been this way before and knew that it led to a plateau nestled a thousand meters up the mountain. There they might find shelter, he believed. But he also knew that reaching the plateau would be extremely hazardous.

They climbed at the side of a craggy ridge beset by snow-covered thornbushes amid the thick pines and firs. The summit seemed insurmountable—so high that it was completely obscured by clouds and mist. Ridge and counterridge broke here and there to allow glimpses of the deep gorges below. The steep climb began in earnest. They fought their way through a deep gash in the mountain wall, wide and craggy, with jutting boulders at every turn. More than once someone stumbled and nearly fell to the frozen ice-lake below. High on the face of towering cliffs they saw the approach to the plateau, a narrow slash in the sheer rock wall. At best it would allow their passage one at a time. To the left, a sheer drop down, was a great V-shaped gorge of snow-covered black granite. To the right stood yet another rock wall, broken only by the slot of another gorge.

Weary and frightened, numb from the bitter wind, they climbed on. Cicero picked his way carefully. Then Snorri, then Stacy right behind. Her hands grappled with the small crevices in the walls, her feet kept a steady footing against treacherously thick ice only inches below the fresh snow.

At last she reached the plateau. Behind her the white silhouettes of the others moved at a crawl. She could see the lumbering figure of Alryc helping the Valley soldiers. Without him, she knew, the lads would never make it.

Moments later Trevor came over the top. He cupped his hands and blew frigid clouds of air into them. His dark eyes searched the ridge. It was desolate. Only an occasional boulder or the bent trunk of a tree blocked the path that led to a sheer smooth wall some hundred meters away. Low against the wall, near the edge of the ridge and overlooking the ice-lake, there was a dark crevice. Half the size of a man in height, it seemed mysterious and forboding but as good a shelter as they were likely to find.

"Not much, is it?" sighed Trevor.

"It will do," grunted the mountain wolf. "I'll lead you."

Trevor shook his head and wiped snow from his eyes. "You stay here and wait for the others. Stacy and I will look together."

Cicero looked warily at the girl.

She nodded. "It's all right. We'll be careful."

Trevor nudged her elbow and pointed to a large drift before the mouth of the cave. "Careful, Stacy," he whispered. "Better let me go first."

The girl nodded and watched him slide forward one step at a time, testing the depth with each step. Suddenly

there was a snap, and Trevor's face contorted in a mask
of pain.

"My leg! It's my leg!" He groaned, trying to hold back
a scream.

With careless abandon the girl gave up all thought of
her own safety and dashed to his side. Taut features
beaded in cold sweat, he held his right leg with both
hands, moaning softly.

Stacy knelt down. "What is it?"

"I . . . don't know. . . . My leg. . . ." He groaned again,
ready to pass out.

She brushed aside loose snow and dug around the
mound in which he had fallen. Cicero bounded to them.
The girl's nimble fingers worked quickly; she exposed a
circular piece of rusting metal. On either side were small
springs, and latched to the springs were two large bars of
iron, with jagged teeth. The teeth had cut deeply into the
leather boot and had taken a firm hold on Trevor's flesh.

Alryc came at a run, carrying a thick branch in his
hand.

"It's a wolf trap, Alryc," panted the girl. "Old One told
me about them. They're used to catch white wolves."

The astronomer grimaced. "This time they've caught a
man," he said grimly. Bending down, he forced the branch
between the soldier's leg and the metal jaw and slowly
began to pry it open. Trevor howled in pain, then fainted.
"Hold him, Stacy! Hold him firm!" The girl nodded and
cradled his head in her lap. She took both of his trembling
hands and held them fast. Alryc pried with all his might,
loosened the teeth and yanked hard. The boot slipped out
and the jaws sprang shut with an echoing roar that made
Stacy shudder.

Alryc wiped his brow and drew a deep breath. It had
been close. A split second more and the trap would have
sprung around the leg once again and pierced it to the
bone.

"He's in a bad way, Stacy," he murmured worriedly.

"I know. What can we do? Have you anything in your pouch?" Stacy looked at him hopefully.

The astronomer frowned. "Only a few herbs and spices. He needs proper care. If that leg becomes infected, we'll have to cut it off."

Stacy put her hand to her mouth and gasped. The very thought made her tremble. Trevor would rather be dead than live like that, she knew, but what else could they do? She could not let him die.

"Maybe it won't come to that," said Alryc, seeing her anguish. "Let's get to the cave. At least there we can take off the boot and dress the wound."

Two soldiers ran over at Alryc's command. Together they lifted the wounded commander and brought him into the depths of the black grotto. Stacy waited outside until Robin, Melinda and the last soldier had entered. Then she got down on her knees and crawled inside as well. Then a sudden rush of warm air startled her. And she saw that, inside, the cave was far larger than any of them had dared hope. About three or four meters from the mouth the ceiling rose to great unexpected heights. There was more than enough room to stand fully erect. The walls seemed to be limestone and sparkled wetly with dull hues of brown and deep reds and purples. From some crevice or other she heard the constant drip-drip of seeping water. The ground was hard near the mouth, but farther back, close to the spot where the light stopped, it seemed to soften considerably. She even saw small weeds growing against the jagged walls and what looked like a narrow tunnel leading down into a shaft of some kind. But these matters could be looked into later. The long night had begun to set in and the snow showed no sign of letting up, so the first order of business was to make certain that Trevor was being cared for and then see that the rest of them did not freeze to death before the blizzard ended.

"How is he?" she asked, standing beside pensive Melinda and peering down at the straining Alryc. Already the astronomer had carefully taken off the torn boot and was washing the swollen gaping wounds with a handful of fresh snow. Then he reached inside a small pouch at his waist and withdrew a soft, clean bandage. Before wrapping the oozing wound, he pressed a small herb tightly against it. "This should help," he mumbled. "I'm not a physician, but the healing arts are familiar to me. This herb is one used by hunters in the Free Lands. They say it works well on wounds like this."

Stacy bit her lip. "But that's not just a wound."

Alryc nodded. "It's a deep gash. Almost straight to the bone. I fear that even if the wound does heal he'll never walk properly again."

A cripple! The words slashed at her like thrown knives. She had let him walk first and test the drifts by himself. She should have known better. It was her fault that he was hurt.

"Well?"

She snapped out of her thought to see Alryc looking at her questioningly. "I'm sorry," she said. "What did you say?"

"I asked if you thought we could find enough dry wood in here to make ourselves a small fire. I have flints."

The girl looked about, caught sight of the weeds again and noticed bits and pieces of dried wood strewn about. "There'll be enough. If not, we can gather some from outside."

"Good. Then why don't you get to that? Leave Trevor to me. There's nothing you can do for him, anyway."

It took but a short while. Melinda and Robin helped search the lighted part of the cave and soon there was more than enough tinder for the fire. Cicero and Snorri kept a careful eye on the mouth of the grotto, watching for signs of either white wolves or the dreaded *things* that had attacked below. Save for the constant fall of the blinding snow they saw nothing.

The fire was lit and brought instant warmth. The walls of the cave came alive in splashes of bright colors. The flames flickered and danced, sending eerie shadows racing above their heads across the concave ceiling. The three Valley soldiers took out their pouches and passed around the few rations they had. Everyone ate somberly, without speaking. Every few moments Trevor would moan in an uneasy sleep and Stacy would turn to him with distraught eyes. He sometimes smiled as she comforted him by running her fingers lightly through his hair or kissing him softly on his brow, tenderly reassuring him.

At last, when the meal was done, when everyone sat huddled together and tried to sleep, Alryc and Stacy slipped away by themselves. The astronomer greeted her with a worried look when they were alone.

"The snows could last for days," he whispered in a husky tone. "And our cave won't make a good shelter for much longer."

Stacy sat with her back against the wall, sifting the soft dirt through her fingers. "That's what I've been thinking. We'll starve up here. We're going to have to go below after all."

"To face the *things* again? No, my lady. In any case, the snows will be too heavy for us to negotiate the tricky path down. Better then to stay up here and take our chances."

"But we can't! What will we eat? And what about Trevor? He needs help. If we can get back to the ship. . . ."

Alryc looked at her kindly but with an awareness in his eyes that told her he knew she was speaking from her heart and not from her forest-sense. "We cannot carry him, Stacy. Perhaps in several days' time, if the wound is better, we can make a splint. Then maybe he can struggle on his own. But not by tomorrow."

The girl sighed. She knew full well that everything Alryc had said was true. There was no way they could leave this place even if Trevor had not been so badly hurt. "What do you suggest, then?"

"That we comb the cave. Go deep into the passageways. I've heard that creatures dwell in places such as this. Lizards, mice." He shrugged. "When you're about to starve, even they'll look good enough to eat. And besides, you've heard the dripping water. There must be underground springs somewhere down there. That will mean some kind of vegetation for us to eat."

Stacy glanced down the narrow passageway and saw that it seemed to wind and twist on an ever downward spiral right into the bowels of the mountain. "How far below might that tunnel lead?"

Alryc shrugged. "Who knows? But what does it matter. We can make torches. We'll mark our path with stones and follow the water. With luck that underground lake or stream will lead us out of here. What do you say, Stacy? Shall we explore?"

She felt taken aback at the way the question was asked. "Why do you say that, Alryc? Am I suddenly in command?"

The astronomer smiled kindly with soft eyes and took her hand in his own. "Ah, my lady. Don't you know it yet? You've been the one to lead ever since the day we reached this strange land. We look to you, not to Trevor or Elias. The Rangers realized it first; your wolves knew it all along. You *are* the leader of this band. You may not realize or accept it yet, but you are."

Stacy sat quietly for a long while. She had always thought of herself as one among the many. Perhaps as a leader of the wolves, or even the Rangers, now that Sandra was gone. But of everyone? On the sea it was Elias they had looked to. Here, on the shores of this wild land, it was supposed to be Trevor. She glanced at the injured soldier and suddenly realized that whether she wanted the job or not, it was forced upon her. There was no one else. She would have to be strong for all their sakes.

"All right, Alryc, tomorrow we'll begin our search of the passageway. Make torches for us and leave one of the soldiers behind with Trevor. The wolves will come with us; we'll be needing their help."

Alryc readily agreed. He took her hand again and squeezed it tightly until Stacy winced. She tried to pull away, but he kept the grip firm, locking his wizened eyes into hers. "This is meant to be, Stacy," he told her. "I have always known it—and I think you knew it, too."

Stacy looked away. "It frightens me, Alryc. I don't know if I'm ready to lead. I don't know if the others behind, at the ship, will want it." She shivered, suddenly feeling the cold as never before.

"You cannot change the stars, my lady. Men such as I will live and die, our names never to be remembered. But yours may well live forever. Keep that thought with you always, even when things appear their blackest. Listen to the wind, child. Does it not speak to you?"

Stacy nodded fearfully. Outside Aleya was howling and screaming in a way she had never known. There was a message upon Aleya's breath, she knew, although she was not yet certain she could understand it. "Aleya always speaks to me, Alryc. I've known it since I was a child. I know her better than the wolves, better than any Dweller."

"And the whale, Salome? She spoke with you, also?"

Again Stacy nodded. "Yes, once. The day we first sighted land. She said she had brought me to safety."

The astronomer smiled a knowing smile. Stacy realized he was keeping other thoughts hidden from her, but she dared not ask why because the answer might only frighten her more. She remembered a dream she had often had these past weeks. In the dream she saw two open roads. One would lead to glory and fame, the other to mystery and danger. One road was as bright as *Balaka,* the other as black as the pits of Hel. The right road was for her to choose. And Aleya sang: *"Khalea, Khalea, let me be your guide. Let me find for you the way; let me take you to the crown. For so long I have waited; for the birth of the Empire Princess."*

CHAPTER TWENTY-ONE

The shaft of the passageway slanted downward at a sharp angle; flames from the torches sent shadows leaping across the walls. Cicero growled at the sight of the winding tunnel, putting his head low and sniffing at the dank, musty air. Stacy peered back over her shoulder, past her companions, to the mouth of the cave. Trevor was sleeping more peacefully now. The young soldier staying behind with him sat close by his side, placing small pieces of kindling onto the smoldering fire. She turned back toward the tunnel, and with both wolves at her side, and Alryc right behind, she led them single file down into the dark.

After a few minutes the tunnel grew wider. At either side stood strange rock formations, pillarlike, rising from the earth. Stony, icicle-shaped stalactites hung down from above as if ready to fall upon them like great swords. Moss spread beneath their feet, weed and slime clung to the walls.

The dripping became louder; the tunnel twisted upward. As they walked, their feet disturbed thick layers of dust. Stacy stumbled among bits of crumbling stone. Suddenly there was a glimmer of daylight. Looking up, shading her eyes from the brightness, she saw a small fissure amid the jumbled rock of the ceiling, allowing strong streams of light to pour down across the tunnel.

Cicero cautiously moved ahead, past the fissure. He

stopped abruptly and snarled. Stacy signaled for the others to wait and followed his sound cautiously.

"What is it, Cicero?" she whispered, her canine eyes darting to and fro.

"The tunnel, Khalea. Look. It opens into two passages. One winds up, the other down, deeper into the earth."

The girl listened intently. Dripping water sounds were coming from the downward passage. "We'll take that one," she said authoritatively.

As the others reached them, she led the way to the shaft on the left and once again they began a sharp descent. Here the earth became hard; sharp stones dug through their boots, slashing through the leather. Torchlight flickered, and small lizards dashed into the grim recesses of the wall.

After a while, the tunnel flattened and became wide again. It opened quite suddenly into a vast cavern of pillars and scattered boulders. In the middle there was a dark pool of water with what seemed to be a small stream feeding it as it wound down from somewhere above.

Stacy and Alryc knelt beside it and put the water to their mouths. "It's fresh," said the astronomer. "There must be a constant supply coming down from above."

Stacy agreed. They all rested for a while after they drank their fill. The water was cold and good, pure and fresh. As the others relaxed, rubbing at blistered feet and stretching aching muscles, Stacy used the time to explore a little bit deeper. Using a torch borrowed from one of the soldiers, she moved from the cavern into the twisting shaft that began across the water. It was long and deep and would take a long time to fully explore. But its steady downward slant convinced her that it might eventually lead them to the base of the mountain, perhaps to some hidden exit. And if there were one, they could go down the mountain without having to make the treacherous descent in snow. She ran back and brought Alryc to see.

The astronomer concurred, much to her relief. "Shall we continue, then?" he asked.

Stacy nodded. "We might as well. Call the others." Then Cicero and Snorri, eyes glowing, moved out into the dark and were soon well ahead, out of sight.

Stacy led the band forward. Suddenly the air began to heat. After a short while, they were forced to slow down, discard their jackets. Strange, thought Stacy, she had expected the depths of the cave to be warm, sheltered as it was from the outside world, but not like this. It was a lulling warmth like a fire, making them drowsy.

"Can't we rest a while?" asked Melinda with a yawn.

Stacy shook her head violently. "Absolutely not! We've got to keep going—" A distant sound sent them whirling.

The Ranger girl's mouth hung open. "Stacy! Listen!"

Stacy froze in her place; so did everyone else. A low sound came again, dull and far away—but strangely familiar.

"Fara above!" cried Stacy. She recognized the sound— and it sent chills down her spine. *Things!*

She glanced back in the direction of the pool. A shadow passed beneath the dim light of Alryc's torch.

"They're behind us!" cried Robin, tightening her fingers around her bow.

The grunts grew louder. Fiercer. Descending down the shaft came a pack of hairy creatures, half baboon, half man. Alryc pushed his torch at arm's length, toward them. For the first time they stood face to face with the dreaded *things*.

They were large creatures, although smaller than men, long-limbed with sharp razorlike claws at the end of long bony fingers. Their faces were muzzled, more or less apelike, but the small eyes showed a measure of cunning and intelligence. Fangs projected from the lips of gaping mouths. In their hands they wielded sticks and clubs and sharp swordlike pieces of rock. Then they began to advance.

They shrieked warcries and abruptly leaped down the passage with savage swiftness. Stacy whirled, plunging her dagger into the gut of the foul-smelling lead attacker. The creature moaned and tore madly at her with his claws. She dodged deftly to the side, drew out the bloody blade and plunged it again and again into the furry cap of light-colored hair at the back of its neck. The animal staggered, then slumped down in a heap at her feet.

Twang!

Melinda's bow sang brightly. The arrow smacked cleanly between the eyes of another dreaded *thing*. Its companions pushed it aside and came charging, heaving clubs and rock swords. The soldiers met the blows with their blades. Metal clashed on rock, sparks flew. Alryc pushed his torch against the fur of another. Its coat ablaze, the *thing* ran shrieking down the passage, a living ball of flame, howling in torment.

Again Melinda let loose an arrow. Yet another *thing* crumpled at her feet, groping about darkly as the girl drew her dagger and slit its throat. The grunting and wailing became terrible. The band moved back and huddled closely together as the creatures began to regroup and charge again.

"We've got to get out of here!" cried Alryc frantically.

But to where? Stacy peered over her shoulder. The passage seemed blacker and more frightening than ever before. But then she smiled. From out of that dimness came the racing wolves. From their advance position they had heard the fray and were now bounding back to help. Cicero leaped high and brought down another attacker. The *thing* screamed in abject terror as the wolf's weight slammed it across hard ground. Other *things* stumbled over it, waving rock swords, and charged again in strength. Stacy gasped at the sight. There seemed to be no end to their numbers!

A scream from behind. She spun to see one of the soldiers fall, a *thing* climbing over his back. Again she plunged the silver dagger. Snorri crouched, then leaped high. Another *thing* fell back dazed. Fangs sunk ever deeper. The creature moaned and doubled over. As it did, Alryc's sword severed its head from its massive shoulders and sent it rolling down the passageway.

"Into the depths, Khalea!" snarled Cicero, dark blood dripping from his fangs. "We can't hold our ground much longer!"

The band pressed themselves ever deeper into the passage. The *things* grouped to follow. Stacy and Cicero covered the others as they fled. At their feet lay no less than a dozen fallen fiends. Wolf cries filled the air, above the frantic wails of the enemy. With each moment Cicero and the girl gained in courage, even as the *things* began to cower. Stacy fought like a true huntress, Cicero like the wild mountain wolf he was. Slowly the creatures fell back to lick their wounds. Then Stacy and Cicero turned and fled down the passage, to where the others crouched in wait.

"What now?" asked a pale and drawn Melinda who rested with her crossbow between her legs. The exhausted group sat scattered about gloomily, except for Alryc who was busy dressing a deep wound that a soldier had sustained. He gave little consideration to the needle-thin cuts crisscrossed over his own body. Stacy glanced about pensively and said, "We can't go back the way we came, that's certain. We'll have to keep moving and hope this tunnel will finally take us down the mountain."

"But what about Trevor?" asked a shaking Robin. "Shouldn't we try to get back for him?"

Ruefully, Stacy shook her head. "We can't go back. We'd never make it. But he'll be safe at the cave. I don't think the *things* will look for him. They're too concerned about us. We're the enemy now, and they'll be back to deal with us."

"Then we'd better not tarry," said Alryc glumly. "Those *things* won't be licking their wounds for long."

Off again they went, farther into the bowels of the mountain, alert for the return of the fiends. Gradually the tunnel became hotter. Stacy touched the walls. Warm as an oven, she realized with trepidation. Neither she nor any of the others had any explanation for this phenomenon. At length the tunnel once again straightened, then opened into what could only be described as a vast underground canyon. On either side loomed huge bluffs and pillars of tinted purple-red granite beneath a high ceiling. At the end of the canyon, high above a crooked archway, there was a distant shaft, and from the shaft came a gleam of light, pale and fine as a needle. It was then, and only then, that they began to realize they had long ago passed the ground level of the mountain. They were now beneath it, far underground, and with still no sign of a hidden exit that would bring them back into the open.

It was there, exhausted and hungry, that they rested beside a shallow stream and ate the last of their meager provisions. It was a glum meal. Meanwhile, Cicero and Snorri used the time to scout the tunnel ahead again.

"Very strange, Khalea," snorted the mountain wolf when he came back. "Ahead are more tunnels, all leading deeper into other great shafts."

Stacy raised her brows. "What do you make of it?"

"I think the shafts lead into other mountains. Very odd, Khalea. The walls are sheer, smooth as stones in the sea."

"Perhaps we'd better have a look," she said, becoming increasingly curious about this forboding world.

She and Alryc followed the wolf through the maze of tunnels. At the end of the first they stood and gaped in the light of Alryc's torch. Before them stood no less than four concave shafts, all running at slight downward angles; all, as the wolf had said, smooth as marble. Stacy went to examine the first. Alryc stood peering from behind, and when the girl glanced at him, he whispered, "These tunnels were made by men, it seems to me."

The girl's eyes widened at this astounding statement.

"Man-made? Are you sure, Alryc? Maybe the walls are smooth like this because they've had no contact with the elements for thousands of years."

The astronomer ran his fingers gently along the closest wall. Then he bent down and touched the floor. Dust gave way, exposing what appeared to be a pattern in the surface. Dim colors, badly faded, criss-crossed from one side to the next, a pattern that could have been a mosaic of some kind chiseled into the stone.

"Alryc," said Stacy with puzzlement, "is it possible that men might still dwell down here? Under the mountains?"

The astronomer shrugged and looked hard down the dark tunnel. "Perhaps, my lady. Men may have been forced down here at one time because of hostile elements above."

"Like *things*?"

He nodded darkly. "Or even white wolves. Who can say? But these tunnels have been unused for years. See how thick the dust is."

"They must lead somewhere," said Stacy. "There's got to be a way out, wherever it takes us. We'll get some sleep, then start afresh in a few hours. Meanwhile let's get back to the others. I don't like leaving them alone."

The astronomer nodded and smiled. Stacy, despite her own doubts about herself, had assumed her new role quite easily.

A few hours later, rested, they set out again. The air became more stuffy and dank. They moved more swiftly now, since the floor was firm. From time to time Stacy marveled at the intensity of the colors that marked the strange passage. Even though long centuries had probably passed since the tunnels were last used, the walls still glittered and shone. Spiders and small mice abounded, especially as the dim light at the end of the tunnel began to grow larger. What at first had been little more than a pinprick of light soon gave way to a dazzling swell of almost blinding color. They came to a bright-crimson open corridor, with a ceiling so far above their heads it made them dizzy to look up. The walls were smooth, the broken tile floor now covered with dust. At the far end of the corridor stood an archway, man-made, and behind it, what appeared to be a sheet of solid rock from floor to ceiling.

Alryc gently ran his hands up and down the sides, then said, "I think this might be some kind of secret door. But see how firmly it's constructed. We'll never be able to push it open, I fear."

"Perhaps we won't have to," replied the girl. She ran her own hands over it. "There must be a hidden spring, something that will unlatch———"

Just as she spoke there was a dull moan. Her finger had pressed against a well-hidden recess. As the rock slid slowly to the side, they were met with a sudden gust of cold air. Stacy threw her jacket over her shoulders and peered inside. There were alarming noises within, and she stepped back.

"Things?" asked Alryc, fondling his weapon nervously.

The girl shook her head. "I don't think so. Listen."

From far away came a series of soft, ethereal sounds. Alryc looked perplexed. Melinda strained her ears to listen and then said, "It sounds like bells. Little bells."

"It's black as Hel inside there," said Robin uneasily.

"But maybe it offers a way out," replied Stacy. "Alryc, give me your torch." The astronomer reluctantly handed it to her, and the girl boldly stepped inside. A strong gust of air blew out the fire. Shivering from the cold, she came back out puzzled and worried.

"It's like a blizzard in there," she said. "And the winds———" She held up the blown-out torch. The soldier relit it with his own.

"It must be a draft wind," said Alryc, "sweeping down from the mountaintops."

Stacy sighed with worry. If they were to continue, it would have to be in the dark, the almost total darkness that she had just experienced.

"Perhaps we should go back and choose another tunnel," said Alryc.

"No. There's something to be found at the end of this cavern, I'm sure. You hear those bells, don't you? Cicero, go first. Snorri and I will lead the others."

And as she expected, within seconds the other torches had blown out. The wind whooshed down from above. They pulled their collars tightly about them and formed a single line. It took long minutes until Stacy's eyes adjusted to the dark. Then she saw new massive walls looming on either side of their path. The tinkling of bells grew louder all around them. Stacy peered up, straining to determine from where the sound was coming. But the blowing winds and echoes made it impossible.

Suddenly there came another sound: the low grunt of *things!*

From all around the grunts and wails intensified. Stacy realized they were trapped. And where could they possibly run? "Keep moving!" she cried, sensing the terror of her sightless companions. The *things* stood back, lurking in the dark shadows, small eyes glowing. But they had yet to make a move to fight.

The *things* began to circle, pressing forward. Alryc made a frantic effort to light his torch. The flints struck brightly for an instant, revealing the ugly faces of the creatures. Stacy wielded her dagger menacingly in their direction. They grunted among themselves and snarled but still they seemed reluctant to attack. Stacy couldn't understand why. Her group was outnumbered, caught in total darkness in a place they neither knew nor understood. It was a perfect trap. Why did the *things* linger? What were they waiting for?

An alarming note sounded; one of the creatures darted directly into Stacy's path, emitting squeals and barks that sounded uncannily canine. Frightened, Stacy thrust her knife. The *thing* dodged and ran off to the shadows. Another noise—one from above. Stacy whirled as a huge net abruptly descended, entangling them all. Stacy squirmed and wheeled about, caught in its knotted folds. The cord was rough and thick; she worked her dagger with a frenzy. Around her, Robin and Melinda fell to the floor, entangled and screaming for help. Cicero growled and fought to free himself, but the more he twisted and turned the tighter the grip of the net became. They were snared—like beasts!

Screams of *things* filled the night as other forms, dark, swarthy, literally seemed to leap from hidden walls. Alryc stumbled and grappled with the net as the twine wound around his throat. The *things* were now running all about, leaping and climbing all over the net, but they seemed unconcerned about Stacy and her companions, concerned only with fleeing the net as fast as possible.

Panic raced through Stacy like a thunderbolt. Her eyes could make out only the scantest of images. Blurs. *Things* wailing and falling, heaving rock swords in futility as other, more furious, weapons flashed and swept upon them. Bright lights flashed, and she felt her head spin like a whirlpool. The growls of the wolves grew dim—where were they? With all her effort, amid the raging tumult, she tried to raise herself to her knees. A blinding white light flashed before her eyes; a thousand stars came rushing at her. There was a sharp pain in the back of her neck, and clumsily she fell, a fall that felt like the descent into a bottomless pit. And that was the last thing she knew.

CHAPTER TWENTY-TWO

She awoke in semidarkness. Very, very slowly and painfully, bit by bit, she let her eyes focus and became aware of the shapes around her. Above was a stone ceiling, seamed, and she realized that she was lying on something soft, a cot or a bed. The room itself, if you could call it that, was quite small, not much larger than the cabin she had shared with Melinda aboard the *Brora*. There were no windows, at least within her view, and no light save for the dim globe light that glowed from above. Soft hands were busy massaging the back of her neck. She barely had the energy to turn her head and see who they belonged to.

"Feeling better?" said a friendly voice.

She managed to twist around and peered up into the worried but smiling face of Melinda. The girl's tunic was torn at the shoulder and hem, as though she had grappled with some unknown attacker. Her long hair was windblown, but she held herself with the poise and calm that were a Ranger's trademark.

Lifting herself, Stacy saw that one of her wrists was encircled by an iron ringlet attached to a long heavy chain secured to yet another ring embedded in the opposite wall. Clearing a dry throat, she managed to ask, "Where are we?"

Melinda laughed bitterly. "I don't even know *how* we got here, let alone where."

Stacy frowned. "Well, how long have we been here?"

"More than a day, I think. But I've yet to see anything besides these walls and these chains." She held up her hand and showed Stacy that she, too, was attached to an iron bracelet.

"Where's Robin?"

Melinda shrugged, sighing deeply.

"Alryc?"

"Don't know that, either, Stacy. But I do know I'm frightened." She bit her trembling lip.

Stacy forced herself to sit up. She reached out and took Melinda's hand. "Don't worry, Melinda. We'll find some way out of this," she assured her bravely.

The Ranger sniffed and smiled, then gestured to the corner of the prison. "There's food here, Stacy. That is, if you can stomach eating."

Stacy glanced to the corner and saw two large bowls, each filled with a cold muttonlike stew, and beside them, a pitcher, a colorful clay urn.

"It's water. I found it there when I awoke," Melinda said.

Stacy took a long draft from the pitcher, ignoring the food. The water was cold and fresh.

"What will become of us now?" Melinda said with a quiver in her voice. "I keep thinking that everyone else is dead, killed by *things,* and they've taken us here as prisoners. Toys to play with when they're bored."

"It wasn't *things* that brought us here," said Stacy, frowning in recollection.

Melinda's eyes widened. "How do you know?"

"Don't you remember what happened after the net fell? There was some sort of a fight. It happened so fast I'm unclear about it myself. But the *things* were attacked by something else. Some kind of shadowy, furry figures. I don't know, Melinda. I'm confused, too. But believe me, it wasn't *things* that caught us. It was something else."

Melinda sat on the edge of her own cot and put her

head in her hands. Stacy leaned over, the iron chain now taut, and touched her friend's cheek gently. "We're both still alive," she said gently, "and that means the others probably are, too. Whoever caught us can't be too cruel, otherwise they'd never have left that food for us. We'll be safe, Melinda. You'll see."

"Do you really think so, Stacy? I mean really?"

Stacy lied. "Yes. And I'll wager we're a lot better off here than down in the caves."

"If you ask me, I'd say we still *are* in the caves. Look, the walls are limestone. And if you touch them, you'll see that they're warm, the same way they were in the tunnels."

Stacy reached out to the rough stone above her cot. It *was* warm. And where the room should have been damp and stuffy, it was quite the opposite. The air was fresh. Hidden vents must have brought down fresh air from above; the room temperature was comfortable.

She let her eyes glance to the hinged door of solid rock set into the opposite wall. A small catch clicked, and a long metal bar slid open. Stacy gasped at the sight of two dark eyes peering at her. She leaped to the door, but her chain prevented her from reaching it. "Who are you?" she demanded. No answer came. The eyes continued to watch. "I demand that you release us right now!"

The strange eyes glared for a moment longer, cold and aloof, then the window slid shut. Frustration and anger burned inside Stacy, but there was nothing she could do. With a scowl she dropped back onto her cot and seethed. Melinda looked at her nervously. "I'm frightened again, Stacy."

Stacy sighed. "Me, too. But at least those were human eyes. We're not being held by *things*."

Melinda's eyes widened, and she put her hand to her mouth. "Hush, Stacy!"

Stacy froze. From beyond the door came a heavy shuffling of boots and the soft murmur of speech. A rattle of keys, the sound of a lock opening, and then the door was pushed wide open. Two stout men, bearded, wearing scarlet cloaks and belts of mail, shortswords dangling, pushed into the room. Their eyes were dark and fiery, faces lined and rugged. Crests above their hearts told her instantly that they were soldiers of some sort. They stood at either side of the door, barely glancing at the two frightened girls, who jumped to their feet, hearts racing.

Then into the room strode a woman—young, perhaps several years older than Stacy. Tall, with long, flowing, yellow hair, she stopped by the entrance, eyes examining the two captives. Ice-blue eyes, deep and brooding, with calculating intelligence behind them. On her head she wore a resplendent gold diadem. A gold bracelet inlaid with intricate design dangled loosely from a slim wrist. She wore a caftan, blue to match her eyes. Fastened at her left shoulder was a silver brooch, a fleur-de-lis, with a tiny translucent emerald that glowed and dazzled in the light.

A snap of her fingers brought a third soldier into the room. He grabbed Melinda's wrist and unlocked the chain. Then he did the same for Stacy. And all the while the yellow-haired girl kept her eyes, cold and mistrustful, locked on Stacy's. There was a definite regal air about her. She whispered in a low voice and the soldiers left the room. The language was rough and guttural, yet it did not seem entirely different from that of the Empire. Stacy wondered at the curious similarity between these people and those of her own Empire.

The yellow-haired girl said something directly to her. Something about "dark" and "nets." Stacy was puzzled and shook her head in bewilderment.

The girl fumed and this time spoke slowly, in a clear distinct voice. "Can you understand now?" she asked.

Stacy nodded.

"How came you to the nets?"

"You mean the net that snared us? By accident. We were seeking a way from the tunnels."

A hard slap across the face staggered her. She regained her posture and glared back at her captor.

"You will address me by my title!" snapped the girl.

Stacy rubbed gently at the side of her face, felt the sting linger. "What title is that?"

Her questioner looked at her with astonishment. "From which *shala* do you come?" she demanded.

A voice boomed from the corridor. "That will be all, Rani!"

The yellow-haired girl spun around and lowered her eyes at the sight of a tall hawk-nosed man entering the room. She crossed her arms over her breasts and lowered her head respectfully. "I was told to unchain them, Minister," she said curtly. "Are you questioning my authority?"

The man frowned and looked to Stacy and Melinda, then back to her. "To unchain them, no, Mistress Sigried. To interrogate them, yes."

Sigried flushed with anger but said nothing. Stacy took a quick measure of the man and saw that he, too, wore a crest above his heart, the image of a black peregrine falcon emblazoned into his robe. Whoever he was, it was apparent to her that his own rank was superior to the Rani, Sigried.

"You may leave, Rani," he said with a note of authority. "I shall take charge now."

Yellow-haired Sigried shook her head vehemently. "I have as much right to be at the questioning as you do," she hissed, fire burning in her ice-blue eyes.

The older man sighed. "Very well. We'll *both* escort them. Have the others been taken from their cells?"

Stacy felt her heart leap. *The others!* Alryc and the rest were all alive after all!

"They are waiting at the hall," replied Sigried dourly, but still with respect. "These two women are the last."

The man nodded. "Very thorough, Rani. As usual." He clapped his hands and the soldiers outside snapped to attention. Then he turned to Stacy and Melinda. "Follow me, please. Your companions are waiting for you."

With the soldiers following directly behind, the minister and Sigried in front, Stacy and Melinda were led silently down the long dim passage. Stacy let her hand slide down to her dagger. It was then, for the first time, she realized it was missing. The scabbard was still there, but the blade had been lifted. Her eyes glanced briefly at Melinda's waist. Her blade, too, was gone.

Shadows leaped across the high rock ceilings as they reached the incline of the corridor. To their right stretched another passage, parallel to this one, divided from it by a low wall. The roof above gradually became lower as they continued, increasing the multitude of shadows. Ironwood torches grew in frequency, suspended at sharp angles from the walls. Melinda seemed to hesitate with almost every step, but Stacy found herself walking with a strong stride that surprised her. If nothing else, she was determined to appear calm and relaxed and not let her mounting fears show—at least not while Sigried was there. *But only she could see the sky!*

As they walked, the passage sloped increasingly upward. Stacy became certain they were winding their way higher inside what could only be an enormous mountain. And she wondered just how far from the original cave they really were. At length they emerged from the labyrinth into what was no less than the most spectacular sight she had ever seen.

Above, the mica-encrusted ceiling rose to what must have been a hundred meters high. And from somewhere, far above, thin streams of brilliant sunlight poured throughout, bathing the cavern in warmth and light. What a cavern it was! A great hall, worthy of the finest king in a book of fables. As big as a castle!

Hanging from the walls were large disks of silver and bronze, each depicting scenes of snow-swept mountains and vast panoramas of the sea and the hills of the lowlands. Huge torches of ironwood burned at every turn. And beneath them stood more guards. Stacy's mind flashed. She stared at the furs and realized that it was these men, hidden as they had been by the blackness, who had been the dark furry beasts that fought with the *things* in the black cavern when the nets fell.

The floors were lined with thick-piled rugs, and here and there the pelt or head of an enormous bear. A long carpet, dyed a deep indigo that recalled the spires of Rhonnda, ran from the entrance to a low platform far at the other end of the hall. On each side of the carpet stood throngs of onlookers. Bearded men dressed in colorful togas and long, fitted robes; women wearing soft linen fabric. Whispers and murmurs filled the hall; Stacy felt as though she were being gaped at like some strange animal.

The minister turned and faced Stacy, signaling with his hand for them to wait. From another entrance, leading from another tunnel, Stacy supposed, came a handful of soldiers. One yanked roughly at a chain behind him. And it was then that she saw Cicero and Snorri. Both wolves had heavy choke collars around their necks—so tight that even the slightest movement of their heads made them wince with pain. The wolves were being dragged into the chamber, the sharp tips of the guards' spears jabbing at them from either side.

As the crowd caught sight of the wolves, they gasped; some cringed, some looked in horror. Cicero's eyes caught Stacy's and he growled. The chain pulled fiercely, the collar tightened. In pain the wolf stumbled, a spear swiftly at his throat. The minister waved a hand and the soldier lifted the spear. The other soldier holding the chain loosened his grip. Cicero bounded to his feet, snarling.

"Enough of this!" hissed Sigried. She looked around, glared at Stacy, then said, "The prince awaits you."

Across the purple carpet they walked, the wolves right behind. More gasps rose from the crowd as they recoiled at the sight of these unknown strangers.

Upon the platform toward which they walked was a man

sitting on a throne, dressed in a crested woolen tunic, with thin black stripes running from the V of the neck across his heart. His face was stern but not cruel. Dark, deep-set, intelligent eyes studied the strangers.

The minister stepped forward, crossed his arms over his chest and bowed respectfully. Sigried did the same. The prince nodded and gestured for them to stand. He looked at Stacy, to Melinda, then to the wolves. "And the others?" he asked casually of the minister.

The minister gestured grandly. From behind thick curtains strode Alryc, his hands bound with heavy iron shackles. Behind him came Robin, and after her the Valley soldier, Kent. Alryc walked proud and tall, the way Stacy knew he would. Written across his lined face was a scowl and a look of defiance. Even his chains had not diminished his fiery stance. If anything, they intensified it. Shoulders back, chin high, he gazed coolly at the man on the throne.

Robin and Kent, however, showed none of his courage. Unbound they walked slowly, heads bowed, nervously darting their eyes at the glistening blades of scimitars.

"There is still another prisoner," announced the minister after the group had been gathered before the prince.

The prince raised his brows in speculation. "Oh?"

"A wounded one," added Sigried, with open contempt aimed directly at Stacy. "We found him huddled at the mouth of a cave with a companion. The companion was dead."

Trevor! They had found Trevor! Stacy breathed with thankful relief.

"The man is being attended to by our physicians," informed the minister. "His leg has been severely injured and he is in high fever. I thought it best to let him be until later."

The prince looked at Alryc, then directed his words to the hawk-nosed minister. "And why is *this* man in chains?"

"He gave us much trouble, my liege. We were forced to keep him bound lest he strike at us like a madman."

The prince appraised Alryc's powerful frame. "I see. Are you the leader?" he asked. "What is your name?"

The astronomer scowled and rattled his chains menacingly. "I am Alryc of the Blue Fires. And if my hands were free, I would show you whether I am a leader or a follower!"

The prince's eyes narrowed angrily. "You seem to beg for your death, Alryc of the Blue Fires. Are you so eager to die?"

"I am eager only that my chains be lifted," shot back the astronomer. "And that I be treated more like a man than a dog!"

Sigried sneered. "Let me deal with them, my liege."

The prince shook his head. "No, Rani. At least not yet. They are strangers. Better that we know more about them."

"Spies, you mean! Have done with them *now*—before more ill comes of it!" She shot a hateful glance at Stacy and said; "Speak, girls! From what *shala* have you come?"

Stacy drew a long breath and gritted her teeth. "I told you before, I don't know what you mean. I don't even know what a *shala* is."

"Ha!" cooed the blustery Sigried. "Do you see? She will answer none of our questions! Let me put my knife to her pretty face, my lord! *Then* she might have a few things to say!"

She waved a tiny dagger at Stacy's face, pointing the tip at her jugular. It all happened in a flash. Stacy whirled and grabbed the startled Rani by the arm and hauled her to the floor. Alryc raised his powerful arms, brought the iron manacle down on the neck of an unsuspecting soldier. Melinda kicked swiftly, literally wrenching the scimitar from another, and threw it to Stacy, while Snorri threw his weight against the guard holding his leash and broke free. Screams of panic swept throughout the hall. Bowstrings twanged, and Snorri slumped to the floor, an arrow through his neck. A dozen fierce soldiers came racing from behind. The prince rose from his throne and raised his hands. "Hold!" he thundered.

Everyone froze in their spots.

Stacy crouched, scimitar in hand, and pressed it at Sigried's neck. "Move one of your men and I'll kill your Rani! I swear it!"

"Do so," replied the prince coolly, "and all your lives are forfeit. Is it worth it? Would you see your companions die?"

Stacy bit her trembling lips and looked around. At that moment she would have given her own life gladly, but how could she bear the blame for the deaths of her companions? Reluctantly she took the curved blade and flung it down. A harried soldier ran and hastily picked it up. As other soldiers drew around the captives with their drawn swords, Stacy knelt down and gently closed Snorri's eyes. Blood ran over her hands. Onlookers, horrified, watched with amazement. Even the prince stared. "Why do you have pity for the wolf?" he asked, astonished.

Stacy glanced up through watery eyes. "Not pity. I cry for a friend."

"She is bewitched!" cried the shaken Sigried. "I demand their deaths! All of them!"

The prince ignored her. He was completely intrigued by the sight of the girl and her tears for the dead wolf. "Why have you such love for a beast?" he asked.

Stacy lowered her eyes. At her side Cicero stood frozen. "I told you. He was a friend," she replied. "He once risked his life for me."

Sigried raised a hand to her mouth; her face whitened. "She *is* a sorceress! And the giant—he is a sorcerer! They must be dealt with at once." She glared at her liege.

"Be still, Rani!" the prince commanded. "This is not your father's city! It is mine! And I will decide what is to be done!"

Sigried bowed her head and crossed her arms. "As you

will, Prince Sumavand. But know that my father shall hear of it."

Sumavand's eyes narrowed. "I am certain of that, Rani. I give you permission to withdraw." His tone was bitter.

The girl stepped back a few paces, turned, then raised her head and strode into the crowd, two burly bodyguards behind her. The prince watched her leave, sighed, then turned back to the hawk-nosed minister.

"What say you, Sebelius? Is the Rani right?"

The man glanced at Stacy and the small band of captives. "I know not, my liege. But this I *do* know: it is better to let them speak for themselves before we speak for them, as Sigried does."

Sumavand leaned back and smiled. "Wise counsel," he agreed. Then to Alryc: "I repeat my question. Do you lead among your companions?"

"*I* lead," said Stacy, boldly stepping forward but well aware of the blade pointed at her back.

Sumavand raised his brows. "You?" He took a long hard look at her. "And may I ask *your* name?"

Stacy stood proud and tall, head thrown back, eyes fixed on his. "Anastasia. Lady Anastasia of the Haven."

"And what is the Haven, Lady Anastasia?"

"The capital city of the Empire," she replied.

"Oh? Forgive me, Anastasia, but what empire is that? You say you came from no *shala.*"

Stacy was taken aback. Again she said, "I don't know what a *shala* is. Perhaps if you explain it to me . . ."

"A mountain city," offered Sebelius, the minister. "Here there are many, each ruled freely of others. I think you might call each one an empire of itself."

I see, thought Stacy, for the first time beginning to grasp something of the strange new world in which they found themselves.

"We come from no *shala,* Prince Sumavand. Our Empire lies far away, five hundred leagues and more across the sea."

The prince and the minister exchanged dubious glances.

"You sailed across the *sea?*" the minister asked, incredulous.

Stacy nodded firmly. "And Alryc was our guide. From his star charts we found the way."

Loud murmuring rose from the court.

"Is this possible, Minister?" Sumavand asked, clutching the carved arms of his throne.

Sebelius shrugged. "Never in any *shala* have I seen garb such as theirs." His fingers fondled Stacy's tunic. "Our women weave not like this."

"Cloth can be cut in many ways," observed Sūmavand.

Sebelius agreed. "True, my liege. But I think you should also see their weapons." He snapped his fingers and from behind the curtains two soldiers came, briskly carrying a large woven basket. They placed the basket at Sumavand's feet, then withdrew. The prince leaned forward and eyed the weapons carefully. He ran a finger along the side of Alryc's sword, then picked up a crossbow and examined it. He loosened the winch and squeezed the hair trigger. At a glance Stacy could tell that he was no stranger to such weapons.

"Whose is this?" he asked suddenly, looking up at their faces.

Melinda stepped forward. "Mine, my lord," she said with a polite but reserved curtsy.

Sumavand smiled at her warmly. "You need not be frightened, girl. But tell me, where did you learn to use it?"

"In the forests, sire."

The prince frowned. "It's clumsy. Far too heavy when you have to move quickly and the enemy is close behind. Yet it *is* well designed. Where was it crafted?"

"In the city called Rhonnda-by-the-Sea, my lord."

"An odd name. But, of course, the very fact that a woman uses a crossbow is odd to us. Are you, er, a . . . warrior?"

"Not a warrior, my lord. A huntress. There's a difference." Melinda grinned.

Sumavand laughed, his eyes crinkling at the corners. Stacy noticed that for an instant the stern, hard look was gone, replaced instead by a gentle one that reminded her very much of Elias.

At length Sumavand put down the crossbow and Melinda stepped back. Then the prince took out the silver dagger and eyed it admiringly.

"Who claims the knife?" he asked, looking about.

"The dagger is mine," acknowledged Stacy.

He grinned. "I should have known. It's most handsome, Lady Anastasia. Forged from silver, I see."

"And steel, my lord. The blade is virtually invincible. My father gave it to me many years ago."

"Judging by your age, not too many years ago," retorted the prince. "Can you use it?"

"When I have to, yes." She met his gaze evenly. "May I have it back?"

He smiled thinly and shook his head. "I think not, Anastasia. I saw how easily you handled the Rani. Such a blade is far too dangerous to be in such skilled hands as your own. But enough of this. I see indeed that you are all from some far land, be it a *shala* or not. The Rani calls you out as spies—and that may very well be. How you came upon the nets or even the tunnels is no longer of any consequence. I ask you one simple question: What do you want here?"

"We came across the sea in peace," answered Alryc, now ready to speak, "to find out the lost city of which we were told."

Sumavand frowned. "A lost city? How came you *here?*"

"Our ship lies anchored in an inlet some leagues away," replied Stacy. "A hunting party was sent out to the hills to follow the herds of caribou. There we were caught in a blizzard. And during the storm we were attacked by what we call *things*. Baboonlike creatures with long fangs and an unquenchable thirst for blood."

Sumavand nodded knowingly. "We have a different name for them," he said grimly. "But *things* will do. Their ghastly work remains the same under any name."

The girl continued. "Lost and weary, we sought shelter from the snow in the cave of your mountain. It was there that : . . that our first leader was snared by your trap. We spent the night and the next morning we followed the caverns, seeking food and a way out."

Sumavand sighed. "If this tale is true, then you are most fortunate merely to be alive. All of you. The caverns are infested with what you call *things*."

Stacy smiled grimly. "We found that out for ourselves, my lord. One of our own and a dozen of them are lying dead in darkness to prove it."

The prince said, "Tell me, all of you, what do you know of this land?"

"Very little," replied Stacy, answering for everyone.

"The Ritual Wars are strange to you?" he marveled.

A puzzled Stacy shrugged. "We don't know what you mean."

Sumavand threw up his hands in exasperation. "You are all either fools or liars! Don't you know, can't you tell what happens here? Don't you realize why we live beneath these mountains?"

"We're strangers here," protested the girl. "How can we possibly know or understand what you're telling me? As Alryc told you, we came here in peace, to seek out a lost city with which our Empire hoped to trade and exchange goodwill. Instead we've found ourselves beset by savage *things*, thrown in your cells and shackled like animals."

The prince searched her face with thoughtful eyes. "We know nothing of trade or goodwill. Only war—and how to survive. We designed the pits and the nets you stumbled upon for one purpose: to kill *things* before their armies gather in ritual to march upon us before summer. We also set traps along the mountain slopes to snare wild white wolves. Their packs run savage and free in summer; they attack our farms, our livestock. The forests harbor fearsome beasts that prowl upon us. The *shaleen* try to band together for mutual protection. But often as not, we find ourselves at one another's throats. *This* is the nature of the land into which you have come."

Stacy and the others stood breathless, glancing at each other and unable to speak.

"Tell me, girl," said the prince. "In your own land, do men revere the Fates?"

Stacy nodded slowly. "We are a religious people."

"Then pray," said Sumavand. "Pray for your life—and for mine. And for those helpless souls still aboard your ship. When the snows melt, war will come. Your companions will be slaughtered. The war will spread throughout our land, to every *shala,* across every river. Men against wolves, men against *things.* Sometimes men against other men, when the barbarians attack from the lowlands. Each year is the same—only worse than the one before. You say you believe in the Fates and in heaven. Then you must also know of the demons below. Here you have come, and here you must stay. Welcome to our *shala,* Lady Anastasia. Welcome to Satra. And welcome to Hel."

CHAPTER TWENTY-THREE

Back at the inlet, Elias was chopping wood when Ashcroft came to say that the patrol the captain had sent out was returning from the hills. Elias put down his axe, his heart beginning to pound. Perhaps this time they had success, he told himself. Perhaps this time Heather would have some answers.

The band of warmly bundled Rangers and Valley soldiers moved slowly, dragging behind them makeshift sleds laden with carcasses. Casca slunk along at Heather's side. A great cheer went up from the camp. Tools were cast aside, and everyone gathered in front of the roughly built sled, knee-deep in snow.

"They're dragging fresh meat," cried an astounded Ashcroft. "This time they must have found Trevor's camp!"

There was a glum sort of smile from Elias because he hoped against hope that the Rangers had found more than just the camp.

Heather came on ahead as eager sailors raced to help her companions pull the sleds down to the ridge. Elias, face masked with a scarf, greeted her halfway up the slope. "What happened? Any luck?"

The Ranger shook her head. "It took us better than a day to find Trevor's tents. There were no tracks anywhere; everything was obliterated in the blizzard. We found some fresh meat, wrapped and bundled, ready to be carted away, and a small stock of their own provisions."

"But didn't you find *them?*"

Heather lowered her eyes. "Nothing. We searched everywhere. Knowing how Stacy and Melinda think, the next morning we followed the path of a stream toward the mountains."

"And?" Elias clenched his fists, clinging onto any hope.

The girl shuddered, but not from the cold. "Beneath a drift we found the body of one of Trevor's lads. Frozen solid."

Elias winced. "He died of the cold?"

"Not of cold," whispered Heather, meeting the captain's forlorn eyes. "The soldier's face had been clawed. His throat was cut." Again she shivered, the memory all too vivid.

"What did it?" asked Elias. "Were there bears in the hills? Big cats?"

"I don't know what it was, Elias. But it was frightful. I've fought against grizzly bears in the Free Lands, but I never saw slashes and cuts as vicious as that."

Elias's face turned sour with alarm. "Then they must have been under attack," he said flatly.

Heather shook her head ruefully. "They never made it back to their camp, that's for certain."

"Were there markers around?" he asked. "Stacy would do that. Leave signs for us."

Again Heather shook her head. "No markers, Elias. Not even signs from Cicero. Casca searched high and low. There was nothing. Only fresh snow."

"And bodies buried under it," muttered Elias.

The girl sighed. "We can't know for certain before the snows melt. Sending another search party now is futile. We've done all we could." She burst into tears. Elias put his arm around her and let her sink her head against his chest.

"We're not ready to give up yet," he told her softly. "Stacy's too smart to let herself get trapped out in the open like that. Maybe they reached some sort of shelter."

Heather looked at him through wet, large eyes. "If that's

true, then why haven't they come back? The blizzard ended days ago. I keep thinking that they're dead." Again she began to cry. Elias comforted her quietly and led her down the slope.

"You did well, Heather. Fates know, better than I could have done. But I'm still not ready to give up. If they're dead, I want proof of it. We're going to stay put here on this ridge, carry on as usual and get the *Brora* fit and trim. And the day, the very first day, that the snows begin to melt I'm going out there. Alone if I have to. We'll turn this blasted land upside down."

They walked for a while, Heather with her head low. The sun had paled and from beyond the mountains she could see more snow clouds racing. "They might have fled to the mountains," she mumbled hopefully.

In his gloom Elias's eyes suddenly brightened. "Could they have, Heather? I mean, could they have gone that far? Even in a storm?"

"It's possible."

He bit his lip and stared up at the snowcapped peaks. And in them he saw a glimmer of hope. "There might be shelter up there," he conjectured.

Heather nodded. "There might. Caves, perhaps. But there'd also be white wolves. I heard their cries while we searched."

Elias took both of the Ranger's hands and clasped them in his own. "They won't frighten Stacy," he said. "Nor Cicero. Take heart, Heather. Common sense tells me they should all be dead, but I've always been short on common sense."

Heather laughed, a sparkle returning to her eyes. "None of us have any. Otherwise we wouldn't be here."

"Stacy's alive, Heather. I know it," he insisted. "I *feel* it. I *believe* it. And so are the others. If they don't find us, we'll find them. Until we do, the *Brora* stays put. We're all in this together, and I'm not going to give up—no matter what the dangers."

CHAPTER TWENTY-FOUR

This time the room was well lighted. Thick rugs were scattered across the floor. There were no windows, and Stacy wondered if there were any at all in this bedazzling *shala* called Satra. In lieu of chairs the room was peppered with plush pillows of gold and maroon, comfortable and soft. Again there were no beds, only cots hugging the walls, held in place by sturdy chains. At the center of the room was a low oblong table made of heavy oak. Atop it stood a copper pitcher, filled to the brim with sweet, honeyed wine.

Stacy sat cross-legged on a circular laced pillow and sipped slowly from a small goblet. Beside her, lying across the dark pelted rug, was a tunic, a new one, brought in to her minutes before by a fair-haired Satrian girl who served as both companion and guard. The dress was magnificent, a sheer pale green that seemed to darken as it turned from light. On her cot the girl had also placed a vanity case—small, leather-crafted, with brushes, combs and perfumes. The sight of it delighted Stacy and already she had spent her time running the brush through her hair, frowning at the tangle of knots.

From the tiny vents that criss-crossed the smooth rock ceiling came the soft, constant sound of bells. The same sounds she had heard in the cavern, ethereal and harplike. The bells were found virtually everywhere, a constant in the day-to-day life of Satra, but she didn't know what purpose they were intended to serve.

She smiled, leaned back on the floor and reflected upon these past few days. No longer were she and her companions kept in cells, no longer were there chains or shackles. Save for the fact they were prisoners, they were now being treated like honored guests. Guests with locked doors and a guard posted outside every one. This difference in attitude puzzled and disturbed her. At times they were given complete freedom to wander— at least through the carefully guarded palace corridors. They ate the best food, drank the finest wine. Except for questioning by the minister, no one bothered them. And even his questions had not been harsh, merely understandable curiosity about who they were, why they came, and what they expected from Satra.

Also, Trevor had been well cared for. Stacy had seen him only once and then but for a fleeting moment, but she realized that the Satrian physicians were doing all they could to reduce his fever and save his infected leg.

So far, though, none of them had yet to see the city itself. And another thing bothered her: Not once had they been allowed to gather together. At times she had been able to speak with Melinda, once with Alryc, once with Robin. But only briefly and even then with their guards looking suspicious and apprehensive. What caused even more concern was what Prince Sumavand had said about danger to those aboard the *Brora*. And what else was it that Sumavand had said? *Here you have come, and here you must stay.*

Was that a threat? Or was it his way of warning of the dangers to those who leave his *shala*?

A brisk knock on the door broke into her thoughts.

"May I come in, my lady?"

At once she recognized the soft voice of Shaina, her guard-companion. "You have the key, Shaina. Open the door whenever you like. I'm not going anywhere."

Fingers fumbled with the lock. There was a dull click and the slim-waisted hazel-eyed girl with long-braided hair slipped inside, closing the door behind her.

Shaina looked at the tunic and frowned. "Your dress, my lady! Why haven't you put it on? It was chosen especially for you. Don't you like it?"

"I like it fine. It's lovely. But who can I show it off to? I'm still your prisoner, remember?"

Shaina sighed and casually plopped herself onto the large cushion opposite Stacy. The hilt of a dagger showed from behind the folds of her colorful robe. "A poor choice of words, my lady," she said. "You are to be watched, even guarded. But is that so strange? Consider: If you were spies sent here from some distant *shala,* could you expect us to act otherwise?"

"But we're not spies, Shaina. You know that."

"I believe you, Anastasia. But still we must be careful. There are those here who do not trust you."

"Like your Rani?"

Shaina laughed. "Like the Rani."

"Who is she, Shaina? Is she Sumavand's mistress? Or his wife?"

The guard smiled wryly and shook her head. "Sigried is here at the behest of her father, a very powerful lord of another *shala,* to the west. She has no love for our prince, nor he for her, as you must have observed. The Rani's father needs Satra and its resources, but we also have need of his. It is a shrewd political game our liege plays, my lady. I understand it not, nor do I desire to."

"But the Rani seems to have considerable power here."

Shaina's thin mouth turned down at the corners. She thought long before answering, and Stacy realized she was weighing her words carefully.

"The Rani has . . . friends in Satra. Those who would. . . . The Rani is a powerful woman. Her name is known throughout the city."

"And when can I see your city?" asked Stacy eagerly.

"Soon, my lady."

"And when can I see my companions? Why can't we be allowed to speak freely among ourselves?"

"You will," Shaina assured her, "when the minister permits it. But for now, why not be content to hold your questions until this evening? Take a long hot bath, my lady. Let me tend to your makeup and prepare your new robe, and make you look beautiful."

Stacy furrowed her brows in puzzlement. "What's all this about, Shaina? What's going on?"

Shaina lowered her voice and smiled coyly. "I was told the prince has requested to dine with you this evening."

Stacy wrinkled her nose. "Another interrogation?"

"Oh, no! Please, my lady, believe me! He wants only to speak with you and hear more about your own land."

Stacy smiled to herself. It would be an interrogation after all, she knew, despite what Shaina believed. Yet if she were clever about it, she might just be able to use her wiles to gain some freedoms for herself and her friends. After all, Sumavand, prince or no, was a man. And an attractive one at that.

"Will the prince come here?" she asked innocently.

Shaina laughed. "No, my lady. You will be brought to *him*. The minister will send word when the time has arrived."

So the tiger beckons to the lamb, thought Stacy, with a feline smile. "I'll take that bath, Shaina. But let's hurry. It'll take me a long time to get ready, and I'm not one to keep a prince waiting."

Afterward, Shaina accompanied her to the prince's chamber and left her there to wait alone. The room was bright and airy; the soft tinkle of hidden bells filled the air. Colorful tapestries hung from the walls; the curtains were made of velvet and lace. From the ceiling hung dimly lit glowing globes. Dark cushions served as chairs, Satrian-fashion, beside them a thick pile rug. Stacy stared

for a moment, then gasped. The fur was white—wolf fur!
Of the white wolves!

From an arched doorway on the opposite side of the chamber, Sumavand suddenly appeared. His face was cast in shadows, but Stacy could see his eyes clearly. They were like a cat's eyes, she thought. Small, piercing, intelligent. A broad smile crossed the prince's handsome face; he stepped into the light. Long dark hair, peppered with gray, fell to his shoulders. The silver clasps of his purple tunic gayly reflected the burning fires of the globes' dancing light above.

Instinctively Stacy lowered her head in a respectful bow. "My lord, I am honored at your invitation."

"It is good to see you again, Anastasia," he said with a pleased smile, gesturing for her to sit. "I see you've already adapted our own dress."

"My . . . companion brought it to me. It's quite lovely. She chose well."

Sumavand looked at it admiringly and nodded; he had chosen it himself. "Green suits you well. It is your color. It sets off the fire in your eyes." He reached over to the table and filled two copper goblets with heavy sweet wine. Stacy took hers and sipped slowly, aware of his eyes keenly watching her every move.

"Where is this place?" she asked. "Are these your personal chambers?"

"No, this is what you might call a greeting chamber. My own rooms are far above, through many levels. Here we greet friends and visitors from other *shaleen*. Perhaps you would like to sit in the garden?"

The very thought of there being a garden in Satra puzzled her. It certainly was the last thing she expected inside the middle of a mountain. "I'd love to see it," she replied, excited. "Which way?"

Sumavand gestured for her to follow. "I think you'll be pleasantly surprised, Anastasia. Come."

And was she! Once past the curtains huge windows

opened onto a spacious veranda. Stunned, she looked out onto a large rock garden. *Fully in bloom!* In random pattern there were rows of fully budded flowers, all interspersed with shrubs and bushes. The garden led upward at a slight angle onto a stone terrace twirling and twisting with thick boughs of ivy.

"I . . . think I'm confused," she murmured. "It's winter —but I see flowers."

Sumavand laughed. "Our climate is controlled," he replied, looking at her with a warm, full smile. "But tell me, Anastasia, in your own land do you not grow or plant underground?"

Stacy sat comfortably on a stone bench; Sumavand sat beside her. "In my Empire, my lord, we grow all food above ground. Under the sun."

"But we also have sun here," he protested. "The light pours down from fissures above."

"Then you never farm outside?" she asked inquisitively.

"In summer, yes. But less and less with each year. We no longer need to. Everything can be done within the confines of the *shala*."

"Everything?"

Sumavand grinned. "You said you wanted to see our city, Anastasia. Do you still?"

Stacy nodded eagerly. "I've been dying to see it," she confided, "if it's anything like this."

He took her by the hand. "Then come!"

It was a short walk through another glass door on the far side of the garden. At the entrance a burly guard snapped sharply to attention. Sumavand acknowledged him, then led her up another flight of stone steps, one that seemed to have no end. Higher and higher they climbed until she was exhausted. The prince smiled at her. "A bit further, but you'll be glad you came. I promise."

At last the end was in sight, an oval door hinged upon a wall of smoothed limestone. A light tap of his fingers on the door released a hidden lock. The door swung open onto another balcony.

"This way, Anastasia." He took her firmly by the hand and led her to the edge of the balcony. And there she stood, frozen in wonder.

"Behold Satra!" whispered Sumavand.

Below, in a grand sweep, like nothing she could ever have imagined, was a glistening city of light. Towers, domes, steeples and spires rose high into the air. But from where she stood the tallest seemed small enough to hold in her hand. "The hollow of the mountain," she marveled.

Sumavand grinned. "Many mountains, Anastasia. Look!" He gestured to the massive rock walls all around. "It took our engineers centuries to construct it," he told her proudly. "Our *shala* rests on the floor of Mount Satra. Below it, where you have been, are a thousand tunnels winding from the city through other mountains leading to other *shaleen*. One need never step out into open lands. Our fields, our vineyards, our groves all lie in the hollow of the mountain."

"It's beautiful," she whispered, recalling the first day she had seen Rhonnda. She focused her eyes on the burning dome of what looked like nothing less than a splendid palace. At the sides of the marble structure were winding steps, all leading to a central square. "What is that?" asked Stacy. "Another wing of your palace?"

"The Great Temple," replied the prince solemnly. "From there the priestesses give the blessing before Ritual begins."

"The Ritual? You mean the wars?"

He avoided the question. "Look beyond the temple," he said.

She did and stared down on what at first glance seemed a large park but then showed itself to be a garden, the most magnificent she had ever seen, bedazzling, bejeweled, it sprang to life with vivid, splendorous color.

"In summer it's even more beautiful," promised Sumavand with a glow. "Even with our controls many species
will not bloom in winter. But we are working on that problem. Satra is the finest *shala* that exists."

"Are there many *shaleen?*"

He frowned. "Once, there were *shaleen* to be found
from one end of our land to the other, but now we are
few, mere remnants of what once was . . ."

Again Stacy thought of the wars, the strange Ritual
he had mentioned previously. She decided not to press,
though. "My companion, Shaina, tells me that the Rani
is not Satrian, that she comes from another *shala*. A renowned one, to the west."

Sumavand nodded sourly. "The Rani comes from
across the *Jazeel,* the Thunder Plain. Her father rules
an . . . empire. Yes, you might call it that. One that once
could have. . . . But such talk is only dreams of our history." He laughed again. "I had hoped to hear wondrous
tales of *your* land, Anastasia, but instead I've been the
one to answer questions. Shall we go back to the chamber?
Our supper is being prepared. We can eat, then perhaps
talk some more."

As the servants withdrew the dishes after dinner, the
prince lay back on a large cushion and relaxed. "Who
governs in your land? Who is your regent?" The questions
were abrupt and unexpected.

"We don't have a regent, my lord. The Empire for
as long as history records has been ruled by the Council.
A body of men who make decisions jointly."

"And what if your lords are not of the same will? What
happens when there is disagreement?"

"The matter is solved by count. The elder of the
Council will bend to the will of the majority."

Sumavand leaned forward, displaying eager curiosity.
"And there is no war? The warlords do not call out their
troops into battle?"

"We have no warlords among men. The decision of the Council is supreme." Of course, she purposely did not speak of her own brush with Empire law when the *Brora* set sail, wisely leaving that moment for posterity.

He pondered on this, twirling his finger rings. Then: "Our Rani still insists you come from some distant unknown *shala*. She would claim that a land such as yours cannot exist."

Stacy scowled. "The Rani is wrong."

"The Rani is a smart woman. Few things escape her eyes."

"So I've been led to believe," answered the girl curtly. "Shaina tells me that she's been listening as your minister questions us in his chambers."

"You need not fear in that respect. Anastasia. Siggy will not harm you—nor your companions. If she proves right, and you are indeed here to spy upon us, you will see that Satra has its own methods of dealing with treachery."

"My lord!" Stacy was aghast. "How can you suspect——"

Sumavand waved his hand. "Let me finish. If you did plot against Satra, then it would be my matter, not Sigried's. But I think no. I think you are who you claim to be. Strangers from across the sea."

"It can easily be proved, my lord. Send some of your men to my ship. You'll see we spoke the truth. Or better, let me take you there."

"That cannot be," he said sharply. "The weather makes it impossible. And there are other dangers."

Again the references to war! This time Stacy decided to ask.

"What are these risks, my lord, that a simple trip across the hills is impossible?"

Sumavand's eyes darkened. "With time," he said in a low voice, "you will come to understand all of these things. But this much I can tell you now: If Satra were a *shala* on open land, it would not stand today. We are beset by enemies."

"Like the white wolves?"

He sneered at the thought. "Vermin. They steal from us and slaughter our sheep when they graze among the grasses. They are treacherous, yes. But wolves are not what we fear."

"Then what is the *real* threat? What is the Ritual?"

He shot her a mistrustful glance. "You've been through the tunnels, have you not? Once men moved freely among them, between the *shaleen*. There was commerce and trade, just as you speak of it. But now such movement is impossible. Six summers ago the *shala* beneath Aris fell. It was wanton massacre, as in the Old Time, as in the days before the Cataclysm."

"I don't know of these things," admitted Stacy. "Although I do know of the ancient days, of the Old Time. When the world was freely sailed and men crossed every sea."

"Then at least we share this common knowledge, your land and mine," he said. "But our world is not the same. Here blackness has covered everything."

"It was once the same in my land, my lord. Our Forest Wars lasted for almost two thousand years. But now they are past, spoken of only in books and upon the lips of balladeers. The blackness you spoke of has been lifted across the Newfoundland Sea. I was sent here to offer you the help of my Empire. *We* do not live in *shaleen* but above the soil. Under sun and stars. My Empire seeks your friendship and to share your knowledge with our own. An alliance, my lord. Not one built on soft sands like that of *shaleen*, which plot against each other behind their backs, but an open treaty. Built on rock as solid as the walls of Satra."

The prince's face softened. "Tell me more of your Empire, Anastasia. Tell me how it was that you, a woman, was sent to us." He seemed genuinely interested.

"Many were sent to you, my lord. It has been my personal fortune to be here with you now. But had any of my companions been chosen for your company tonight you would see that nothing would be different."

"Tell me of these Forest Wars, Anastasia. And of the Haven, and your Council. And speak of the city called Rhonnda-by-the-Sea that the girl called Melinda spoke of. And tell me of the forests and the rivers and the sea." His eyes sparkled. "Yes! Of the sea."

Stacy told of the building of the Haven; of the expansion of the Empire; recounted for him the many tales of heroism against the ancient enemies of the forests. She spoke of men long since dead, and of others yet alive. And none more proudly than that of her father's own contributions to Empire peace.

When she had finished, the prince sat back thoughtfully and said, "I am truly impressed, Anastasia. But my heart is sad. I fear that Satra can never attain what you have. You say your Empire would help us in any way it can. I would gladly accept such help—but have you ten thousand soldiers to send to my banner?" He shook his head. "I think not. Have you swift fleets of fighting ships that I might command for but a single year? I think not. No, come spring, again we shall be under siege. The tunnels will reek with the corpses of *things,* the mountains will groan beneath the weight of barbaric Nomads, come to plunder and loot, murder and maim. For so long have we suffered these barbarities that now even *shaleen* mistrust and plot against one another. Even in Kuba! Fates in the heavens! Kuba, the city of the Rani! Even *they* plot against the Satrian throne!"

"But surely you are safe behind your walls? Your enemies cannot hope to gain entry."

Sumavand held up his hand. "Satra is large and powerful, the greatest *shala,* but even our resources are taxed to the limit. Believe it, Anastasia. The Nomads and *things* would tear Satra apart. Nomads call themselves men, but they are not. They are savages—and cruel. Had they found you instead of us, when they were done with you it would be a kindness if they slit your throat. Sometimes they give their unwanted captives to wandering *things*. I know what has been done in the past to foolish Satrian girls who left the *shala* on their own. Shall I tell you how the Nomads use them?"

Stacy swallowed hard. At least now she understood Satra's mistrust and why Sumavand had called this land Hel. It was strange and sad, she thought, to see how differently their two disparate lands had developed over the same years, with but a sea between them.

Concerned, the prince asked, "Have I upset you?"

She looked up and shook her head. "No, my liege. It's all right . . ."

"Now you are *not* telling me the truth," he replied, knowingly. "I see I *have* upset you. Forgive me, Anastasia. But I do not want you to harbor false illusions. These matters are not pleasant, I know, but I felt you should be told. But, look! We must have spoken all night!" said Sumavand suddenly, seeing that a morning member of his palace guard had slipped into the room to speak with him. "Tell me, Anastasia. Is there anything I can do for you to make you and your companions more comfortable here?"

"As a matter of fact," said Stacy, realizing that the "interrogation" was over, "there *are* a few things. I meant to bring them up myself. For one thing, you could unlock your doors. It's most disconcerting——"

He laughed loudly. "Done! What else?"

"I would like for my companions and myself to be allowed to mix freely with one another and not have your guards follow behind. Also, I'd like your permission to allow us to see your city. To walk among the people, speak with them—learn about Satra firsthand."

"Again done. I shall instruct the minister. I no longer think you need to be watched like prisoners. Now, is there anything else?" he asked, feigning exasperation.

Stacy smiled at him fully. "I, er, I would like to have my dagger back."

The prince grinned and shook his head bemusedly. "I have your word that you won't plunge it into anyone's back?" he asked, arching over the table that separated them.

She laughed as loudly as he. "You have it, my lord. Not even the Rani's." And she winked with her mirth.

"Siggy will be pleased to hear it, I'm sure," he remarked wryly. "Very well. But now you must go. Leave me here to sulk over matters of state. And go quickly, before I wind up turning over my throne to you!" They both laughed heartily.

With a full Satrian bow, arms spread across her breasts, Stacy stood, stepped backward a few paces and slipped out of sight behind the curtains, buoyant at this pleasant first confrontation.

CHAPTER TWENTY-FIVE

Stacy tenderly put her fingertips to Trevor's lips. Trevor stirred slightly and flexed his jaw. Opening his eyes, he stared dumbly for a moment, then broke into a broad grin. Standing over him was Alryc, dressed in a blue toga and Satrian sandals; beside him, a smiling Melinda; but best of all, her fingers still on his lips, Stacy.

"How are you feeling?" she whispered.

"Better, much better. They tell me I've been out of it for days." He tried to clear a still-foggy head.

"More than that, Commander," said Alryc. He glanced briefly at the heavy bandage wrapped around Trevor's leg. "We've been in Satra over two weeks.

"What happened?" asked Stacy. "That morning we left you in the cave, how did you get captured by the Satrians?"

The soldier sighed and tried to recollect hazed thoughts, "I don't really know. I remember the snow, then there were sounds. The soldier you left behind went to look. Then there was a scream—his, I think. There were one or two of those *things*. It's all so dim."

"The Satrians must have been searching the tunnels after they found us," said Alryc to Stacy. "Either that or they were chasing *things* when they chanced upon Trevor."

"You'll be all right now," said Stacy soothingly. "And that's all that matters. We have our leader back. They say your leg will heal and that you'll be on your feet in no time."

"So they assure me," he said rather glumly. "This morning I was visited by a man who called himself Sebelius. Seemed like a nice sort, very proper and all, but a nice sort."

"He's the minister," Stacy told him. "If it weren't for him, I think we might all still be in chains."

"The minister?" Trevor was puzzled.

"Kind of like a governor, I guess you'd say. Prince Sumavand gives the orders and he carries them out."

Trevor nodded knowingly. "This Sumavand, have you met him?"

Stacy nodded. "We all have. He's an unusual man. At first glance you'd think him a barbarian. But he isn't. He's a no-nonsense fellow, and he rules Satra by sheer will alone."

"Does he know about us? About why we came?"

"He knows. I've told him everything about the Empire." She turned away her eyes.

"What's the matter?" Trevor asked.

Stacy sighed. "I can't really explain it to you, Trevor. You'll see for yourself, I'm sure. But this whole place. . . ."

Alryc's face darkened, lips pressed tightly together in something of a scowl. "We've come to a strange land, Commander. As unlike our own as the sun from the stars. Here men view one another with suspicion and mistrust. Some have accused us of being spies."

"But that doesn't make any sense! Who would we spy for?" cried Trevor.

"Very little around here makes sense," grumbled Melinda. "They've been treating us this past week like honored guests, yet we remain prisoners."

"We're being kept from contacting the ship," added Stacy.

Trevor tried to sit up but managed to raise himself only a few inches off the pillows. "Why?"

"They keep telling us it's not possible to travel during

winter, that heavy snow forces everyone to remain within the confines of the *shala.*"

"But you don't believe that?" he asked.

The girl shook her head emphatically. "Not for a minute! These people are not backward, Trevor. You should see the things they do! They harvest beneath the mountains, control the climate. They even grow flowers in winter!"

"And their city, *shala,* as they say it," added Alryc. "It's the richest a mortal man will ever see. They have temples with walls of inlaid gold, jewels and statues of marble that dazzle."

"And a war machine like our Empire has never dreamed," said Stacy. "Satra is a fortress of solid rock. And the tunnels below it lead across the lands to yet other *shaleen.* A vast network of underground cities that covers the breadth of this whole land."

Trevor took it all in slowly. "Sounds to me that a city that could do all this should be able to send a few men out into the snow."

"Exactly," said Stacy. "But they don't—or won't."

"Why do you think they're holding us like this?"

Alryc glanced from one to the other. "If you ask me, I think they're frightened of us."

"That's ridiculous," said Melinda. "They have well-armed soldiers crawling all over the place. They fight wars against *things* and Nomads continually. How can we harm them, a handful of strangers without weapons?"

"There is more to fear than merely the blades of scimitars," replied the stargazer. "We offer our hand to a people who are bred on suspicions. We tell them of mighty ships that ply our rivers; Satra has no ships. We speak of knowledge of the forests; Satra fears the forests. We tell them our understanding of wolves. Wolves are their enemies. *All* outsiders are their enemies. So then, they ask, who are these strangers with ships that sail the sea? Who are they who can speak with wolves and fight beside them?"

"I see your point," frowned Stacy. "Here, under their watch, we pose no threat. But if freed, if allowed to go back to our ship. . . ."

Alryc nodded sadly. "I fear we have come to this wondrous city a thousand years too late. Suspicions are too deeply embedded. Perhaps Sumavand envisions a fleet of Empire ships crossing the sea to war upon him. Perhaps he envisions ten thousand hunters upon those ships."

"The prince is a good man," insisted Stacy firmly. "He is not rash and always listens with an open mind."

The stargazer raised his brows. "Ah! But does he?"

Melinda looked gloomily at Stacy. "Remember what we were told when we came? 'Here you have come——' "

" 'And here you must stay,' " replied Stacy, completing the thought. "But he knows about the ship. He knows Elias will look for us."

Alryc sighed. "He hopes they will lift anchor and sail away across the sea. But if Elias doesn't, and I agree he won't, the prince knows what will happen to him. The Ritual of War will deal with our companions. *Things* will sweep down, Nomads will ravish the ship. What chance will Elias and his pitiful band have against such armies? Even Satra itself reels under such blows."

Stacy put her hand to her mouth. Goosebumps crawled down her flesh. *"Fara above!* They'll be slaughtered! They've got to be warned!"

"It makes no matter," drawled the stargazer. "They will be found. The white wolves already know of their presence; the Nomads must, also. The battle will come whether they search for us or not."

"I must speak to the prince again!" she cried. "He must let us send word!"

"But what if Alryc's right?" Trevor asked. "What if he doesn't care?"

"We'll have to do it ourselves," she whispered.

"And how are we to do that?" wondered Alryc. "I have spent many hours pondering an escape. I have observed the passages and the gates that lead from the *shala*. The gates have doors of steel, and stern guards stand at every one."

"But we can try!" blurted the girl frantically.

Alryc peered at her darkly. "You know what will happen if they catch us?"

She nodded sourly. The answer was as clear as Satrian water. "The Rani will have her way. She will demand our deaths, and the prince will be compelled to assent."

There was a long moment of silence; each one thinking of the risks and consequences. It was Trevor who finally spoke. "Where are the others? Where's Robin? And Kent? And Cicero?"

"Robin is in the city," said Stacy. "She's asked to be taken to see the temple, but she knows to keep her eyes open. Kent must be around somewhere."

"And Cicero is kept carefully guarded," said Melinda. "They may allow us some freedoms, but they'd never let a wolf free in their midst. The mere sight of him sent Sumavand's court into a frenzy. They were terrified."

"Then he won't be able to help us."

"Help us what?" asked Stacy.

Trevor pushed himself up with his elbows. "From all I've gathered, no war begins until spring, right?"

Stacy nodded. "They call it the Ritual. It starts when the snows melt."

"Good," sighed Trevor. "Then we have plenty of time. From now on we're going to learn as much about this place as we can. We're going to befriend the Satrians and be taught everything and anything about the *shala*. How it operates, where they hunt, how they control the entrances to the tunnels. And we'll pool our knowledge. Every bit of information, no matter how trivial, will be noted. I want to know when the guards are changed, when troops are sent into the pits. I want us to learn the streets of the city as well as we know the streets of Rhonnda. Every alley, every gate, every bloody stairway."

"Sounds good," grunted Alryc. "Given time we may

learn a way to get out. But we must be careful. The
Satrians watch us carefully. If they suspect——"

Trevor dismissed the thought with a wave of his hand.
"They want us to adopt their ways, don't they? Let's make
ourselves eager. That knowledge will show us how to get
out of here."

"So far they've been pretty tight-lipped," ruminated
Melinda.

"Shaina, my 'companion,' is pretty open," offered Stacy.
"I know I can learn from her."

"That's a beginning," said Trevor. "Learn all you can.
Make her trust you."

Stacy frowned. "She already does. But I don't want to
hurt her, Trevor. If we *are* prisoners, it's not her fault.
Shaina's been a friend. The only one we've had in Satra."

"No one's going to be hurt, Stacy. But the information
she has can be invaluable to us. Let her be your guide.
Let her show you *everything*. No one will question you
with a Satrian guard on your arm."

Stacy nodded, understanding what had to be done.

Trevor smiled and looked at the others. "We all know
what we have to do. Melinda, speak with Robin. I'll talk
to Kent myself. If we keep our eyes open and our heads
calm, we'll make it out of here. Elias and the others
risked their lives to get us here, now we've to do the
same for them."

It was a broad avenue, the air filled with the fragrance
of spice from the stalls of Satrian merchants. Shaina
led Stacy by the hand across a tiny tree-lined square to
a domed building with large marble columns at the
arched entrance, fountains in the open courtyard.

"What place is this, Shaina?" Stacy asked, impressed
by the ten-meter-high statues that flanked the entrance.

"A temple, my lady," came the reply as they made
their way up the polished steps. "A temple of Kuba."

Stacy furrowed her brows. "Isn't that another *shala?*"

The girl laughed. "You know it is, my lady. The city

of the Rani. Satra pays her homage with this temple of priestesses. You *asked* to see the priestess. Today she will dance. Today the Firebird rises from the flames. It's an ancient belief that Kuba celebrates."

Stacy shrugged. The more she found out, the better. They passed through a filmy lace curtain and entered a large hall with polished marble floors. Tapestries hung from the walls, deep blue velvet with leaping yellow fires. There were tall, carved columns of white marble at the podium, brightly burning glowing globes suspended from the high ceiling.

Already a small crowd had gathered, well back from the raised platform. Behind the platform hung a large silver disk, mirrorlike, engraved with the image of a mythical bird with enormous wings spread toward a golden sun. The crowd, mostly well-dressed Satrian women wearing dazzling jewels and elegant saris, stood solemn and quiet, awaiting the entrance of the priestesses. Suddenly Stacy's eyes widened. There was a tall yellow-haired girl among the crowd at the front. Her head was bowed, her eyes closed in silent prayer. Sigried!

"What's the Rani doing here?" whispered Stacy, a bit shaken.

"Shhh! She has come for the rites. The priestess is of Kuba, her *shala*. She is obligated to be here."

The soft lulling sounds of bells came from behind the curtain. Shaina fell silent as a long row of robed young women stepped from behind the curtains and walked in carefully measured steps toward the center of the podium. Their eyes were darkly painted, lips soft and full. On their hands were finger bells, tiny chimes that rang in musical variance. Gracefully, with a slight swaying of the hips, they took their places in a semi-circle before the platform.

Seductively the priestesses raised their hands above their heads. Then, in one broad sweeping gesture, they bowed, then knelt with faces inches from the floor, arms outstretched.

From somewhere came the slow, steady beat of a drum. It rose steadily higher in pitch, then it was joined by another. Stacy stood breathlessly as a slim form, silhouetted by the shadows, moved from behind the curtains. Around her neck was a gold band in the image of a snake, with tiny rubies for eyes. The priestess shook her head in rhythm with the bells and long black hair shimmered. She wore a silken dress, flowing, cut low at the neck so that her breasts could be seen moving with every breath. Broad-hipped, shoulders high, her arms outstretched, the priestess of Kuba began to sway her hips. A mellow-toned flute flooded its sounds through the hall; the light from the globes began to fade. The room became dark, but as it did so a flaming torch appeared. The silver disk on the platform glowed and burned. All around the room dulled colors glimmered, blended with shadows and twisted into curious shapes.

The priestess leaned forward, shoulders swaying, eyes blazing. She spun and her dress flared. Soft flesh was exposed, wide thighs, long legs. Her arms reached out, fingers beckoning.

The priestess of Kuba threw back her head. Her hair flowed wildly. She laughed seductively and swirled across the black floor, eyes flashing with mystery. She crouched and reached out as if to some unseen lover, ran her hands down her body and along the sides of her breasts. On her feet again she danced, swaying, sliding, faster and faster. The drums beat in frenzy. She unfastened a clasp from her shoulder and bared her shoulders. Oiled and smooth, the skin gleamed in reddish light. She cried wildly, thrashed herself down upon the floor and swung her hips higher and higher in time with the drums.

From behind, the bowed priestesses rose and also began to sway, their large eyes flashing. The priestess of Kuba cried out to them in some strange dialect. Then like a whirlwind she threw up her head and arched backward. The other priestesses repeated the prayer, raising their arms above their heads. And together they spun to the music. The silver disk glowed more intensely, sending splashes of form and color dancing across the walls.

The priestess turned in a slow circle, the drums began to soften, their pace ebbed. From somewhere above, a great light began to burn, first dimly, then more brightly, until it finally blazed like a white-hot sun. Stacy shaded her eyes from it, wincing.

The priestess of Kuba lay sprawled across the floor, panting, totally still. The others lay prostrate at her feet. White light turned to red, softening until only the glow remained. The Firebird had risen from the flames. The dance was done.

Stacy snapped out of it as if awakening from a dream. It did not take her long to realize that her trance was no different from that of the other observers.

The priestess of Kuba, golden skin smothered in tiny beads of perspiration, stood, bowed fully to the Rani, hands across her breasts, then strode back behind the curtains.

The Rani spoke quietly to her companions for a moment, then suddenly froze at the sight of Stacy. She approached with fire in her ice-blue eyes. "How dare you bring *this* one into the temple!" she flared at Shaina.

Shaina bowed her head, her eyes fixed on the Rani's. "Lady Anastasia has the freedom of the *shala,* Rani. The minister has given her the right."

"This is a Temple of Kuba! She has *no* right!"

Stacy met Sigried's glare evenly. "No blame rests with Shaina. I asked to be brought here today. If my presence offends you, I do not apologize."

Sigried fumed. "I told you once before, wolf bitch, if you speak to me, address me by my title! Slut! Who do you think you are?"

Stacy felt the hand of Shaina tugging at her sleeve, pulling her away. She yanked free, resisting the urge to tighten her hands around Sigried's throat.

"My lady! Please!" cried Shaina. "She draws you purposely into an argument!"

The Rani laughed caustically. "I need no pretense for this one! Be warned, Shaina! Keep your distance from her lest you be dragged down beside her!" And with a haughty swirl, hair tossing over her shoulders, she turned and strode through the now opened arched doors to the streets below.

Shaina gazed at Stacy with fearful eyes. "Take care, Anastasia. The Rani is a powerful enemy. I should never have brought you here."

Stacy smiled warmly. "Her anger goes back further than today, Shaina," she said, recalling the tip of the scimitar pointed at the yellow-haired girl's throat. "But never mind her. She's not going to spoil the day. What shall we do next?"

As the Satrian began to answer, a sudden shrill blast of a horn rang through the *shala*. Shaina stood perfectly still, her hand unconsciously moving toward her hidden dagger. Twice more the blast came.

"What was *that?*" Stacy asked.

"The alarm, my lady," whispered the girl.

Stacy glanced toward the street. Everything seemed normal, Satrians busily moving along the square to the avenue. But from the corner of her eye she caught sight of mail-vested soldiers running down into what seemed a spiral stairwell leading underground. "What's happening, Shaina? she demanded. "Don't lie to me."

The girl bit at her lip. "There must have been a breach in the tunnels——" She cut the words short.

Stacy stared. "What does that mean?"

Shaina regained her composure and forced a weak smile. "Nothing we should concern ourselves with, Anastasia. There matters are swiftly dealt with. You need have no fear. But come! Let me take you to our gardens, I think you'll enjoy them." She literally pulled Stacy by the arm and brought her down into the square.

There were no more blasts; the street remained quiet.

But as they crossed toward the open boulevard, a Satrian soldier came racing toward them. Stacy recognized the man at once. It was Rald, the tall guard from outside Sumavand's quarters.

"Mistress Shaina," he said, catching his breath. "Please return at once to the minister's post."

The girl nodded without a moment's hesitation. "But what about Lady Anastasia? She'll have to be brought back to the palace."

"I'll escort her, mistress. But hurry. All officers are being called at once."

"I'll have to leave, my lady," said Shaina. "Follow Rald. He'll bring you home." With that and a quick smile Shaina disappeared among the crowds.

The guard sighed, then grinned at the startled girl. "Do not worry, my lady. Things are well."

Just the quickest glance into his deep-set eyes told her that they were not well at all. There was more happening than either one was willing to say. But she knew that questioning Rald was futile. He was as close-mouthed as every other Satrian.

The guard pointed. "This way, my lady. Please follow me."

Stacy nodded and followed him along the street. There was something important going on, and she was going to find out what it was, even if it meant being chained again. Bit by bit, without the guard even realizing it, she slipped a quarter pace behind. Ahead was a busy avenue filled with veiled Satrian women in saris similar to hers. Stacy took a deep breath and pushed Rald hard so that he stumbled. Before he could turn around she was gone, hidden among a hundred women bustling among the stalls.

Stacy walked at a fast clip toward the spiral stairwell, yet slow enough not to attract attention. She covered her face with her veil and bent her head low. Then, certain that no one had seen, she took hold of the metal banister and dashed two steps at a time down into the darkness. She found herself on a small landing, faced with a tall iron door blocking her path. If there was a guard on the other side, her game was done, she knew. But if there was no one. . . .

She held her breath and pushed at the concealed recess near the lower hinge. Metal groaned; the door opened. She passed through easily and stepped inside a luminous passageway that led farther below. The door shut behind her on its own.

Down, down she went. Shouting voices echoed in the distance, yet here the tunnel was empty. Save for an occasional mouse, she was alone. At length the tunnel grew dim, the earth beneath her feet softer. Holding the wall with her hand, she moved slowly and cautiously, letting her eyes become accustomed to the new light. Canine instinct warned her of danger ahead; her keen sense of smell picked up a scent of blood.

A frantic cry sent her reeling back. Ahead a soldier came running, his eyes ablaze. At the sight of her he stopped. "The canal! They've broken across the canal!"

Stacy thought fast. "I know! Others are to follow! Get above and bring as many reinforcements as you can find!"

The soldier nodded. "Yes, mistress!"

She saw that he was young, not really more than a boy—yet from the look of his sunken, ravished eyes, she knew he had already seen long service in the tunnels fighting *things*.

He ran frantically on, in the direction of the stairwell she had just descended.

Stacy pressed forward, heart pounding like the drums in the temple. An underground canal! No one had told her of that! If there was a canal, there would probably be a river—and that would lead outside the mountain!

More cries from ahead. The passage grew wider and wider with every step, and wind began to howl down from hidden fissures. It became cold, winter cold. She stopped at the foot of a ledge and peered down into a vast cavern below. The pits! A dark, endless, windswept canyon filled with boulders and rocky ledges. Across the floor lay the bodies of *things,* bloodied and mangled, intertwined with corpses of Satrian soldiers, their weapons shimmering dully in dim light.

She edged her way along the edge of the tunnel, hands feeling their way along the wall. Suddenly her fingers touched metal. Handholds! To climb down below, she knew. She grasped the first hold, lowered herself down the ladder and swiftly made the descent. Her feet dropped into a thin layer of mud, splashing dully.

Nauseated by the stench of death, she retched. Soon she caught sight of a dim tunnel far to her right. It was from there the screams were coming; it was there the battle was being fought. She drew her dagger from inside her sari.

She heard the sound of rushing water and knew the river and canal must be close. The dim light grew closer; she hugged the wall. Once past the pit she saw a sight that she would never forget.

A vast cavern loomed, a hundred meters high. From below came a steady flow of water spilling over a deep wooded channel dug into the earth. Below the ledge on which she crouched the battle raged in eerie light, Satrian soldiers wielding scimitars in wild frenzy as a countless number of fierce droop-jawed creatures swarmed around them.

The column of men was pressing steadily backward below her ledge, in the direction of yet another tunnel. Corpses were littered everywhere. The *things* grunted and wailed, swinging huge rock swords over their heads. The clash was terrible. Now a trumpet blast screamed and a wall began to move on the far side of the canal. Stacy saw the wall mysteriously slide open; a hail of arrows rained down upon the confused *things*. They tried to scatter but were caught in a crossfire. Stumbling and shrieking, many fell into the canal, their bodies borne swiftly away by the rushing black water.

A company of fierce mail-clad Satrians charged through the opening in the wall. The men tossed ropes, secured them on both sides of the water and began to cross the canal. Again came a clashing of swords and the shattering sound of smashed bone. A row of the enemy fell back. As they did, the original defenders of the tunnel broke forward with renewed fury, shouting warcries.

Everywhere, men became blurs, *things* grotesque silhouettes against the limestone walls. Stacy felt her head swim, the stench of blood and death heavy in the air. Onward the Satrian army pressed, now clearly regaining the upper hand. *Things* squirmed, writhed; rock swords clanged hollowly against scimitars. Crossbows sang a song of death. Swarming from ledges and tunnels, the Satrians swiftly took control of both sides of the canal. Bodies mingled, twisted, lunged. The earth became soaked in blood.

Stacy shuddered. She staggered backward, back toward the dark. She had seen a taste of the Ritual Wars, and a taste was more than she could bear.

Welcome to my city, Anastasia. Welcome to Hel!

Blindly, she ran back in the direction of the pit, trying in vain to block out the dreadful images of battle. She found herself leaning against the wall of the handhold ladder, panting, drenched in perspiration. Drawing a deep breath, she scrambled up the ladder and ran along the now familiar tunnel. She did not stop until the rock door was opened and the spiral stairwell leading to the *shala* was in sight.

Head sunk on her pillow, she tossed about in an uneasy sleep. There was a *thing* coming for her. Its eyes were wild, face twisted and laughing. She tried to move but found herself frozen. The creature threw back its head and bared horrible fangs. Then she screamed.

Then she awoke.

Her room was light, the globe above her head burning brightly. The sound of bells was soft; they helped calm her nerves. On the table was a pitcher of wine and with shaky hands she poured a goblet full to the brim.

There was a soft knock at the door.

"My lady? May I enter?"

Stacy sat up on the edge of the bed. "Come in, Shaina," she answered, glad for the familiar voice.

The Satrian girl entered with a worried look. "You caused us great concern, Anastasia," she said. "Rald reported your disappearance to his superiors. The minister was very upset."

"I got lost in the crowds," Stacy lied, shying her eyes.

Shaina eyed her coolly. "I think not, my lady. A soldier returning from the tunnels reported seeing someone very much like you headed toward the pits."

Stacy sighed. "You're right, Shaina. I was below. I followed your soldiers to the canal. And I saw the battle. Will you report me?"

The Satrian shook her head sadly and sank into one of the cushioned seats beside the table. "But you promised not to enter any restricted area. No one is allowed below, my lady. You've caused great anger."

"You may not believe this, Shaina, but I'm sorry I went. What I saw——"

"What you saw is never to be repeated!" snapped the girl.

Stacy stared with surprise at this first outbreak of temper she had seen from Shaina. "What's happening, Shaina? Tell me. Please. Satra's in great danger, isn't it? The wars go badly, worse than you would have your people believe."

Shaina put her head in her hands. "This is not the first time our defenses have been breached. But all is under control." The words were flat, dry, as if she were repeating a standard reply to such a query.

Stacy didn't believe her for an instant. "You are holding back, Shaina. Why?"

"Because to speak of military matters is forbidden! Ah, Anastasia, your own eyes have seen it. What can

I add? Yes, Satra is in danger. The tunnels are infested as never before. Last week the caravan from Kuba was attacked and they made it through only by their wits. What they reported has frightened us."

"What was that?"

The girl looked at her ruefully. "I should not be repeating this to you, my lady. I can be punished."

"I'll tell no one, Shaina. I give my oath as a friend. Tell me."

"Armies have begun to group. In spring we would expect it. But not now. The enemy gathers force and moves to Satra's perimeter. Skirmishes have already begun, soldiers have been dispatched. Kuba itself is reported under siege. The Rani's father has requested our aid, but we can do little for him. The Rani now accuses our prince of responsibility if Kuba falls. I fear she will rally support from within Satra and force Sumavand's hand by her cunning and prowess. If that happens and we are forced to send large contingents to Kuba, Satra may well be left defenseless when the true onslaught begins. Patrols from the hills already tell of a large force of Nomads approaching the mountains——"

"Stop there!" Stacy's eyes displayed fiery anger of her own. "You lied to me, Shaina! You all did—even your prince! You said that no Satrian ever leaves the mountain during winter. Now you speak of your patrols in the hills! You could have sent word to our ship, couldn't you? You could have warned our companions of the danger!"

Shaina wept openly. "Forgive me, my lady. I was commanded never to speak of our patrols. You were not to know."

Stacy wiped tears from her own eyes. "But why? You want them to be killed? What harm have they done to you?" And she shook Shaina by the shoulders.

"It's too late! Don't you understand? They're already doomed! Already the Nomads have seen your ship. Their columns have been sighted, moving in the direction of the inlet. There is nothing to be done."

"How can you say that? Send a force of your own soldiers to their side! Help them! Save their lives!"

The girl shook her head. "We dare not. We cannot!"

Stacy stared in shocked silence. Alryc had been right all along. The Satrians would do nothing to aid them. Elias and his band would be left to defend themselves as best they could against the havoc that was being wreaked upon them. "Get out, Shaina," she said angrily. "I'll take my cause directly to the prince. He'll listen to reason even if you won't!"

Shaina shook her head. "No, Anastasia. It was Suma-vand who gave the command; no patrol must approach your camp. We've seen it from a safe distance. But they did not see us."

"You've been there? Yet you didn't warn them?"

The Satrian sighed. "We were forbidden."

"Everything here is forbidden!" flared Stacy. "What's the matter with you people? You call yourself my friend, but you're not! You're as poisoned as Sigried! Now get out!"

Shaina stood, bowed in Satrian fashion. Then she spun around, skirt flaring, and strode tearfully from the room, slamming the door.

Stacy threw herself down on a pillow and cried for a long while. Elias and the others would be helpless against what was coming, she knew, but there was nothing to be done. Trevor's plan for escape would be too little, too late. They could not wait until spring. They had to leave now. Every day lost would bring the war that much closer.

But they were prisoners here, as surely as if they had been thrown into the deepest dungeon. Prisoners in a golden cage. Eyes flushed with tears, Stacy vowed to break free.

She got dressed in her sari, hid her dagger beneath the skirt and made her way to the small meeting room at the end of the corridor. It was with surprise that she saw Melinda and Alryc already there. They looked up, startled, as she entered.

"Stacy!" cried Melinda. "We've been so frightened! What happened to you yesterday? Our guards were frantic. Even the minister was here. He said you fled your escort."

Stacy slumped dejectedly down on the cushions. The ringing chimes in the background began to annoy her. Gazing about, she made sure no Satrian guards or servants were near and then searched the faces of her friends.

"I've been below, beyond the pits," she confided.

"How? Where?" her companion's demanded.

"Shhh! Listen to me, both of you. The war has already begun. I saw it. *Things* are already on the march, moving toward the *shala*. I don't know all the details, but Satra is preparing for an all-out attack. And they lied to us when they said no one ever goes above. Satrian patrols have been in the hills and seen the *Brora*. They also reported an army of Nomads massing and heading in the direction of our camp."

Melinda gasped in alarm, her trembling hand at her lips.

"But the Satrians won't help," Stacy continued. "The ship's in grave peril, but Sumavand won't lift a finger. You were right, Alryc. They're afraid of us. If Nomads wipe out our camp, they'll consider it a threat removed."

The Ranger's eyes glowed. "We've got to *do* something!"

"There's an underground canal—and a river. I've seen it. It leads out of here. With a lot of luck someone might just make it to daylight."

"And that someone is *you?*" asked Alryc darkly.

Stacy nodded. "It has to be. I'm the only one with any idea how to get away. Trevor's plan is no longer any good. Time counts, so there's none to waste. Elias must be warned right away. If he's not. . . ." She didn't have to draw any pictures of what would happen.

"How will you make it to the ship, Stacy? Satrian soldiers will be on your heels the moment you flee through the tunnels. And this time I fear the Rani will be given her way. Your life will be in her hands."

Stacy scoffed. "She doesn't frighten me. And I can elude the soldiers. I know the tunnels; I'll get by."

"But what about *things?*" cried Melinda. "They'll swarm all over you, like they did to us before. And even if you make it to daylight, you'll have to elude Nomads. They'll want you, too. Remember the tales we've heard about what they do to captives?"

"I'll have to risk it, Melinda," said Stacy with a frown. "Too many lives are at stake. I know I can't make it all the way to the ship by myself. I will need help—and I intend to get it."

"Stacy!" rasped Melinda, "Have you lost your senses? There's nothing between you and the ship except snow and ice. Who will come to your aid? Where will you find shelter?"

"In the only place I've ever found shelter," she replied dourly. "Among wolves."

"The *white wolves?*"

"They'll take me in. They have to. I'm one of them, remember?"

"This is not the Empire, girl!" boomed Alryc. "They have no love for men. Do you expect them to fight for us?"

"It's a slim thread, I know. They might even take me for a Satrian and kill me. But I doubt it. If I can reach their dens, I'll find the only safety we've known since that day we left camp." Her tone of voice showed she would not be deterred.

"When will you leave, little wolf princess?" asked Alryc.

"Tonight. After midnight. That's when the guard is changed. Melinda, can you steal a warm cloak for me? And maybe some boots? Mine are pretty ragged." She glanced down and frowned.

"I'll find what you need, Stacy. Don't worry. What about weapons?"

She shook her head. "I have my dagger. It's enough. But right now I have a lot to do. Melinda, meet me later at the entrance to the palace wing. Six bells will be a good time. Right now I'm going to find Shaina. I treated her like dirt a while ago and I want to apologize."

Craggy walls dimly lit by torches loomed along the unfamiliar passage. It was the women's quarter, set aside for girls in service of the throne—girls like Shaina. Stacy had expected to hear laughter from the chambers, but instead there was no sound, no sign of anyone. Cautiously she passed an endless number of closed gray iron doors. Where was everyone? Surely someone was about! A guard, a servant, anyone.

Nothing.

Stacy began to feel uneasy. She slid her hand to the hilt of her dagger. Which chamber opened into Shaina's room? She knocked on a door; no one was inside. Then another door, then a third. Something was wrong. An attack, perhaps? Had all the girls been called to duty?

Suddenly she froze. From somewhere down the hall she heard a moan, soft, almost a whimper. A door stood ajar, spilling light into the hall. Uneasily she came to it and pushed the door fully open. Lying on the floor was Shaina, hands bound behind her back, mouth gagged with a scarf. Her dress was torn and small threads of blood trickled down her arms, breasts, legs.

Stacy, shocked, knelt down beside the injured girl. "Shaina," she whispered. "Shaina! Can you hear me?"

A long groan came in reply. Gently, Stacy lifted the girl's head and recoiled with shock. Shaina's lovely face was bruised and cut—the work of a finely sharpened knife, she knew. One expertly wielded to do minimum cosmetic damage but to inflict the greatest amount of pain.

"Oh, Shaina," she cried softly, "who did this to you? Who did this to you?"

Slowly the Satrian girl managed to open her eyes. They

were clouded, showing the effects of forced drugs. "Anastasia? Is . . . it really you. . . ?"

"What happened, Shaina? What animal did this to you?"

The girl coughed as she tried to speak. She took hold of the soft fabric of Stacy's sari. "You must not go back. . . . You must *not*. . . ."

"What are you talking about? Go back where?"

"Your chamber, my lady. You must run!"

"What's going on, Shaina? Is there trouble?"

The girl nodded weakly. "The Rani . . ."

"Did *she* do this to you? Is this Sigried's doing?"

Shaina began to weep. "She hurt me, Anastasia. She hurt me badly, she and her friends. They demanded I answer their questions. I refused. . . . I. . . ."

"Does the minister know of this?"

"Sebelius has been taken. All of us under his authority have been arrested and held for treason against Satra."

"Treason? Impossible!"

"The Rani has seen to it. Sumavand has left the *shala* to direct our defenses across the river. Sigried, in his absence, has accused the minister of treachery against the throne. It is a lie, but many warlords have sided with her. Do you realize what that means? She will use her authority to get at you and your companions. Flee, my lady! And forgive me for not being truthful with you before."

Stacy cradled her closely and wept unashamedly. "Forgive *me*, Shaina. I said terrible things to you before. None of them were true. You have been my friend. I shan't forget."

The girl pointed to a small chest at the foot of her bed. "Open it, my lady. In there you will find a crest. A black dragon. It is the insignia of my rank. Veil your face and wear the crest above your heart. Few know your features, so no soldier will stop you. You can pass as me."

Stacy did as she said and pinned the crest onto her sari.

"Take my cloak, my lady—there, beside the bed. Now go—swiftly! Fly before her soldiers come again!"

"I can't! You're hurt. You need help!"

Shaina gritted her teeth and coughed again. "My wounds will heal, my lady. Now leave! And go with your Fates!"

Stacy kissed her gently and placed her head against a cushion. Shaina shut her eyes and groaned.

"Good-bye, my friend," whispered Stacy. "We *will* meet again. That is *my* vow. And by Fara I'll keep it!"

She threw the cloak over her shoulders, drew the dagger from her sari and fastened it securely around her waist. Then back into the corridor she went, trying to erase the picture of Shaina lying bloody and bruised on the floor. *By Fara, there will one day be justice in Satra! And I'll be there to see it.*

It was an hour before she managed to work her way into the city. Twice she had been forced to hide as soldiers stomped heavily across the passages and hallways, seeking her. She no sooner eluded one patrol than another appeared. But finally she emerged onto open streets.

As before, people bustled along the avenues, busy with their errands and work. Stacy realized that they were all totally uninformed of the intrigues being hatched this very moment in the grand palace above. She swung her veil over her face, leaving only her dark eyes exposed. With a quick gait, not at all unusual for a girl of military rank, she pushed past a host of vendors and shoppers.

A guard beside a fountain stared for a moment, then bowed as he saw the black crest. Stacy nodded curtly and passed him quickly. The spiral stairwell loomed ahead. Here she slowed, making certain no one was watching. She dashed down the steps. At the heavy door stood a soldier, a large bearded man with what seemed to be a perpetual scowl across his face.

"Open it!" she demanded. "I must reach the canal!"

"Mistress?"

"You heard me! Open the door!"

The man looked at her coolly. "What business are you on?"

"The Rani's business, dolt! Now open it quickly before I have you demoted to gravedigger!"

The scowl darkened. "You speak strangely, mistress. Are you not foreign?"

"I am as Satrian as you are, idiot! Now open that door!"

The man frowned, looked again at the crest and did as she asked. Once inside, the door shut, Stacy leaned against the wall, recovering from her fright. Had he questioned her further she would have had to kill him.

Then down the tunnel she ran, her eyes slowly becoming accustomed to the dim light. The closer she came to the pit the heavier the rancid smell of death became. She held her breath as long as she could and hurried to reach the ladder. With cold hands she grasped at the iron holds and climbed down swiftly. Her worn boots touched soil, and she stood motionless, peering into the darkness.

Her eyes focused along the passage that led to the canal. From here on she would have to be doubly careful. She now had two enemies—Satrian guards as well as lurking *things*.

A pebble rolled across the ground behind her. She whirled. Black shadows fell upon black rock. A rat darted into a corner. Stacy relaxed and told herself she was getting a touch too jumpy.

Or was she?

"I've been expecting you."

The voice was a whisper from behind. She spun, dagger in hand. She could see nothing, but the voice was familiar, disconcertingly familiar.

"Step closer," came the whisper again. "I want to see your lovely face. That's right, closer. Keep coming, *wolf bitch!*"

Sigried!

Stacy froze in her tracks as the yellow-haired girl stepped out from behind the shadows. Her hair was flowing freely, held back by a slim black velvet band. Like Stacy, she wore a heavy cloak, clasped at her shoulders, a loose-fitting sari and long black leather boots. In one hand she wielded a curved dagger, bejeweled at the hilt with glowing stones. In the other hand was a whip.

"I suspected you'd come this way," she hissed in a dry matter-of-fact tone. "But just in case you didn't I had all the other caverns posted with my troops. Indeed, it's been my fortune you came so soon. I was beginning to get a chill waiting for you." The whip cracked against a rock, and Stacy jumped back a pace. Sigried laughed. "You've never seen my whip before, have you?" Again the whip cracked at Sigried's side. "I'm going to kill you, Empire whore, but first I'm going to teach you a lesson."

"You like to hurt people, don't you, Siggy?"

The yellow-haired girl winced at being called by her familiar name. Her eyes narrowed with contempt.

Stacy stalled for time until she could get a sure footing and familiarize herself with the surroundings. "That bothers you, does it, Siggy? Know what I think? I think you're afraid of women who attract men. I heard the priestesses whispering about you in the temple. They say you sleep with the lowest Satrian soldier."

"Liar!" flared Sigried.

The whip cracked inches from Stacy's feet.

Stacy stayed cool and calm. She took a slow backward step and the Rani followed.

"Siggy, I've always wanted to know about Kuba, about your father's throne. Someone said your mother was a harlot and that you gave your virginity to your father when you were ten. What was it like? Making love to your own father, I mean?"

"You filthy-mouthed whore!"

The whip stung hard against Stacy's arm. She drew back in pain, biting her lip. The Rani followed again. *Good,* thought Stacy. *She's letting me draw her out more; gives me more room to work.*

The Rani lunged at Stacy. Stacy met the blade with her dagger and pushed the blonde back before the whip could be brought high enough to lash. Then she crouched low, held her knife at a level with her eyes and began to pace in a slow circle around the enraged Rani of Kuba.

"Angry, aren't you, Siggy? What's the matter? Upset because I'm not as easy a mark as Shaina was?"

Sigried kicked dirt at her face. "Slut!"

Stacy lithely sidestepped it, laughing.

The silver dagger lashed. Sigried reeled as warm blood pulsed down her arm.

Again Stacy circled. "Keep your guard up, Siggy. Watch it! I'm fast!" She snarled like a wolf, baring sharp teeth. "Know how I got this way, Siggy? Wolves trained me. I can stalk like a cat, run like a fawn, fight like a hunter. But look! I've torn your pretty dress with my knife. How clumsy of me!"

With a single movement Sigried unfastened her cloak and let it fall to the ground. "I won't be needing this," she said. Then she pretended to lunge with the dagger and with her injured arm lashed the whip high. It caught Stacy off balance, the tip cutting across her shoulder, tearing through her cloak. Stacy reeled with the sting.

For long moments the two women paced each other, probing, testing.

Rani's curved blade flashed in an upward stroke. Stacy twisted sideways and met the knife with her own. Metal clashed on metal. Both pulled slightly back. Stacy shifted her weight to her left side. Sigried hesitated, then lunged. Up went the dagger; crack went the whip. Sigried reeled back, a thin stream of blood trickling down her shoulder. Stacy grimaced as the whip's sting raced along the seams of her torn dress.

Cold, ice-blue eyes laughed tauntingly. "A nasty cut, wolf bitch," said the Rani, trying to close the space between them.

Stacy feinted, then brought the dagger down in a flash.

Sigried screamed and hurled herself backward, her body smacking against a boulder. For an instant she took her eyes off the dark-haired girl and glanced down at the cut. It was deep. The bitch had slashed her whip arm from the shoulder almost down to the elbow.

Stacy snarled, her eyes glowing. Again she began to circle, again she began to probe her opponent's weakened defenses.

Sigried's eyes tightened, and her jaw became set. Her whip arm was virtually useless; she tossed the whip into the dark. The bitch could have killed her, she knew, that moment when she had been pressed against the rock—but she hadn't. Why? Her whip must have done more damage than she realized. Why else had Stacy hesitated?

She knows, thought Stacy, her face in a stony grimace. Her arm began to throb. She shifted the dagger from hand to hand, keeping her expression constant.

"You grow weaker, whore," hissed the Rani, leering.

Stacy smiled also, darting her eyes to the Rani's bleeding arm. "You, too, Siggy. Your cut's deeper than mine. Better kill me quick, if you can. Otherwise you'll bleed to death—and I'll be fighting a corpse."

"Strumpet!" Dirt swirled as the Rani kicked.

Stacy staggered, the tip of Sigried's boot in her stomach. Sigried lurched and slammed the back of her wounded arm against Stacy's face. Stacy was all over her, smashing her elbow into Sigried's ribs, clawing at her face with sharp hawklike nails.

Sigried pushed with all her force and slammed Stacy back against a rock. Before the girl could even wince from the blow, the Rani's boot was up, the kick knocking the silver dagger into the dirt.

Stacy scrambled to her feet, then crouched while Sigried drew around and poised her blade toward her throat. "Where is your weapon, tart?" she panted, blood now covering both her arms.

Stacy leaped, knocked the blonde over and literally wrenched her arm around, tossing her into the dirt like a bag of rubbish. Sigried was stunned. Stacy moved like

Helfire, picked up the fallen dagger and with a single swoop slashed it fiercely across Rani's midriff. Sigried's eyes widened. Staring at her adversary in utter disbelief, she whispered, "You think you've won, don't you? Not yet. Escape above, if you will. But you'll wish you had died at my hands instead of *theirs!*"

Stacy looked away as the Rani moaned in pain. The girl was bleeding to death. And she no longer looked like the cruel sadist she was, but like a small whimpering child. In that moment Stacy felt sorrow and shame. On many occasions she had used her dagger in violence, but never before on a human being. She had been about to take a human life, and the knowledge of it sickened her.

Head low, she said, "I'm sorry it came to this, Sigried."

"Go to Hel, Anastasia! Must you hover over me like an ape? Let me die alone. If you want to show mercy, plunge your dagger through my heart!"

"I can't do it, Rani. I want to, but I can't." Sheathing the dagger, she looked at the wound in Sigried's stomach. It was a long gash, bleeding. If left alone, the Rani would be dead in minutes. Yet if she could receive help quickly, there was a chance she might live. Ripping the hem of her dress, Stacy pressed the fabric firmly against the wound. "Hold it tight, Rani," she said. "It'll help to stop the bleeding."

The yellow-haired girl looked at her incredulously. "You . . . you want me to live?"

"I want the world to be rid of you! You're a black-hearted witch! But you're also human, and I'm not a murderess. I'm leaving Satra. I'm going to warn my people of the war. But I give you fair warning, Sigried. If in my absence you try to harm anyone who's close to me, I *will* kill you—with no regrets. Now, before you bleed to death, tell me how I can alert your soldiers!"

Sigried turned her eyes toward the pit. "Trip wires," she rasped, trying not to cough. "Walk across one and the nets will fall. The alarm will sound, the lights. . . ."

Stacy nodded. "Save your breath. I understand." She stood up, peered about and began to move away.

Sigried grasped her sleeve. "But now I give *you* warning, Anastasia! I told you that if you go above you'd wish you had died at my hand. I meant it! Escape from the mountains is impossible!"

Stacy stared at her. "Why?"

"Nomads. Our soldiers have seen their armies."

"I'll make it," Stacy replied. Then, without looking back, she said: "Good-bye, Rani," and began to walk into the black, purposely tripping the wires.

The nets fell, lights began to flash. Stacy pressed hard against the wall. Within seconds came distant shouts and a multitude of running footsteps. She bounded from the pit and into a side tunnel. Soldiers would be every where, she knew; she would have to hide until they had scattered out in search parties.

At the crook of the shaft she crouched, breathing heavily. She could hear shouts of shock and dismay as the Satrians came upon the bleeding Rani. There was frantic scrambling and a shout for physicians above to be alerted. Then a dark voice saying, "Who did this to you, Rani?"

"Who do you think?" came an infuriated wail. "There's a Nomad loose in the pit! Find him and slit his throat!"

"Yes, Rani! Which way did he go?"

"The canal, you dolt! Ouch! Lift me carefully! Do you think I'm a rag?"

A group of men dashed down the adjacent tunnel, the *wrong* tunnel—and Sigried had sent them that way purposely. Stacy smiled. She had saved the Rani's life, and now Sigried was trying to do the same for her.

She rose and ran through the totally black passage, far away from the pit, far from the canal, entering a strange world of total darkness that she prayed would eventually lead out into the light of day. Rats darted between her feet. Large spiders danced across immense webs above her head. Water began to drip from the invisible ceiling. Strong drafts of wind rushed down at her. She strained her eyes for some distant glimmer of light. There was none.

Her heart began to pound with a growing sense of panic. The sting of the whip felt like dry ice pressing against her. Which way? *Which way now?* Ahead she could see nothing, only an endless stretch of darkness.

Forward she went. More dripping water, more strong downdrafts of wind. It became cold, colder than in the pits. She drew her cloak tightly around her. Unseen boulders tore at the sides of her dress. Upward, ever upward. The tunnel began to narrow, then widen, then widen even more. Pillars of limestone reached down from the ceiling like huge dripping icicles, like large beckoning fingers. Ahead, the tunnel seemed to wind endlessly, a labyrinth of darkness, a maze of enclosing rock, twisting forever upward.

After an hour, the blackness gave way to the dimmest glow. After a steep ascent she came into a large cavern, its limestone walls giving off a soft glow of dullish red. At the side of the wall ran a small stream of cold, fresh water. Beside the stream Stacy finally rested. She took a cloth from her dress, soaked it, then washed and cleaned her wounds. The touch of the water felt good, soothing. Her neck and shoulders stung from multiple scratches, her shoulders also from the lash of the whip. She slumped with her back against the wall and sighed. It was dangerous to stop here, she knew—and even more dangerous to sleep. But she was so tired, and she had walked for so long.

Without even realizing it, she fell asleep. A peaceful slumber, filled with dreams of pleasant forest streams and a warm gentle sun.

CHAPTER TWENTY-SIX

"Pretty, ain't she?"

Startled, she awoke. She tried to get up but couldn't. A large furred boot was pressing down firmly on her stomach. Fear rising like smoke, she peered up into the face of a tall man with small beady eyes, an unkempt beard flecked with fresh snow. He wore what appeared to be a fur hunting jacket, heavily lined, and an animal skin hat with two small horns. The flaps of the skin were pulled down tight over his ears.

"Who . . . who are you?" she gasped, eyes widening.

The man put his hands on his hips and roared with laughter. He peered over his shoulder and called to a companion. A brute of a man, Stacy saw, with a long pointed nose and a cruel sneer. Mean eyes stared down at her; the sneer turned into a grin.

"She'll warm us tonight, won't she, Kral?" the second man said with a mean growl, throaty and hoarse.

Kral snickered. Bending down, he pressed dirty fingers into her flesh. Stacy squirmed.

"We haven't had a Satrian woman to keep us company for a long time, eh, Vlask? And she's a looker, too! And young! The chief will be pleased."

Vlask came closer, still grinning. He showed a mouth full of decayed teeth.

Stacy turned away, sickened.

"Don't think she takes to you, Vlask," observed Kral.

"What's the matter, precious? Do we frighten you?" The grip tightened and he laughed again.

"I . . . can't . . . breathe."

Fingers loosened slightly. "Don't worry! We won't hurt you, girl. You're too valuable."

Vlask put his face close to hers and ran a filthy hand up and down her body. Stacy cringed. "Let's have her now, Kral. What do you say? Come on, it's warm here and——"

Kral shook his head firmly. "You know the rules. The chief gets her first."

Vlask spat on the floor. "There's little left after he's done. Remember that last one? She was useless. Couldn't even recall her name. Let's enjoy this one now. We don't have to bring her back at all. We can use her for a few days and return without her. Come on, Kral! Let's have 'er now!"

"No!"

Kral pulled Stacy to her feet. "Bundle up, precious. We're going to take a long walk in the snow."

She followed him with her eyes as he swept up a nearby knapsack and flung it over his shoulder. Vlask stared at her and sneered again. "This way," he said, pushing her. And before she knew it they had followed the stream and came out onto a windy ledge. The sun was burning down brightly. Fresh air filled her lungs. They were high above a range of lower mountains, she saw, very close to the summit of an enormous snow-swept peak. Below was a treacherous descent and a huge gorge with even higher mountains across it.

Kral walked in front, Vlask in back of her. They took long strides in the snow, so it was hard for her to keep up. But a shove now and then from Vlask made sure that she did.

Stacy struggled along the rocky ledges of the ridge, barely able to keep her footing. Under the fresh snow was a sheer sheet of ice, and one slip, one twist the wrong way, and she would plunge into the canyon below. She realized that even thinking of ways to escape from the barbarians was foolish. On terrain like this she was better off with them. They knew these lands and knew what to watch out for, but she didn't. If nothing else, ugly Kral and stinking Vlask would lead her to safer ground.

After a perilous hour of negotiating the ridge, they crested the mountain. Swirling snow almost blinded her; the Nomads slid dark visors over their eyes.

"Keep going!" barked Kral.

Stacy looked at him helplessly, hands frigid with cold. "Which way?" she stammered.

The Nomad grunted and pointed ahead. "There. Now just keep moving!"

It was a shelter, she saw. Not a cave by any means but a large crevice in the wall of the mountain. Kral pulled her roughly by the arm and literally threw her inside. She fell onto soft, damp earth, scattered with bits of dried wood. At the center of the floor was a clumsily built fireplace, a circle of stones sheltering a shallow hole in the ground. Inside the hole lay cold embers from what she guessed was last night's fire. And she wondered what had brought these two so high up. Logic told her they did not live here and that they were just using this place as a makeshift camp.

Vlask gathered wood and with scrawny flints set the fire. Kral spread a blanket across the floor and took pieces of dried meat from his sack. He threw one to her. "Here. Eat. It's all you'll get until we reach camp." He turned to Vlask. "Keep your eyes open," he said through a mouthful of the slightly spoiled meat. "And don't go too far. I want you within earshot."

Vlask grunted and wiped greasy hands on his fur jacket. Then he lowered the visor and stepped back outside into the snow.

"Eat, eat!" said Kral, turning his attention back to her.

Stacy shook her head and threw the putrid meat back to him. "You eat it! The smell is sickening."

The Nomad laughed. "Spoiled, eh? Used to good hot food, eh? You'll have little more of that, precious. Not where we're going."

"And where is that?"

Kral laughed. "Curious, too, ain't you? Well, never you mind, precious. But our work ain't done yet, see? Vlask here's going to look around a bit more—while I keep my eyes on you."

"What does he look for?" she asked casually.

"Most times, anything. But these days is special, ain't they? Look." He reached inside the sack and pulled out a small jeweled knife. She saw at once it was Satrian.

"Took it yesterday off some soldier clown. Won't be needin' it anymore, will he? Satrians been crawling 'round for days now. Must be bloody doings underground. But don't get your hopes up, precious. Won't be any soldiers coming for you. Too busy with their apes."

"You've *seen* them?"

"Seen them? Hordes of them! Old Sumavand's got his hands full this time, eh? Won't be bothered much about men like me and Vlask. No, not this winter. Chief he says to me: 'Kral, you go up the mountain. You find out what you can. Catch me a Satrian soldier.'" Kral's eyes twinkled. "Did as he said, I did. Always do. Whenever something's needed, who does the boss call? Kral, that's who. Knows I can get the job done right."

Stacy leaned back and sighed. It seemed the Nomads were on top of everything; they knew just where to find information and how to get it. And they weren't very concerned about going down into the tunnels, either, which both impressed and frightened her simultaneously.

"Where do you live, er, Kral?"

"Live?" He said the word as if it had no meaning to him. "The land, of course. Wherever our tents are set is where we live. Sometimes near Satra, other times Kuba.

Any *shala*. It makes no matter. Not as long as there're men to fight and women to warm my bed." He looked at her with growing lust.

The seeds of a plan for her escape were born. She forced a smile and brushed at her hair. "I must look terrible," she said in a seductive voice.

Kral stared at she purposely leaned over, letting her breasts show above the ripped sari.

"Why must I be given to the chief?" she asked.

"Why? It's law! The boss would cut off my——"

"I see," she replied. "But laws are broken, aren't they? I mean, even in Satra men break laws for the women they desire."

The barbarian stopped chewing and looked at her long and hard.

She flung her cloak back, exposing her thighs, and gazed into his eyes. "When does your friend come back? Vlask, I mean."

Kral grunted. "Too soon."

"Keep him away, Kral. I don't like him. I like you much better. I think you know how to handle a woman. A woman like me." She spoke to him in seductive whispers, leaning towards him, wetting her lips.

He swallowed his food, then wiped his hands in the dirt. "I never met a Satrian woman who didn't kick and scream until she had to be knocked unconscious," he said.

Stacy's eyes flashed with passion. "Then you don't know who I am, do you? I'm a priestess from the temple. I've been trained, trained how to please."

Kral had to clear his throat. "What was a priestess doing in the tunnels?"

"Running away. I killed someone. A woman. She stole my lover."

Kral leaned forward and studied her eyes, her face.

She took a stick of wood and fondled it with her hands.

"Shall I dance for you, Kral? Or shall I do other things for you? Things you'll like and appreciate."

The barbarian pulled off his fur and tossed it to the side. He leaned over and brushed his hand along her leg, fingers running from her ankle almost to her thigh. Stacy sucked in air, then let it out with a soft moan. He drew his body close to hers; she pushed him back gently. "Slowly, Kral," she whispered. "We have time, lots of time. And I want to make it nice for you." She let go of the piece of wood and ran her hand through his thick matted hair. Kral put his hand on her bosom, and she tried desperately not to cringe. "Gently, Kral. Don't hurt me." She pushed him all the way down until he was on his back, then she opened the front of her dress.

Kral gaped at the firm bare breasts, the golden skin.

"Do you like it?"

Kral nodded, and ran a dry tongue over his thick lips.

"Good, Kral. I'm glad. Shall I continue?"

The barbarian grinned, entranced, thinking only of the pleasures ahead. *A priestess! What luck!*

Stacy lifted her hands in back of her head and pretended to unclasp her sari. "Aren't you going to slip out of your clothes?" she asked. "In Satra we *never* make love wearing clothes."

Kral almost tore his jacket off, then yanked off the rag of a shirt, pulled off his boots and peeled off his breeches. All the while he kept his eyes on her, goggling at her graceful sway as she pretended to slip out of her sari. In his eagerness he did not realize that by the time he was completely naked she was as fully dressed as ever.

"Lie back, Kral," she whispered. "It'll just take me a minute more. There's a belt under my dress." Her hand swung behind the cloak and drew slowly toward the unseen dagger. "I'll be with you in a second, Kral."

He stirred as her body drew close to his, her free hand touching his shoulders. He opened his arms to embrace her. She purred softly, warm and inviting.

"Worm!"

The dagger slashed across his face. Stunned, Kral tried to lift himself up, but a swift kick in the groin threw him back. Blood streamed down his face and onto his chest.

"I'm blind!" he wailed. His hands went to his face, fingers and hands covered with thick pulsing red. "Daughter of Hel; I'll kill you!"

Stacy whirled, horrified at what she had done, and ran frantically out of the cavern.

"Come back! Come back, you bitch!"

Crawling, stumbling, he followed, naked into the cold. She was running along the same trail they had taken to come to the shelter. She looked back and saw he was hobbling, falling. If she could only make it across the crest to the other side. . . .

Something smacked her hard from behind. She fell and slid across a sheet of ice. The dagger dropped; she strained to reach it. A heavy boot stomped hard across her hand. She groaned and looked up into the cruel eyes of Vlask.

"Well, well!" he laughed, seeing the naked Kral stumbling on his knees. "This is a pretty sight! A pretty sight, indeed!"

Vlask's twisted face turned as ugly as Kral's. A bitter scowl crossed his heavy features. *"I* do the saying now! Look at you. Kral the Mighty! Ha! You can't even handle a girl half your size!"

Vlask yanked Stacy by the hair and stared meanly into her blurry eyes. "I'm going to show you how a man really does it," he rasped. "Hear me?"

She moaned and dropped her head helplessly to the side. Vlask grimaced, then took a handful of snow and wiped it across her face. She still did not come around. A powerful lash with the back of his hand across her mouth did the trick.

"Wake up, bitch! I want you to know what's happening!" Grubby hands tore at her sari, exposing soft, bruiséd flesh.

She could not stop him. She felt his sickening fingers touching her, probing her. She made one last effort to move, but just a look from him stopped her cold.

"We don't want to do that again, do we?" he asked meanly.

She shook her head in fear and put her hands to her ears to wipe out the sounds of his laugh. Everything began to blur; the world started to spin. His body was bearing down, trying to have its way.

"Aiiiii!"

His scream filled the air. He fell back, moaning and whimpering, writhing upon the ground.

Stacy forced her eyes open and saw huge white forms leaping from the snow mound above, tearing at the throats of the barbaric Nomads. Warm blood melted paths in the mounds of soft snow.

White wolves!

The carnage took only seconds. Fangs bared, dripping blood, the wolves hovered over the two motionless bodies. There were about six wolves, she saw, all with great glowing manes as white as the snow. Long-snouted, with small slanted eyes, they sniffed at the tracks of the men and sought the scent of other Nomads. Then one, the largest—and clearly the pack leader—howled a shrill call to other unseen companions. He told them that the job was done. Then he looked to Stacy, studying her.

"Shall we end her life?" growled a wolf from behind.

The big one shook his shaggy head. "The female is already near death. She can trouble no one. Better to leave her here and let the cold do its work."

Stacy looked up, and with all the effort she could muster, spoke. "Please, my lord. Don't let me die. Take me. . . ."

Each and every one of them froze in their tracks.

"She speaks!" cried a third wolf. "She speaks as we do!"

The leader pressed closer, even as the others stepped back in fear. His eyes were suspicious, fangs menacingly bared.

"No, don't! I am of the pack!" She was frantic.

The wolves glanced incredulously at each other.

"You? Of the pack? You are a daughter of men!"

"I swear it! Of the packs across the sea! I am one of you."

The leader stared in utter disbelief. "Who are you? What manner of man-trick is this?"

Stacy tried hard not to faint from the throb in her head. "My . . . my name is Khalea. I come from the Northern Forest across the sea."

"Khalea? How come you by such a name? It is one given only to the Chosen."

She closed her eyes. "Fara wished it so, my lord. The name was bestowed on me by the finest lord my forest has ever known."

"This is impossible!" barked a voice from behind. "A man-trick, nothing more!"

The leader growled menacingly. "That is not for you to say! She speaks as one of us."

"Take me with you," pleaded Stacy. "I'm hurt. Would one of the pack turn away another who is injured and seeks shelter?"

"You ask that we take you to our den?"

"I beg it, my lord. Let the sage and the elders judge me."

A worried wolf stepped forward to the leader. "This one is cunning," he growled. "She carries a tooth! I saw what she did to the naked one."

The hunter pouted. "But he was an enemy. And she claims to be of us. If that is so, she acted well, like a huntress."

"I . . . I *am* a huntress!"

"She is badly hurt," came another voice. "There will be no danger if we take her to the elders."

The leader nodded reluctantly. "Very well, Suli. Let cooler heads prevail on this matter. As you say, she cannot harm us. And the sage will be most curious to question her. Perhaps he will call for the Circle of Lords. What know I of such things?"

The friendly one concurred. "The sage must consult *Balaka*. Perhaps Fara has written of this across the sky. I do not know. But this much I can say: If we do not leave with her soon, she will surely die."

CHAPTER TWENTY-SEVEN

Outside, the glow of Lea penetrated softly through the deepest recesses of the den. If not warm, the den was at least comfortable, and Stacy had managed to rest, eat and regain a bit of her diminished strength. The entrance to the den, a pyramid shape of natural erosion, was hidden by weighty branches and large rocks, an indication that even wolves dared not live openly under the sun.

The white wolves had treated her well since she had been brought here the previous day. Yet she was a stranger. They spoke little, if at all, and then only when necessary. Suspicious and wary, they kept their distance and were careful not to let her see very much of their den. The size of this cave told her this was a meeting place; the center floor was surrounded by a pattern of large rocks in a circle. Such a meeting place could only be for warlords and the sage. She knew she was here at their pleasure, a prisoner until they had gathered and could question her. And the busy coming and going of hunters all day made it clear that the time of the questioning would be soon.

The arrival of a magnificent wolf with a flowing mane and large intelligent eyes told her the first of the lords had come. He grunted as the hunters at the entrance bowed, then took up a place atop one of the rocks in the circle. Paws dangling over the side, he watched and studied her as she smiled awkwardly and drew her cloak more tightly around her. A few minutes later another lord came, this one a massive animal with a long pointed snout and the largest gleaming fangs she had ever seen. He, too, took a place atop a rock and lazily stretched out.

The third lord to arrive did so with bluster. Growling and snarling, she heard him command those at the entrance to stand taller and firmer. They arched their backs, complying with haste. This wolf was clearly more than a lord, she knew. More likely the warlord—with long years of experience in battle.

Within minutes the cavern was full; at least two dozen wolves were present. The last to enter was a lumbering giant of a wolf with small slanted eyes and a shock of white fur that fell over his face. He shook his pelt, sending off a wave of wet snow, then took his place atop the highest rock of all. The cavern became still, and the whispering and beating of tails ceased.

Stacy looked up in awe at the stern but gentle face of the sage. She drew a deep breath and sat with her knees up, arms folded tightly around them. Then breathlessly she waited for the questions to begin.

The sage glanced from one lord to the next and nodded his head in short greeting. "Who is it that shall tell us of how the daughter of men was found?"

Another wolf approached from the shadows. She saw that it was the one who had spoken with compassion, the one called Suli.

"We came upon this *man-child*," he said, looking at her, "as she was brought from the tunnels by men of the Lowlands. We followed behind, poised to attack. But they came upon shelter before we were prepared. As they burned their fire, I came close and hid beside the drifts. There I saw this *girl*, the daughter of men, draw a tooth from her garment and strike the man across the face. She fled the shelter in fear. We were set to close in when the second man came back from his search. He hit her and tried to force her to submit to him, but before he could we struck. The men were killed."

The sage looked to the girl and saw that she was trembling. "And?"

"And we were ready to leave when she spoke. Fara above! We thought a demon was upon us! She spoke softly, as one who is hurt, and pleaded that we take her with us. She claimed to be of the pack."

Here there was much murmuring among the lords. They began to watch and observe the girl all the more closely.

The sage let this pass. "Why did you listen to her? Why did you take her?"

Suli looked confused. "She was injured, my lord. And she spoke as one of us."

The sage growled discontentedly. "Can a man be a wolf?" he barked. "Can this girl be of the pack, as she claims?"

Suli shook his head ruefully. "I do not know, my lord. But your question can be answered if you ask *her*."

"I intend to, young hunter. Go now. You have said what had to be said."

He turned to Stacy as Suli left. She felt a cold shiver run down her spine. The sage narrowed his eyes.

"Do you know who I am??" he asked.

Stacy nodded. "I do, my lord. You are the sage."

There were literal gasps from the lords, who now heard her speak the canine tongue for the first time.

"You have understood all that has been said here?" asked the sage.

Stacy nodded once more. "I have, my lord."

"What is your name, daughter of men?"

She raised her chin proudly. "I am called Khalea."

"You know why you have been brought to us?"

"To answer questions. I, a child of men, have sought your shelter. I seek to be known as one of your own. You are here now to deem whether or not I am worthy."

The sage kept a solemn face and nodded slowly. But

his heart pounded with astonishment. Here before him was this creature who looked as a woman, yet spoke and acted as a wolf. "How came you by the name Khalea? Do you know its meaning?"

In true humility she bowed her head. "It is an honored and revered name, my lord, one that I have tried to be worthy of. When I was a cub, the tests were given to me. I was sent alone into the wilds. I returned a huntress. The name Khalea was bestowed on me by the greatest lord of the Northern Forest, Hector the Gray."

"We know not the name you speak of, Khalea. Nor the wood of which you tell. But Fara's kingdom is vast. Far beyond our mountains are dense forests. Is it from there you have come?"

"No, my lord. The forest of which I speak is to be found only across the great waters men call the sea."

Here the sage's eyes darkened.

"You spin a strange tale for us, Khalea-of-the-Forest. How came you across the Great Waters?"

"Upon a sailing ship. A mighty vessel that carried us to your shores."

"The ship of men!" barked a warlord in wonder.

Grim eyes flashed to the wolf who had spoken. The sage paused and glanced back and forth from him to the girl. "You have seen this ship?"

The warlord growled. "I have, my lord. A strange thing. A man-thing. Like a foul serpent it rests beside a cove near the Lowland hills."

"That's the one!" cried Stacy. "Then you must have seen my friends who came with me! Wolves from my own land, with coats of blazing red, others as black as night."

The warlord growled again. "I have seen these things," he said. "Wolves, yes, yet not like wolves at all. They aid and serve men."

There were gasps again from the Circle of Lords. The sage drew back. "They aid men? Do man's bidding?"

"Not as servants, my lord, but as *friends*," Stacy protested. "In my land there is friendship between us."

"Now the truth is plain!" shouted another. "She belongs not among us, my lord, but among men! Her ways are those of deceit and lies! She can never claim the free rights of a huntress!"

Howls of agreement filled the air.

Stacy saw that the Circle of Lords was heavily against her. "Am I to be treated as an outsider without benefit of trial?" she growled. "Will I be judged by what others think with no search for truth? I ask for pack justice! I ask the right of the test, my lord."

"Another man-trick," barked the warlord. "She cannot be trusted and can never be of the pack!"

The sage snarled angrily. Against the shadows he looked awesome, his eyes glowing, his massive frame tensed as if ready to strike. "Enough! The one who calls herself Khalea has asked no more than she deserves. Are we barbarians, or are we of the pack? If we send her to her death without search for truth, would we still be worthy of the gifts Fara has bestowed? I think not, good lords." He looked at her gently. "You know what will happen if you fail the test?"

She nodded glumly. She would be at their mercy. The looks on their faces assured her they would tear her apart.

The law of the pack demanded as much.

As the sage pondered his first question, she did her best to stay calm and prayed that all she had been taught had not been forgotten. She cursed herself for recalling so many days when her lessons had not been given full attention. Those lessons now could either save or cost her her life. It would only take one mistake, then the warlord would call her out as an imposter.

At length the sage looked to her sternly and said, "If you are truly of the forests, Khalea, then you will know its five natural wonders. Name them for me."

She bit her lip pensively and thought carefully before

answering. "First is Phebe, the rain, for without her there is nothing. Second comes Lurilla, the grasses from which all things grow. Then mighty Sythera, the trees, whose boughs and leaves protect all Dwellers. Fourth, sweet Jasmine, the wild flower whose petals bring beauty to the wood. And last is Aleya, the wind. Fickle sister of Fara, who sends us warning of our enemies."

The sage seemed pleased, the lords surprised. She had handled the first question as easily as any of them could.

"And tell me, Khalea, what are the three major tongues of the forest. But take heed! The tongue of cats must not be mentioned lest we invoke Fara's bitter memories."

Stacy nodded. She understood. This one was easy for her, though. Later would be tougher.

"There is Raith, the chatter of all winged creatures; Erusia, the dark tongue of beasts; and Loiré, the canine tongue in all its forms, jackal, hyena."

"That will do," said the sage gruffly. "You need say no more than is asked. Fara has given to us, and all other Dwellers, many gifts. Of all she gave, tell me the five basic wits."

A difficult question, Stacy knew. There would be many variances of the same gift; she would have to search her memory for only the basics and not make the mistake of combining any of them together.

"The five basic wits," she said. "Common sense, cunning, memory, intelligence." She held her breath, then blurted the last. "Skill of the hunter!"

The sage hid a pleased smile. Stacy breathed a long sigh of relief.

His face became stern again as he posed the next question. "Can you read *Balaka?*"

She nodded slowly. "I know some of the readings, my lord, as any huntress must know. But only a sage can read them all."

"That is true, Khalea. But rest assured that I will ask only that which a huntress must know to earn her position. In Fara's universe there are a thousand-thousand stars. Recount for me the seven that the pack turns to for its needs."

Stacy shifted slightly. She closed her eyes and thought deeply. "In reverse order of importance?" she asked.

"Of course. Otherwise it is useless."

She frowned. That would make it harder. But still she was confident. "Solange, the one also known as Mars of Anger. Next in reverse order of importance would be Lycia and Sham, the Twins. From them we glean our way through the night until dawn." That was three. From here on it was easier. "Sabrina, the North Star, which burns brightly from its fixed position in the heavens. Then, of course, AnaFara, daughter of Fara, the star to which a huntress turns in time of need. Then Lea, the moon, and most important of all, the source of all warmth and joy, Khal the sun."

"Khal and Lea," whispered the sage. "From which you received your name."

Stacy smiled. She saw that the Circle of Lords was impressed.

"You have done well, Khalea-of-the-Forest. But I am not quite done. The next question will be the most important of all. For it is from this we govern our very lives. One who would be of our pack must live it and breathe it every moment. Do you know of what I speak, Khalea?"

"I do, my lord. You speak of Fara's works of mercy."

The sage nodded. "As your final question I ask you to recite these works for me."

"Fara demands her works of all Dwellers," she began, recalling days long past when Hector had sat beside her in the sun and made her recite them aloud time and time again. "We must tend the ill, feed the hungry, shelter the destitute and homeless, visit with the motherless and the afflicted and always remember with our prayers those who have passed into her arms."

The sage sighed, closed his eyes and nodded. She had

recounted the works totally, without hesitation. "Your teacher taught you well, Khalea," he said somberly. "You should be proud."

Tears welling, she replied, "I am, my lord. Very proud. Lord Hector is worthy of Fara's kingdom. His memory lives with me always."

The sage nodded. He turned to the Circle of Lords. "The daughter of men has proved herself to be of us. I find her above suspicion, to be as equal as we before Fara's eyes. How say you all?"

One by one the wolves began to nod their heads in assent. If she had proven herself to the sage, they reasoned, there was no doubt that she was worthy, even though her shape and form was that of a woman.

"You are a free member among us, Khalea-of-the-Forest," said the sage. "All dens will be so advised. You may come and go as you will and find your shelter wherever you choose. Let the lords decide who will take you in and into which of the packs you shall prosper as a huntress."

"I am humbled and honored before you," she said gently, bowing low with her arms outstretched on the earth. "You have saved me from the savage barbarian men and given me food and shelter and warmth. Now you have accepted me as one of your own." Soft tears ran down her face, and the Circle saw that her humility was sincere.

"The sage has called you one of our own, Khalea," growled another of the warlords. "We will accept his word. But you have yet to speak of why you came here from the tunnels. Was fear of the barbarians the only reason? Or is there another?"

Stacy dried her eyes as she sat up. "I have come a stranger from a faraway land to seek your aid."

"What is it you ask, Khalea?" asked the sage. "How may we help you?"

She glanced at their faces and knew how difficult this

would be. "In the time I have been in this land I have
seen the shadow of war grow even darker across the sky.
Those I love are in grave peril. I ask that you help in
saving their lives."

The Circle of Lords began to stir uneasily. Many whispered among themselves. "Do you speak of the dark-
furred wolves who came with you across the sea?" she
was asked sternly.

"Yes, my lord. And also the men. They know not
what threatens and will be led like lambs to slaughter if
they are not helped."

One sharp-eyed warlord growled at her fiercely. "You
are asking us to fight for *men?* Men are our enemies! What
happens to them is of little concern to us!" Growls of
agreement filled her ears.

"But these are not the barbarians! These are men of
peaceful ways, friends of the pack."

The lords looked at her as though she were mad. The
sage frowned. "If men and apes wish to battle one another, what business is it of ours? They are all a scourge
upon the earth!"

Stacy bit at her trembling lip and glared up at him.
"And what of those of my ship? They have never harmed
you. Are they to die for the blame of others? When the
wars begin. . . ."

The first warlord glanced sharply at the sage. In reply
the sage nodded to him and gave him permission to speak
his truth.

"The war you speak of has already started," he said
glumly. "Seekers have tracked the barbarian army from
the Far Lands. They have laid siege to the *shala* known
as Kuba and have swept down upon the city in great
numbers. Kuba has fallen."

Stacy winced. *Kuba destroyed!* No wonder Sumavand
had so hastily left his *shala* to direct his defenses across
the river! By now *things* would be swarming through the
tunnels, and his army would be committed against them.

If the Nomads attacked Satra, the *shala* would be defenseless against their onslaught from above. Satra would be destroyed. This new war would be the last.

In desperation she cried; "Satra must be saved! If it falls, then the Nomad armies will conquer all the land!"

The sage sighed and arched his head toward the ceiling. "It is Fara's will. Satra is doomed."

"Fara would not will such terrible destruction," she cried. "You say these things because there is fear in your hearts. Every one of you!"

The warlord stirred angrily. "Who are you to say these things to us?" he barked. "We who have fought men since the creation! Is it not enough that we have saved your life and taken you among us? You are safe, Khalea. No harm will come to you."

"Great harm will come to me and to all of us if the Nomads have their way! Gates of Fara's kingdom! Don't you see? Are you all so blinded by hatred? When Satra falls, who will blunt the thrust of the dark armies? *Things* will clamor from their dark tunnels, Nomads will sweep from the plains to these very mountains!"

"You howl like a jackal," snarled the warlord.

The girl fumed and bared her teeth. "If I do, it's because I am forced to deal not with wolves but with dogs! Common dogs!"

The insult was too much to bear. Every lord felt stung, every lord growled viciously and bared his fangs at the outrage.

But the calm voice of the sage prevailed. "Do you think so little of us, Khalea?" he asked softly.

Stacy lowered her head and let her tears flow freely. "You are not the wolves I was told of," she whispered, "Not the mightly race of white brothers I expected to find."

"Then go back to whence you came!" hissed the warlord angrily.

"I am ashamed," she admitted. "All wolves shall be

ashamed. I give thanks that the old wolf who told me of this land is not here to see what has happened to his brothers. Garth would die of such pain."

None seemed to know what she was talking about, but one wolf among them, an elderly lord who sat far off to the side, suddenly began to tremble. His eyes widened, and his great white tail lifted high behind him. "The name you spoke," he whispered. "What was it?" He pushed his snout closer to her.

Stacy looked at him sadly. "We call him Old One. He, too, is a white wolf, the first any of my forest had ever known."

"But the name, child! *Tell me the name!*"

She appeared puzzled. "I told you. We know him as Old One, but he says his true name is Garth."

At this, the old wolf began to weep.

The sage and the other lords glanced at each other in puzzlement. "What is it, Lord Remus? Perhaps your long journey has made you tired. Would you care to sleep? A den can be prepared."

Remus opened tired, bloodshot eyes. "I am not ill," he growled. Then, looking back to Stacy: "I must know more about this wolf of whom you speak."

Stacy, although confused as the others, readily complied. "He came to our forest many, many years ago. His wanderings took him at long last to the pack of Hector, in which I was raised. His fur is as white as the snow, just as yours is. He tells of once being a bold hunter and leading his pack down from the mountains to seek plentiful game. But then one day, while out searching for his father, he became lost in a blizzard. For days he wandered, starving. He expected to die. But Fara was with him. He found himself floating one morning on a sheet of ice, and that ice took him across the sea."

The old wolf cried again. "He became lost searching for his father, you say?"

Stacy nodded.

Remus howled to the heavens, to the complete surprise of everyone. "My brother!" he barked. "My brother is alive! Fara be praised, *Garth lives!*"

Stacy stared with utter disbelief.

Suddenly the old wolf laughed. "We gave him up for dead," he said, gasping to catch his breath. "We thought he had starved, or that he had fallen into a man-trap. But now you say he lives! What joy! Khalea, do you swear this thing? Do you give your oath?"

"I give it as a huntress. Your brother still lives."

"Is he well? Do the wolves of your pack treat him with kindness?"

She laughed. "They do, Lord Remus. Old One is loved by all! He spends his time spinning tales for the young."

Remus shared the laugh, even as he wept. "That would be just like him! Even when we were young he always loved to fill the heads of the cubs with his fantasies!"

"I share your tears of joy," she told him truthfully, "and I want it known before all wolves that Old One still burns with love both for you and this land he was forced to leave against his will."

"For the tidings you have brought me, Khalea," Remus said, "there is no price I would not pay. Come with me tonight to my dens and let me call out before all my pack that you, Khalea-of-the-Forest, the huntress from across the sea, shall become our leader when my time is done."

Stacy was stunned at the offer. "I am honored, my lord. And I thank you with all my heart. But I must refuse."

"But why, Khalea?" Remus was befuddled by her response.

She glanced at the long faces about her. "I cannot accept because my heart cries out to those I have left behind. They need me; they count on me. I cannot turn away from their plea."

The warlord growled angrily at her. "Foolish girl! You have been offered great honor among us! And you spurn the offer! Why? My seekers have followed the dark tracks of this army; they have seen them deal the death blow to Kuba. You would leave here alone to fight such a force?"

Sadly she bowed her head. "If I abandon those I love, then I am not worthy to dwell among Fara's Chosen. Below, my friends stand on the edge of death's shadow. Men and wolves alike. Alone I came to you, alone I must go back. Satra must be warned, my ship must be warned. A true huntress readily dies for her family. They are mine."

The sage nodded with deep understanding but with sorrow in his eyes. He feared for her life. "Then go with Fara, Khalea-of-the-Forest," he said at last. "And accomplish what you must. Let Fara's will be done."

CHAPTER TWENTY-EIGHT

The burly man knelt over the body and scowled in disgust at the sight. The lad was lying flat on his back, throat slit from ear to ear. Small stab wounds covered his chest and shoulders; thin pieces of wood had been plunged under his fingernails.

With a long sigh Elias reached out and closed the glazed eyes, bowing his head and saying a silent prayer as he did so. Behind him, Heather and two other Rangers stood with their crossbows. Frightened eyes darted back and forth among the dense trees, looking for signs of the ever present danger. Casca stood at the side, ears up, nose sniffing at the wind. There was a foul smell in the air. One that told of savage men, unlike any he had ever known.

Elias stood and wiped the blood from his hands. Glancing to Ashcroft, he whispered, "After they finished their games, they slit his throat."

The sailor paled, then nodded glumly. This was not the first time one of their guards had been murdered while standing at his post at night. In the last week five such men had been found dead. Always this foul work was done at night. Never once had their unseen attackers shown themselves in the light of day.

Elias scanned the landscape. They were helpless, he knew. Whoever was out there was able to prey virtually at will. After the first body was found, the guard had been doubled. Then tripled. But no matter how many men he put on watch there was no stopping the killings. It seemed to have become almost a game—a death each night.

"Let's bury him," he mumbled.

"What about tonight?" asked Ashcroft. "We can't post any more guards."

"We won't. We'll all remain behind the barricade in front of the cabins. If our lurking friends out there want to get at us, they're going to have to show themselves—and fight."

"What makes you think they'll show themselves?" asked Heather.

Casca growled bitterly. "Sooner or later they must. They'll tire of this vile game they play. They'll thirst for more blood."

Elias reached for his shovel and began to dig the grave, tossing mounds of gravel carelessly behind.

Ashcroft started to speak, then hesitated.

Elias looked up at him coldly. "You had something to say, mister?"

The sailor bit his lip. "I . . . you know what I was going to say."

The mariner threw down his shovel. "Yes, mister, I *do* know! Don't you think I've heard the others whisper it? Don't you think I've seen the looks in their eyes?"

Ashcroft turned away. "They're frightened, Capt'n. It's been half a winter since . . . since the others went into the hills."

"You want me to set sail right away, don't you? Not even wait until spring. You don't care if they're still alive somewhere—and waiting for us."

His officer looked at him with pained eyes. "You think that? You think I wouldn't give my own life if there were a chance they're still alive? I'd gladly die if I knew Melinda still needed me."

Elias sighed deeply and put his hand on Ashcroft's

shoulder. "We came into this together," he said. "All of us. If I deserted them now, without knowing for certain if they're dead, I couldn't live with myself. I'd rather die myself."

Ashcroft nodded slowly. "The crew wants to leave this place. The *Brora*'s just about fit. We could sail away to-morrow if you gave the word."

"And how long would we survive on open sea in the middle of winter? We'd be blessed to make it halfway."

"We all know that, Capt'n. We're doomed. But isn't it better to fight for our lives on the sea than to stay here and be butchered one at a time? Towers of Rhonnda, Elias!" He looked at the corpse and shuddered. "We're sailors, not explorers. If we have to die, let's die on the sea, under the stars."

Elias looked away, feeling miserable. If he could choose, such a death was certainly preferable. Far better the sea should claim them all than the horrors of this strange land. Staring into the distance, he saw Casca sniffing about the thick trees. Casca would give anything to go home, also, Elias knew—anything except leave his beloved Khalea behind.

Suddenly Casca turned sharply, tail between his legs, and began running and barking.

"The camp! Get back to the camp!"

Elias stared. Ashcroft bounded to his feet, mouth gaping. Running from the trees came a band of fierce wild men, wielding axes and curved swords. They scrambled across the snow, shrieking warcries in a strange tongue and brandishing their weapons above their heads.

The two Rangers knelt and put crossbows to their shoulders. *Twang!*

A barbarian dropped his sword and put his hands to his face. A second arrow brought him to his knees.

"Get back!" screamed Elias to the Rangers. One girl jumped up and scrambled back toward safety. The second reloaded her bow and tried to get off a second shot. A hairy arm smashed into her face and sent her sprawling into the snow. Then the Nomad was all over her. The girl kicked and tumbled, trying to shield herself from his blows.

Casca did an abrupt about-face and leaped on the barbarian. With fangs bared he tore at the barbarian's throat and brought him shrieking to the ground.

Elias wielded his shovel with abandon. One barbarian staggered, then reeled back as the shovel struck and tumbled him to the ground.

Elias ran to where the girl had fallen. From the corner of his eye he saw Heather leading six more Rangers, firing volleys from behind. With deft speed that amazed him, he swept up the injured Ranger into his arms.

"Run back!" called Heather frantically. "I'll give you cover. There're more of them behind the trees! They're surrounding the camp!"

Elias was aghast. More? More of *them?*

Two sailors sprang from behind the hill and relieved him of the burden of the Ranger. He let her go reluctantly, his head still spinning from his near brush with death. He heard the whizzing of crossbows all around and was numbly aware of screams and warcries of more barbarians lunging from the thickets. Ashcroft's voice shrilled above the others as he barked commands to the running sailors. Swords clanged against axe blades, daggers flashed. For every barbarian that fell to the ground, three more sprang from the trees to take his place.

Elias snapped out of his haziness, now aware of the full force of the fight. A girl named Rhia fell before his eyes, her body crumpling under the gruesome weight of a flying axe. Their band in disarray, Ashcroft and his group were pinned down ahead by a small party of savages hurling long spears. Two sailors fell under the torrent, moaning as they tugged at the razor-sharp sticks embedded in their bellies. Everywhere was mayhem—men dodging and scrambling, barbarians sweeping from all sides.

Elias pushed his way forward, swept up the sword of a fallen soldier and hewed it left and right among charging Nomads, creating a wheel of bloodied chaos.

"Behind you, Elias!"

He swerved as the blade whistled by. Heather's bow sang; the barbarian slumped and thudded.

Slowly and painfully they fought their way to the crest of the closest hill and looked down on the bare cabins of the camp. The barricade was less than fifty meters away—but it would be the longest distance they had ever covered.

From behind the barricade, sailors and soldiers let loose a torrent of arrows. *"Move!"* Elias shouted to his staggering companions. They stumbled their way through heavy snow, spears hurtling above their heads.

The wall was low, no higher at any point than a man's chest. But it afforded a triangular barricade from which they could put up a good fight. The only exposed side was the one to the sea.

Amid the tumult most were able to fight their way back. Casca and his wolves forced open a path, and the wounded Rangers, followed by Heather and Ashcroft, managed to get behind the wall. Elias led a rear guard at the farthest outer point as a number of Nomads slipped through the torrent of arrows and swung widely around the ridge to attack from the side.

Heather rounded up her Rangers and set a line at the outermost position. Casca snarled, then poised his wolves along the top of the wall while Ashcroft led the Valley troops into a tight band around them all. Nomads charged with reckless abandon, whooping, screaming, eyes fiercely ablaze. Mindlessly they pressed on, right into Heather's line of fire. Warcries turned to howls as barbarians stumbled and fell in the snow. But a shrill horn blast brought another band of Nomads racing from the other side.

Elias swung his group to meet this new onslaught, as the wolves and Rangers continued to deal with the first assault. Nomads flooded to the wall like a grim wave of mauling death, axes and swords heaving and glittering. Leading the group was a huge warrior, full-bearded and fierce-eyed, his axe swinging above his head. Elias rushed to meet him, sword horizontal to blunt the blow of the vicious blade. The axe descended. Elias blocked the downward thrust, then with a sharp hammerlike blow his sword plunged deeply into the barbarian's chest. The Nomad careened forward. Elias drew his sword out and thrust the tip high. It caught the wild man under the chin and tore straight up through his mouth. The barbarian tumbled backward, reeling in a ghastly pirouette.

A score more of Nomads lunged ahead. Heather swung her forces and arrows rained, decimating the ranks of the staggering warriors. Wildly the first ranks threw down their weapons and began to flee. Casca leaped on a straggler and brought him down into the snow, biting cleanly through the jugular. Head low to avoid sailing arrows, he began to chase other fleeing Nomads. Other wolves were quickly behind, catching wild men by the calves and bringing them down viciously.

"They're beaten!" shouted Ashcroft gleefully. He sheathed his weapon, watching the babarians dash helter-skelter for the thickets.

Bodies were strewn across the field of battle. Barbarians in the throes of death wailed and moaned. Some crawled and whined, clutching their bleeding wounds. Elias stood with bloody sword in hand, breathing hard. He looked around at his companions. The enemy had been stopped —this time. But neither Elias nor any of the others deluded themselves. The wild men would be back. And next time they would be better prepared.

CHAPTER TWENTY-NINE

The sky was dull and overcast. Aleya blew cold. Stacy walked alone in the swirl of snow, trying to make her way down the steep mountain to the Lowlands. Her heart cried out with her failure. She had counted on the wolves and had been certain that they would understand—and help. But no, like everyone in this strange land, they were too filled with countless years of mistrust.

For hours she had negotiated her way down the ledges, through drifts and pockets of treacherous ice, ever making her way lower. Aleya seemed to mock her, beating against her face, turning tears into cold icy streams down her cheeks. What could she do? How could she possibly find her way clear to the ship? Had she been wrong? she asked herself. Was her true fate to have stayed with Remus?

She came upon a low bluff filled with snow-burdened trees and bushes. Below, there was a deep gorge, a sheer fall of hundreds of meters. How easy it would be for her to end this agony, to do what was forbidden by both men and Dwellers: take her own life. Faces flashed before her: Casca, Cicero, and Melinda and Heather, Alryc and Trevor—and then there was Elias. She remembered him that night in the snow, his face and beard flecked with white, his deep worry for her. *I don't want a good girl, I want a smart one.*

For the first time she admitted to herself the feelings she had for so long ignored. It was Elias who had made her strong; it was he who had made her see the difference between girlish dreams and the desires of a woman. And right now she wanted him to be with her more than anything else she could imagine. To be there to cradle her in his arms and wipe away her tears. *"Elias,"* she wept, *"will I die without telling you that I love you?"*

No tears came to her eyes now, though. Not even tears of bitterness. The dark times had returned. Her visions were lost.

A sudden sound drew her from her thoughts. Her eyes shot to the left, then to the right. She whipped out her dagger and swung around. Dark was closing, and she could see nothing. Again the sound—from behind the bushes. Nomads, she told herself. It had to be! Who else would be lurking on the ledges?

Shadows grew; eyes stared. Stacy gasped. It was a wolf!

"Suli!" She cried with surprise.

The wolf grinned sheepishly, wagged his tail and came running to her. Kneeling, she hugged him tightly, kissed him and ran her fingers through his fur. "What are you doing here?"

"I came to help you, Khalea." He looked around.

From the other side of the ledge two more wolves stepped out of darkness. And behind them were many more. Within moments the entire ridge was filled with young, bold white hunters.

"You . . . you want to help me?" she asked, bewildered and excited. "You want to *fight?* But the sage— and the warlord?"

From somewhere among the milling pack the sage himself stepped forward, his head lowered humbly.

"Before dawn," he said, "I consulted *Balaka.* And the stars wove a tale my heart could not deny. Tell me, Khalea, can it be sheer coincidence that brought you to us? Were Garth's words ordained by Fara herself? I pondered these matters long and hard, Khalea. I know not if you are indeed Fara's messenger, but I do know I cannot let your long journey be ended with your death."

"Then you would fight for men against other men?"

The sage bowed his head. "We will fight for *you*, Khalea. Lead the way and we shall follow."

And a great howl arose from the pack. "Khalea! Khalea! Lead us, Khalea!"

Stacy stood, amazed at the sight. In her possession was an army—as fine an army as anyone could raise. Fierce hunters, cunning trackers, swift seekers as silent as the night. Her heart began to beat wildly. Her bitter prayers had been answered, as only Fara could answer them. Head thrown back, hands on her hips, eyes wet with tears, she cried, "Then to the tunnels! All seekers to the Lowlands to follow the enemies' tracks. Have our trackers find the quickest route to the *shala*."

Even as she spoke, dozens of wolves began to scatter, obeying her commands. Stacy cried at the sight. She would teach the Nomads a lesson they would never forget! They wanted war, they would get war! And the name Khalea would ring in their ears like the howling wind. She wept softly. Cloak flowing behind her, she held her dagger high. "Onward to Satra!"

It was an awesome sight to the wolves, her silhouette black against the glittering stars. The sage watched and shuddered. What he had read in *Balaka* was true; she *was* the one. AnaFara, the one who would alter their destiny forever; Khalea, the bridge between sun and moon —and much more.

Khalea—the wolf queen!

CHAPTER THIRTY

Sinister quiet now prevailed across the dim cavern where only an hour before the screams of battle had been deafening. The stench of death hung heavily in the air.

Prince Sumavand paced solemnly across the battle scene. His face was dirty, his tunic and mail splattered with blood. All around lay corpses of hideous *things,* fallen in combat. The battle was over, but the price of victory had not come cheaply. Mingled with the slain enemy lay hundreds of his own troops, brave and valiant men who had given their lives to keep the gates of Satra clear for yet another day.

For three days this fight had raged, and Sumavand had been there every moment, in the thick of battle. Now he was tired, drained, bone weary. But even more than that, he was sick of heart. The word of mighty Kuba's fall had struck him like the blow of a hammer despite the old antagonisms that had existed between the two *shaleen.* For with Kuba fell the last hope of reaching an alliance, some bargain that might yet have been struck to keep both their cities free of danger. Now Satra, as always, would have to stand alone. And most likely fall alone. For even as he stood here, word had come of the new attack from across the Black Canyon, that vast wasteland beneath the earth that lay between Kuba and Satra.

Yet even all this was not to be the final blow, he

realized. His last patrol above had barely evaded the massing army of Nomads who even now were crossing the Thunder Plain and making breathtaking speed toward Satra. It would be no more than twenty-four hours before both armies converged. Satra would not be able to withstand such a shattering dual blow.

He crossed the battlefield flanked by several of his captains, also grim-faced and glum. "Reinforce the southern gate," said the prince, "and send out a troop of our best archers to fortify the inner wall. The Nomads will press the south first, I fear."

"And attack the *shala* head-on?" asked a captain.

Slowly, Sumavand nodded. "They know too well our situation. While we are pinned in the tunnels, they will waste no time in trying to batter down our doors."

They made their way from the bleak cavern and headed toward the tunnel that led to the palace. An aide came running, crossed his arms and swept low before the prince.

Sumavand glanced down at him wearily. "Well? Speak."

The soldier looked frightened. "The river, my lord. The enemy has crossed the river!"

Sumavand sighed. This was sooner than expected. His hastily fortified defenses across the river had been smashed. "Do we still hold the approaches to the canal?" he asked apprehensively, strong hands upon his hips.

"Yes, my lord. But the waters run muddy with Satrian blood."

The prince cursed softly under his breath. The locusts were swarming as never before, and Satra lay defenseless before them.

"We are forced to commit more forces along the Black Canyon," said a captain.

"We dare not!" replied another. "If Nomads sweep upon our southern flanks, we shall need every able-bodied man in the *shala* to help fend them off!"

"And do what down here?" cried the first captain.

"Let the dark beasts run amok through our tunnels? I tell you the Black Canyon must be defended!"

Sumavand raised his hands to cease the argument. "And what is the news of the Nomad army above?" he asked the frightened messenger.

"The Thunder Plain has been crossed hours ago, my lord. By morning they will have entered the High Cavern."

"Then my guess was right," despaired the prince. "It will be a direct assault upon the southern gate. Gods below! They will have us pinned like a vise!"

They were met at the entrance to the palace tunnel by two men swiftly coming their way. One was the minister, Sebelius, the other a tall slim man who walked with a slight limp. The prince looked closely at the second man. "I know you!" he said astonished. "You are one of those from across the sea!"

Trevor bowed and nodded. "I am, my lord."

The prince turned to his minister. "What is this man doing here? Have you lost your senses, Sebelius? Get above!"

Sebelius crossed his arms over his chest. "Hear me out first, my liege! This man can be of value to us."

"Him?" laughed a captain. "Does he know the battlefield better than we?" He looked at Trevor with unmistakable scorn.

"No, but he can be of service," insisted Sebelius.

Sumavand scowled. "I think you were better off when the Rani put you under lock and key!" he barked. "Now leave here at once lest I regret having freed you!"

Sebelius gazed harshly upon the prince's face. "I will go, my lord. But I beg you, not for my sake but for Satra's, listen to what this man has to say."

Trevor boldly stepped forward. "The minister has let me study the drawings of your system of canals and dams. I understand how you draw your water supplies."

"So? What has this to do with our urgent needs?" demanded Sumavand.

The Valley soldier gazed evenly into the prince's doubting eyes. "I am an engineer, my lord. I understand such workings. Your spillways——"

"Make your point, master engineer!" the prince huffed.

Trevor took a deep breath. "I want to smash your dams and flood the Black Canyon," he replied boldly.

Sumavand acted as though the air were knocked out of him. "Do I hear you properly, engineer?"

Trevor nodded. "Yes, my lord. There is enough water in your reserves to flood the river ten meters above its banks. We can let loose a torrent that will spill from here to Kuba."

"And swallow Satra with it!" barked a captain. "This is foolish talk, my lord! If this plan could work, our own engineers would have thought of it long ago!"

"Satra itself will not be flooded, my lord," replied Trevor as coolly as he could. "I propose that the dams be broken only past the second lock. Satra will be safe; we can dig a channel."

The prince toyed with the edge of his drooping mustache. "It sounds a clever plan, master engineer," he conceded. "But we have no time to dig channels! We have no time to even properly bury our dead! The enemy presses on our heels. By morning they'll be upon us."

"Give me a hundred men!" begged Trevor. "I assure you Satra will be safe. Your buttress wall will hold back the current behind, and your valves will be broken to release the reservoir basin. The fury of that alone will smash the locks and break the wooden walls of your canal. Look, let me speak with your own engineers at once. They'll understand my plan. Let *them* tell you if it makes sense."

"At least do that much," pleaded the minister.

"I have grave doubts," replied Sumavand, "but I suppose we have little to lose."

"If it works, we can place our entire army in defense of the gates," said one captain thoughtfully. "It will take every man we can muster just to hold the Nomads back."

    A single front! thought Sumavand. Satra might have a chance for survival after all. That is, *if* this scheme could work. The prince glared at the stranger. "How do I know I can trust you, master engineer?"

    "I know your predicament, my lord," Trevor replied. "My companions and I are as trapped here as you are. And our throats cut as easily as your own. We'll have to trust each other."

    Sumavand smiled grimly. "I am a desperate man, master engineer. Do your work well and you'll find my gratitude has no bounds. But if you try to make a fool of me——"

    He did not have a chance to finish his words. At that moment a shrill blast sounded from above. Soldiers began running through the tunnels. The first attacks at the gate had begun.

    The High Cavern that was the entrance to the southern gate of the city was a kilometer wide and twice as long. Sheer stone walls rose in places up to a height of fifty meters. The gate of the *shala,* two huge doors of meter-thick solid oak, stood firmly hinged with iron along a high wall of stone solid bedrock.

    Along the crenellated wall five hundred Satrian soldiers watched as the distant entrance grew dark with swarthy Nomads easing their way inside and setting up battle lines. The barbarians began to pour through, axes gleaming, spears sharpened to fine points. Catapults lumbered; wheels groaned. The deadly war machines were lined in a row; broad shouldered barbarians, muscles bulging, began bringing forth large heavy stones to load them.

    Sumavand watched from the parapet, barking commands, instructing junior officers how best to deploy their forces. Trumpets blared, and Satrian banners were raised high. Defiantly they blazed in the faces of the enemy.

The prince paced the wall, hands behind his back. A flurry of noise caught his attention, and he turned to see his guards grappling with a giant of a man straining to get past them.

"What goes on here?" demanded Sumavand.

The guards bowed. "This man, my lord, demands——"

It was Alryc, Sumavand saw. Alryc of the Blue Fires, standing a full head above his soldiers, his eyes burning with anger, his muscles straining to break free.

"Release him," said Sumavand.

The soldiers complied. Alryc looked at him and glared.

"Why have you left your quarters, stargazer?" asked the prince. "Have you come to see our city fall?"

Alryc stood to his full massive height. "I came to fight. I and my companions demand that you let us join you in battle. If we are to die, it will not be while locked in your palace rooms! Now give me a weapon!"

The prince turned sourly to his officers. "Give him a sword."

"My lord!" The officers were aghast.

"Give him one! We need every hand we can get. If he wishes his own death, so be it!"

Alryc was handed a scimitar and he took it with a smile. He ran his thumb across the edge of the blade. "A sharp blade," he said. "Now, what about my companions?"

Sumavand looked behind Alryc and saw Melinda and Robin standing near the top of the stairwell. Instead of their saris they were once again dressed in Ranger tunics, and each was holding a crossbow. "You wish to fight also?" he asked incredulously.

Melinda came to the landing and threw back her head. "That's why we're here. Shaina got us our bows back. Now if you'll kindly have your soldiers bring some arrows."

"Very well. Good archers are valuable. Have my captains position you along the wall."

The girls bowed, then turned on their heels to follow the captains.

"Where shall *I* fight?" growled Alryc.

"Next to me, stargazer. A man of your size will draw many spears away from me."

The large man grinned, and his eyes sparkled. "It will be a pleasure. But there is one more request, my lord."

"And what might that be?"

"The red wolf, Cicero. Remove his chain and bring him forth. He will stand beside us, also."

With a shrug, the prince said, "Why not? This is a day filled with ironies, and I can think of none greater than having a wolf fight at my feet." Then to his startled aides, "Do as the stargazer asks. Release the wolf and bring him here. He wants to fight."

"My lord?"

Sumavand grinned bemusedly. "No, I haven't yet lost my mind. But do as I say and be quick! Our Nomad friends grow restless!"

Glumly the soldier held his torch low, flames dancing in darkness. Trevor ran his eyes over the ancient plans of the underground water system. There were two large reservoirs, it seemed, each connected by the canal, each with long spillways running toward the Black Canyon. A series of locks regulated the flow from the river.

He ran his finger lightly over the lines of the canal and traced the river down from the surface of the mountains. It was a complex system, he saw, one that must have been conceived, planned and executed over many, many long years. At length he glanced up at the two solemn-faced engineers at his side.

"How long are the spillways?" he asked.

"A thousand meters each, Commander. They join at the first lock."

"And how many locks?"

"Six in all."

He smiled grimly. The plans indicated the locks were low walls meant only to regulate a planned flow of water. Free the floodgate completely, and the surging rush of water would smash them into splinters. "You understand what we're going to do?" he asked.

Both engineers nodded hesitantly. "Allow the current to run wild."

"Right. It'll tear down the spillways, flood the canal, and the first lock will give way under the pressure. By the time the water reaches the second lock it will be out of control. By the time the fifth and sixth locks are reached the full force of the river will run rampant through the Black Canyon. Anything alive from here to Kuba will be drowned in water ten meters high."

"It can also flow the other way," added one sourly. "All Satra might be flooded."

"Not with our new wall." He glanced behind at the hundred or so soldiers busily placing stones and beams of thick wood across the concave entrances that led back to the tunnels. "We'll have our side sealed tight as a drum."

"These new walls of yours are hastily built. If the spillway waters hit with too much force, they'll be smashed as easily as the locks."

"They can take the stress. Everything I was ever taught about water pressures tells me they can hold. I feel confident."

An eerie silence prevailed as the last echo of his voice dimmed. A sudden dread and horror fell over them all. Far off in the distance there was a low rumble, so faint they had to strain their ears to hear it. The sound of the marching *thing* army, now more than halfway to Satra.

"Let's get on with it," said one of the engineers in a barely audible whisper. His hands were shaking.

"Good," Trevor said. "All right! Everybody back to work! Every minute counts!"

The ensuing hours passed quickly. The new buttress wall across the tunnels was completed. Guards stood at their posts; the engineers took their places at the valves of the reservoir. Trevor climbed atop the wall and signaled for the Satrian soldiers to put down their tools and take shelter. From his position he would take full view of the cavern, the spillways and also the approach to the canal. Beyond that there was only the edge of the Black Canyon itself and the dread that lay beyond. The rumble of *things* began to grow in intensity; he realized that the first wave of attackers was no more than minutes away.

The captain of the Satrian troops came to his side, sword in hand, beads of perspiration dotted across his forehead. If something went wrong, if the plan did not work, he had but one hundred men to fend off thousands of the dark enemy. With Sumavand directing the battle above, there would be no aid to help them in their fight.

The guards at the outermost post near the first lock of the canal suddenly came running. "They come!" cried one, gripping his scimitar and clambering up the handholds of the new wall.

Trevor gritted his teeth. Each second brought the *things* closer, and he wanted the impact of the water to hit with full intensity upon their first ranks. "Have they reached the approaches to the canal?"

"By now, yes!" panted the guard.

Trevor swung around and looked at the Satrian engineers. "Now! Open the valves!"

The men grappled with the wheel; Trevor heard the slow groan as it began to turn. The gate began to open and water raced down along the spillways—a steady stream pulsing and surging forward. But not enough to flood.

Something was wrong!

With fright in his eyes he confronted the engineers. "Open it all the way! All the way!"

"We can't!" shouted one. "The wheel's stuck!"

He leaped to the handholds and dropped down onto the floor. Wild water splashed from the side of the spillway. The captain of the Satrians was right on his heels.

"It won't open!" cried the engineer. "It's stuck! Gates of Satra, it's stuck!"

Trevor saw that the gate was up about a third, and no matter how much the engineers strained it would raise no farther. He heaved and tugged at the wheel. It gave a little, then jammed tight.

Grunts and growls came louder and louder. A band of *things,* fangs bared, rock swords and spears held high, came lunging forward. They were met by a handful of Satrians who had jumped down from the wall. Metal clashed against rock; echoes filled the air. The first *things* fell quickly, slipping in mud. But on their heels were more, and behind them would come their entire army.

In desperation Trevor grabbed a scimitar from a nearby soldier and looked wildly about. "Where are the chains?" he cried. "The chains that lift the floodgate!"

"Beside the valve!" answered the engineer. "But you can't reach it! You'll have to climb onto the spillway— and you'll be drowned!"

Trevor spun around as a hideous dark beast lunged for him. He swirled his scimitar and almost severed the *thing's* head from its shoulders. Then, without even pausing to take a breath, he leaped onto the spillway itself, feet trying desperately to get a firm hold. Waist-deep in rushing water, he fought to reach the gate. For an instant the scimitar was nearly flung from his hand by rushing water. But he held. He fell, was submerged, and it took all his strength, every ounce within him, to right himself and battle forward.

He fought against the increasing current to reach the gate and the heavy chains on its sides. He hacked and hewed with his blade, frantically struggling to see as the water began to sweep over his head. Again and again.

Something gave. The fury of the water lashed like a whip, and the gate itself went flying from its foundation.

Trevor plunged underwater and lost all balance. With all his strength he grasped the top of the wall and heaved himself over the side of the spillway. He fell into thick mud and lay gasping, safe.

Water raged through the cavern spillways and down into the canal. Terrible screams changed to gurgles, and drowning *things* clawed at the walls. It was like the sea itself, a roaring tide. The first lock cracked like balsam, the second gave way like paper. On and on it went. The third lock flew high in the air. There was no force on the face of the earth that could stop it. Millions and millions of gallons, now freed, running wild and savage, dealing death and destruction. It broke through the fifth gate like a demon, ever rising, pulsing, growing. The sixth gate crumpled under the weight—and now the water was truly free! Nothing for league upon league to hold it!

The main body of the *thing* army had yet to reach the canal. But what they saw coming sent fear through their hearts. It was a tidal wave, pouring over them like the winds of a hurricane. They threw down all weapons and raced back into the dark, back toward the fallen Kuba, back toward the deep bowels of the earth in which they lived. But their speed could not match the speed of the water: they were picked up and flung against the walls, limbs broken and shattered. Heads were bashed, limbs nearly torn from their sockets. The tide swelled and swelled, carried them back, flung corpses pell-mell before it and washed them away in a raging fury.

Ever onward, ever onward, the Black Canyon became again what it had been countless eons ago: a deep river, a treacherous, swirling current.

Great rocks flung from the catapults came crashing down on the Satrian wall. The impact threw many archers off balance and sent them hurtling to the earth below. A thousand frenzied Nomads attacked in waves, swinging axes and swords, whooping foul warcries. Torrents of arrows came whistling down over their heads but were blunted by the animal-skin shields the barbarians held. Then, hauling rope ladders over the top, they began scrambling up the wall. Satrian swords heaved at the ropes and split them asunder. Nomads fell by the score. But no sooner had one rope been cut than another was flung to take its place. Others of the enemy crawled to the foot of the gate. And there, pressed tightly against the wall so that none of Sumavand's archers could see them, they waited with gleaming axes for the battering ram to be brought.

It was a great ram, as long as the walls were high, needing almost a hundred men to carry it. And at its head was a forged fist of iron, so thick and so heavy that twenty men groaned under its weight.

Spears flying right and left, Sumavand dodged and peered over the wall to see the dark, lumbering menace approach. The mere sight of it made his troops quiver. They knew if the gate were breached, the wall could not be held. They would have to retreat behind the second wall of the city, the lower wall, and there rally to make a last fight. And if this second wall were breached as well, there would be nothing at all to stop the enemy from reaching the passages to the floor of the mountain and the *shala* itself, where the city was ripe for the taking.

Melinda and Robin, casting fear aside, stood boldly and openly at the far end of the wall, making every arrow count. Wave upon wave the enemy continued to press until hundreds had reached the wall. Shields held high, they gave good cover to those carrying the battering ram.

Sumavand shouted for all arrows to be directed toward them. But for every Nomad that fell there seemed to be ten replacements. The battering ram drew closer with every second.

"Behind you!" cried Alryc to the prince. In his concern Sumavand had not seen the three wild-eyed barbarians who had managed to climb over the wall behind him.

They brandished their weapons above their heads, swinging them recklessly. As the prince swerved to blunt the blow of the first, Alryc plunged his blade deeply into the back of another. Seemingly from nowhere, Cicero sank sharp fangs into the first attacker's neck. But one barbarian remained. With eyes aflame, he knocked the prince off his feet with the hilt of his axe. It was Cicero who ripped out the wild man's jugular before his blade could descend upon the prince.

Sumavand dizzily and slowly rose to his feet. He was astounded, not because the Nomads had almost killed him but because it had been a wolf that had saved his life. *A wolf!* He wanted to thank him, but before he could the wolf growled and turned to deal death to other attackers along the wall.

Just then there was a mighty crash. The ram had dealt its first blow against the gate. "Heave!" cried the Nomads. *"Heave!"*

The massive ram was drawn back, then like thunder against the gates of Satra a terrible *boom* reverberated right across the High Cavern. Again it drew back and again it was swung forward. The beams groaned and split. The gates plunged open. Great cheers of glee swelled from the attackers.

Waves of wild men came pouring through the entrance, whooping at the tops of their lungs. Two hundred Satrians met them head-on, but the Nomads were driven men, urged on by the knowledge of the plunder that lay before them. From precious stones to tunnels of gold and silver, from the wealth of the palace, to the lust of women, all this and more lay at their feet. Scimitars and arrows would not keep them from it. For so long they had lusted; now it was theirs for the taking!

Sumavand, with Alryc and Cicero at his side, dashed down the long steps from the parapet. The Rangers drew long, curved Satrian daggers and plunged wildly to

Sumavand's side, slashing the air, sending wild men reeling back.

"We are lost," shouted Sumavand in bitter realization.

"Not yet, Prince!" rasped Alryc. The astronomer cut a path before him with his blade; inch by inch the small band began to withdraw. Melinda plunged her knife through the heart of a hairy bestial man lunging at her; Cicero toppled on the ground with two wild men, dodging and swerving, keeping the knives at bay. Sumavand heaved his sword about and brought it crashing against mail and flesh and skins and axe blades. Dizzily he forgot his royal bearing and began to shriek like the savages that surrounded him, dealing death at every turn.

Grisly shouts obliterated all. Sumavand was hardly aware of the din, besieged as he was. But through the fog of his mind he swore he heard the howl of wolves. The ultimate irony, he thought. Now that the *things* have ravished the *shala* from below and the Nomads from above, the wolves would seek their vengeance, too. There had been too many enemies for too long, he knew, and now Satra would pay the price.

It was with incredible shock that he heard the shrill blasts of the Nomad horns sound the retreat. From all around, barbarians who had been pressing upon his very flesh now began to turn pale with fright and to scurry back in the direction of the gate.

Alryc stood, hand to his wound. Melinda and Robin painfully lifted themselves off the floor, panting.

And the wolf howls rose above all, louder and louder. Cicero suddenly bounded up atop the wall.

"What is it?" gasped the prince amid the tumult.

"What are they saying, Cicero?" asked Melinda.

The wolf glanced down with amazement. "Lead us! They are shouting 'lead us, lead us, Khalea!' "

Robin and Melinda hurried to the wall. Alryc and the prince were quick to follow. Hundreds upon hundreds of great fierce white wolves were pouring into the cavern from outside, lunging and leaping, tearing at Nomad throats. And leading them was a woman dressed in a long cloak that swirled behind her, a band of ferocious seekers surrounding and protecting her. As the bitter fight waxed hotly everywhere, the girl strode forward, dagger in hand, barking commands in the canine tongue.

Alryc clapped Sumavand on the shoulder, eyes twinkling. "We've been saved, Prince! *Saved!* The name they shout, Khalea, do you know to whom it belongs?"

Sumavand still could not believe what he saw. "Anastasia!" he gasped. "It can't be. *But it is!*"

"Yes," replied the astronomer dourly. "Anastasia. She has come to fight for us—with the white wolves."

Tears streamed down Melinda's face, tears of joy. "You did it, Stacy," she whispered. "You really did it!"

The battle was brief but savage. The Nomad army, having taken many casualties at the hands of the Satrians, were now completely overrun from behind. The disarray was total. Wild men broke ranks and fled in panic, vainly seeking shelter from the rampaging wolves. The wolves were repaying an old debt. Never again would Lowland men catch and murder them. Never again would they shy from the tips of Nomad spears or the gleaming blades of their axes. Khalea had called them wild and free—and now they truly were. Free wolves of the pack! Wherever she beckoned they would follow, for now she was their queen.

CHAPTER THIRTY-ONE

The long winter snows began to melt. Aleya blew more gently now, and Khal bathed the land in his warmth. Fara had awakened from her slumber at last; the first days of spring were close at hand.

Captain Elias stood at the foot of the ridge, peering out at his ship and the dark blue sea beyond.

The *Brora,* still nestled in the cove, rocked gently with the bobbing waves, her new sail proudly fluttering in the breeze. Gulls filled the sky, and the bright sun peeked from behind fast-rolling, cottonlike clouds.

Alryc stood beside Elias, dressed now not in fine Satrian fabric but in the rougher cloth of his Newfoundland tunic.

"Can you see it all?" he asked softly. "See Bartok's vision coming true?"

Elias nodded. "I think so, yes."

The astronomer sighed and touched lightly at the healing wound under his eye. "Tell me what you see."

"Our ships crossing beside Satra's own," sighed Elias. "Our world and Satra's bound together by bonds that can't be broken. We'll learn from each other."

Alryc nodded somberly. "We both have much to teach. We will bring home new wonders. And some of us will stay behind to work with Satra and forge this bold new world you see."

"And some stay behind in death," added the mariner.

The mystic bowed his head. "Believe that they died with a purpose, my friend. They gave all so that others may follow in their places. The world changes around us. We must accept that."

Elias looked away. Beside the cabins of the camp his crew and most of the Rangers and Valley soldiers were busily making preparations for the prince's arrival. A handful of Satrians were helping, including the hawk-nosed minister called Sebelius. He had been among the first to reach them that day after the wolves had come down from the mountains and sent the Nomads fleeing from the camp. And Elias had to smile at the memory of how terrified he had been. First the wolves, then these strangely garbed men of Satra. With their mail and their scimitars, it looked as if they were there to finish what the Nomads had left undone.

Everything had happened so fast: the news that Stacy and most of the others were alive, that Satra had been found, that the prince of Satra was prepared to form an alliance with the Empire and would send his special emissaries back to Rhonnda aboard the *Brora*. A trumpet blast sounded from the hills. The Satrians began to cheer.

The trumpet blared again, closer. Elias saw the first of the Satrian soldiers, all riding stunted ponies, strange and colorful banners flying high. The minister bowed low as a line of sleek black horses appeared at the crest of the hill. Six black horses, six proud riders dressed in bright saris and togas, cloaks flowing gracefully behind in the wind. He stared dumbly. Riding the finest steed of all was Stacy. She rode tall, with her head thrown back, her hair swirling before her eyes. Next to her was a stout broad-shouldered man with a powerful face and bright intelligent eyes. This one was the prince, Elias knew. Poise and manner alone assured him of that. Flanking him was an aide of some sort and a strikingly beautiful young woman with long yellow hair and eyes the color of the sea. Next to her, hands holding the reins lightly, came Trevor.

At length they dismounted and came into camp. The

minister interceded between them. With a sweeping gesture to his prince he introduced Elias. The captain bowed nervously. The prince looked at him and grinned.

"So, Captain Elias," Sumavand said, hands on hips, fingers at the hilt of his jeweled dagger, "I don't mind telling you your name has been spoken frequently to me."

Elias looked to Stacy. "Good things, I trust," he replied.

"*Very* good things, Captain. Were it not for your own knowledge of the sea and your stargazer's understanding of the sky I would probably not have been alive on this day. But now to business. When will your ship be ready to sail back to your Empire?"

"By the new moon, my lord. Seven days' time from now."

"Ah, sooner than I hoped," said the prince, rubbing his hands together. "But I am rude! Forgive me, Captain. Allow me to introduce those who have accompanied me here today." He pointed to the aide. "This, of course, is General Vela," he said. "My finest soldier. I daresay you two will spend much time together. He will accompany you on your voyage. And it will be he who shall sign in my absence the trade agreements I am told your Council so badly seeks."

The dour soldier smiled and extended his hand to the captain. "I am quite anxious to see this Empire of yours," Vela said. "I have heard tales of your fabulous city called Rhonnda-by-the-Sea."

Elias grinned. "You'll like it," he answered, grasping the hand firmly.

Sumavand beckoned to another. "This is Mistress Shaina," he said. "She, er, has come to know your companions quite well, I'm told." Here he smiled. "Some would say too well, I'm sure."

Elias caught a flustered look in the blonde girl's eye.

"Shaina will also go back with you. When she bargains with your Council on trade, you will find her as capable as any man. She knows how to extract a good price."

Elias laughed. "We have shrewd women at home, too, my lord. I'm sure Mistress Shaina will meet her match."

Sumavand frowned good-naturedly. Then he put his arm around Sigried and the girl bristled. "I've been saving this one for last," he chuckled. "Permit me to introduce the Rani of Kuba, Sigried."

Elias bowed and took her outstretched hand and kissed it.

"The Rani and your own Anastasia have, er, a special relationship. Sigried is to go back with you, also. To Siggy I give the right to decide on the final agreements we strike with you. I'll be blunt, Captain. She doesn't trust your Empire. So I feel that her watchful eyes will guarantee that whatever bargain is struck it will not be to Satra's disadvantage."

"I understand," replied Elias, not realizing Sumavand's delight in having the beautiful Rani out of his hair for a couple of years.

"Now," continued the prince, turning abruptly to Trevor. "This man helped save our *shala* from total catastrophe. He calls himself an engineer. A *master* engineer, I call him. And such title and rank have I bestowed upon him. It took great effort on my part, but I have convinced him to stay with us for a time." He smiled warmly at Trevor. "Build me a new *shala,* master engineer. One that stands above the ground—in the sun. We are free men now, are we not?"

"But I go home when my work is done," protested Trevor.

Sumavand laughed. "Of course! That is if you don't find a young Satrian girl to your liking. We have many to choose from, you know. You might be impressed."

Trevor grinned. "I already have."

Stacy looked on with surprise and joy as Shaina took Trevor's hand and kissed him softly on the cheek.

Sumavan roared. "Ah, master engineer? So Satra has already woven its magic upon you! Then I must see to it that Shaina tarries not too long in this Empire of yours."

"It doesn't matter," said Trevor happily. "I *will* go home one day. But it will cost Satra a prize negotiator."

Stacy came over meekly, clasped both their hands and kissed them. "I wish you . . . I wish you. . . ." She broke into tears.

"Isn't that like a woman!" laughed Sumavand, shaking his head. He pulled Stacy away and looked into her eyes as he spoke. "As for this one," he began, "would you believe I offered her my name and my crown?"

Elias felt his heart begin to pound like a drum.

"And she turned me down! Gods above! Any woman in Satra would give *anything* for such an offer! And this one spurns me as though I were a jester!"

"That's not true!" she pouted, squeezing his hand.

Sumavand shrugged. "True enough, but never mind. To Anastasia, Satra owes everything. She has brought us into the light and taught us that years of hatred beget only further hatred. Because of her the white wolves came to our aid, and because of her we have given solemn oath never to harm them again. No more will our traps be set on the mountains. Even as we speak, the red wolf, Cicero, negotiates a treaty between us. It will take some years, I fear, until we have the special relationship with Dwellers that your own land does. But give us time, I pray you. These ways are still new and strange."

He turned suddenly to his minister. "But we have yet to reward her! And Sebelius will be most unhappy unless I give Anastasia her due."

The minister brought forth a satin pillow on which lay a small golden diadem, laden with tiny jewels.

"Kneel before me, Anastasia," he said. And she did, eyes closed, hands trembling.

He carefully lifted the crown and placed it on her head.

"I know not what honors your own land bestows, my lady. But I do know how Satra treats those who have helped her. Although you are not my bride, I give to you the title of princess of Satra. Bear it well, for it is a heavy role to play. When you leave this land, you must always hold it dear in your heart. Remember that one day our two lands may well become one. Arise, Anastasia of Satra, the Empire princess."

As she stood, every Satrian, including the Rani and Sumavand himself, bowed low before her. And those from the *Brora,* Alryc, Trevor, and Melinda and Robin and Ashcroft, and all the others did the same. But to Elias there was great sadness, for as a princess he knew Stacy could never be his.

With a heavy heart he slipped from the crowd and went back to staring at the ship and the sea. Salty winds bit harshly against salted tears. It took him a long time to realize that she was standing behind him, alone, with tears of her own.

"Hello, Captain," she said.

"Hello, Princess," he replied.

"It's been a long time, hasn't it?"

He tried to smile. "Too long, my lady. I've missed you. How have you been all these weeks?"

She smiled impishly, batting her wet eyes. "Well, I haven't been very *good,* but I sure have been *smart.*"

He grabbed her in his arms and squeezed her as tightly as he could. She could hardly breathe, but she didn't care as she smothered him with wet kisses. "I *love* you, Elias. I think I always did."

"And I've loved you, too, Stacy. You've always known it."

"I've always hoped it."

Hand in hand they gazed out toward the sea and the setting sun, glowing with the excitement of having at last found each other again.

"You'll be going home with great honor and glory, Stacy," Elias said softly.

"All of us will," she sighed.

"It's not the same. You've found more than just the answers you sought, Stacy."

"I know I did. I found myself. And I know for the first time in my life just who I am. Not in title; titles mean nothing to me. But within myself. I left Rhonnda a frightened girl."

"And now?"

She shrugged, kissing him gently. "And now I'm going to use everything given to me to create a better world for us all."

Puzzled, he stared into her dark, mysterious eyes; eyes he so adored.

"Oh, Elias," she sniffed, pressing herself closer. "I do need you, and I do need your help. We *are* alike, you know. Cut from the same cloth, just as Trevor once said we were. Maybe we were meant to be wild and free. I doubt either one of us will ever change. And there'll be so much for us to accomplish when we return to Rhonnda."

Home to Rhonnda. It could have brought tears even to a sailor's eyes. "I suppose we won't be sailing the river anymore," he said wistfully.

Stacy laughed, her saucy eyes dancing. "You won't need the river anymore, Elias. Think of the sea! We'll sail the seas together, and we'll change the face of the world!"

He nodded reflectively. "Just as Bartok foretold."

"The seven seas that the ancients spoke of," whispered Stacy. "And we'll sail them all. Maybe even find that land where Fara never sleeps and Khal always shines."

The captain closed his arms around her and drew her close against his chest. "And there are going to be children, Stacy. Our children."

She looked at him warmly and began to cry. *How very much she wanted to have children!* "As many as we want, Elias—and they're all going to be just like you."

Elias shook his head. "I don't think so, little wolf queen. Their mother will be a princess among men, but still too much of a wolf herself to keep her children away from the forest. You'll bring them to Casca, just as your father brought you to Hector. And I'm going to be proud."

Her tears were running more freely now, and she laughed with happiness. Elias smiled, wiped them away, grinning as he thought, *"Isn't that just like a woman!"*

OTHER SELECTIONS
FROM
PLAYBOY PRESS

THE HAVEN $1.95
GRAHAM DIAMOND
An army of cunning, vicious dogs in league with a horde of vampire bats comes to destroy the last remaining bastion of human civilization on earth.

CITY OF MASQUES $1.75
ALAN BRENNERT
A bone-chiller about a Hollywood studio that would make anyone a star: simply replace thought patterns electronically with those of the person you want to become. The results: overnight fame—and overnight terror.

WOLF MOUNTAIN $1.95
PETER LARS SANDBERG
A woman takes her climbing club of girls into the mountains, where they are taken captive by two psychopathic killers. A first-rate cliff-hanger.

THE DEATH CONNECTION $1.50
ROGER BRANDT
The U.S. Border Patrol tangles with a ruthless alien smuggler in one of the boldest and bloodiest novels written about the U.S.-Mexican alien smuggling problem.

THE MINOTAUR FACTOR $1.95
STUART STERN
A mysterious killer disease is striking teenagers all over the world. The only way to stop it is a hideous experiment using human guinea pigs.

THE TRANSFORMATION $1.95
JOY FIELDING
Three star-struck women, disenchanted by Hollywood, become involved in a bizarre ritual murder.